# Part One

## May-July 1908

# The Rage
## of the
# Vulture

*Books by Barry Unsworth*

BARRY UNSWORTH

# The Rage
## of the
# Vulture

W. W. Norton & Company
New York   •   London

Printed in the United States of America

First published as a Norton paperback 1995

Manufacturing by the Haddon Craftsmen, Inc.

Library of Congress Cataloging-in-Publication Data
Unsworth, Barry, 1930–
The rage of the vulture.
I. Title.
PR6071.N8R3   1983   823′.914   82-23249


ISBN 0-393-31308-5

W. W. Norton & Company, Inc.
500 Fifth Avenue, New York, N.Y. 10110
www.wwnorton.com


W. W. Norton & Company Ltd.
Castle House, 75/76 Wells Street, London W1T 3QT


6 7 8 9 0

To John Lennox Cook

Know ye the land where the cypress and myrtle
Are emblems of deeds that are done in their clime,
Where the rage of the vulture, the love of the turtle
Now melt into sorrow, now madden to crime?

*Byron*

# List of Characters

| | |
|---|---|
| Abdul Hamid II | Sultan of Turkey |
| Captain Robert Markham | British army officer stationed in Constantinople |
| Henry Markham | Markham's son |
| Elizabeth Markham | Markham's wife |
| Miss Mary Taverner | Henry's governess |

Mehmet Agha ⎱
Nevres Badji ⎰    Servants in Markham's house

| | |
|---|---|
| Miss Munro | a visitor to Constantinople |
| Captain Blake | a colleague of Markham's |
| Kyriakos | a Greek doctor |
| Somerville | a financier, member of the Ottoman Debt Commission |
| Ayshe | a little Turkish girl, friend of Henry's |
| Colonel Nesbitt | British Military Attaché in Constantinople |

Tahsin Bey, First Secretary ⎫
Izzet, Chamberlain       ⎬
Djavad Agha,                 Members of the Palace
   Chief of the Black Eunuchs    clique
Abdul Hudar,             ⎭
   Court Astrologer

| | |
|---|---|
| Said Pasha | Grand Vizier |
| Arturo Zimin | a Levantine spy |
| Skafidis | a Greek shopkeeper |

| | |
|---|---|
| Essad Pasha | Commander of anti-guerrilla forces in Macedonia |
| Worseley-Jones<br>Morrison<br>Ramsay<br>Straker<br>Clissold | Members of the Embassy staff in Constantinople |
| Nejib | a Turkish officer, member of the Committee of Union and Progress |
| Mr and Mrs Wallisch<br>Colin-Olivier | Acquaintances of Markham's |
| Henderson | an American journalist |
| Hartunian | an Armenian merchant |
| Tarquin | Hartunian's secretary |
| Mara | a gypsy dancing girl |
| Mesté Alem | a slave girl in the Harem |
| Miss Ada Lamb | a singer |
| Alex | barman at the Pera Club |
| Commander Phelps | a naval officer |
| Major Godard | a French army officer, colleague of Markham's |
| Willis | Nesbitt's batman |
| Missakian | an Armenian nationalist |
| Narsan | a negro eunuch |
| Hassan Fehmi | editor of *Serbesti*, a right-wing newspaper |
| Madame Clara | a brothel-keeper |
| Irma | one of Madame Clara's girls |
| Kebali | a Turkish orderly officer |
| Rassim Bey | the Sultan's Chief of Secret Police |
| A Macedonian sentry | |

Plus sundry dancers, gypsies, officials, etc.

# 1

By that summer, the last of his long and blood-stained reign, Abdul Hamid's fears had become so great that they threatened to paralyse him altogether. To stave off this ultimate immobility of panic he grew to rely more and more on certain set procedures, habits that took on the force of ritual. The business of the telescopes was one of these. He had four of them, installed in a domed observatory on the roof of Yildiz Kiosk, the 'Star Pavilion' of his palace, and from one or the other he was able to scan all the cardinal points of a threatening world. Every day, at fixed times, he did this.

Directly before him lay his park and pleasure grounds. The walls of his harem and theatre, the labyrinth of walks and passages and interconnected pavilions that made up his palace of Yildiz. Beyond the massive walls that enclosed all this, amidst the foliage of the outer grounds, he could catch occasional reflections from the gilt bars of his menagerie and from the water of his artificial lake; and see, with comfort, the whitewashed barracks of the palace guard, his trusty Albanians, the only troops in the Ottoman Empire, it was said, not in arrears of pay. He could look down past these, over the high outer walls, at the white palace of Cheragan on the Bosphoros, where his mad brother Murad had been immured for thirty years; then at the glittering waterway itself, busy with sails, ruffled with currents and fish, free - for that moment at least - from the shapes of hostile warships. Across the strait rose the green, unmutinous slopes of Asia.

To the south, the whole of Constantinople lay open to his view: Pera and the European Embassies and business houses; the Golden Horn, crowded with ships of every nation, among them the dilapidated, totally unserviceable ironclads of the

11

Imperial Navy, which he had allowed to rot there, for fear they might be used against him - now chicken coops and vegetable gardens flourished among the decaying hulks. Through the lattice of masts and spars he could see Stambul, the old city, with its skyline of minaret and dome, the wooded grounds of the Seraglio, the Old Palace of the Sultans, his predecessors. Finally the placid blue of the Marmara, flecked here and there with sails.

On this particular afternoon, however - and we have this on the authority of his favourite, the Syrian Izzet Bey, to whom he spoke of it and who mentions it in his Memoirs, written after the collapse of the régime, as typical of the small anxieties that preyed on his master during those last months - it was not the larger view which occupied him, but a gathering or party of some kind in a suburb adjoining the palace grounds to the southeast, a suburb named Beshiktash, built on the slopes above the Bosphoros, a mesh, from Abdul Hamid's height above it, of dusty lanes and mottled plane trees and big wooden houses set in walled gardens.

In one of these gardens there were small groups of people, standing, moving. The telescope rested on them, swung away, returned; noted with weary disapproval the unveiled faces of the women, registered their hats and summer dresses and parasols, the light-coloured clothes and uniforms of the men. Remote as the moon, this scene, for all the detail in which he could see it. Inconceivable he should ever set foot there - he never left the precincts of his palace now. The movements of the people were like a performance of some kind, a dance of which he did not know the measure. He did not like it that they moved at all, within his sight yet independent. He was accustomed to think that all movement began with him.

These people were Europeans. Again, like a slight wince of pain or an involuntary flutter of the nerves, tuning note in the orchestra of his anxieties, the reminder came that an English officer had elected to live here, in this Turkish suburb, rather than in the European quarter of Pera, among his colleagues.

An unusual thing. Files were kept on all foreign residents in Constantinople, civil and military. He knew the man's name and a certain number of facts about him. His name was Markham and he spoke Turkish. Another unusual thing. The telescope dwelt on the faces of the men, did not know which was his, swung away finally in search of fresh phantoms.

It was a good year for roses. Markham's ten-year-old son Henry had heard several people remark on this during the brief time he had been living there. He thought it quite likely they were saying the same thing now. Or something similar, he thought, peering out through the narrow aperture. He had to guess, because he was out of earshot here in the ramshackle summer-house among the trees at the bottom of the garden, where he had gone to be out of the way, read, spy on the guests.

He had discovered the summer-house on the day of his arrival. It was safe because no one would suspect that he knew how to get in. The blistered white door was kept locked always, but on the side away from the house there were lilac bushes and he could approach without being seen, squeeze his thin body through the gap in the ruined shutters, then through the window where for long there had been no panes. Here, after the stealth of the approach and the scrambling entry, he felt safe from everyone. He sat on the dusty cushions of the windowseat, aware of the silence, smelling the mould and the flaked paint and cobwebs.

One window gave a view of part of the house and rear terrace, and the upper part of the garden. Vision was reduced by the honeysuckle that grew half over the window, but Henry did not regret this. It concealed him, for one thing. And it meant that anyone in the narrow compass of his view was held in intense focus, was offered, in a way, to his scrutiny. He had always liked watching and listening, from screened, secret places – the secrecy of it made him aware of himself, excited him as nothing else did. Since his arrival here the impulse had grown, nourished by his unhappiness, the strangeness of the place, the change he had found in his father. It was necessary to spy on the world, to know what was going on, not to be taken by surprise.

At the moment he could see two ladies in wide-brimmed hats and wide-sleeved dresses, one white, one pale blue. They were standing near the rose trellis and were partly obscured from the boy's view by the rose leaves and by the thickly clustering, pale pink roses. Because of this, and because they seemed to be looking at the roses, Henry felt that this was what they must be talking about, and he began trying to shape the words and accents of the ladies, moving his mouth and eyes in soundless imitation. *Yes, my dear, the roses are simply splendid this year. I don't think I've ever seen roses like them, certainly not here.*

The pale blue one was thinner and smiled more. The brim of her hat seemed softer, it dipped with the movements of her head. *I have seen better ones in Bury St Edmunds.*

This was the only English town that came into his mind. It was where their house was, where he had gone to school and lived with his mother, before they came out here.

Suddenly his governess, Miss Taverner, appeared in the picture. She did not join the two ladies but came and stood near them. She did not look at them either, but glanced around the garden in different directions. Henry knew at once that she was looking for him. She was bare-headed and dressed differently from the others, in darker clothes. He guessed that she had just come out of the house to look for him. Henry would have done a lot to please Miss Taverner, who was beautiful, but he was unwilling to run the gauntlet of the guests, so he decided to stay where he was for the time being. She did not in any case remain long there, moving away, further down the garden, almost at once.

With the mimicry born of his loneliness Henry continued some moments longer to shape his mouth to the ladies' imagined speech, trying from his meagre stock to supply

14

words for them. But Miss Taverner's appearance had changed everything, like a wash of colour. With her dark hair and her glances and her plain brown dress she had made the other ladies seem unreal. He did not care what they were saying now.

He edged forward on the smooth, warped wood of the windowseat, which ran like a bench round three walls of the summer-house, and rested his face against the corner of the window in an effort to increase his field of vision. He could not see where Miss Taverner had gone but the shift enabled him to see a larger section of the rear of the house with its white wooden walls and clustering wisteria – Miss Taverner herself had told him that name. He saw his father's Turkish manservant, Mehmet Agha, pass from the deep shade at the edge of the terrace into the sunlight. He was carrying a tray with glasses on it, and the glasses lost shape suddenly, dissolved into gleams of light. Mehmet Agha was dressed in his best for the occasion, in white silk turban, short-bodied waistcoat embroidered in blue and gold, and full white trousers. He was tall and fair-bearded and dignified. A fine fellow, Henry had once heard his father say, and the phrase had stayed in his mind, preserved by his envy of such approval.

Mehmet Agha crossed that part of the terrace that the boy could see, then vanished again as if absorbed by the sunlight. But Henry now saw, at the extreme edge of his vision, what he immediately knew was the dark smooth back of his father's head, and part of the back of his grey suit. He was talking to someone beyond, whom the boy could not see. Henry tried to imagine what his father might be saying, made a brief forlorn attempt at his father's clipped and precise way of speaking, the slightly metallic quality of the voice, the way the mouth set firm and motionless after each group of words; but his invention failed at once, his attempt at mimicry faltered and died. His father was too powerful.

After a moment or two he opened his book and began to

read. The book was called *Magic and Religion Among the Moslems*, which, because of the first word, had seemed one of the more promising titles on the shelves of his father's study, from where, without permission, he had taken it. It had gilt lines down the borders and the first letter on each page was decorated in red and blue. The colours had run a little, perhaps through some long process of damp, and this made an effect that the boy found beautiful. He was a precocious reader, not much deterred by unfamiliar words, even enjoying their mystery. He was reading now about Azrael, the Angel of Death, one of the most powerful among the ranks of the angels, whose special duty it was to separate the soul from the body. If the dead person had lived a good life and kept his soul unpolluted by sin, this presented no difficulty. In that case the soul was loose within the body and easily separated, and Azrael did his job with great gentleness. That person became one with Allah immediately. But if the dead person had been a sinner it was a very different matter. His soul was still attached to his body and had to be wrenched out. His whole body had to be torn apart for Azrael to get at his soul . . .

Henry looked up from his book. Unpolluted by sin, he thought. The words had a dark sound. But how could it be done? The soul would still have shreds of body sticking to it. It would be all covered with blood. It seemed hardly possible. He could ask Miss Taverner, of course, but that would mean revealing that he had taken the book, and he could not rely on her yet not to tell his parents things. Perhaps it was she his father had been talking to, out there on the terrace. No, she was not one of the guests. All the same, his father did talk to Miss Taverner, quite often. He spoke in a joking kind of way usually. Miss Taverner laughed and colour came into her face.

The words which had defeated his son's imagination came from Markham's lips perfectly clear and measured, involving no change in the rather cold set of the features. 'No,' he said, 'I don't think I would call Constantinople a romantic city exactly.'

'Oh, but surely,' the lady said. 'All these contrasts it affords . . . Diverse worlds rubbing shoulders. East and West meet here, don't they? I mean, *surely?*'

Markham looked at her for a moment, aware of dislike. Worlds rubbing shoulders – it did not augur well for the style of the articles she had said she was proposing to write. 'Well, that is true,' he said. 'There's no point in arguing about words, anyway. I really don't know what the word means.'

However, she was a person who persisted. 'It is what has mostly struck me since my arrival,' she said, 'that very thing.'

'You have been here less than a week, you said.' He had forgotten for the moment the woman's name. He sought to recall it, the better to attach disparaging epithets to her in his mind. She was the niece of someone at the Embassy. She was engaged to write some articles for a magazine. His wife had met her at a tea party. Scottish name . . . Miss Munro.

'I know it is not very long,' she said.

'Piquant contrasts,' he said. 'The exotic and the squalid, all that kind of thing?' It was almost a sneer.

'Thank you for the suggestion,' she said. Her small grey eyes were regarding him narrowly. He saw that she found him disagreeable and this, quite unreasonably, surprised him. A belated sense of his duty as host came to him. His features relaxed from the rather mask-like composure they took on when he was at all tense or angry.

'No reason why it shouldn't be said again,' he said.

'I have no intention of repeating other people's judgements of the city,' Miss Munro said stiffly. 'I hope I have enough sense to form my own.'

'Quite so,' he said. This was better. Priggish but sturdy. Why had he been so rude?

'And that includes yours,' she said, obviously not placated yet.

17

He looked at her, smiling slightly. A long, pale, bony face that the short, fashionably-bobbed hair did not suit. Sharp shoulders beneath the white muslin dress. She would be in her late twenties. Late to be unmarried. The sort of age when women begin to cultivate fine responses, in the absence of grosser pleasures . . . He was at once slightly ashamed of this thought. Why had he reacted so strongly to her harmless remark? Perhaps the gesture that had gone with it, that raising of one thin arm, the opening and closing of the white glove, as if she wished to grasp the city. Twenty centuries of blood, he thought suddenly – that glove should return to her side red with blood, red to the wrist. *Romantic*. Yes, that was it, probably: the predatory gesture and the facile word.

'I intend to get my experience at first hand,' she said. 'From the Turks themselves.'

'You won't find any Turks here,' he said, 'other than the servants.'

'Don't you invite Turks?'

'They wouldn't come,' he said patiently. 'None of them would dare to come to the house of a foreigner. Once on the Sultan's list you never get off it. Men disappear without trace in this city, this *romantic* city. Sometimes hours after being reported, sometimes years. This is a police state, Miss Munro, run by a man who has been insane for a long time.' His voice had risen as he spoke, but had not varied in its rather flat, uninflected delivery. Now he lowered it again, to say, 'But surely your uncle will have spoken to you about all this?'

'Well, yes,' she said. 'He did describe the régime as harsh, but he says the Sultan has many difficulties to contend with, and the country needs a firm hand.'

'Firm hand?' A sharp sound broke from Markham, something between a cough and a laugh. 'That's the sort of phrase you would use for a horse,' he said. He glanced up over her head, glimpsed at that moment the flash of a mirror or window, some reflecting surface, from somewhere high up among the distant rooftops of the Palace, which were visible

18

from here only as a haze of white marble through the foliage of the Sultan's park. The flash came and went, came again, remained steady for a few moments. It was as though someone up there were signalling.

'I expect the Palace executioners have firm hands,' he said, looking back at Miss Munro. It seemed to him that her expression had become wary. He was conscious that his words and manner were not appropriate for an occasion of this kind, but the desire to disturb Miss Munro was rising in him like a kind of cruelty, and he felt for the moment unable to stop or change, as if he were committing atrocities in a dream. He glanced up again, but the flash had gone. 'Firm hands for the bastinado and the boiling oil,' he said.

She did not reply to this, and in the silence that fell between them, Markham glanced aside and saw his wife standing just below the terrace, talking to Blake. Something characteristic caught and held him in that brief moment, a quality of tension in her figure. She was *coping* – a word she often used. It was as though her being here among these people were the result of some obscure self-conquest. Courage is not measured by the issues of the battle, and there was something poignant to him in his wife's posture at this moment, the set of her shoulders and head. This almost visible quiver of duty seemed in a way to sum up all his knowledge of her.

He began to glance round the garden, as if in search of someone or something there that would relieve him from this knowledge or provide a contrast, but found nothing. With a vague sense of dissatisfaction, as at expectation cheated, he returned his attention to Miss Munro. She had begun to speak again about her uncle, his views of the present situation.

'Yes,' he said, barely listening, 'that's true, I suppose.' His sense of dissatisfaction continued. He caught the arm of Kyriakos, the Embassy doctor, who was passing. 'Well, Doctor,' he said, 'tell me, would you call Constantinople a romantic city?'

'Romantic?'

Markham looked seriously at the cynical, good-humoured face of the Greek. It was not a word likely to mean much to him. 'I don't think you've met Miss Munro, have you?' he said.

'Romantic?' Kyriakos said again, after the formalities of introduction were over. 'The place where you live is never romantic. Taking a pulse is taking a pulse.'

'But you must see things beyond your mere professional concerns,' Miss Munro said. 'Surely.' She laughed slightly as she spoke, at the absurdity of anyone not seeing this.

Kyriakos smiled, but Markham thought it probable that he was not much drawn to Miss Munro. Indeed, she seemed to have a gift for antagonizing people.

'I mean, *surely*?' she said.

Suddenly Markham saw his son's governess coming up the terrace steps towards them. She was bareheaded and her head was lowered slightly. She was not looking at them but at the steps before her. She was wearing a brown cotton dress of very simple cut, high-necked, close-fitting on the arms and shoulders, and no jewellery of any kind. This severity made the fulness and beauty of her figure more striking. The steps were rather deep and in mounting them her knees were given brief alternate prominence by the stuff of her dress. The moment he caught sight of her Markham realized, without surprise – indeed with a sense of naturalness and inevitability – that it was she he had been looking for earlier, in his glances round the garden.

He did not ask himself yet why this was so, but was content merely to feel it. He watched her reach the top of the steps, hesitate for some moments, then move across the terrace, through the french windows into the house. Looking for Henry, no doubt – the boy had a gift for disappearing. When he returned his attention to Miss Munro and Kyriakos, it was with a sense of the world having changed in some way.

* * *

20

'No,' Elizabeth Markham said. 'It is not his health exactly. As a matter of fact I was wondering whether there might be something troubling him, you know.'

The mildness of her words gave no indication of the effort it had been to bring them out. It was an effort for her to confide in anyone, particularly about matters so close to her, and to a man of only a month's acquaintance. But then, no acquaintance she had in Constantinople went further back than this. And she had sensed from the beginning, from the moment of meeting him, that Captain Blake would be one whom she could turn to, sensed it in the quality of his attentiveness to her – recognized it rather, as it was something she had seen in other men from time to time and felt grateful for, without conscious disloyalty to Markham, though the men who seemed to admire her were always of a different type from her husband, as Captain Blake was, large, inarticulate, protective. She herself was touched, and attracted too, by the chivalry with which such men treated her. She met Captain Blake's eyes. They were furious with the honesty of his desire to be of help.

'Your husband is a very reserved man, Mrs Markham,' he said. 'I mean where his feelings are concerned, of course.' He sought for further words, pushing his shoulders back as if this might help. The movement strained his broad chest against the polished diagonal strap of his Sam Browne – he had come to the luncheon party straight from the offices of the Military Commission in Stambul and was still in uniform. 'Not what you'd call a demonstrative man,' he said. 'At least, not . . . If there were anything amiss he would not readily talk about it.'

'No, quite,' she said instantly, proudly. It humiliated her to seem to know so little about her husband, to seem to be asking for advice in an area where she should know best – almost as if she were complaining that he did not confide in her. 'I didn't mean that, really,' she said. 'I thought perhaps you might have noticed something.'

She looked away from the open, fair-skinned face divided

21

between kindness and embarrassment, towards the sun-filled terrace and the narrow back of her husband as he stood there talking to someone. Miss Munro. He would not be enjoying that. He was standing very straight and it seemed to her unnaturally still, with the immobility of someone threatened. Then he raised his head and the illusion was broken.

'No,' Blake said, 'I can't say I have.'

She was still looking towards her husband and saw him now draw Doctor Kyriakos into the conversation, no doubt the first step in a move to escape. Miss Taverner, wearing a dark-coloured dress that made her strangely conspicuous, was standing below the terrace looking towards the garden. Looking for Henry, no doubt. Elizabeth frowned a little at the thought of how difficult and secretive Henry was getting. Difficult to cope with . . . *My husband is a changed man*, she wanted to say to Captain Blake. *Being here, in this city, has changed him. I saw it at once, the moment I arrived. You must have seen it too.*

'Well,' she said, 'if you notice anything . . .'

But that is the wrong way to put it, she thought, the wrong way to ask him. It was impossible, really, to give expression, at least in any coherent way, to what was troubling her. There were the symptoms of strain in her husband, the sleeplessness, the hours of the night spent in his study or walking in the garden. But what chiefly worried her, and even at times frightened her, was his retreat during the three months they had been separated, into some narrow territory of his own. He seemed to live behind some contrived fence, as ill or afflicted people do.

'He has a consuming interest in the Sultan,' she said. 'It is almost an obsession with him. The most various things are often brought round to that.'

Blake glanced at the face of the woman as once again, in some constraint, she looked away. The sun, so much hotter than at home, had not yet touched her face. It was slightly flushed now, with the embarrassment of what she had been driven to say. Breeding in every line of her, Blake thought. He was moved by the appeal implicit in her words, by the sense of what it cost her to violate reticence in this way. But he could not think of anything. He and Markham were not close. He was not drawn to the other man, disliking the dandified style, the sardonic fluency of speech.

'He has been very busy lately,' he said. 'The situation in Macedonia is critical, you know.'

She nodded. 'He is responsible for organizing the local militia, isn't he?' she said. 'You and he work together.'

'It is quite a headache,' Blake said. He looked at her for a moment, wondering how much she knew about Markham's work, whether he confided in her. It was obvious that there must be more than the militia business behind Markham's posting. There were people up in Macedonia handling that, at least as far as the formation of the units was concerned. The Powers That Be had wanted Markham in Constantinople for reasons of their own. Blake was not particularly curious, however. He had been in the army long enough to mind his own business where matters like that were concerned.

'If you do see anything—' she began, then changed the form of her words. 'I'd be terribly grateful if you would keep an eye on him for me,' she said.

'I'll do my best,' Blake said, and the brusqueness of his tone did not deceive her. The desire to be of service to her was writ large on his face. 'I'll have to be going,' he said now. 'I have to be back at the office this afternoon. It was very nice of you to ask me.'

'You are always welcome here,' she said. She saw Miss Taverner mount the steps to the terrace, cross it, and disappear into the house. The group around her husband was beginning to break up. Miss Munro had begun moving across the terrace towards her, no doubt to take her leave. Elizabeth smiled once more at Blake, then moved forward still smiling, though differently, towards Miss Munro. As she did so she noticed that her husband and Doctor Kyriakos had been joined by another man, whom she recognized as Mr Somerville. She knew little of Mr Somerville except that he talked a great deal, and always enthusiastically, about money.

The door of the summer-house made a sudden rattling sound. Henry looked up vaguely from his book, his vision still occupied with the sinner's body all mangled after the struggle to extract his soul. Like a pulpy fig. The rattling came again, and with a shock of alarm he saw the flimsy door move to and fro against the frame several times. Someone was rattling the door from outside.

Taking great care to make no noise, and keeping his finger inside the book to mark his place, Henry slid down from the windowseat to the floor. He was directly below the window here. He was about to move further towards the corner, when he saw the peering face of Miss Taverner suddenly loom up against the window, framed by the sprays of honeysuckle. Instinct told him that any movement now would be detected. He lay still, pressed against the base of the windowseat, looking upwards. Her face was immense, so close against the window, just above him – it was not more than three feet away. But the wide brown eyes were not regarding anything, merely striving to see. The interior was too dim, the window too dirty. Some seconds passed and with cautious delight Henry realized that Miss Taverner's face was there for him to look at, just as if it were a picture in a book. His heart was ticking in his ears as he studied Miss Taverner's broad cheekbones, creamy skin, her beautiful wide eyes, like a cow's, gazing without focus through the dusty pane, her mouth with the full underlip – the lips were parted a little now, as she vainly peered. Then the face receded, disappeared, leaving him with a feeling of breathlessness.

He waited some moments longer, then got up on the seat and looked out. There were not so many people now. The ladies had gone from the rose garden. A tall lady in a

24

billowing sort of dress and a little white hat moved slowly across the terrace. His father was still in the same place, talking to two men. There was no sign of Miss Taverner.

*The Angel of Death*, the boy whispered to himself. He would have to leave the summer-house soon. By keeping to the edge of the garden, among the bushes, he might be able to pass below the terrace and reach his room undetected. His father would already be angry with him, so the longer he could keep out of the way the better – experience had taught him that time dilutes wrath. Perhaps it would be better to stay where he was for the time being . . . Not for too long, he thought, or my mother will be worried. He began to read again, shaping his lips to the words:

> When the interment has been concluded and the mourners have dispersed, the *imam* remains a short time longer by the grave in order to prompt the dead man in his replies to the Questioners. These are two angels, Mounkir and Nekir, whose task it is to interrogate the newly dead concerning their faith. They are armed with specially fashioned rods, the shafts being of iron, the end a heavy copper knob. They stand at the head of the grave and put their questions. *Who is thy creator? Who is thy prophet?* If the dead man has been a devout Moslem, his reply will be: *My God is Allah; my prophet Mohammad; my religion Islam; and my kibla the Holy Kaaba.* If, however, he has been lax in his religious observances he will not be able to remember the words of his creed. No matter how carefully he has committed them to memory, he will infallibly forget them when the time comes for him to answer. And when he stammers and fails to answer, the knobs of the rods which the angels carry in their hands will fall heavily on his head, beating it relentlessly . . .

'I'm not talking about concession-hunting,' Somerville said, wrinkling his nose as he spoke, so that his glasses moved briefly up and down. This was a frequent mannerism of his, and gave him a sniffing sort of eagerness, markedly at odds with the judicious set of the mouth below the thin moustache. 'If things were on a sounder footing here,' he said, 'there'd be much less of that too. No, I'm talking about planned investment in the country's economy by the European powers. Controlled through the proper channels, of course.'

'Proper channels?' Kyriakos glanced humorously from face to face, then looked upward as if searching for something in the sky. 'Where are they,' he said, 'these proper channels, which you take for granted?'

'Do you realize,' Somerville said, speaking directly to Markham, 'the opportunities for investment this country affords, the enormous potential for development . . .?' He paused, wrinkling his nose again. His glasses had slipped down a little, and he raised a hand to adjust them. Kyriakos continued his play-acting, glancing about him on the ground as if in search of something there.

Markham watched them for a moment or two without speaking, the thin, fair-browed Englishman with that odd contrast in his face between eagerness and dispassion, the curious suppressed fervour with which he talked about finance; and the Greek of the Phanar, with his ease of gesture, his quickness of wit, his suppleness, in which there was, to English eyes at least, less than full dignity. Kyriakos was the wiser man, he reflected: at ease with his body and his world. But it suddenly seemed not at all surprising to Markham, seeing them together, that the English were the dominant race. There was aspiration in Somerville's small eyes – all that was most imaginative in him was fired by thoughts of securing the eight per cent for the British shareholders he represented, along with his fellow commissioners in the Ottoman Consolidated Loan Company; whereas Kyriakos's face, full of intelligence as it was, reflected merely application to particular immediate ends: the performance of his medical

26

duties, the choice of the right restaurant or the right gift for his mistress, a Jewess of Polish extraction whom he kept in Pera, just off the Grande Rue. Kyriakos did not know, of course, that he, Markham, was in possession of this last piece of information. Files were kept on all persons connected in any way with the Embassy.

'I think you are wrong, Somerville,' he said, 'if what you are saying is that the remedy for Turkish ills is simply pouring more money in. Very little of it would go where it is needed. Most would go where most goes already, into the pockets of the gang around Abdul Hamid.'

'That is what I meant,' Somerville said, 'when I referred to the proper channels.'

Kyriakos smiled at Elizabeth Markham who had just joined them, with Blake beside her. 'I see only improper channels in the Ottoman lands,' he said.

Markham saw his wife smile back, with a slight, conscious lift of the chin. Rising to the occasion again. She would not like the insinuating quality in the Greek's manner, nor his cynicism.

'After all,' Somerville said, 'it is official British policy to maintain the Sultan and preserve the Empire, and money is the best way of preserving governments, in my view.'

'Like embalming fluid?' Kyriakos said.

Markham caught the flash of light again, from high up on the wooded hill of Yildiz, among the dark green of foliage, the white latticed façades. Suddenly he realized what it was.

'Old Baba Hamid,' he said involuntarily. 'He's keeping an eye on us.'

'More like an injection,' Blake said. He was pleased with this thought which it had taken him some time to arrive at. 'What do you mean?' he said. He half turned to glance in the direction of Yildiz, then looked curiously at Markham's face, which was as usual so composed as to be mask-like. There was something disturbing in this immobility, in the contrast between the vividness of the face, with its strongly marked

27

brows, luminous dark eyes, wide sensuous mouth, and this stillness of the features, the almost unvarying composure. At times, in certain lights, it was possible to think of the face as an actual mask. 'What do you mean?' he said again.

'Father Hamid,' Markham said, in the same tone. 'As the Turks call him.'

'Though there have been better fathers,' Kyriakos said. 'Chronos, for example.'

'Chronos?' Blake had not understood the reference.

'He made a practice of eating his children, if you remember.'

Blake nodded coldly, not caring to be instructed by the Greek. It occurred to him that he had already taken leave of his hostess, more or less, but he felt a certain reluctance to go.

'He's keeping an eye on us,' Markham repeated. 'He has got a telescope up there.'

He at once regretted having said this, had time fractionally to wonder at himself, feel dismayed at such a lapse of taste, no, more like a betrayal of the special relationship, for so he felt it, between himself and the man up there on the roof – who of course knew nothing about it. It was disquieting, too, how near the threshold of sound his words had been lying, as if the merest twitch of a nerve had elicited those few syllables from his throat. This induced no caution, however; again when he spoke it was with a sense of words uttered almost by reflex, only just within the limits of control.

'A very distinguished autocrat,' he said. 'More blood on his hands than any ruler of modern times.'

Blake twisted his head round on his short neck to peer up again towards Yildiz. He did this as much out of embarrassment as curiosity. There had been too much seriousness in Markham's words for the occasion, his manner had too much edge to it; and the sudden portentousness had seemed wrong, somehow – it was as though Markham had made some unexpected personal confession.

'Well, my dear,' Elizabeth Markham said, in a laughing

28

tone, and several moments too late to prevent a rather awkward pause in the conversation, 'if you had one of the best views in Constantinople, you would probably get yourself a telescope too, I should think. Poor old man, he must be lonely up there.'

'Lonely?' Kyriakos said. 'With three hundred women at his disposal?'

He smiled at Elizabeth rather too lingeringly. Blake felt his prejudice against foreigners reinforced: an Englishman making the same remark would have smiled at the other men. What made it all worse of course was the fellow's impeccable English. Markham himself did not seem to be paying much attention to any of this.

'You take an interest in him, don't you?' Blake said quietly. 'In the Sultan, I mean.' He thought at first that Markham had not heard him. His expression did not change, the regard remained steady, the mouth faintly smiling. Then he saw, or thought he saw, some impulse to speak, something impetuous, rise to the mouth and the eyes, something checked instantly and almost visibly. When Markham did at last reply, it was in a cool and indifferent manner.

'Well, after all, he's a neighbour of ours,' he said. Then, after a pause, he added, 'So you think the treatment is money, do you?'

So abrupt a reversion to the former topic seemed like a snub, a reproof to Blake for pressing him too close.

'Yes,' Blake said, 'I agree with Somerville.' I must be careful, he thought. The fellow's state of mind is not really my business. He had been over-sensitized somehow, by the attractiveness of the man's wife and the fact that she had chosen him to confide in. It occurred to him once again that he ought to be getting along. He saw with distaste that the Greek had commenced his play-acting again.

'Money,' Kyriakos said, placing his fingertips together, 'is generally a good and efficacious remedy for all kinds of disorder and distress. However, the patient in question is suffering from a terminal disease. There is no cure for decaying Empires.' Kyriakos dropped his hands to his sides and looked around but not for applause. The quality of his smile changed, became blander. 'As you yourselves will find,' he said.

Markham nodded and smiled, forestalling any sharper reaction from his fellow-countrymen. 'We must cross that bridge when we come to it,' he said. He glanced up again in the direction of Yildiz. He knew, sensed, that Abdul Hamid's scrutiny of the world was over for the time being; and he felt suddenly empty in that knowledge, drained of identity, as if his most vividly realized life was at the end of the Sultan's telescope.

# 2

When Abdul Hamid left the roof of his Star Pavilion, the guests had all gone, the garden was deserted – it was there that he looked last, before retiring from the roof. He went down by the internal staircase, which was to his own design, straight and very narrow, so that only one at a time could go up or down, only one at a time come face to face with him. Of one man, at a distance, he was not so much afraid. He always carried two pistols on him, in pockets specially sewn in his clothes, and constant practice had made him extremely adept with them.

The staircase ended in a door, concealed on the side of the passage to which it gave access by a large rug hanging on the wall. The passage appeared to be blocked off at both ends, though at one end there was merely a screen of plastered laths which could be lifted aside. This opened on to a complicated system of narrower passages, many of which led nowhere at all. Following a certain route through these passages the Sultan came at last to the secret entrance to his study, another, much narrower screen, covered on the interior side by heavy draperies. Two quick steps brought the Sultan through these hangings into the security of his study, which was guarded at the official entrance, both outside and inside the anteroom doors, by his faithful Albanians. It had taken him six minutes to traverse what was by direct measurement a very short distance indeed, certainly no more than a hundred metres. No one else could have done it at all, without getting lost. Certain routes to the vicinity of the Sultan were known to certain persons: the Commander of the Palace Guard, for example, senior officials of the Secretariat, Abdul Hudar the Court Astrologer; one or two had a more comprehensive knowledge, like Tahsin Bey, the First Secretary, or Izzet, or the Chief of the Black Eunuchs, Djavad Agha, but only the Sultan himself, who ordered and supervised the changes that were constantly being made (but never by the same workmen), could have known in its entirety or carried in his mind the labyrinth of passages linking the offices and state rooms of the Palace itself, all the connexions between the various buildings within the enclosure of the inner walls, together with the blind alleys, blocked-off entrances, false fronts, detours and intersections designed to confuse would-be assassins. Even he, who had contrived this labyrinth through thirty years of slowly intensifying fear, sometimes made mistakes; sometimes it happened that he gave orders, perhaps for a certain corridor to be narrowed, only to be told by the workmen concerned that this corridor existed no longer, having been filled in in the time of their fathers.

'Well,' Markham said, 'I wasn't sorry, really, to see them go. Were you?'

This sentiment was so heart-felt that he took his wife's assent for granted, did not listen to her murmured words of reply. 'Blake's not a bad fellow, of course,' he went on. 'Rather heavy-going. Somerville talked about money as usual. Amazing the faith these people have in money.'

'He's rather sweet, I think,' Elizabeth Markham said, in her low, slightly vibrant voice – even in ordinary conversations like this one, her voice always seemed to contain a note of feeling not completely suppressed.

'Who do you mean?' he said. 'Somerville?'

'No, Captain Blake.'

'Do you really?' He turned to look at her more fully. The directness of her remark had seemed like a mild reproof to him, especially as it was not the kind of thing she often said – she would usually have expressed her opinion more obliquely. 'Hardly the word . . .' he said, smiling slightly, waiting for the incongruity to strike her. But he saw no answering smile on

32

her face and after a moment he said, 'The kind of man your father would have approved of, I should think.' A decent stupidity was what the Brigadier had liked best – he himself had been set down as too clever, unstable. All the same he was already regretting the remark. It sounded too like a complaint.

'Probably,' she said vaguely. She half turned away from him to look into an oval mirror on the wall. After a moment or two she raised her hands to her head, beginning to take out some of the pins which had been holding up her hair.

They were alone together in the larger of the two interconnecting *salons* that occupied the central part of the ground floor, running the whole depth of the house from front to rear. This, the front one, afforded a magnificent view of the Bosphoros and the Asian shore beyond. It was furnished, as was the whole house, in early nineteenth-century Ottoman style, rather bare, with low alabaster tables in wrought-iron frames, woven rugs, a long, high-backed sofa against one wall. As usual with Turkish houses of the older sort, the main decorative element was the view. The window was deeply recessed and took up most of one wall. A broad divan covered in faded green velvet, with cushions of the same material, ran round all three sides of the window. One could recline here and admire the blue water below, the cypresses and white villas of Scutari, on the Asian side.

The shutters were open and light flooded in through the tall uncurtained windows. Perhaps because of this fulness of light, which was by now a familiar experience to him; perhaps because of something he felt as characteristic in their respective attitudes – he standing lounging at the window, she inclined forward in slightly strained attention to her image in the mirror, letting down her hair as if in obedience to precise instructions inscribed there – Markham felt suddenly that the things they were saying to each other were in the nature of afterthoughts to some previous conversation, conducted long before. Perhaps, he thought, we are adding some vital element.

'That woman,' he said, 'I must say . . . She is an example of the New Woman, I suppose. What can she possibly find to say about the situation here? She has only just arrived for one thing.'

'Why is it, I wonder,' she said smiling, 'that whenever a woman is unmarried, and ventures to express an opinion of her own these days, men put on that expression you are putting on now and call her the New Woman?' She looked away from her reflection, towards the window where her husband was standing with shoulders raised a little, hands in his jacket pockets. 'People must be allowed to see things in their own way, Robert,' she said.

'That's true, I suppose.' All the same, he could not rid himself completely of the resentment he had felt at the way the woman seemed to take the city over, make it into an abstraction, a sort of manageable idea – this intractable city, whose sounds and sights and smells were acting from day to day like caustic on his memory, scraping off protective skins, exposing the twelve-year-old wound, still raw. It was experience of pain that had made him proprietorial about the city. His wife, of course, knew nothing of this, did not know, even, that he had been in Constantinople at that time, the time of the massacres. And it was too late now to tell her. She thought him possessive of the place by virtue simply of residence, of official status – petty reasons. His own fault, of course, that she misjudged him: he had feared her judgement too much to speak of the past to her. Now as she stood there, the light hair down to her shoulders, he was visited by a tenderness for her, a feeling almost of pity for her ignorance of him.

He was about to move towards her when he saw Mehmet Agha enter the farther room from the terrace beyond. The double doors connecting the two rooms stood open, so that it was possible from where Markham was standing to see right through to the trees of the garden. He watched the servant approach against this background of sunlight and leaves and

34

then pause in the doorway. He had come to inquire whether the *effendis* had more needs. Markham considered him a moment as he stood there, dignified in his bulk, impassive, with his fair beard and blue eyes, which were direct and steady yet without familiarity or boldness. The hands, loosely crossed in deference across his broad chest, were heavy-looking, tanned and roughened by his thirty years at sea, first as a Trabzon fisherman then on a customs launch, patrolling the southern shores of the Black Sea for smugglers. This was before he had married Nevres Badji, the Abyssinian freedwoman who kept house for the Markhams.

'No,' Markham said in Turkish, 'there's nothing else. Thank you Mehmet, you did very well. *Bu isi cok guzel yaptin.*'

'*Bir sey degil,*' the servant said, inclining his head slightly.

'Thank you, Mehmet,' his wife said in English, and she smiled.

Mehmet's gravity, proof against Markham's praises, was dissolved by this smile. He smiled in his turn, broadly, and salaamed low as he left.

'We were lucky in that fellow,' Markham said. 'He's completely reliable. But then, you show me an Anatolian Turk who isn't.'

'They are fine people,' she said, but this was so much an expression of her own steadfastness as to seem almost self-approving, and it brought out a kind of immediate impiety in him.

'Why are we talking like Blake?' he said. 'The trouble is that they never look critically at what they are relied upon to do. The Turks, I mean. Like all races renowned for their fidelity. They can be relied upon to commit atrocities too.'

She moved and sat on the edge of the divan, leaning forward a little. 'I don't see that man committing atrocities,' she said.

'If he thought it was his duty . . .' Into Markham's mind, unbidden, came leaping memories of what men not much different to look at had done, memories of what he had seen or

35

had been told, images not separate but coalescing, blood-cemented: clubbed Armenians, bleeding their lives away in the gutters of Galata; the human bonfires of Urfa; the lines of blinded Bulgarians. He shook his head very slightly to dispel these images, and the images went, but the collective agony pulsed still in his mind, slowly, like the slow beat of his own heart.

He went over to his wife and stood above her, looking down. Her hair lay in a smooth, burnished unbroken sweep to her shoulders. He moved the hair aside to uncover the pale narrow nape of her neck. He bent his head and kissed her there, pressing his lips against the slightly muscled softness just below the hair-line. Still that pulsing of the memory continued. She sat still for some moments then she put up her hand to the side of his face, still without speaking. For a moment or two they were still, as if waiting for something that could bring them closer or take them further apart. Markham's eyes had been closed. He opened them now to see in blurred close-up the grain of his wife's skin. He smelled the warm crepe of her dress and the odour of her perfume, distinct but unassertive, like some gentle violation. Without warning or any sort of preliminary – and this casualness was itself part of the nightmare – he began to feel the now familiar sense of suffocation, her scent and closeness stopped his breathing, like a scented pad over his mouth. With deliberate lack of haste he raised his head, straightened himself, moved away into the centre of the recess. He breathed deeply, aware once more of the wide vista of water and wooded hills framed by the window.

'Well,' he said, 'I shall have to be getting on. I have to go over and see Nesbitt.'

'You will be careful, won't you?' she said.

'Careful? Of course. I'm always careful when I talk to Nesbitt.'

She half-turned so that she was facing inwards towards him. He stood with his back to the window now. His features

36

had settled into their customary, rather cold composure. She made a vague, half-completed gesture with her arm, causing the sleeve of her dress to fall away almost to the elbow. 'I wasn't really talking about Nesbitt,' she said. 'It's about that man who was killed in Smyrna, isn't it?'

'Turgut, yes. But his being killed doesn't alter the equation for the rest of us.'

'I don't see why you had to go at all,' she said.

This she had said before, at the time of his going. There seemed to him a curious wilfulness in her taking it up now, as if her anxiety was reason enough for resuming the debate, even after the event.

'But my love, I've told you already,' he said. 'Someone had to go, and I speak Turkish, so I could talk to the police, as well as the consul there. He was a British subject, after all. Though how he managed that nobody quite knows.'

'I still think someone on the spot could have done it,' she said.

This obstinacy sprang from her love, he knew that; yet at the same time there was hostility in it, as if in some way she blamed him. He wondered briefly if she had sensed his fear, just now, sensed the quality of recoil in the way he had moved away from her. No, probably not. He had controlled it well. Besides, he had heard it in her voice quite often lately, this obscure reproach.

'It could be important,' he said. 'It's not just one isolated case. The Sultan's informers, people like this Turgut, have plied their trade openly for years, making no attempt to hide what they were. In fact, it helped if their power was believed in; it gave them more influence locally.'

'How do you mean?' she said.

Markham paused a moment. He knew he could rely absolutely on his wife's discretion. All the same it went against the grain to discuss these things too fully with her. They belonged to his work, and the outside world, from which he was accustomed to think women should be excluded.

'Well, opportunities for blackmail,' he said. 'An accredited agent of the Palace will always be believed, if it is his word against those he accuses. People will pay to avoid being accused. That's why the spy system is so vicious. Anyway, the wind is changing. These fine fellows, who have been strutting about for years, are now being set upon, beaten, in some cases killed. Old scores are being paid off. In the last fortnight alone, agents of the Sultan have been assassinated in Monastir, in Jannina, in Aleppo. And now in Smyrna. This must mean some change of mood in the people, a new heart—'

'What, even for such cowardly acts?' In her tone, and in the sudden raising of her face, there was contempt for these backstreet murders, a contempt which extended to him as their advocate – or so he felt at this moment, sensitive as he was to her reproaches.

He paused, looking at her with a sort of baffled irritation which he dared not express. Partly he was disabled by the suggestion of cowardice, partly by being caught in unwilling respect for what he recognized as the blind operation of the code in her, the voice of her landowning forebears, privileged generations who had never had to resort to meanness and deceit. Whether these ancestral voices were gruff or soft, the message was always the same. And she could never see beyond it, never. It was not feeling she lacked, but the kind of imagination that can make routes to other, possibly baser, hearts and minds.

'Yes,' he said, 'even for such cowardly acts.' It was an effort for him now to argue the matter, break free from his own corrupted respect; however, he persisted, speaking with a sort of conscious care and deliberateness. 'You must try to imagine what thirty years of oppression will do to a people,' he said. 'Possibly you do not realize how hopeless of redress wrongs will seem after thirty years of tyranny, how in a generation brought up to see no protection in the law fear of the authorities will be endemic. Surely you see this? Under

38

certain circumstances, to plant a knife between a man's shoulderblades takes a good deal of courage.' He glanced at her face. It was slightly turned away from him, the eyes lowered. When he spoke again, his voice was duller, as if he had recognized a defeat. 'Circumstances alter cases, Elizabeth,' he said. 'It is what you have never seen. Sir Henry Newbolt and Abdul Hamid simply do not mix.'

At once, quite involuntarily, with the mention of that name, he glanced at his watch. What would the Sultan be doing now? 'He sits up there,' he said. 'Can you imagine it? One motion of the pen and who knows the lives blasted, ruined? Now it's coming home to him . . .'

He had begun to walk back and forth with short rapid strides down the centre of the *kilim* on the floor. This was a broad rectangle in shape, Anatolian weaving of some fifty years before, in which tones of brown and red formed a sinuous pattern beguiling to the eye. Markham measured it with his steps, eight forward, eight back, keeping carefully within the confines of the rectangle. She watched him, sitting back against the cushions, hands loosely clasped in her lap.

'He won't see it, of course,' he said. 'Not until too late. His people will keep it from him. He employs more spies than police but he learns nothing essential. His informers invent plots to keep him entertained. People continue to be arrested but the real forces of change go on undetected. He can't see, in any case. None of that gang at the Palace can see. They have grown old together in tyranny. Old dogs with glazed eyes.'

In his growing absorption Markham had begun to walk more carelessly and in this way he overshot the limits of the *kilim* at the end farthest from the window, in the interior of the room. In making his turn he caught sight of a small black shoe and a few inches of thickly wrinkled grey stocking behind the sofa which stood against the wall. Abstractedly, his mind still occupied with what he had been saying, he knelt on the sofa and looked down over the high curving back. His son was lying there in a roughly foetal position but with one leg more

39

extended than the other – it was this incautiously extended leg that had given him away. The boy was facing inwards towards the room so that when Markham looked down his eyes met those of his son immediately.

'Good God!' Markham said violently. 'What—?' He stared down, speechless for the moment, at the recumbent form. It had not stirred, and it was this perhaps, the fact that the boy made no attempt to move, that Markham found most outrageous of all. 'Get out from there,' he said. 'At once.'

Henry Markham came out quietly on hands and knees, straightened, and stood with his back against the wall. He was holding a book. He stood against the wall, well away from his father. There was nothing submissive in his attitude, however. He lowered his eyes for a moment or two, then raised them to glance towards his mother.

'What are you doing here?' Markham said, only slightly less loudly. Behind him he heard his wife say his name, warningly, but he was not angry so much as shocked. Pacing the *kilim*, talking of the Sultan, he had been as heedless and yet as vulnerable to interruption as a person sleepwalking. It was as if the sight of the boy had shaken him awake. 'What are you doing?' he said again.

'I was reading,' the boy said. 'I was here when you came in, sir. I was here first.' He said this with confidence, as if it constituted an irreproachable defence.

'Don't you know,' Markham said, 'that you must not listen to other people's conversations without their knowledge? That is eavesdropping. No person of breeding does that. Don't you *know* that?'

'Yes, sir,' the boy said. 'But you and Mamma were talking as you came in, and I was already here.'

Markham felt a pang of sympathy for the boy. Thrust out into the light he was reacting to danger as predictably as any other solitary mammal. That stillness against the wall, the composure of the face, the precocious self-possession – speech so deliberate as almost to seem learned beforehand – were

40

devices that Markham recognized with the beginnings of sorrow as his own. His own too the thinness and tallness of the form before him, the shape and moulding of the face, the thick, slightly curling dark hair. The boy's eyes were like his mother's: blue, set wide in the head, long-lashed.

'So you were waiting,' Markham said sarcastically, 'for the right moment?'

'I was waiting for you to leave,' the boy said.

Markham paused, at a loss, obscurely ashamed of himself, and of the boy, who showed no sign of shame.

'You should be lying down, shouldn't you?' Elizabeth Markham said. 'You know this is your time for resting. You'd better go to your room straightaway.'

'Yes,' Henry said. He moved at once to the door but paused there. He looked at his mother.

'What is it?' Markham said. 'What are you waiting for?' He spoke sharply, knowing well that the boy was waiting for some last-moment word, some sign of relenting from his mother.

'Go along,' Elizabeth said.

The boy nodded, and it seemed to Markham that he had flushed slightly. Then he turned and was gone.

'That boy . . .' Markham said. He could not understand now the violence of his reaction. It had not been the eavesdropping merely, but something more, some deeper transgression which was his own, just as the face which had looked up at him was his own. He steered away from the mystery, took refuge in a sort of half-humorous complaint. 'He seemed to think we had invaded his privacy,' he said.

'He was embarrassed,' she said.

'*Embarrassed*? I should think he was. No boy with the right instincts would have stayed silent there.'

'Nonsense, Robert. He was simply caught off his guard.'

It was strange, he thought, with mingled jealousy and resentment, that her strong sense of code, of the decencies of behaviour, which made him always strive to conceal his own weaknesses from her, should be so invariably relaxed when it

41

came to her son. He felt at this some of the rage of injustice he had sometimes felt as a child against his own parents.

'He must have heard every word,' he said. 'I suppose he got . . . Do you think he got behind the sofa when he heard us coming?'

'You don't really think that, do you? You know how he likes to creep into corners and narrow places. He's always been like that, from a very small child. Those dens he was always making in the garden at home . . . Don't you remember? And it has got worse, since we came here. He's always hiding himself away.'

'Yes,' he said, remembering suddenly. 'Today Miss Taverner was looking for him . . . You think I've let him down, don't you? You think I haven't been enough of a father to him since he came here.'

'He's going through a difficult phase just now.'

'All his phases seem to be difficult,' Markham said gloomily. 'I've been very busy lately, you know. There've been a lot of things to see to. You ought never to have brought him out here with you. It was against my wishes from the first. He would have been far better off at school in England.'

'He is only ten, you know. Besides, we had the whole business of school out in our letters. We couldn't have left him alone all through the long vacation, with both of us so far away, and not even any other boys about.'

'No,' he said. 'I suppose not.' She would always find reasons, he knew that, sensible arguments to cover the one thing there was no arguing about: her determination, at whatever cost, to keep the boy by her side. 'All the same,' he said, 'I don't want you to go up there. He must be made to realize we think he has behaved badly. Both of us. So leave him to himself this afternoon.'

After a pause that seemed long to him, long enough at least for him to wonder if he was speaking as the boy's parent or his rival, she raised her head and said, 'Very well.'

'Actually,' he said, 'he has got away with things rather. I

42

was going to take him to task about the way he disappeared after lunch, but this business drove it out of my mind. Miss Taverner was looking all over for him . . .' Into his mind, swift and resistless, sprang the immensely potent image of Miss Taverner climbing the steps in her dark dress, head lowered, her long thighs alternately defined as she mounted. 'I haven't time now,' he said. 'It will have to wait.' He moved over to her and kissed her on the brow. She did not move. 'I'd better be off,' he said heavily. 'I should try and rest if I were you. I don't like these headaches you've been having lately.'

He had to overcome a temptation to stop at the door, turn there, wait as his son had waited, disguising his need with the same composure, for some sign, some help from the woman sitting there.

Henry Markham, sent upstairs for his afternoon rest, found rest impossible, and even remaining still very difficult to achieve. Part of this tension was due to the fact that he was waiting for his mother to come, knowing however that she would not. That pause by the door had been all that pride would allow in the way of a plea. But his father would have told her not to – he knew this in a way that did not admit of doubt, though it did not preclude hope either. The hope was like a defiance of his father, a small flag held up before a much stronger enemy.

It lessened, however, as time passed, and he began to feel unhappy. Without the assurance of his mother's kiss and her touch on his face and the smell of her perfume, his room seemed still a strange inimical place, though he had been sleeping here for a month now.

He lay on his back, the sheet drawn up to his chin, staring up at the gilt and pink moulding on the high ceiling, at the pattern of interlaced stars that ran along the top of the windows. The windows were open but the latticed shutters were closed, so that the room was dim. Narrow bars of light came through the chinks in the lattice and fell in haphazard

43

patterns, striping the bed and performing very faint spirals on the walls.

Though he did not feel he had been wrong to listen, he did not feel unjustly punished either, so he could have no recourse to self-pity. He sought to deflect his unhappiness by imagining, with a faint resurgence of his mimicry in the summer-house, how the conversation had continued after his departure, what his parents might have said about him; but he gave this up almost at once.

A man with a knife planted between his shoulderblades. This was what he chiefly recalled from the conversation. The delicacy and care of planting the blade, making sure that the flesh closed round it; but it was to kill the man, not to make anything grow . . . His father's voice when he talked about the man had been like a sort of rising and falling drone, the sort of sound that would go on whether there was anyone there to listen or not, like the lonely organ music in the chapel at his school in England. His face had looked shocked, the mouth could scarcely stretch to make more words . . . Henry put his head below the sheet to escape from that stiff face, but in this roseate dimness there awaited him the man with the knife planted in his back, between the shoulderblades, planted and growing, watered by the blood. Blackmail was a word he didn't know, but supposed envelopes with black borders. Under the sheet too things seemed to get blacker, with his father suddenly stammering and uncertain how to proceed, and the Questioners raising their iron rods . . .

Henry got up and went to the window, eager for more light. Cautiously he pushed open the heavy shutter until he had made a gap wide enough for him to look out into the glare of the afternoon. All traces of the luncheon party had now been removed. Immediately below him was the terrace with its crumbling stone balustrade, its paving stones picked out in green by the moss growing along the joins, its plants in pitted stone urns set at the edges of the steps. Beyond this he could see the little pagoda-shaped roof of the summer-house set among its bushes and trees. But the further reaches of the garden, the fountain and pool and sunken court, and the shrubbery beyond, were invisible from here: there was only a large stationary mass of green without apparent form or order. Bounding all this, he knew, was the high wall of pink brick.

He turned away with the whole garden present to his mind; vividly present too his own power of moving about in it. This sense of power was all the decision he was conscious of. But as he got quickly out of his pyjamas and into his clothes he made calculations of a sort. He had not slept yet, so he had all the time before him that he would have spent sleeping. His mother would not come now, his father had gone out. His lessons did not begin again until after tea and he would know when it was tea-time because Nevres Badji would beat the brass plate, as she did every day.

The problem was to avoid being seen. For some moments Henry considered the matter. He moved over to the mirror on the wall and watched his face while he was considering. Strange and momentous, this image of himself in a room which had somehow become stealthy, rustling with rebellion. He looked at his serious, narrow, straight-browed face, printing the reflection on his mind, at this moment of being about to disobey his parents. Mehmet Agha probably, and Nevres Badji almost certainly, would be in the kitchen, restoring things to order after the luncheon party. There was really only Ibrahim, the gardener, to worry about, and he slept in the afternoons.

He decided to use the main staircase, which led down to the front part of the house. This was a bold stroke, but would lessen the risk of being seen by any of the servants. Miss Taverner's room was at the front, and if she was at her window she might see him emerge, but this was a risk he would have to take.

Carrying his shoes in one hand Henry opened the bedroom door quietly and slipped out into the corridor. He trod softly down the centre of the worn, plum-coloured stair carpet, counting the polished bosses on the bannister as he went. Reaching the ground floor he went quickly and with bated breath past the door of the drawing room where he supposed his mother would still be. There was a side door off the main hall which took him out on to the narrow front terrace. No one challenged him, and a few short steps took him into the cover of the shrubs bordering the path at the side of the house.

He sat down here to put his shoes on. His heart was beating fast. An acrid smell of dust and dead twigs came to him from underneath the bushes. The hot shiny surfaces of the leaves were close to his eyes. He began to move through the bushes, making towards the bottom of the garden, past the roses where the ladies had recently chatted. He was among trees now, low, thin-leaved trees with white, cone-shaped clusters of flowers. For the first time he became aware of the concert of insect sounds around him. This seemed to have a very rapid pulse to it, a sort of vibrant humming, as if someone had struck a huge tuning fork somewhere, and the note had just gone on. There were white petals scattered on the ground below the trees and sunlight lay broken on them. The flowers had a heavy smell, brackishly sweet.

At first he was frightened, partly at his own temerity, partly at the strangeness of the hot garden. He had been here before often enough, but never at this forbidden time of day. The smell of the flowers and the sustained note of the insects seemed like symptoms of alarm too, as if everything was being alerted by his approach. Gradually, however, as he cautiously proceeded, past the summer house into the denser shade of the umbrella pines beyond, his own slow movement seemed to absorb the noises and smells, and he began to feel that everything depended on him, everything would stop if he stopped. With this, his heart grew quieter. He was moving along a sort of complex track, or continuum of sound, crawling along it, almost, through the garden. It was like a rope he was following hand over hand.

Now, too, there was the sound of the fountain, notes of

46

falling water. He passed under a ramshackle vine-trellis, the trailings of the leaves hanging low to make a tunnel. The grapes were small and hard. He tried one as he passed, spat it out. It was too bitter.

Emerging from this he found the long oval-shaped pool before him, with its lilypads and low stone parapet and the marble fountain beyond. The fountain had three shallow basins one below the other, each of the lower two bigger than the one above. The water came welling out of the fountainhead, ran down a marble gutter into the first basin. Water displaced from this slid over the rim and fell into the larger basin below, causing further displacement in its turn. Each of the basins was so full that the merest drop overcharged it. From the lowest basin water brimmed over into the pool.

Henry stood for some while here, fascinated as usual by the complexities of sound caused by drops falling from different levels into varying quantities of water, a multitudinous tinkling and splashing, which thickened with extra strands of melody that rope of sound he had been following through the garden. The water brimmed and slid over the marble and the sunlight expanded the water into thin bright sheets over the shallow ledges. No ear could make a single thread of sound from this, nor eye make a simple pattern of the falls and glitters of the water. All the same the sounds blended into a single whole, Henry had discovered, which came to you when you stopped trying to hear it.

In the pool itself there were lily pads and ancient fish, slowly breathing, irregularly mottled red and silver. Henry broke the spell of the fountain by trying to bomb these denizens with bits of gravel from the path, but the fish whisked lower, out of sight, as soon as the stone broke the surface. A blue dragonfly hovered briefly over the water, then darted off. As he skirted the pool, the hot sharp pieces of gravel in his hands, he saw the flicker of a green lizard. He threw the gravel in a handful into the water, heard the plopping sounds merge briefly into the general concert. He

47

moved round the pool, past the Judas tree – Miss Taverner had told him this name, and the story that Judas's blood had stained the flowers. These had all fallen now, and lay in a scattering of faded magenta on the ground below.

Now he was at the end of the garden, near the high brick wall. The path ended in a wooden gate set in the wall. This gate was always kept padlocked with a thick rusty chain. Today, driven by some spirit of curiosity or defiance, he went up to the gate and examined it more closely. There was a metal bar bolted into the centre, and this acted as a handle. He gave it a tug, tautening the chain, and noticed as he did so a distinct movement of the clip in the padlock. He forced the padlock against the chain and saw at once that although the chain went through it, the clip was loose in its socket. The door in fact was not locked at all. He pulled the clip up and slipped off the chain. He pulled again on the handle, and the door moved towards him with a reluctant grating sound. He hesitated, but only briefly, before slipping through.

Outside he stood for some moments, breathing quickly, in mingled fear and exhilaration. He was on an earth path which ran close to the wall of the garden and then continued past it. On the other side was a dry stream bed, tangled with bushes along its low banks, a line of smooth whitish stones down the middle. Beyond this again was a wall of stone much too high for him to see over – he supposed it to be the boundary wall of gardens on that side. The two walls made a sort of alley, about half of which was taken up by the stream bed.

Henry turned to his right and began to walk along the path in the shadow cast by the wall. He was led on at first by a spirit of exploration, but as wall succeeded wall, with gates at intervals, and the path continued to follow the line of the stream bed, he grew uneasy at the distance he was putting between himself and the house. He would not hear the tea gong from here. Also, he was beginning to feel worried now by the business of getting back to his room undetected. He stopped and retraced his steps. He was on the point of pushing open the gate and re-entering the garden when he heard a few notes of song, a girl's voice, coming from a little further down in the other direction, on his left, from beyond the opposite wall. He walked towards this sound and after a dozen yards or so, he drew level with a gate set in the wall, a heavy metal gate with a grill across the upper part. The bank was higher on that side, and Henry was unable to see more than some of the higher foliage of the garden through the bars. The voice came to him again, thin but curiously sweet and lingering, singing words he could not understand.

He began at once to negotiate the bushes on his side of the stream bed. That he should investigate this singing without delay seemed natural and indeed inevitable to him. He scrambled down the bank and up the other side. However, he was still not tall enough to see through the grill. He went down again, found a flat stone, clambered awkwardly up with it. This he did three times, a further snatch of song coming to him as he laboured. He scratched his leg, quite a deep scratch, but hardly noticed, so intent was he on finding the right sort of stones and getting them up the bankside.

He made a platform of the stones by placing one on top of another to a height of about two feet. Standing precariously on this he was able to look through the thin bars of the grill into the garden. Immediately before him, in an open space of bare earth backed by trees, he saw a thin, dark-haired little girl in very colourful clothes, standing quite still with her back to him, one arm held out a little from her body, elbow bent, palm extended downwards, finger rigidly straight. Her hair was black and very long, falling well below her shoulders. It was gathered loosely at the nape with a thick yellow ribbon. Her skirt was yellow too, bright yellow, and sewn all over with little patches of silver. She was wearing a pale blue sash and a pink blouse of some shiny, satiny material. At first Henry could not believe his eyes, so strange and vivid was the girl's appearance. She stood with head slightly lowered, body

49

tense, arm stiffly extended, as if waiting for some signal or command. Then, while he watched, his face close to the bars of the grill, she took several short steps sideways, at the same time raising her other arm to the same level. She broke into the same curiously sweet and drawn-out notes of the song, as incomprehensible to him as the song of a bird. Then she twirled once in a pirouette that raised the yellow skirt in a brief swirl round her thin bare legs and caused the little metal pieces sewn on to her skirt to glitter in the sunshine. The turn completed, she again took a series of sideways steps, raising her arms still higher. It was now, in the midst of the dance, that she saw him, saw his face through the grill looking directly at her. She stopped at once, lowering her arms. She stood still for a moment or two, then backed some steps away, towards the shadow of the trees.

'*Ne istiyorsen?*' she said. Her voice was high-pitched, rather reedy.

Henry tried to smile at her through the bars. 'It's all right,' he said. 'I was just . . .' He sought for some form of words that would explain his presence there, reassure her. 'I was passing by,' he said, remembering a phrase he had heard adults use.

'*Ne istiyorsen?*' she said again. She was standing still now, but she looked frightened. Her eyes were dark, huge in the thin face.

Henry realized quite suddenly that she didn't understand English. 'It's all right,' he repeated. In his embarrassment and perplexity, unable to make any reassuring gesture, with only his face visible to the girl, Henry could think of nothing to do but put a funny expression on. He had had some success as an imitator and face-puller at school in England, and now he decided to try the furious stare of the maths master there. He drew his brows together, puffed out his cheeks, then opened his eyes as wide as they would go in a fixed glare. The effort involved in this made his face red and congested-looking, thus adding to the effect. The girl stared in wonder, all fear forgotten. However, Henry was not able to glare thus furiously for long. He had shifted his feet on the platform of stones, disturbing their precarious balance. Now he felt them move under him. For a second or two he scrabbled with his feet for balance. The comic fury of his expression gave way to the real anguish of one about to fall. Then the stones collapsed and Henry disappeared abruptly from the girl's view. Because the path was so narrow his fall took him crashing down through the bushes to lie sprawling in the stream bed. He lay there dazed and winded for some time. Then, looking up, he saw the girl's pale face against the grill of the gate, gazing down at him. She had climbed up on to something in her turn, in order to follow his progress. As he stared up he saw the flash of white teeth, and heard the sound of high, partly suppressed laughter. She was laughing at him. Instinctively, ignoring his hurts and bruises, with the true instinct of the entertainer, Henry sat up and began looking round him with a sort of pop-eyed, outraged astonishment, as if unable to understand how he came to be there. He was rewarded by the continuing sounds of her laughter.

# 3

Abdul Hamid was back once more in the narrow world of his study with its green baize desk, divan against the wall, ashtrays and cigarette boxes everywhere – he smoked incessantly.

He was absorbed in his reading of the day's *djournals*, which he had interrupted earlier to perform the ritual of the telescopes. Shut up here in his Palace of Yildiz, he had continued for more than thirty years to receive from his agents reports, or *djournals* – strange corruption, this, of the French *journal*. These reports fed his fears, and as his fears had increased his appetite had grown, so that he was now such a passionate reader that sometimes, when he received an interesting *djournal*, he became so engrossed with it that he forgot everything else. The *djournals* had become an addiction, and if it happened on a particular day that he did not receive one, he became, as Izzet Bey records in his Memoirs, 'in the highest degree unhappy'. However, there were very few such days. On an average day he received scores of them and, as he never destroyed any, by that summer of 1908 he had accumulated almost a million. The collection occupied a building to itself in the Imperial War Museum. Owing to faults in the filing system, however, and the corrupt and petrified nature of the civil service – petrified at an advanced state of corruption – no proper records had been kept, so it was not completely known, in all cases, what were the date, subject matter, author or place of origin. They lay on long shelves, ranged from floor to ceiling, in stiff official folders piled one above the other, prey to mice and dust and damp, vast archives of treachery.

Much of it was invented, wholly or in part. There were so

many spies, a veritable army of them, and not enough plotting to go round. The spies had to earn their money and justify their existence somehow. Besides, their master needed constant conspiracies. He consumed them. He believed everything, however trivial or absurd. For example, he had devoted hours of anxious thought to the investigation of a warning against the plumbing system in the Palace, expressed in the vaguest terms. The author had not even specified the way in which the pipes could be used for assassination purposes – though he did accuse the Armenians of being behind the conspiracy. Various Armenians were arrested and tortured in the hope of finding out the details. (All torture took place in the Malta Kiosk, near the Menagerie, so that the screams of the victims could be attributed to the animals.) The Sultan, as was his custom, had sat behind a screen and listened to their confessions, but the Armenians, demented with pain, had confessed to such improbable ways of using the pipes, and their confessions were so various, that Abdul Hamid had ended up more frightened and confused than ever. Finally he ordered all the water pipes in the Palace, well over a thousand metres of them, to be exhumed in his presence and replaced by others only a few inches below ground, so that any attempt to use them for purposes of assassination might be instantly detected . . .

Now, in the silence of his study, in his black skull cap and thick grey caftan, he sat absorbed in the latest threats to his person, while outside, in his capital city, where he almost never set foot, the afternoon passed in customary business.

Emerging from his house, Markham exchanged glances with a man in fez and dark caftan standing on the corner, who might or might not have been a spy – Markham thought he had seen the face before but was not sure. It did not matter really: all movements of foreigners were reported as a matter of course; and many who were not regular spies would pass on information if they saw the chance of a few piastres.

53

He walked down the steep cobbled street towards the landing stage for the Bosphoros ferryboats. There were always fiacres waiting down there. However, he found one before that, outside the courtyard of the mosque, and asked the driver to take him to the British Embassy in Pera. They went by way of the quiet narrow streets below the Galata Serai, more or less deserted at this time of day. It was a district that Markham liked, with its innumerable tiny cafés, awnings of vine-trellis, quiet squares and carved marble street fountains.

The regular hoof beats, the jingle of the harness, the steady back of the Greek driver in its dirty calico, combined to make him feel sleepy – he was tired in any case, having spent the day before in Smyrna, enquiring into the circumstances of Turgut's death, returning to Constantinople by the overnight train.

Relaxed now, in the shade of the black leather canopy, he thought again about this death. Third known police spy to be murdered in Smyrna in the last month. Well known to the local people – he had lived in their midst and grown fat on extortion. Stabbed in broad daylight. The Consul in Smyrna, a Greek named Pavlidis. His face broad, pale, moist, the eyes black as currants, quick eyes and a slow body. 'Now, you see,' he had said, 'now my good sir, they are killing them. This is a new sport in Smyrna.' Not only Smyrna of course: it was the same story in Aleppo, Damascus, Beirut, Salonika, as if the news had spread somehow, carried on wings: forget your fears, the day of the spies is over . . . His day is over. Innumerable cups of sweet black coffee. Swatting the flies. Hot in that little office of Pavlidis. Turgut was from Caesarea. Fat. Bad teeth. An exporter of olive oil. Last seen with death lying heavy on his jowls. His day was over. Turgut's, yes. And that of the man behind him. Surely it meant that. They would not act so openly . . . Abdul Hamid, Vice-Regent of God on earth, who twelve years ago with a word here and a word there and a few strokes of the pen brought death to fifty thousand obscure Armenians, in round figures, among them a

54

girl named Miriam Krikorian, whose fiancé had been not an Armenian but an Englishman. *I am not Armenian. My name is Robert Markham* . . . Markham sat forward. He was wide-awake suddenly with a desolate sense of loss. It was not grief. He could not, even now, mourn properly for Miriam, could not separate her violation and death from the horror of the traitor's part he had played. The loss was rather of something in himself. Something essential, some vital component, extracted that August evening. At the time fear had acted as a sort of anaesthetic, but he had felt pain since, at certain seasons, like an ache in his bones. Now however, back in this city, he was remembering too easily, too often. The horror was too quick, too mercurial: it rose to the surface of consciousness without warning, giving him no chance to control it.

They came to the Grande Rue de Pera with its throng of traffic and pedestrians, followed it for some distance then turned off down the short street leading to the Embassy. Markham paid the driver and passed through the high, wrought-iron gates. As he approached the broad façade of the Embassy building with its white marble shrouded partially by the dark green cypress trees, he was struck once again by the impressiveness yet absurdity of the architecture. Tuscan Gothic, copied from the Palazzo Pitti in Florence, built to the orders of a former ambassador who left little mark on Ottoman policy perhaps, but certainly a lasting mark on the city.

Hartley, the security guard and general odd-job man, was sitting in his little cubby hole in the entrance hall. Markham nodded to him, crossed the hall and began to climb the stairs – there was no lift in the building. Colonel Nesbitt's office was on the second floor. Markham knocked and at once heard the harsh voice bid him enter. He stood for a moment in the doorway, hands by his sides, in a position of slightly negligent attention.

Nesbitt looked up from his desk. 'Come in,' he said. 'You're back then. Come in and sit down.' The voice was grating and strained, as if the muscles of articulation were clenched in some deep reluctance. He was in shirt sleeves, an army shirt, with the badges of rank sewn on to the epaulettes. Traces of cigar smoke hung in the air, mingled with the scent of acacia flowers from the garden below.

Markham sat down opposite him at the large desk. From here he could look through the tall windows, open now, clear across the Petits Champs des Morts to the waters of the Golden Horn. It was typical of Nesbitt, he thought, that he should choose to sit with his back to this marvellous view. It was in such ways that he expressed his dedication – and his contempt. Typical, too, that he should continue working here in Pera, through the heat and bad smells, when almost everyone else had moved to the summer Embassy at Therapia on the Bosphoros. The Embassy here was almost empty except for a few security men and secretaries. This year, of course, the move to summer quarters had not been so concerted, nor marked by the usual festivities of inauguration, balls, sporting events and outings of various kinds, because the death of the Ambassador was still too recent – he had died the previous April – and his successor had not yet been appointed.

Nesbitt was looking steadily at him across the space of the desk. He was leaning against the back of his chair, thick pale forearms resting exactly parallel on the desk, hands loosely curled. A bulky square-shouldered man, with grey hair cut short on his large blunt head, and a lined shrewd face in which the pale eyes were steady and curiously patient – at odds with the contemptuous brusqueness of his manner.

'Well,' he said, 'did you get anything?'

'Not very much.' Markham described the inglorious end of Turgut. 'He was killed in broad daylight,' he said, 'as he was coming out of a restaurant in the Konak district. There must have been witnesses but no one has come forward. According to the police, that is. They may be holding something back.'

56

'Why should they do that?'

'They may have reason to think it was the work of the Committee.'

Nesbitt made a derisive grunting sound. 'You've got a bee in your bonnet about the Committee, Markham,' he said. 'Someone saw a chance and put a knife into him, that's all.'

'Perhaps so, sir.' It was odd, Markham thought, how Nesbitt invariably sneered at any reference to the Young Turks and their underground revolutionary society. It was as if, in spite of all evidence, he wished not to acknowledge the existence of the Committee. Now was not the time to argue about it, however.

'Was anyone with him?' Nesbitt asked.

'He had a girl with him, an Algerian, a dancer at a cabaret in the European quarter. She says she knows nothing about it, and I think she's telling the truth. Anyway, there's no apparent connexion between them. He doesn't seem to have been set up for it in any way. Someone walked up to him in the crowd, knifed him, then disappeared – the district is a maze of little streets. I've asked Pavlidis, the Consul there, to have the girl watched, but I don't think anything will come of it. Besides, sir, as you know, local officials have their own sympathies and are not necessarily on our side.'

Nesbitt nodded slowly, his face impassive. Two dark patches of sweat had appeared below the shoulders of his shirt. 'Our side,' he repeated softly. 'Yours and mine, Markham.'

Again there was the edge of sarcasm, almost a sneer, in the voice. Markham reacted as he always did to his superior's hostility, by injecting his own tone with a sort of slightly offensive briskness. 'Yes, sir,' he said. 'Exactly so. Our common cause.'

He saw Nesbitt's eyes widen slightly and the heavy hands move on the desk. 'Anyway,' he added quickly. 'I don't know how useful he was to us. Turgut, I mean. You will know that better, sir.'

He had expected Nesbitt to assent to this, even though not volunteering any information. If the dead man had occasionally passed things on to the British, it must have been through Nesbitt, who had for years been responsible for the collection of intelligence in Constantinople. He was surprised, therefore, to see the other man frown slightly and hear him say, 'No, I know nothing much about the fellow.'

'I see,' Markham said. 'Well, that's that, then.' He took care to make his tone normally conversational. In fact a certain caution had suddenly descended on him. It seemed to him probable that Nesbitt was not telling the truth. Nesbitt was a ranker, an old campaigner, a man who had grown grey in this corrupting city, in the surveillance of treachery. No creature more devious than the honest old soldier, especially when his cynicism about authority becomes universal, as Nesbitt's was.

'He was Turgutted right enough,' Nesbitt said. He laughed, expecting Markham to laugh with him. 'Aptly named,' he said.

Markham's answering smile was polite, masking his deep distaste at the joke. Ten years of army service had familiarized him with the forms of death, but familiarity had not made death seem a subject for humour. 'Well,' he said, 'I'll be on my way. If there's nothing further, sir.' He waited a moment then got to his feet.

Nesbitt looked up at him. The laughter had faded from his face, leaving it heavy, contemptuously impassive. 'Useless to look for a conspiracy,' he said. 'All the same, there is something in it, something in the air. Perhaps you would say it is the breath of freedom?' Something of the sneer was back in his voice now. 'But we are not concerned with freedom, are we, Markham?' He reached out and took a cigar from the box on the desk before him. Markham watched him trim the end, light it. 'It's not our business,' Nesbitt said, between puffs. 'Help yourself, if you want one.'

'No, thank you.'

'The persecuted minorities are not our business either, are they?'

'No, I suppose not.'

'Damn right they're not,' Nesbitt said, his voice straining more harshly with the emphasis of the words. 'Persecuted minorities ... The Jews and Armenians between them run the whole blasted Empire.'

Markham remained silent for a while, then he said, with deliberate indifference, 'By the way, could I take the stuff we've got on the other killings? I'd like to have a look at it.'

'If you like.' Nesbitt heaved himself out of his chair, went round the desk and through into the small room where the files were kept.

Markham moved towards the window and looked down at the terraced gardens of the Embassy. He was aware that his hands were trembling slightly. He tried to reiterate, in his mind, the inflections of that harsh voice, tried to detect some particular meaning or intention. Nothing, probably. Merely a coincidence, that reference to the Armenians. Nesbitt suspected him of liberal views, had wanted to bully him a little, that was all. Nesbitt was something of a brute, and had not liked him from the first. Natural in any case that he should feel hostile. After running the show himself all these years it must be galling to have someone foisted on him like this. It was a clear sign that he was not fully trusted, and Nesbitt, not being a fool, would know this.

As he turned away from the window he glanced down at Nesbitt's desk. There were only a few papers on it, and these were arranged in an orderly manner – Nesbitt was a careful, methodical man. He was about to move on round the desk when his eye fell on a single sheet with the name *Hartunian, A.* at the top, as a heading. Below this were some twelve lines of writing in Arabic characters. The date, however, which was written at the top left hand of the document, was *alla franca* and was that day's.

He did not, in the first moments, remember this name. At

least, he did not remember whose name it was. It was therefore rather absentmindedly, without conscious curiosity, that he bent lower over the desk in an attempt to read what was written on the paper. But the ink was very pale and the characters difficult to read without actually picking the paper up and looking closely at it. All he could make out was that it was a report of some kind, and that the language was Turkish. He saw a reference to Yeni Mahalleh, one of the suburbs on the Asian side of the Bosphoros.

He heard Nesbitt close the metal drawer of the filing cabinet and at once moved away from the desk into the middle of the room. A moment later Nesbitt came through the door, carrying a stiff grey official folder. 'Here you are,' he said. 'There's a variety of lingoes here, but that won't deter a chap like you, will it?'

It was only gradually, while answering this gibe, that Markham became aware of the strangeness of seeing the name there on Nesbitt's desk, the subject of an official enquiry – for such at first he supposed it to be. It was the name of his dead fiancée's mother – Miriam's mother too had been killed at the same time, on that same evening, twelve years before. So preoccupied was he by this coincidence that he took leave of Nesbitt quite mechanically, without any conscious sense of what he was doing or saying.

He was still absorbed in it as he went down the stairs, but now already certain questions were beginning to come into his mind. These were mainly as to how such a document could have found its way on to Nesbitt's desk. Before he could think any further about this, he saw Somerville talking to one of the Embassy secretaries. He called a greeting, nodded to the secretary. He was not intending to stop, but Somerville followed him to the main door.

'How are things?' he said. 'Hot, isn't it?'

'What are you doing here?' Markham said. He had for a moment or two a curious sense of not really being near enough to Somerville to talk to him. The sight of that name on

Nesbitt's desk seemed to have set everything at a distance from him. This feeling lessened as he looked into the bespectacled, lightly freckled face of the young man before him.

'I came over with the latest trade figures,' Somerville said. He looked at Markham with his usual peering enthusiasm. 'They're terrible,' he said. It was one of his endearing qualities – to Markham at least – that he took the monthly trade figures with such intense seriousness.

'I can't stop to hear about them now,' Markham said. 'Tell me about them on Friday. You haven't forgotten you are coming to us for supper on Friday evening?'

'No fear,' Somerville said promptly. 'I'm looking forward to it.' He said this in the same tone as when speaking of the trade figures, and this made Markham smile again.

As he walked back through the grounds, however, the oppression of the name returned to him; he experienced a kind of rebellious misery. Why now, after so many years, should such things be thrust into his consciousness? Why had he been such a fool as to come back? Already, however, before the question was even formulated, the answer was instantly present in his mind. Or rather, that desolate knowledge of himself that made the question superfluous. The truth was, he had never left the city, never left the scene of his 'lapse', as he sometimes called it to himself – seeking with the playful word to mitigate the gravity of it. Now, with the intrusion of Hartunian's name, the city had put another loop round him, bound him more tightly to herself. The twelve years of his life since, years of his marriage and his army career, were as if they had never been.

He had been intending to go over to his office, in Stambul on the other side of the Golden Horn, to see what papers had accumulated in his absence; but he felt tired suddenly, and bored by the idea of sitting at a desk. He wanted something else, some relief from the tension he had felt since seeing the report. He would go home, he decided. He had a strong sense of his house, the quiet rooms, the sunlit terraces, the garden with its smells of acacia flowers and roses. Something else, too, that he was vaguely aware of as an inducement, a reason for returning. He hailed a fiacre as he emerged on to the Grande Rue, and asked the driver to take him to Beshiktash. They went down past the church of St Gregory and followed the coast road, the Dolmabache Caddesi, which ran along by the Bosphoros, past the gilt and marble splendours of the Dolmabache Palace. As they approached Beshiktash, Markham, acting on an impulse, asked the driver not to turn off into the suburb, but to go some way further along the Caddesi. When they came to a point more or less directly below the slopes of Yildiz, he told the man to stop. He got out and held up the money, aware of the compound reek of horse and driver. He stood watching as the fiacre turned and headed back towards the city. Then he looked up at the slopes of the Sultan's park, the dark mulberry trees, the groves of walnut and birch interspersed with huge glowing copper beeches. Through this thick greenery could be seen glimpses of white – the lower buildings of the Palace.

Markham stood there for some time, looking upward. Several people passed but he took no notice of them. The vegetation of the park, seen thus from below, seemed to him to possess an unnatural luxuriance, sinister somehow, as if it was fed by blood – his impression really of the whole city, the way he had thought of it in his absence, blood holding together the mortar, greening the plants, keeping the fixed shape of dome and minaret. And at the centre, up there in his Palace, crouched the Shadow of God on Earth, who was so slight and desiccated he seemed to have no blood in him.

The thought was like a blow, painless, but slowing him down, settling him to a deeper, steadier rhythm. He had seen it only twice so far, and then fleetingly and at a distance, the thin rouged face, the hooked nose. The fez always too large for the small compass of the brows. Small and slight and feeble of appetite to be an ogre. Wasted by the iniquities of his régime . . . In all the changes that had taken place since those deaths that summer evening, the man up there was the one constant element Markham could grasp. The men who had done the murder and rape, their hour of fanaticism and bloodlust over, had scattered again, gone their several ways, for ever. They would never reassemble again. He did not remember their faces, except for one. There was only the Sultan, and Yildiz his monument, as a focus for thought and memory. These and the streets of the city. Otherwise what reality had the past? Miriam dust now, even the place of her burial unknown to him – he had looked for her grave in the Armenian cemetery, without success. All the others, guests and killers, gone, fallen away. Only the Sultan, who had signed the order, who had duplicated in a thousand hearts the loss in his, only he remained to answer for the past.

Markham turned and began to walk slowly back towards Beshiktash and his house. As he did so thoughts of Miss Taverner came into his mind, thoughts accompanied by the same, almost obsessive, deliberateness with which he had thought of the Sultan, the same slow pulse. He saw her mount the steps again, cross the terrace, very slowly. There was no relief in this image, as there had been before. It was oppressive, inappropriate somehow. He began to walk more quickly, trying as he did so to keep his mind clear of all thought.

Near the Beshiktash landing stage a man was selling carnations, white and red. Markham went past, then returned and asked for a bunch of the white ones. He took up the flowers, paid for them hastily, abstractedly, and left without waiting for his change.

Opposite his house, in the shade of the plane tree on the corner, the man was still waiting. This time, perhaps out of embarrassment, he avoided Markham's gaze. Markham could still see him from the window of his study, on the ground floor. This surveillance to which he was being subjected was extremely inefficient because it was not continuous, and yet quite predictable. There was never anyone there before about half-past nine in the morning, or between one o'clock and three o'clock in the afternoon, presumably because all the watchers were taking their rest then. In any case there was a way out, Markham had discovered, through the garden behind the house, by means of a gate in the wall. Whether or not this possibility had occurred to the authorities, there was certainly no watch kept at the back – Markham had ascertained this for himself. Perhaps, he thought, as he looked past the man at the garden of the house opposite and the ruffled blue of the Bosphoros beyond, perhaps it was simply the fixed custom to have a watch of some kind kept on the comings and goings of all foreigners in the city, irrespective of occupation or status, with no one caring very much how effective it was. This, in its combination of punctilio and slackness, its overuse of human resources, was typical of the system as a whole, he thought, and was probably the truth of the matter.

Passing out of the study, still carrying the carnations, he looked briefly into the room where he had left his wife earlier in the afternoon. It was empty. She would be upstairs, lying down. He stood for some seconds, undecided. The double doors connecting the two room were open, giving him a long vista through the french windows, also open, to the terrace at the rear of the house where Ibrahim was working, watering the plants along the stone balustrade. There was no sound from within the house but he could hear, or thought he could, the faint hiss of the water and the sound of insects from the garden. He experienced a vague disappointment, as though cheated in some expectation. The rooms were full of sunlight, softer now, more golden, the sunlight of late afternoon. They smelled of polish and the flowers which his wife had arranged in vases. Her watercolours were here and there on the walls, street scenes of Constantinople, one or two landscapes with ruined temples; all painted with accomplishment, all depicting the changeless world of the picturesque, of interesting perspectives. She would paint a Berkshire village in the same way, he thought, as she painted this suffering city. Perhaps it was the sense of propriety so strongly developed in her that restricted her range so much, kept her to the quaint and charming. Or perhaps, he thought, she was a healer, practising a sort of instantaneous healer's art. But one couldn't dress wounds without seeing them first, surely . . .

He went out of the room, along the short wide passage with its stucco decorations and moulded arches, and up the short flight of steps to the first floor. On the landing, he hesitated again. Then, instead of going left towards the front of the house where their bedroom was, he turned in the other direction. At once, with the first steps, he was aware that his breathing had quickened.

'*Et Pierre?*' Miss Taverner said. '*Qu'est-ce qu'il fait?*'

'*Il joue avec ses* toy soldiers,' Henry said.

'The French for toy soldiers is *soldats de plomb*,' Miss Taverner said. 'It's there in your book. Say it again, will you?'

'*Il joue avec ses soldats de plomb*,' Henry said obediently. He thought Miss Taverner was looking particularly beautiful this afternoon, with her dark hair pinned up on her head and her dark shining eyes. They were in the nursery at the square table against the window. Late afternoon sunshine fell over Miss Taverner, lighting up her hair and lashes and glowing along her cheeks, defining the form of shoulders and arms through the white muslin dress she was wearing. One pale hand was on the table before her, the other out of sight, resting in her lap below the table. Henry could smell the scent she had used, a faint, musky smell. The smell of her and the roseate outlines of her arms inside her dress and the expectancy of her face each time she asked him a question combined to make a sort of knot of tension inside him. He could not decide whether this was a happy feeling or not. He looked at her gravely, awaiting the next question.

'*Et Marie? Que fait-elle?*'

65

Henry looked down at the picture in his book, at the little domestic world portrayed there, father, mother, little boy, little girl. They were fixed for ever on the one thing they were doing in the picture. All you had to do to please Miss Taverner was to say what they were doing, or what they were wearing, or where the furniture was situated. She never asked what they were thinking, or whether they were happy, questions like that. All their faces were the same colour, one tone of pink, and all wore the same contented smile. Marie was in a blue dress with bows on the shoulders. She was sitting on the floor, holding a doll. Henry wondered what colour her knickers would be.

He looked up again at Miss Taverner, who was still regarding him with the same expectant expression, her lips parted slightly, as if to formulate the first syllable of the answer for him. He felt sure that Miss Taverner's would be white.

'*Marie joue avec sa poupée*,' he said.

Miss Taverner smiled and relaxed her posture slightly. '*Très bien*,' she said. 'It took you rather a long time, though, didn't it? You're not ready to carry on a conversation in French yet. Not without a lot of patience on both sides.'

Henry thought suddenly about the little girl in the neighbouring house, whom he had met that afternoon. They had had a kind of conversation without using any words at all . . . He had managed to get back undetected, even managed to wash the blood off his legs before tea. The blood had run into his stockings, but he had folded them over in a way that concealed this.

'So much patience as that is not very common,' Miss Taverner said. '*Et le père de famille? Qu'est-ce qu'il fait?*'

'*Il lit son journal.*'

'*Journal*,' Miss Taverner leaned forward a little and held Henry with her eyes. '*Journal*,' she said again. Henry watched the word form on her lips. This happened in two stages: first Miss Taverner's mouth, which had a rather full underlip, drew forward in a pout; then the lips opened softly and the upper one was raised so that the teeth showed a little. '*Journal*,' he said, trying to imitate this.

'*Journal*,' said Miss Taverner again.

It was at this point that they heard the door open, and both turned to look. Henry saw his father standing in the doorway, holding a bunch of white flowers. He took in at once the slight awkwardness and hesitation in his father's manner. With instinctive curiosity he glanced at Miss Taverner and saw the wave of colour that had risen in her face.

'Oh, excuse me,' Markham said. He had a hasty impression of books open on the table, of a conversation interrupted, of their two heads turning at the same time to look at him. He saw his son register his presence, saw too the boy's quick glance at the governess's face. He himself did not seem to see her face clearly. It was as though the sunlight diffused her outlines somehow.

'I am sorry to disturb your lesson,' he said. 'Please don't get up.' But they were both standing now. He advanced a few paces into the room. 'I was looking for my wife, as a matter of fact,' he said, and felt at once the foolishness of this, its inadequacy as an explanation for his presence there.

'I think she went up to her room,' Miss Taverner said.

'Of course,' Markham said. 'I should have looked there first.' He smiled. He could see her more clearly now, and was beginning to feel more composed. She was somehow taller than he had thought her, not more than two or three inches below his six feet. He was aware of the strong, well-formed body inside the delicate material of the dress. 'I'm not very often home at this time, you know,' he said.

'No,' Miss Taverner said, smiling back at him. There was a certain knowledge of him in the way she uttered this monosyllable, a familiarity with the general pattern of his life, which was to strike him more forcibly later.

'How is he getting on?' Markham indicated his son with a movement of the head. 'I hope he does what you tell him.'

'Oh yes,' she said, serious now that it was a question of her professional duties. 'He's doing very well.'

Markham glanced at his son, who was smiling slightly now – smiling, Markham knew, in response to the jocularity in his father's voice. Henry was sensitive to tone, and malleable enough to meet others' expectations of him; provided, of course, that he was not forced into a corner . . . Markham reflected again how like him his son was, and with this recognition there returned to him something of the anguish of childhood days, when one is talked about, scrutinized, an object of appraisal whose attributes can be discussed quite openly. He caught his son's eye and grimaced in sympathy, but saw no change on the boy's faintly smiling face.

'Keep him up to the mark,' he said.

'Yes' she said, though this time uncertainly, as though not quite sure what this last phrase meant.

Markham smiled and nodded and turned away. 'I'll let you get on with it,' he said. Then abruptly he turned to her again. He took one of the carnations and held it out. 'I'd like you to have this,' he said. He was smiling a little but his face looked serious to Henry, who was never to forget the grace and formality of this moment. Miss Taverner had flushed again. She took the flower without speaking, and made as if to lay it on the table, then changed her mind and kept it in her hand. Markham himself said nothing more. After a moment he turned and walked rapidly out of the room. Closing the door behind him, walking away, he found himself breathing deeply, as after some exertion.

His wife was in the bedroom. She was sitting at her dressing table when he entered, and she turned in her chair and smiled at him as he crossed the room towards her. She was wearing a peignoir of pale green silk, which he did not remember having seen before, and her abundant fair hair was tied up in a chignon of green ribbon.

'Hallo, darling,' she said. 'You're back early.'

'These are for you,' he said, laying the carnations on the dressing table.

'They're beautiful,' she said.

The pleasure in her voice touched him. He put his hands on her shoulders and kissed her on the side of the neck. Her skin was warm and smelled of eau de cologne. 'Did you have a rest?' he said.

'Yes, I slept for an hour or so.'

A thin sash was all that held the peignoir together. She was wearing nothing beneath it, and her turning to greet him had caused it to fall open at the neck, revealing the pale, almost marmoreal perfection of her chest and the upper part of her breasts – Elizabeth's skin was flawless, both on face and body.

Markham looked at her, smiling, the smile concealing, as always nowadays, the tension that he felt when alone with his wife. 'You're feeling all right, aren't you?' he asked.

'Oh, yes,' she said. She stood up and took a few steps across the room, then stopped and faced him. 'Nevres Badji brought me up some camomile tea,' she said. 'It seems to be her remedy for everything.'

'Well,' he said, 'it's good stuff.'

She smiled, half turning away as if to return to the dressing table. 'I don't suppose you've ever had any in your life,' she said.

'I haven't, actually.' Markham noticed again the straightness of his wife's back, the sense she gave of disciplined movement. She had been considered a promising dancer when a child, and had gone on with lessons longer than most children. Why she had stopped had never been clear to him; he sometimes suspected that the Brigadier, her father, had not considered it suitable. What she had retained was not so much any evident gracefulness of movement, but the braced posture of the trainee at the *barre*, waiting for the piano note that would signal the next exercise. She moved always with that

69

conscious control, as if waiting for some authentic music that would launch her.

'How did your little chat with Colonel Nesbitt go?' she asked.

'Predictably unpleasant.' Markham wrinkled his nose to indicate distaste. 'We don't get on,' he said. He thought again of Nesbitt's strained voice, the contemptuous steadiness of the pale eyes. The man could not be so ignorant of the Committee as he made himself out to be, not after so many years here. They had intelligence in London, let alone here, that the organization was well established and spreading fast . . .

'I don't like Colonel Nesbitt much,' he heard his wife say. She had seated herself once again at the dressing table.

'Why not?'

'He doesn't believe in anything,' she said. 'I must put these flowers in water.'

'And I do?'

'Well, you get cross about things, don't you? I don't think he does. I think he believed in things once. I would be sorry for him, but he blames other people for it, I mean for what has happened to him. He is quite horrid to people, and I'm sure that's the reason.'

Typical of his wife, he thought, to think of Nesbitt's moral nature while he himself was only concerned with the devious workings of the man's mind – he had taken corruption for granted.

'You dislike him because he's not a gentleman,' he said. He spoke lightly, but there was an undercurrent of bitterness in his voice. As always, she judged by the code. For her it was very simple: a man must embody certain values and these must not be talked about but must be evident through behaviour. It was this that made it – had always made it – impossible for him to confide in her. She had been bred to be a succour to the strong, not a solace to the weak. She could not come down to the level where he needed her.

'That is not true, Robert,' she said. 'I try to look at people as they are.'

'Well, you may be right.' Markham felt a sudden weariness, a desire to end the conversation. He had been standing in the middle of the room, while she continued to sit half-turned towards him, before the dressing table. Now he came towards her and knelt, laying his head for a moment in her lap, then raising it to kiss her arm and her breasts through the thin material of her robe.

These actions on his part had expressed no more really than the desire to end the talking between them, which with every syllable had been making him feel more estranged from her. No more than this; but he felt at once the stirred warmth of her body, the yielding of response to his kisses; and responding in his turn to this, constrained almost to seem desirous of her in a degree greater than her desire, he again lowered his face to her breasts, finding them now through the opened front of her robe. He felt some return of that scented suffocation he had experienced earlier, but not so strongly now, not strongly enough to cause fear.

She stirred and her breath came quickly. Her hand was in his hair with that kind of perfunctory caress which he recognized in her as the beginning of excitement. 'Robert,' she said, 'the door . . . perhaps the servants . . .'

'Yes,' Markham said. He got up and went to the door. He felt as yet no real desire, but knew as he turned the key in the lock that they were committed to love-making.

He moved back towards her with the intention of kneeling as before, but she rose as he approached. He put his arms round her and held her close against him, experiencing a tenderness for her at this moment that was akin to pity. So far he was acting like a man in a dream, as if under some sort of duress or constraint. He put his hands on her shoulders under the robe. They were warm and smooth. He slipped the robe off her shoulders, raised his head to look closely at the flawless

71

texture of the skin. With what seemed like shyness she pressed herself against him, avoiding his scrutiny. They moved together still half-embraced towards the bed.

There were almost no preliminaries between them, almost no interval before they were joined and moving together like a slow, rhythmic palpitation or breathing of the whole creature, one two-toned body, the lower half several degrees lighter-hued than the upper.

Almost at once Markham began to lose his sense of time and space. It seemed that the light itself in which they moved had a buoyant quality, sustaining their bodies, not allowing them to sink. It was a light Markham seemed to recognize as the invariable accompaniment to the love-making, yellowish and thick somehow, like a denser element in which they floated and grappled; in it their movements were gentled and blurred, lost all urgency, lost even the tactile value of gestures made in other circumstances and other light, so that touching was a strangely numb proceeding, or was for him at least, and it seemed natural to assume the same state of numbness in both parts of the slowly pulsing creature, so that he was surprised to hear the quick moaning intake of his wife's breath, and the quickening movements of her body under him.

He himself was sweating now, despite the sense of numbness, aware of sweat breaking out all over him as their bodies moved together and slightly apart, like gills, he thought, or a dance of some kind. He heard a quick anticipatory cry from her. He was moving more strongly, more urgently against her now and though unresisting she seemed like a barrier, like a reef to him, he was a wave constantly breaking against her, like water scattered time and again. He heard her cry again, distant, like a voice heard through the scudding of waves. Through this distance the cry was equally of pleasure and of pain, reminding him of another cry no more distant, and he was moving in his wife's arms as he had moved in those other arms that had held him,

Miriam's first, in the dance, then the others . . . Abruptly, quite unexpectedly, he was in the grip of the nightmare, as if there had been no pause, no interval, since that other dance, and his wife's cry came to him and he felt his own preliminary throbs of release and heard, or remembered, his own voice, accented mysteriously, dreadfully charged with supplication, though stating a simple fact: *I am an Englishman. I am Robert Markham, an Englishman*, and saw the slow smile on the Kurd's face, the knowledge of him, the mockery of deference on receipt of that announcement. *Evet effendim. Ingilizsiniz. Bac. Bac.* Courteously inviting him to look at what they were doing . . .

It was with that face before him that Markham felt his own face contort, felt himself throb back to stillness, though not peace. He lay beside his wife, half embracing her still, feeling the sweat cool on him. He glanced at her face. Her eyes were closed and she was breathing deeply, regularly. She was deeply flushed. He did not think she was asleep because of the firmness with which her arms continued to hold him. She is at peace, he thought, with a sudden rush of affection, grateful at least that they were two creatures and not one, so that the horrors his mind produced remained in the one chamber.

He looked away from her towards the window where light filtered through the stiff lace curtains – Brusa lace, made in patterns of tulips. Light lay glazed on the alabaster surface of the dressing table, gleamed in the oval mirror above it, lay along the backs of the pink rattan chairs and the threads of brocade in the dark red cushions. He would get up soon, he thought, and dress and go downstairs and Mehmet would bring him a whisky and soda. He thought lovingly of the peace and solitude of his study. The watcher would still be out there, probably. He or another . . . Markham thought again about the name at the head of the report on Nesbitt's desk. Like the resumption of an ache, the questions began to come: why was Nesbitt having a prominent member of the Armenian community watched in the first place? Or was it

73

simply a police report which had been sent to him for some reason? But in that case, why written out in longhand, and why not on an official report form? Trivial questions perhaps; but his intelligence training had taught him the importance of noting even the slightest departure from routine. There was something odd, irregular, about the document, he sensed it instinctively. And then, the name, that particular name, and the accident of his seeing it . . .

Involuntarily, in flight from these thoughts, which he knew already and with foreboding would make some sort of action on his part necessary, his mind fastened on Miss Taverner, fastened gently, and with a dawning sense of gratitude. He thought of the dark eyes, shy and assured at the same time; of her confusion when he had spoken to her - and of his own; of the knowledge she had displayed of his movements. Lying there, spent as he was, he felt desire for the governess quicken in him, a desire without compunction yet strangely obscure. It was as if her knowledge stirred him, as if he sought to be enfolded in her knowledge.

# 4

Abdul Hamid, worried by the reports from his spies, and by the deaths and woundings of some of them in distant parts of his possessions, summoned his close advisers to a conference in the Little Mabeyn, his personal quarters in the Palace. This took place early in the morning, when people in the city were just beginning to wake. Present were Tahsin, his First Secretary; Izzet, his Chamberlain; Djavad Agha, the Chief of the Black Eunuchs; Abdul Hudar, the Court Astrologer. All these lived in the Palace. The Grand Vizier, Ferid Pasha, arrived late, having been summoned by messenger from his house in Bebek.

The Sultan, in long quilted coat and thick felt skullcap – he felt the cold badly – opened the proceedings. The mood of the people was changing, he said. There were these attacks on faithful servants of the state. The authors of them were never apprehended. Confessions obtained from prisoners led nowhere. There was Macedonia, source of trouble from time immemorial, constantly inviting intervention from the Great Powers, an open sore in the Ottoman state. Not only that, but the reports he was receiving indicated that the secret revolutionary society known as the Committee of Union and Progress, dedicated to the restoration of the Constitution, was gaining ground and spreading rapidly in the army, especially in the ranks of the Third Army Corps in Macedonia – those nearest, the Sultan said bitterly, the beastly contagion of Europe and its atheist political systems.

As he spoke he looked from face to face with his huge haunted eyes, dilated and slow like those of some nocturnal creature. When he had finished he watched them in silence for some moments, these men whom he did not trust: Tahsin,

75

head of his Secretariat, mild, brown-haired, clerkly, European in appearance; Syrian Izzet, delicate-boned, quick-tongued, peering; the Chief Eunuch, head of the Harem, a Nubian, obscenely fat, with soft, girlish voice; his Astrologer, also an Arab, from Mersin; lastly his Grand Vizier, Ferid, with his bony, seventy-year-old face, quicker in expression than that of the eastern Turk – Ferid was from the Aegean littoral, had Greek blood in him.

The long pause of majesty over, he invited them to speak. Tahsin began. Speaking quietly and with eyes for the most part downcast, he said that all information sources at his disposal indicated that the Committee of Union and Progress, while certainly a potential threat to His Majesty, was basically a movement among political exiles and malcontents and had its bases and its funds abroad, mainly in Paris and Geneva. In those foreign capitals they sat and dreamed of parliaments and deputies, and so on. It was a foreign movement, not indigenous to Turkey. He did not think it was true that they were gaining ground in Turkey. His Majesty's regiments were loyal to him as Supreme Commander.

The quiet voice came to a stop. After a brief silence Abdul Hudar, the astrologer, spoke in emphatic agreement. All signs were favourable, he said. The heavens revealed no threat. The Chief Eunuch nodded his enormous head. In his soft voice he spoke in concurrence, saying that the country was solidly behind its Sultan and Caliph.

Then Ferid, the Grand Vizier, spoke, breaking this flattering chorus. He pointed out the connections between the Committee and the Free Masons – the Grand Order of the Orient as it was called. This was gaining membership rapidly, no one denied that. It was run by Jews and foreigners as a cover for the Committee. The Sultan should take steps to make this organization illegal, even at the risk of offending foreign powers. Also the policy of banishing dissident officers to distant, disease-ridden parts of the empire was dangerous for peace, as the men were made more discontented still by these unpopular postings, and spread their discontent. They should be recalled, kept close by, watched carefully.

The Sultan looked coldly at his Prime Minister, though he said nothing. In any advice he detected self-interest. Izzet, always adroit at maintaining himself in favour, seeing this displeasure, suggested that Ferid was seeking to extend the authority of the government, the Sublime Porte, at the expense of the Palace. The balance of power between these two had for long determined the nature of the administration. Ferid was beginning, with more heat than was seemly, to deny this accusation, when the Sultan with a gesture of the hand and a slight movement of the head, brought an end to the squabble and an instant later dismissed them. They went, taking care to move slowly, to keep their arms by their sides, remembering the fate of their colleague Hakki Bey who had been shot through the throat for forgetting to do this.

Markham woke early to a feeling of expectation which he did not altogether understand. He heard no sound from his wife's room, which adjoined his – during the last few weeks they had slept in separate rooms, Markham being unwilling to disturb his wife with his late hours and sleeplessness. He gave the bell-rope beside his bed a tug, which was the signal that he wanted his shaving water brought up to the bathroom. The water was never more than lukewarm in the morning; the antiquated cistern, though capacious, required several hours of heating from a wood fire in the kitchen, so that mid-afternoon onwards was the best time for baths.

His shaving water was brought up almost at once by Mehmet Agha in a copper bucket. 'What is the weather like?' he asked, his invariable question, and one that was by now expected of him.

'*Iyi dir*,' Mehmet replied gravely. 'It is a fine day. There are no clouds in the sky. There is a little wind and it is coming from the east.' He had learned that this Englishman took a great interest in the weather, which he himself regarded with indifference, and he made a point each morning of noticing the details so that he could report them.

'Thank you,' Markham said, with equal gravity, and Mehmet salaamed and withdrew, leaving him to get on with the business of shaving and getting into uniform.

Afterwards he went down to the small room adjoining the kitchen where his wife and he had their meals when not entertaining. He had his usual breakfast brought in by Mehmet, fruit, boiled eggs, bread and butter, and tea – made in the Turkish fashion, without milk, and served in a glass. He had a second glass of tea when he had finished eating, and carried it with him to the sitting room at the front of the house.

He loved this room for its spaciousness and lack of clutter and the views it gave of the Bosphoros and the Asian shore. Now, today, with his senses quickened by some feeling of expectation, half-pleasurable, half-apprehensive, he felt the beauty of the room particularly, felt glad of the Turkish willingness to let space and light and good proportion do the main work of embellishment.

He sat at the window for a few minutes, finishing his tea. Almost the whole of this side of the room was taken up with windows, three large rectangular ones separated by plain strips of wood – there was no woodcarving anywhere, but on the wall opposite the window, on either side of the communicating doors, there were wooden cupboards and recesses decorated with painted flowers and gilt moulding. The ceiling was treated in the same way, the strips of moulding applied in a simple design of linking curves and coloured in pink and dark blue. Markham sat with his back in an angle of the window, sipping his tea, looking out across mild blue spaces and the still tops of trees, over the roofs and gardens of the lower suburb, down to the shining waterway below and the fertile slopes of the Asian shore.

When he had finished his tea he went quietly upstairs to his wife's room. Usually they chatted for a few minutes, he sitting on the edge of the bed, she propped against her pillows with

78

the tea that she rang for as soon as she woke. This morning, however, she was still asleep. He stood in the doorway for some moments, looking at her face in profile. It was very flushed and the lips were parted a little, as if in slight anxiety. She was breathing heavily, audibly.

'Elizabeth,' he said softly.

She made no movement, nor was there any check in the slightly laboured breathing. After a further moment, in which a certain disquiet was confused with indecision about waking her, Markham went back downstairs, collected his cap and cane and left the house. Once outside, in the open, he experienced a feeling of relief. There was no one waiting under the plane tree, no one in sight at all. It was too early still for the spies.

He walked down the dusty, tree-lined street, past the café on the corner and the little marble fountain with its design of leaves round the edge. He loved this time of day in the Constantinople summer, coolness still lying over everything, but with the promise of heat somehow in the smell of things, a sharp smell of earth and masonry. Across the water, beyond the slender minarets of the Beshiktash mosque, rose the slopes of Scutari, crowned with its cypresses and cemeteries. This morning, high above the cemeteries, he counted four kites slowly circling, saw the whitish gleams of their wings. There were some Turkish labourers in dark headcloths and calico aprons drinking coffee at a table outside the café: porters from the street market nearby, the greater part of their day's work done already. They regarded Markham gravely, steadily, offering no salutation. The owner of the café, however, a stocky, pock-marked Turk from Thrace, who knew the English officer by sight, greeted him with a sonorous '*Gunaydin*', which Markham returned.

He kept a horse, or rather paid for its keep, in some stables owned by an Albanian just above the Beshiktash market; he usually rode to Galata, as there was reasonable stabling behind the offices of the Military Mission, and one of the

79

orderlies, who was from a cavalry regiment, acted as groom. Today, however, because he was not certain of his movements once he had got to his office, with that sense of expectation still present in him, he decided to go by boat. He went down to the landing stage, past the small mosque built by the architect Sinan, with its grassy terrace beside the water and the simple grey stone marking the grave of the sea-lord Barbarossa. There was a boat already waiting with people in it - elderly Greek women in black talking in their harsh, plangent voices, who looked at him with open curiosity in their dark eyes; a Turk of the official class, in a fez and frock coat; and two men standing apart in long coats and white skullcaps, whom Markham thought were probably Bosnian Moslems. With his arrival the boatman, who was a Greek, apparently decided that they had a full complement, and began poling his boat out from the moorings.

Markham descended from the boat at Tophane and made his way up to the headquarters of the Military Mission which was in the polyglot, ramshackle neighbourhood below Galata Tower, overlooking the Golden Horn. He let himself into his office and at once, almost before he had crossed the threshold, before the familiar odours of the place closed around him, he knew what he had come here this morning to do; the foreboding he had felt since seeing that name on Nesbitt's desk had not been of something further happening, but of something he himself would be driven to. All the same, habit and discipline took him to his desk, to the papers that had accumulated during his brief absence in Smyrna. These related mainly to the work of the Mission and in particular to his official function, which was to advise on the reforming of the gendarmerie in bandit-infested areas of the Empire. Dutifully he went through these documents, mainly reports of recent outrages in Macedonia committed both by bandits and gendarmes - except for the fact that the former were Christians and the latter Moslems, there was little difference between them. Also among the papers was a memo from

Nesbitt reminding him of the conference to be held the following morning at the War Ministry, and expressing the hope that he would come prepared with all relevant facts, since the gendarmerie issue was going to be the main item.

Even when all this had been looked at, Markham still did nothing for a while. He sat at his desk, looking before him, possessed by a certain feeling of unreality. Never before in his years of service had he used the apparatus, either official or unofficial, on his own behalf. He had taken short cuts occasionally, used his own judgement; but this had been with clearly defined purposes, the purposes of his country, as he saw them, not his own. Now, because of an Armenian name seen casually, and a shame time could not mute, he was about to break this rule, no, principle rather – for he had felt it as a value, something he had had in common with others, something involved in the idea of service. He thought of the man he was going to use. He had only the name, Zimin, and a phone number in Stambul. They had been given to him by the officer he had replaced, who had gone now with his regiment to India. 'He's a scoundrel, of course,' Wetherby had said, 'but you can rely on him up to a point. And he's outside the circuit, not part of Nesbitt's lot.' That was the main thing, the thing that made him a natural choice now, though Wetherby could have been mistaken – a man who sells information will sell to all comers, such at least was Markham's experience. Still, it was worth taking a chance. Zimin might well know something of Hartunian already – enough to give some indication of why Nesbitt was interested in him. Useless asking Nesbitt himself, of course. It was Wetherby who had warned him to be wary of Nesbitt. 'Something funny there, old boy. Nesbitt keeps a woman in Nishantash, a separate establishment, you understand. He spends a lot. Spends more than his pay.' This might only be gossip, of course. Still, in a régime like this one, the implication was clear . . .

Markham stirred, unlocked his desk, took out the notebook

in which he kept names, numbers, addresses. He found the number, copied it onto a scrap of paper, returned the notebook to its drawer. The provision of telephones was not generous; there was only one on this floor, on the landing outside his room, and this was also used by Captain Blake who worked further along the corridor, and a subaltern named Winters whose room was opposite his own. However, Winters was away in the south engaged in some sort of land-survey – he was an engineer – and Blake had not yet arrived. It seemed a good time to phone.

Markham opened his door, glanced up and down the corridor. There was no one in sight. From the floor below he could hear the sound of a typewriter. He crossed to the phone, moving quickly, decisively, now that his mind was made up. It seemed too that everything conspired to help him. Making telephone calls in Constantinople was an extremely unpredictable and time-wasting process normally, because of the overloading of existing lines. On this occasion, however, he was connected at once to the number he asked for. A female voice answered in Turkish. Using the same language, Markham asked for Zimin.

'He is not here,' she said. 'Who is that?'

Markham told her, giving his name and rank. There was a pause, then he heard her say '*Ingiliz*' rather distantly, as if to someone else there with her.

'How can I get in touch with him?' he asked.

There was a further pause, quite lengthy, then she said, 'He can meet you. Do you know the street in the Bazaar where they sell old things, antiques?'

'The Covered Bazaar? Yes, I can find it.'

'There is a Greek named Skafidis there. Ask him and he will arrange things.'

'Skafidis. When shall I go?'

'Any time,' she said. 'He is always there.' Quite abruptly, the phone at the other end was replaced. Markham replaced his slowly and went back into his office.

It was still possible, of course, for him not to go. He was not really committed in any way by the phone call. All the same, standing there at the dusty window, looking out over the small interior courtyard where the horses were kept, he knew beyond any doubt that he was going to go, knew it in a way that seemed to preclude questioning or choice. It was awkward that he was in uniform, it might make him conspicuous, but after all he would merely be visiting the Bazaar, which many foreigners did. Even if seen entering the Greek's shop he would be taken for a prospective buyer.

At the foot of the stairs he met Blake, who was just coming in.

'Nice morning,' Blake said. He had ridden over from Tacsim, where he had his quarters, and looked flushed and heated from the exercise. 'Finished for the day?' he said. Extremely regular in his own hours of work, he made something of a joke of Markham's erratic habits.

'Official business, old boy.' Markham smiled. He rather liked Blake, though thinking him dull, and sensing too the edge of disapproval that lay behind the jokes. Throughout his service he had heard it, that tone from men like Blake, and even before, at school, from boys who would grow up into men like Blake, good-humoured for the most part, though not always: the tone reserved for those who are odd, suspect in some way. 'You'll find a missive from Nesbitt on your desk, probably,' he said. 'I had one. About the conference tomorrow morning. Apparently the gendarmerie issue is going to loom large.'

'It'll be the usual thing,' Blake said gloomily. 'Talking and getting nowhere.'

For months now they had been subjected to Ottoman diplomacy at its most maddeningly evasive and procrastinatory. Agreement on all the main points concerning the peace-keeping force in Macedonia had been reached – or so it seemed to the British: its basic constitution and role, and even the vexed question of the powers of its European officers. But so far nothing had been done. The Turkish officers with whom they dealt were unfailingly courteous and quite rational in discussion; but there seemed to be no link in their minds between agreement and implementation. This was frustrating for a practical man like Blake, in whose mind the two elements were inseparable.

'Well,' he said, gloomily, 'I'll see you later, I expect.'

He continued up the stairs, treading heavily. Markham went along the uncarpeted corridor and left the building by means of a side door. He descended through the steep fetid streets, little more than alleys, that led to the Galata Bridge. He gave his two piastres to the white-coated tollkeeper and began to make his way across, walking slowly because of the press of the crowd. Every race of the Empire was represented here on this narrow thoroughfare between the European quarter of Pera and Stambul, the old city, city of the Turkish conquerors. There were a good number of foreigners in the crowd, and Markham recognized here and there a fellow countryman by his manner and style of dress, the men in light-coloured high-lapelled suits and soft collars, the women in straw hats and narrow-waisted dresses. It always struck him as strange to see compatriots of his in this fantastic miscellany, as if he had decided somehow that the English belonged on their own, were not a people able to be mixed with others; and he himself did not feel he belonged in the variegated crowd, among the veiled women in their high-heeled slippers and long mantles, the green-turbaned priests, the Greek dignitaries in white petticoats and embroidered vests, fat Turkish pashas under sunshades held by attendants. Yet he did belong, he acknowledged it to himself, in a way that transcended his sense of apartness. He was bound to the city, the idea of it, its every physical aspect, as intimately as any of those who jostled around him now; he had suffered as greatly through it, in his own fashion of suffering, as the ragged street vendors with the half-snarl of poverty on their faces, the maimed beggars crouched back against the railings

84

of the bridge – he saw their mouths moving but heard no words: their plaints merged into the din of the place, whoops of steamers from the Bosphoros, rumble of wheels on the bridge, voices of the crowd. The boards of the bridge creaked under all this weight of bodies, the joints heaved up and down, parting to show the water beneath. He was beginning to feel a certain nausea at this weltering humanity, and was glad to get off the bridge into the quieter, though still crowded, streets surrounding the New Mosque.

The Covered Bazaar was not far. Markham approached it from the side of the Nuru Osmaniye Mosque. Between the courtyard of the mosque and the entrance to the Bazaar there was a wide cobbled space with stalls around the outside. Acrobats and fire-eaters and jugglers were performing here, before little groups of spectators. Markham made a detour to avoid these groups, joining the narrower flow of pedestrians who were moving along the side of the square close to the stalls, towards the gates that led into the labyrinth of the Bazaar. However, in some unaccountable way, this steadily moving current suddenly seemed to be blocked, caught in a local eddy, the nature of which he could not see because of the press of bodies. Side-tracked, unable for the moment to go directly forward, he allowed himself to move with the crowd. At the same time he heard the strains of a hurdy-gurdy, jangling and desolate, playing what he recognized after some moments as the triumphal march from *Aida*. People seemed to thin out around him and he found himself near the front rank of a crowd that had formed, apparently to listen to the music.

The crowd was composed of the poorer sort of Turk for the most part, people in ragged, greasy clothes and threadbare turbans, with faces marked by poverty and hardship. They were watching a short ragged man turning the handle of the hurdy-gurdy. For some reason the man was standing with his back to the crowd. There was a small grey monkey crouched on top of the hurdy-gurdy. A thin chain ran from its neck to the man's left wrist, which he kept down by his side.

The music of the march continued to issue forth, even in this distorted guise still grandiose. Then the man swung round to face the crowd with a sudden clown's smile. He had no nose, only a slight bump in the middle of his face, with two holes in it. The holes looked large and they stretched widely sideways with the man's smile. The effect was striking, as he had also daubed large circles of white on his cheeks. There was a ripple of half-mocking, half-awed comment from the crowd. The man turned his back again, continuing to turn the handle. The march went on, interminably as it seemed to Markham. He was held to the spot, however, for the moment, fascinated in some way by the performance, at once insolent and abject. The monkey sat hunched and disconsolate, a collar of blue beads round his scrawny, elderly neck, staring with round, grey-filmed eyes at the crowd. It shivered frequently, perhaps from cold, though it made no other movement. It seemed probable to Markham that the creature had spent its lifetime thus, travelling the roads of the Empire, chained and sick, but tenacious of life, while the loud music sounded in its ears . . . Suddenly the man moved across the instrument, turned to face the crowd, unsmiling now. He crouched level with the monkey, brought his face close until it was side by side with the creature's, almost touching, and the two faces were staring solemnly at the crowd, the same intense stare of an animal, while the jangling pomp of the music continued.

There was some uncertain laughter from the crowd. '*Delhi dir*,' he heard from somewhere behind him, in a tone almost reverent. 'He has lost his wits.' Markham began to feel oppressed by the heat, by the pressure of the crowd, by something horrific in the two juxtaposed faces. He could hear the blood beat at his temples, and his vision blurred slightly. He turned and broke through the spectators on the side of the courtyard that led into the Bazaar. The crowd was still thick here and he did not feel equal to elbowing a way through. However, there was a low doorway in the wall, half-open, leading into a shop of some kind. Bending to avoid striking his head on the crosspost, Markham plunged away from the music, the two heraldic faces, the staring people, into the welcome dimness. Once inside he paused, leaning back against the wall, still with his head lowered, as if under the impression that the ceiling was as low as the doorway had been. He took off his cap and loosened his shirt collar. At once he began to feel better. The music from outside continued, loud still but without insistence now. The shop was empty but for himself. It was cluttered with objects and garments in which at first, still recovering from the dizziness that had attacked him in the square, he could find no common property, no identifying principle. Then he saw that one wall was covered with masks and masquerade costumes of various kinds, from silver and black dominoes to heavy full-face masks with expressions ranging from grotesque to sinister. Clowns and demons looked down at him. There was a jester's belled cap hanging there, and a spiked helmet, and several kinds of crown. Near these, standing in a corner, was a half-length tailor's dummy dressed in the uniform of a Janissary, with a clip of glass gems in his turban. Markham understood suddenly that he was in some kind of theatrical shop or costumiers. At the same time, a thin elderly man emerged from a recess in the depths of the shop and came towards him.

'Good day, sir,' he said. 'Can I help you?' The voice was thin, slightly asthmatic. For a moment or two Markham felt surprise that the shopkeeper should so unerringly address him in English; then he remembered that he was wearing uniform.

'I don't think so,' he said. 'I was just having a look round.'

'By all means.' The man took several steps back, as if to give Markham more room for his investigations, and stood against a cane screen on which hung a set of the painted marionettes used in the *Karaguz*, the Turkish shadow theatre.

Markham looked along a rack of military uniforms, most of them too splendid to seem very probable, except in the world of musical comedy. He fingered the gilt and silver thread of epaulettes and sleeves, pale-blue, grey, scarlet. There was a long table devoted to headgear of various kinds, peasant caps with earpieces, Tyrolean hats, fezzes, top hats, billycock hats, turbans, embroidered skullcaps. From the low ceiling various other items dangled down: scarves, a diamanté tiara, a plume of dyed feathers. The whole place was a repository of borrowed robes and borrowed faces.

He returned to the inner part of the shop. The shopkeeper was standing in the same place, in the same attitude.

'You have an extraordinary collection here,' Markham said. 'Do you hire things out to theatres, that kind of thing?'

'Yes,' the man said, 'theatres, and also private persons. Especially at Carnival time there is a demand.'

He spoke with a kind of eagerness, as if grateful for Markham's interest. His face was sallow, gentle in expression, and he had a habit of blinking slightly and frequently, which gave him a scholarly look.

'The Greeks hire them, then?' Markham did not know why he was remaining in the shop, prolonging the conversation. He was conscious of some kind of idea or interest here which made him reluctant to leave.

'Greeks, Slavs, all the Christian peoples. Also the Turks, at the time of Ramazan. And of course the Europeans for their fancy dress parties and balls.'

'You are not Turkish, then?'

'No. I am a Parsee. I am the best shop for costumes in the whole of Stambul.'

Beside him, below where the puppets were hanging, Markham saw trays of wigs, beards, moustaches.

'It is surprising,' the shopkeeper said, seeing the direction of his gaze, 'how appearances can be changed.' He moved round the screen, turning his back on Markham for some moments and bending over the counter. When he turned round again his face was altogether transformed. His cheeks looked fatter, he was bald except for two strips of hair over his ears and he wore a thin, Jewish beard. 'You see,' he said, and even his voice sounded different to Markham, deeper, slightly guttural. The effect was startling, uncanny. He stood still for a moment, then raised his hands to his face and peeled away the skin mask. Returned once more to his own likeness, he stood smiling and blinking at Markham. 'Just for a joke,' he said.

'Amazing,' Markham said.

'In this light, you know, it is not difficult.'

The shopkeeper's diffident smile, and these last words of his, remained in Markham's mind for some time after he had left the shop and re-emerged on to the open area outside. The music had ceased without him noticing, and there was no sign now of the man with the hurdy-gurdy. The crowd too had thinned out and he was able to make his way directly through the gates leading into the Bazaar.

Once in the covered labyrinth of the market he breathed more easily. It was as if, in this warren, he felt more secure. He went deeper and deeper into the maze of narrow alleys, first past the streets of the artisans, the coppersmiths, weavers, harness-makers; then, further in, the dealers in commodities, carpets, jewellery, antiques. Dusty shafts of sunlight fell through high windows and skylights, lighting up a rich confusion of fabrics, weapons, rugs, objects in porcelain, glass, metal. The crowd moving around him was as varied, every race of the Empire jostled and rubbed shoulders here, in the narrow streets, in the doorways to the shops, in the numerous tiny cafés – no more than two or three metal tables alongside a wall or in a recess. Markham heard bargaining in Arabic, French, Greek, Yiddish. The noise of voices was loud, continuous; one escaped into shops as into secluded gardens from a main thoroughfare.

In the street of the antique-dealers Markham enlisted the services of a boy about the same age as his son who spoke to him in a shop doorway inviting him inside, one of the many children who frequented the market, slept and ate in corners of it, made a living as touts, coffee-boys, porters. Markham gave the boy a five-piastre piece and uttered the name he had been given. In the space of a minute he was taken to the doorway of the Greek's shop, ushered in.

It seemed dim and quiet inside, after the clamour. Markham had a confused impression of a long counter, with shelves behind, dolls in Greek costume, some beadwork purses and bags, a large box with panels of shell. These looked more like souvenirs than antiques. Three German sailors in white uniforms stood together at one end of the counter, looking down at something, muttering among themselves.

After a moment or two a man approached him, a fattish balding man with shining, chestnut-coloured eyes and a smile full of gold gleams. '*Kali mera, kyrie,*' he said, and waited, smiling.

'Mr Skafidis?' Markham said.

'At your service.'

'I want to get in touch with a person named Zimin,' Markham said, in low tones. 'I was told to come here.'

The Greek's smile became more brilliant. In the pause that followed Markham felt he was being looked at carefully. He was glad now that he was wearing uniform: it gave him an unambiguous identity.

'*Kala,*' Skafidis said. 'You will wait a minute – yes? – while I deal with these gentlemen.' He jerked his head slightly. 'Our German friends,' he said, with what seemed an ironical intonation. '*Par ici.*' He showed Markham through a narrow passage at the side of the counter into a small bare room apparently serving as an office, which contained a table scarred with cigarette burns and a surprisingly elegant writing desk against the wall. There was a door beside this which Markham thought probably led to the living quarters.

After several minutes, Skafidis returned, still with the same unwavering smile. 'So,' he said, 'you will leave a note, yes?'

'Zimin isn't here, then?' Markham felt at once disappointed.

'He doesn't live here,' Skafidis said. 'He calls to collect his post.'

90

'Where does he live?'

'I do not know,' Skafidis said. 'You will leave a note?'

'Very well.'

He was given notepaper and an envelope, shown to the writing desk, left once more alone. There was no chair, so he wrote standing at the desk. He said who he was, said he would wait at seven the following evening opposite the courtyard of the Rustem Pasha mosque. He did not say what the business was about, but hinted that there might be something in it for Zimin.

He bent over the desk, writing these things, conscious of his imprudence in committing himself thus in writing – a practice that broke a cardinal rule of his training. He was making a gift of his identity to an informer. His breathing quickened, he experienced a return of the excited foreboding he had felt earlier. It did not occur to him, however, to question what he was doing. He had no second thoughts about it. It was as if he were responding in the only possible way to the urgent signal of the name on Nesbitt's desk. Everything he had done since seeing that had the same curious quality of being unattended by alternatives.

He sealed the envelope and wrote the single name, without title, on the back. The shop was empty of customers. Skafidis stood alone at the counter, picking his teeth. 'That will be fifty piastres,' he said, taking the envelope. He was quite serious now, as though with this mention of money he had at last reached essential truth. Markham paid, wondering as he did so how many others Skafidis provided this service for.

He was glad to get outside, away from the shop, leaving his note to burn like a fuse there. He walked on through the market, past the bric-a-brac stalls at its heart, where grave-faced men sat crosslegged before wares of amazing profusion and variety, then out on to the wider cobbled alleys on the north side of the Bazaar behind the Ministry of Finance buildings.

Here there was more space, and the crowds were thinner.

Markham was making towards the front of the Ministry where there was a wide square with a fiacre rank, when he caught sight of Miss Taverner some distance in front of him entering one of the streets that led into the Bazaar. The glimpse he had of her before she disappeared into the crowd, no more than a second or two in duration, was sufficient – and he had a vague sense of surprise at this – for a recognition that was utterly certain; as if he had learned her attributes somehow, carried them fixed in his mind, so that he was ready to pounce on any sign of her, even the smallest, as now on this momentary sight of the set of her shoulders, sway of her body, brief profile of her face below the little straw hat.

He set off at once in pursuit. All thoughts of Zimin and Hartunian and his note went out of his mind. Jostling, making his way after her through the crowd, he was aware of nothing but a kind of predatory excitement, as if the press and obstruction of bodies were Miss Taverner's cover, through which he was stalking her.

However, on reaching the entrance to the street he saw no sign of her. It was a street of dressmakers' shops for the most part, with bales of cloth cluttering the doorways and swathes hanging down behind the counters in a variety of colours and textures. The shopkeepers stood among their wares, urging passers-by to stop and look more closely.

These insistent voices and the whole gaudy clutter of the place confused Markham, overlaid his excitement. He went a little way down the street, peering into the dimness of the shops' interiors. Then suddenly he saw her again. She was standing in a space between two open stalls and appeared to be hemmed in there by the people around her. He knew at once from her face that something was amiss: it was flushed and wore an expression both annoyed and distressed. A second later he understood the cause. Two Turkish soldiers were standing near her, and even as Markham watched he saw one of them move up close against her, forcing her to press back against the side of the stall. Markham saw the smile on the man's broad Mongolian face, and then he was moving as quickly as possible through the crowd towards her. As he advanced he called out to her over the heads of the crowd and waved. She turned and saw him, did not smile, but nodded slightly, strangely as if she had been expecting him to appear. The soldiers had seen him too. By the time he reached her side, they had removed themselves to some distance, though still glancing insolently. It was as much of a retreat as pride and hostility for non-Moslems would allow, and Markham decided to take no action against them, though inwardly furious.

'Don't you know,' he said, turning his back on the two men, 'that it is extremely unwise for European ladies to go out unaccompanied in Constantinople? Especially these days. This is not Tunbridge Wells, you know.'

His annoyance that she had been exposed to insult gave a certain asperity to his tone, largely unintentional. He looked at her face, impersonally almost, noting its pallor, now that the flush had faded, registering the tremulous mouth with its full lower lip. Suddenly, without any conscious transition on his part, his mood changed. These marks of her distress seemed now wholly appropriate, the appropriate marks of a creature pursued. He was excited by them, and appalled at his excitement.

'That was horrid,' she said. 'I'm so glad you appeared – it seemed like a miracle. I know it was silly of me, but it seemed a good opportunity to do some shopping. Henry is with Mrs Markham this morning, they're sketching together.'

He nodded, still looking at her with a fixity which made her finally turn away her eyes. 'It's bound up with their religion, you know,' he said slowly. 'No Turk would molest a veiled woman. But foreign women who go round with bare faces . . . that's a different matter. They feel that the law of the Prophet is being flouted. So they are free to insult you. Also, they are starved of women.'

She made no reply to this, and did not look at him. He took

93

her arm lightly and together they moved out into the middle of the street. 'Nowadays,' he continued, 'it's even worse, because of the hostility towards Europeans. Among the people as a whole, I mean. They resent the way we interfere in Turkey's internal affairs, especially in Macedonia. And of course the British have not been popular since we took Egypt away from them.'

He was conscious all the time he talked of his fingers lightly enclosing a section of Miss Taverner's arm below the thin material of her dress. 'What did you want to buy?' he asked.

'Oh, nothing much. Some silk, I thought, for a dress.'

'The Anatolian silk is good,' he said.

'I can get it another time,' she said.

They stopped at an open stall and Markham asked the man to show them what silks he had. He watched her touching and smoothing the different coloured silks, crumpling them to see how well they resisted creasing. Standing slightly back from her, he could see the smooth, slightly sun-freckled nape of her neck between the white linen collar of her dress and the beginning of the upward sweep of her hair. He watched her hands turning over the softly glinting material, pale, long-fingered hands.

She chose what she wanted, and Markham bargained for her with the shopkeeper, not knowing what the silk was worth, offering half of what was asked.

'We probably paid too much,' he said, smiling at her.

'It doesn't matter.'

Seeing her beam with the pleasure of her purchase he thought, she is little more than a child really, and he strove to remember her age. Twenty? Twenty-one? At least ten years younger than he was.

'I'd better be getting back,' she said. 'Thank you for helping me. And thank you so much for rescuing me. You appeared like a knight of old.'

Markham laughed. 'Not much of a knight,' he said. 'I'll walk part of the way back with you, if you like.'

They walked back towards the Ministry of Finance buildings, then turned left between the Bazaar and the *Medresseh* of the Beyazit Mosque. Markham stopped to point out a large triangular piece of marble embedded in the wall of a bathhouse, with helmeted warriors carved in relief on it.

'All that's left of the Column of Theodosius,' he said. 'Byzantium only exists in fragments now, apart from its churches.'

'I must study Byzantine history,' she said, with a note of earnest determination, and again he thought how young she was – the age still when one makes programmes of study. Her remark had been an indirect admission of ignorance too, so he told her something as they went along about the great column of Theodosius the First, erected in the fourth century, pulled down by Sultan Beyazit a thousand years later.

'That bit of marble has seen some blood spilt,' he said with sudden sombreness. 'Like all the fragments of Byzantium.' He had forgotten to whom he was talking. 'It's a wonder they're not stained red,' he said. 'A favourite form of execution was throwing people off these triumphal columns, preferably onto spiked railings. That's what happened to Alexius the Fourth, among others. Apparently it took him several—'

Recollecting himself suddenly, he broke off and glanced at her. 'Sorry,' he said. 'Gloomy subject. I don't know why it is, but I don't seem able to separate myself very easily from things like that. Odd, isn't it?'

'Things in the past, you mean? But when it is so long ago . . .'

'Yes,' he said. 'Quite. Unreasonable, isn't it?'

'How is it that you know so much about it?' she asked. 'About the city, I mean.'

'I've always been interested,' he said. He paused, then said more deliberately, 'I've been here before you know. Years ago.'

'I didn't know that.'

'Oh yes,' Markham said. 'Twelve years ago.' It came out

95

easily enough, though his breathing had quickened. She would have asked more, but they had now emerged on to the wide courtyard of the mosque, where, in the corner nearest them, a crowd had gathered in a semicircle round a ragged, elderly man sitting crosslegged on a small mat. He was talking, looking from face to face. His voice was slow, rather hoarse, with a deliberate rise and fall, as if he were reciting.

'What is happening there?' Miss Taverner asked and there was something childlike about the question, trusting and imperious at the same time, claiming the right to be informed.

'He's a story-teller,' Markham said. 'He's telling the people a story. Would you like to listen? I could probably give you the gist of it.'

'Well,' she said, hesitating, clearly wanting to stay, 'I should be going really.'

Her unease, he knew, was due to the fact that they were alone together – the alien people milling round them did not count. It was there between them, this sense that they had already stayed together longer than was seemly; there in the glances they gave each other, the inflections of their voices. One does nothing, Markham thought. One merely allows time to lapse, perhaps only minutes; and that changes things, that acts for us. He watched the irresolution on her face. 'Just for a minute or two,' he said.

She smiled briefly and nodded and they moved towards the crowd. The sun was high in the sky now and it was hot in the courtyard. Miss Taverner put up her parasol and the sunlight filtered through the white shade onto her face and the front of her cotton dress. The story-teller's voice continued, sing-song, curiously compelling. His head did not move but his heavy-lidded eyes paused on various faces, paused on Markham's and Miss Taverner's.

'He's telling the story of Kerem and Asli,' Markham said quietly. 'Just now he is talking about the hazards of Kerem's journey to find Asli, his betrothed. He can spin these out for hours if he wants to. Do you know the story?'

She shook her head.

'Well, the Shah of Isphahan had a beautiful son, Prince Kerem, who fell in love with the daughter of an Armenian priest. The priest, being a fanatical Christian, did not want his daughter to marry a Moslem, but he was too afraid of the Shah to refuse, so he was obliged to name the wedding day. However, when Kerem went to claim his bride he found the doors open and the house empty. The family had fled. Kerem became a poet on the spot and began to sing to the various belongings of his beloved, her embroidery frame, her divan, and so on. They answered him, also in song. Kerem then set off in search of her with his lute – that's the bit he's telling now. He had all sorts of adventures on the way. As he went along he sang songs to the clouds and trees and so on, asking for news of Asli. Can you hear how the old chap's voice goes up into a sort of crooning note? He's imitating the replies given to Kerem by these various things.'

The story-teller broke off abruptly to raise a copper bowl and rattle the coins inside it.

'That's for our benefit really,' Markham said. 'He won't go on till he's been paid.' He went forward, beneath the impassive stare of the other listeners, and dropped some kurus into the man's bowl.

'I don't think we'd better wait till he reaches the end,' Miss Taverner said, when he returned.

'No, perhaps not. It could take a long time. That's the only commodity these people seem to be rich in. I'll see you across to the cab-rank, if you like. There's one in front of the Ministry of Finance.'

'What happened?' she asked, as they walked along. 'How did it end?'

'He finally ran her to earth, if that's the right phrase, in an Anatolian town. Charmed by Kerem's singing, the notables of the town forced the priest to give his daughter in marriage. But the old devil had one last trick up his sleeve. He made a magic dress for Asli, which buttoned from the neck right

97

down to the hem of the skirt, and the thing about this dress was that no one could unbutton it. Using his enchanted lute Kerem succeeded in getting the buttons to open one after the other, down to the bottom, but no sooner were they opened than the top ones started closing again. This lasted till morning.'

Glancing at Miss Taverner, Markham saw that she was blushing. 'Just imagine it,' he said.

'What a terrible predicament to be in,' she said.

'Indeed, yes,' Markham said. 'By the time dawn broke poor old Kerem was in the last stages of torture. The fever in his heart was turning to real flame. He gave one last sigh, a fire broke from his mouth and then he just turned into a heap of ashes. Not what you'd call a happy ending.'

'No,' she said. 'Poor man.'

'It's really an anti-Christian story,' he said. 'Or perhaps just anti-Armenian.'

They were walking along beside the outer wall of the courtyard now. This was lined with narrow stalls selling rosaries, women's trinkets, dried fruits, spices.

'I do like Constantinople,' she said suddenly, and with enthusiasm. 'I think it's a marvellous city.'

'The most marvellous thing about it at the moment,' he said, 'is that it contains you and me.'

At once he felt he had said too much, gone too far. She looked at him a moment, then lowered her eyes. The expression of enthusiasm left her face.

'Now I have made you serious,' he said. 'I can't take it back, though, can I? Let's have a look at these things.'

They stopped before a stall with a tall pale Arab behind it, and red and blue leather tubes laid out in rows. 'Let me get you some *kohl*,' he said. He wanted to give her something to mark the occasion; but a trinket or any object of that kind he felt would be too intimate, inappropriate. 'May I?' he asked.

'*Kohl?*' she said. 'Yes, if you like. What is it?'

'It's what Moslem women use on their eyes,' he said.

He spoke to the man behind the stall and the man answered gravely, courteously.

'He says the *kohl* has been brought from Mecca,' Markham smiled. 'They always say that. Holy tradition has it that it's pleasing to Mohammed for women to use *kohl* on their eyes, to make them beautiful.'

She chose a red tube, put it carefully in her bag. They walked the rest of the way to the fiacre rank in silence for the most part but not now uneasy with each other. He found a fiacre for her, instructed the driver. As the vehicle began to pull away, she turned to him, clutching parcel, parasol and bag. She smiled good-bye but said nothing – all her sense of occasion was in her smile. He watched the fiacre disappear round the corner of the Ministry buildings.

There was only one other fiacre in the rank and this was taken by a group of young men just before he reached it. Markham swung round in some impatience and began to walk past the main entrance to the Ministry in the hope of catching a fiacre as it approached the square. On the corner, he saw a man hesitate then move away behind the columns flanking the entrance. In that second Markham recognized the beaky, ill-nourished face, the ragged caftan: it was the man he had seen outside his house sometimes.

Peering through the delicate wrought-iron grill of the gate, standing on his platform of stones, Henry watched the little girl dancing. He was slightly bored but fascinated too. She was dressed today as vividly as ever in a red blouse and yellow trousers of the kind Henry had seen Turkish women wear, baggy round the upper part of the legs, fitting closely at the ankles. On her feet she wore shiny black slippers.

She stepped this way and that, holding her hands out on either side of her as if balancing. Intermittently she sang a few notes in her clear bird-like voice. She kept her head lowered

99

most of the time, watching the motions of her feet, but she glanced up occasionally to make sure that Henry was still looking at her.

He had come earlier than last time, his mother having released him from the sketching lesson well before lunch, on the grounds of a headache. She had left him in the nursery to prepare for his afternoon lessons with Miss Taverner, and he had seized the occasion, driven by some restless curiosity, to slip out and make his way here. He had not found her in the garden and had been disappointed. On the point of returning, it had occurred to him to make the sound he had amused her with on his last visit, the extraordinarily loud, tearing noise which can be achieved by blowing in a certain way against the edge of a grass blade. As if waiting somewhere for this signal, she had appeared almost at once, come down the garden towards him, in her red blouse and yellow trousers.

Now, however, he was uneasy. It was time for him to be going back. The muezzin had just called from the mosque below, and Henry knew from experience that the high-pitched, wavering voice was quite soon followed by lunch.

He waved to the little girl, moving his hand from side to side across the bars. She stopped her dance at once, advanced towards the gate a few steps, stopped again. She regarded him expectantly, but he could think of nothing more to entertain her. The light was behind her now and he could see the shape of her legs through the thin material of her trousers. She waited some seconds more, then turned away with an abrupt, petulant movement of her shoulders. The movement expressed annoyance, but whether this was at his interrupting her dance or for some other reason he did not know.

# 5

Abdul Hamid rose at his usual time of five. After brief ablutions in cold water he passed into his study where he drank a cup of Turkish coffee prepared in his presence by his *kafeji-bashi*, Ali. Then he settled down to studying the reports laid on his desk by his first aide-de-camp, Tcherkess Mehmet Pasha. He had become over the years incapable of delegating authority and often found himself dealing with very small matters, such as a complaint against some minor official, or repairs to a bridge in an unimportant provincial town. Decisions about these and larger matters were transmitted via his secretaries to the ministers concerned, and couriers employed for the purpose were constantly passing from Yildiz to the Sublime Porte in Stambul. The secretaries themselves were extremely harassed these days by the sheer volume of spies' reports; indeed many of them, unable to get home, had taken up quarters in the Palace, and worked all day and half the night deciphering reports from Paris, London, Geneva, Cairo.

Halfway through the morning the Sultan had an interview, alone save for the interpreter and Furad, his chamberlain, with two American financiers who offered him large sums in return for concessions to prospect for oil in Mesopotamia. The offers were tempting, but Abdul Hamid had committed himself, in private, to the German Ambassador, Baron Marshall von Biberstein, and he was determined to honour this promise. Gratitude was always strong in his nature, and in these closing months of his reign, as he sensed everywhere the dissolution of his empire and the end of his dynasty, and as personal fear grew daily more overwhelming, he remembered how during the Armenian massacres of the nineties only

Germany among all the nations of Europe had not condemned him. The Kaiser had actually paid him a state visit during that time. Abdul Hamid had never forgotten this. It was to the Germans that the contract to build the great Baghdad railway had gone, and this contract contained secret clauses giving Germany the sole right to exploit any mineral resources for thirty kilometres on either side of the line.

However, he did not reject the American offers outright. Following his usual custom, he temporized, putting the men off with half-promises, vague assurances.

Later, after his siesta, he walked for a while through his park inside the inner walls of the palace. He wore a suit of European style, dark brown in colour – he never wore light-coloured clothes, fearing they would make him too easy a target. By contrast, however, all those who were employed out of doors in the park – gardeners, zookeepers, people of that kind – were obliged as a condition of their service to wear white clothes at all times, and to move with deliberate slowness when in the vicinity of their master. These regulations were due to an unfortunate accident the previous year when a gardener, a lad of only eighteen, meeting the Sultan at a turn in the path had startled him with a too hasty salaam and been shot between the eyes.

Now, with his mulatto Hassan going before him, two of the palace guards some distance behind, and with a small revolver in each of his side pockets, he walked between the double row of birch trees that separated the Imperial Pavilion from the Harem. As he passed he could hear the laughter of women and the sound of a banjo and a voice uttering a snatch of song, a Caucasian song – he did not understand the words. The voice was high and sweet, with a languor in it redolent of all the longing, the poignant sense of waste, of the Harem. Abdul Hamid slowed his steps to listen. He loved the collective sense of the Harem, the comfort and consolation that awaited him there among the women, to whom he was as the sun. He could not enter now, however: etiquette demanded that visits be announced in advance, except in greatly exceptional circumstances.

He skirted the white walls with their high, latticed windows. Red macaws stared at him with greedy and maniacal eyes from the cages against the walls, and one of them uttered a prolonged chattering screech at his approach. Other screeches came occasionally from different parts of the grounds, loud harsh sounds that seemed to leave an extra quality of silence, like a small devastation, in their wake; there were at least four hundred parrots and macaws caged here and there in the park and a man was employed with no other duty but that of caring for them – an important post, as the Sultan set great store by these birds, believing that their outcries would warn him of enemies.

He had reached the lakeside now. Kingfishers flashed across the lake, and cranes and flamingos dipped their graceful necks into the water. Briefly he inspected the little mooring stage with the pleasure boats tied up there, then he proceeded towards the menagerie, acknowledging the salutes of the two Albanian guards at their post against the wall. He had recently purchased a black leopard and it was pride in this acquisition which had drawn him here today. That and the desire to see that the animal was being properly fed. He suspected the keepers of cheating him on the foodstuffs, knew it in fact, but wished to make sure it was not excessive.

The leopard was half-maddened by confinement and paced ceaselessly back and forth across the floor of its cage. At each turn there was a golden blaze from its eyes, then its head went down again. Abdul Hamid watched for some time but that obsessive loping walk unnerved him, and he moved down to his marmosets. These were his favourites. He had bananas specially sent from Alanya to feed them – there were some now, in a crate outside the cage.

Hassan the mulatto and the two guards stood off at a respectful distance, not presuming to look directly at their master. Abdul Hamid smoked a cigarette in the sunshine.

103

Birds and animals in their cages stared at him with eyes deepset or prominent, slit or round, myopic or keen. He returned these looks. When he had finished his cigarette, he took a banana, peeled it, and threw the peel onto the floor of the cage. With astonishing speed and agility the monkeys swung down for it. When the one who snatched it first realized he had been cheated he chattered and shrieked with rage, threw the peel down again. The Sultan laughed, for the only time that day.

The conference was scheduled to begin at ten o'clock and it was almost that when Markham was ushered by an orderly into the large room at the Ministry of War where it was to take place. However, of the British contingent only Blake had arrived so far. He was standing alone on one side of the room. Two Turkish subalterns stood together quietly talking on the other side. Portraits of pashas and military notables hung on the walls. The long table gleamed with polish and the chairs ranged along it were of padded leather with high backs and carved wooden arms.

Markham moved over to where Blake was standing. 'We haven't had a lot of time to sort this out between us,' he said. 'For one reason or another. You're doing the talking, aren't you?'

'I suppose so,' Blake said. 'Just the general picture. Unless Nesbitt wants to do it.'

'Not much chance of that,' Markham said. 'I expect he'll make a token appearance here today.'

Blake was silent, pushing his neck back against the collar of his uniform, as he did when feeling uneasy or put out.

'It's really just a question of going over old ground,' Markham said. Privately, however, he did not altogether believe this. Relations between the British and Turkish military authorities were becoming increasingly strained. The murderous chaos in Macedonia still continued, after months of patient negotiations over the setting up of a peace-keeping force. The man who had been the driving force behind these discussions, the British ambassador, Sir Nicholas O'Connor, had died at the beginning of the previous April, and the new Ambassador had not been appointed yet. In this interval Turkish hostility to the idea of European officers for the gendarmerie – crucial to the whole scheme – had hardened considerably.

Several people now entered the room, among them Nesbitt and the Second Secretary from the embassy, Charles Worseley-Jones. Markham recognized the close-cropped head and heavy clean-shaven face of Essad Pasha who commanded the Turkish regular forces employed against the various guerrilla bands in Macedonia. He had attended several of these conferences, though rarely saying much. With him were two youngish officers, both majors, one of whom was known to Markham already. The other, however, a man with pale steady eyes and a short scar on his cheek, he had not seen before. In their blue and silver dress uniforms the Turks looked resplendent against the drab olive of the British.

Nesbitt made the introductions, punctiliously but with the slight surliness inseparable from him. The Turks bowed, unsmiling, then moved in a body to seat themselves at the far end of the table. With them went the interpreter, a man in a fez and long, buttoned tunic.

Worseley-Jones began the proceedings, referring in general terms to the ground already covered and to the great interest shown in the pacification of Macedonia by the late Ambassador. He spoke easily and well, looking from face to face along the table, pausing for the interpreter. The Turks listened impassively. Markham found himself noticing the newcomer among the officers, who had been introduced as Nejib Bey. There was something about him which compelled attention, some quality of latent strength or energy. He could only be Caucasian, with those pale eyes, full, slow-moving, arrogant in effect. The scar was thin and straight, probably the result of a sword-cut.

Worseley-Jones's level-browed, good-looking face was smiling now. 'My military colleagues,' Markham heard him say. He was about to hand things over. Markham wondered once again why he had not taken more to Worseley-Jones. They were about of an age, and not too dissimilar in background. Perhaps it was that the man was too perfect a specimen, too completely defined by his caste . . . He remembered that the Worseley-Joneses were coming to dinner on Friday. Blake too. On the wall above Nesbitt's head he noticed a large photograph of Abdul Hamid as a young man, soon after his accession. He was in ceremonial dress, with a sword, and looked sulky and abashed somehow, as if he had been chidden, not a man to originate massacres . . .

'Well,' Worseley-Jones said, 'I'll hand you over to Colonel Nesbitt.'

'You have something to say on this, Blake, haven't you?' Nesbitt said, in his harsh voice, looking down the table.

Blake said, 'Yes, sir,' and even in the habitual briskness of this response there was distaste for what he had to do. Looking frequently at the notes on the table before him, he began to speak in some detail about the proposed constitution of the gendarmerie. The strength of the force was to be fifteen thousand men, recruited and trained in stages, organized into small mobile columns each under the command of a trustworthy officer.

Blake was not impressive as a speaker. He avoided people's eyes and spoke in a voice that was both hasty and flat. Markham noticed that his thick fingers trembled slightly and thought how odd it was that Blake, a good officer and a brave man – he had distinguished himself in Afghanistan and had won the Military Cross – should sit there trembling with nerves because he had to speak in formal circumstances.

Everything Blake said had been agreed in principle anyway. Markham allowed his attention to wander. He looked back at the portrait. The Sultan was leaning back in his high chair. Right at the beginning of his remarkably blood-stained career, with all the rapes and tortures still to instigate . . . Involuntarily he glanced across at Nesbitt, remembering the name he had seen on the other's desk. Any Armenian name suggested pain and death to him now, the very syllables seemed clothed with suffering. Well, he would know more about the Hartunian business if he could effect the meeting with Zimin. The Sultan himself had an Armenian type of face, a fact which had often been remarked on. It was particularly noticeable in this picture, Markham thought, the wide, long-lashed eyes, the big nose. His mother, of course, had been Armenian, an Armenian slave-girl.

The officer with the scarred cheek was speaking now. He spoke clearly and fluently with what looked like a slight humorous twitching of the lips below the thick straight moustache. Even before he had begun to take in the words, Markham saw Nesbitt turn his head suddenly towards the speaker, sensed from that the unexpected nature of what was being said. He began to listen carefully, not waiting for the interpreter.

Nejib was talking about money, the situation of his country's finances, but in a detached, unemotional, even rather fastidious way. It was clear he was an educated man, though not, Markham thought, of established family; he had none of the courtliness of the Ottoman ruling class.

'The government,' he was saying, very clearly and distinctly, 'cannot at this stage afford to increase the strength of the gendarmerie in Macedonia.'

'Increase the strength?' Markham said, barely waiting for the interpreter to finish. 'I do not understand what that means. There is no force whatsoever at the moment, at least no organized force. All this was agreed last June.'

He found the pale eyes of the Turk regarding him coldly. 'The situation must be extensively reviewed,' Nejib said, 'before any further decisions.'

'Further decisions?' Quite without warning Markham felt rage beginning to climb with terrible agility up his throat and

107

into his voice. 'Further to what?' he said. 'Good heavens!' He tried to caution himself, but it was too late. 'All this was decided a year ago,' he said in a loud voice. 'In the time of my predecessor here. We and the French agreed to accept increased customs dues in order to meet the costs and avoid extra charge on your government. We are not here today to discuss that, but the organization of the militia units and the scope of their officers.' It was this, he knew, that they baulked at, whatever they might say about money: European officers with executive powers. 'Can we return to the point at issue?' he said.

He heard Nesbitt cough loudly, perhaps with a warning intention. Nejib's mouth twitched again, in that humorous way. His eyes, however, reflected nothing humorous.

'Times change,' he said, in English.

'What do you mean by that?' Markham said. 'Will you please explain that remark?'

'Perhaps,' Worseley-Jones said, 'there has been some change in the situation which we have not been informed about?'

No reply was made to this. After some moments of silence, Essad Pasha began to speak in dignified tones, looking straight before him. He reminded his hearers of the successes gained by the flying columns under his command in Macedonia. He had used the five thousand regular troops allocated to him by personal decree of the Sultan for a massive drive again the *comitadjis* and had inflicted heavy losses, particularly on the Greeks and Bulgarians.

The effort to control his anger, to betray nothing of it, imposed a sort of stillness on Markham's face, lent a measured quality to his words.

'It is not a question of inflicting losses,' he said, 'if the Pasha will forgive me. There are always plenty of recruits for the partisans. You cannot, after all, wipe out the whole population. It is a question of protecting the village people from rape and pillage. And – again if Your Excellency will pardon me – according to our information, which we have no reason to doubt, the losses inflicted by your flying columns have been mainly on the civilian population, and seem to have included a fair number of women and children.'

On finishing this speech Markham was aware of a sort of snorting exclamation from Nesbitt. He did not look at him, however, but across at Blake who was tight-lipped as if in some degree of shock but who nodded briefly in agreement.

Essad Pasha listened in total immobility until the interpreter had finished, then he at once rose to his feet. He looked at Nesbitt. '*Su subayir adi nedir?*' he said. 'What is the officer's name?' It was the old, menacing army trick of identifying an inferior – Essad knew his name perfectly well.

'*Izmin* Markham, *Bey effendi*. Captain Robert Markham,' Nesbitt said.

Essad nodded once, turned on his heel and walked out, followed closely by the rest of the Turkish contingent, though not before Nejib and Markham had stared at each other for some moments more.

'Do you realize what you've done?' Nesbitt's face was dark red, congested-looking. 'You have criticized, to his face, a senior officer's conduct of a campaign.' He lumbered to his feet and stood glaring across the table at Markham.

'No, sir,' Markham said.

'He did not criticize the conduct of the Pasha, sir,' Blake said, 'only the conduct of the troops.'

'Don't split hairs with me,' Nesbitt said, with such savagery that Markham saw Worseley-Jones, though not Blake, recoil slightly. Nesbitt picked up his hat and stick. 'I intend to make a full report of these proceedings,' he said. He made as if to leave, then checked and said, with a marked change of tone. 'You coming, Blake?'

Blake paused appreciably before replying. It was an unmistakable claim for his support, and more than this, for his endorsement of Nesbitt's view of the matter. Blake knew this, as did the others. Unlike Markham, he was a regimental

109

officer – an adverse report here could dog his career for years. He looked at Markham's white face. The fellow was not strong enough to contain his own emotions, he thought, with faint contempt. A picture of Elizabeth Markham as he had last seen her came into his mind, the delicate skin flushed slightly, the appeal in the clear blue eyes. He cleared his throat. 'I think I'll stay on here a bit, if you don't mind, sir,' he said.

'Very well.'

Without looking at anyone else, Nesbitt stalked out of the room. There was silence for some moments, then Worseley-Jones said, 'I shouldn't worry too much, if I were you.' He had spoken with peculiar significance but neither Markham nor Blake made any rejoinder – they were united with Nesbitt for the moment in automatic defence against any civilian intrusion. All the same, Markham was to remember later the intonation Worseley-Jones gave to this remark. 'Well,' he said, 'we'd better be going, I suppose.'

'Can I give you a lift?' Worseley-Jones said. 'I've got one of the Embassy landaus outside.'

'I'd rather walk, I think,' Blake said. 'Stretch my legs a bit. It's just round the corner anyway.'

'Of course,' Worseley-Jones said, with a tact that was too immediate, too palpable. However, he remained some moments longer, lounging irresolutely against the wall in his well-cut grey flannel suit, fair brows drawn together in a slight frown. 'There's been a change of some kind,' he said. 'I don't like it at all.'

'Who was that fellow?' Markham said. 'The one with the scar.'

'Nejib Bey, you mean? He's one of the new men. Seconded from the Third Army Corps in Salonika. Very bright. He speaks English well, though I noticed he affected not to. German too, of course – he was trained by the Germans, like so many of them nowadays. Not much of a Moslem, one gathers – that's the great gulf between some of these junior officers and men like Essad, the Sultan's men. Look, I'm not happy about what's happened here today and I don't suppose you are either. The chargé d'affaires has saddled me with this business until the new Ambassador is appointed, and I shall be responsible to him when he arrives. I wonder if you two would mind coming over to the Embassy one day soon and giving me the benefit of your ideas? Morrison would probably want to be in on that too, and one or two others probably.'

'You are both coming to dinner with us on Friday evening,' Markham said.

'Oh, are we? Well, I know *I* am, of course.' Worseley-Jones smiled at Blake. 'But we won't be able to talk much then, will we? Shall we say Monday, next Monday morning?'

Both Blake and Markham said this would be all right. Worseley-Jones looked relieved, as if arranging the meeting had more or less solved all problems. He straightened up to his full six feet and moved towards the door. 'About ten o'clock?' he said. 'Splendid, I'll send the Embassy launch down for you, Markham.'

Markham accepted this offer and the two officers waited some moments further, then followed Worseley-Jones out. The streets were quiet now, in mid-afternoon. It was very hot. Fetid odours hung in the air, exuded it seemed from the walls of the houses and stones of the streets. Street dogs licked their sores in the sun or lay twitching with dreams in doorways. The two men did not speak much on the way back, as if swayed by some common reluctance to refer to what had just taken place. Blake complained about the heat, and smells, as he often did.

'This must be the most evil-smelling city in the world,' he said. 'Bar none.'

'Have you been to Cairo?'

'No,' Blake said, 'but if it's worse than this I don't even want to think about it. Thank God I've got some leave coming

111

up. I'd hate to think I was going to be here all through the summer.'

'Yes, you're lucky,' Markham said. He glanced briefly, curiously, at the face of the man walking beside him. Blake actually wanted to get out of Constantinople – the wish made him seem almost like a creature of another species. He tried to imagine how he himself would feel if he was recalled now. He found the thought almost unendurable. To leave the city – even on official orders – would be to leave the past unchanged, himself unchanged . . .

Markham did not stay long in his office. Thoughts of the coming meeting with Zimin, uncertainty as to whether the fellow would turn up, unsettled him. He made, for his own reference, a summary of what had been said at the conference, locked it in his desk, then left. He had to get home reasonably early, in any case, so as to change into civilian clothes – it would be unwise to wear uniform for the meeting.

When he got home he found his wife having tea on the narrow terrace at the front of the house, which got the late afternoon sunshine. She was sitting under the large blue sunshade which Mehmet had contrived there for her. This was of thick canvas, not admitting much light through it, so that Elizabeth seemed enclosed by the shade, cut off from the rest of the bright, empty terrace. There was a book open in her lap. Markham sat beside her, half in and half out of the shade. He took off his belt and the tunic of his jacket and leaned back against his chair.

'What a day,' he said.

'Would you like some tea?' she said. 'It's just been made. We'll have to get an extra cup from Nevres Badji.'

'I'll go and get it,' he said. She looked tired, he thought, very pale in the shadow cast by the umbrella.

'No,' she said, 'Henry can go.' She raised her voice. 'Henry,' she called, 'where are you?'

'Not hiding again, is he?' Markham said.

'He was here a moment ago.'

112

'He probably makes himself scarce when he sees me,' Markham said. 'I think he regards me as an intruder.' He got up and went through the house to the kitchen at the rear. Nevres was not there, but he found a cup and saucer and brought them back with him.

'It's not that,' she said, as she poured out tea for him.

'Not what?'

'He doesn't regard you as an intruder. He's simply not at ease with you, Robert. You must try and see it from his point of view.'

'How do you mean?' Markham sipped his tea rather gloomily. He had wanted to complain about his day, about the fiasco of the conference, and now instead he saw that he was to be criticized.

'He didn't see you for over three months,' Elizabeth said. 'And now you seem to be a completely different person from the one he knew.'

'Has he told you this?'

'Not in so many words.'

'I'll tell you what, Elizabeth,' Markham said, 'I think you're quite mistaken. Or at any rate you're exaggerating.'

'Perhaps you don't realize it yourself,' she said. He heard in her voice the slight quiver below the reasonable form of the words and was warned by it. 'I don't know,' he said. 'It's difficult to know how we seem to other people.'

'It's true,' she said. 'I don't want to go into it now, but you're not the same. The man I said goodbye to in England and the man I found here are not the same.'

He said nothing. After a moment or two he saw her lift her chin slightly as if in pride or resignation.

'Anyway,' she said, 'it's just as well perhaps that he isn't here, because something has cropped up. Did you know that he has been in the habit of wandering around the neighbourhood while he's supposed to be resting in the afternoons?'

'Good Lord,' Markham said. 'No, of course I didn't.'

113

'This only came to me in a roundabout way,' she said. 'Through Electra.'

He nodded. Electra was the daily maid, a Greek girl from Alexandria who spoke some English. 'She saw him, did she?' he said.

'No, apparently Ibrahim saw him going out through the gate at the end of the garden, and he told Electra and Electra told me. I asked Nevres if she knew anything about it – using Electra as an interpreter of course – and she said she had washed some stockings with bloodstains on them and also that his shirt sleeves and the seat of his shorts had thick clay on them as if he had been sliding down somewhere. Then Mehmet put the seal on the whole thing. He said that he'd been talking to a friend of his at the market, an Albanian apparently who is a sort of odd-job man for a Turkish family near us somewhere, and this man said he had seen a little boy, a little foreign boy, climbing up to look through a gate into somebody's garden. It seems incredible, but there it is. Apparently they have all known about it for days.'

'Well, well,' Markham said. 'Henry has been leading a double life. No small achievement at the age of ten.'

He spoke lightly, but this account of his son's doings had disturbed him in a way he found difficult to define. It was the secrecy, for one thing – though that was typical of course. And then the accumulation of incriminating details, the bloodstains, the marks of the clay, the exit from the garden, the evidence of the Albanian odd-job man. A net closing round Henry ... Markham was suddenly aware of his own irregularities, the clandestine meeting he was trying to arrange with Zimin. He was behaving not much differently from his son. Somewhere, already, there might be people pooling information about him, assembling the odd things noticed, tightening the net ...

'I'll speak to him about it,' he said.

'As a matter of fact, I'd rather you didn't,' Elizabeth said. 'I wanted to ask you not to mention it to him.'

114

'Why not? He must simply be forbidden to do it. We can't have him wandering about and not know where he is. It's damn risky for one thing.'

'Yes, I know. But let me talk to him, will you?'

Markham hesitated. The boy should be spoken to straight, not cajoled and treated with tact by his mother. Any shame or indignity involved for him in the process should be faced square-on, not all melted away by Elizabeth's 'understanding.' Just another name for indulgence, he thought. But there was a look of appeal on his wife's face, and it came to Markham suddenly that he was being more severe on the boy than he was on himself. Was he not looking for indulgence too? Not from the woman before him, however. Before indulgence there must come *knowledge*. Into his mind, unbidden, came the picture of the governess as he had last seen her, sitting in the cab, clutching her purchases.

'Very well,' he said. 'I agree. He's extraordinary that boy. He goes his own way entirely.'

# 6

Late in the afternoon Abdul Hamid spoke to representatives of the European powers at a hastily convened meeting in the Imperial Pavilion. Present at this meeting were the French, Italian and German Ambassadors, the British Chargé d'Affaires and the First Secretary from the Russian Embassy. The Grand Vizier was there, and of course Izzet Bey, who later, in exile, wrote of this meeting in his Memoirs. The Sultan, who was obviously in a state of high nervous tension, spoke at some length and very emphatically. Turkey, he said, would under no circumstances allow any further intervention in her domestic affairs, and particularly in Macedonia. The programme of reforms agreed upon would be adhered to, but no further concessions or powers would be granted.

He looked round the table at the attentive faces of the Europeans. Turkey's sovereign rights in Macedonia must be clearly recognized, he said. His voice was uneven, barely under control. Izzet records the cynical opinion that his words were for Turkish internal consumption, designed to allay patriotic indignation about concessions already granted rather than make an impression on the Europeans. Izzet does not try to account for the Sultan's state of nerves on this occasion. It was in any case a fairly frequent thing with him during those final months. And there were pressures on him, particularly from the army, which Izzet knew nothing about.

The Italian, Pallavicini, asked about guarantees for the protection of the Christian minorities in Macedonia, but Abdul Hamid refused to answer. He got to his feet, bringing the meeting abruptly to an end. Afterwards, when the foreign diplomats had gone, he took some valerian to calm himself, and lay down for an hour.

Markham was early for his appointment with Zimin. He did not therefore make his way directly to the Rustem Pasha mosque, but spent some time lounging at the harbour wall near the second, inner bridge across the Golden Horn, known as Mahmoud Bridge. He felt fairly sure he had not been followed – at least not by any of the men who watched his house. None of them in fact had been in evidence when he had glanced out of his study window, but he had decided to use the garden exit just in case. He had walked along the path, between the high walls and the dry stream-bed, seeing nobody. Emerging on to the street he had turned away from the sea, gone some way higher up towards Nishantash, and taken a fiacre from there.

He watched a small cargo boat laden with hides edge out into the middle of the waterway and move slowly down towards the entrance to the Marmara. The small flurry of its departure was over almost at once, the little knot of people at the dockside dispersed, the wake was smoothed instantly. Something like a sneeze, he thought vaguely: violent in a way, quickly settled, meaningless.

The sun was declining, laying flames on the harbour water beyond the bridge. The lead-coloured dome of the Sultan Selim Mosque further inland was hazed with gold. Already the sky was thickening, filling with the grain of a sunset that promised to be splendid – one of those spectacular skies of Constantinople's summer, dramatized as it seemed to Markham by the violence and cruelty of the city itself, which he knew, which he remembered so well. Nothing more terrible at times than this splendour. Yes, he remembered it well, from the August evenings of twelve years ago. Twelve years was a long time, by some modes of measurement. Time for marriage and children, time to establish a career. He had thought of it as a thick pad of time when he had learned he

117

was to be posted here. But three months had sufficed to reduce it to the thinnest of membranes, soft and porous, so that sensation was indistinguishable from memory, touching his nerves with an immediacy against which he had no defence, as did now this flame on the water, the slow graining of the sky, the conjunction of beauty and indifference in the scene before him.

He turned away and began to climb upward through the streets towards the small mosque near which he had offered to meet Zimin. He could not see it from here, though he could see the minarets of the great Sulimaniyé Mosque nearby. Two street dogs snarled and snapped at each other in an alley as he passed, quarrelling over a scrap of offal. He caught a glint of water from an open drain. Already there was a sense of nightfall in the air, in these narrow streets whose tall balconied houses almost met overhead, shutting out most of the sky. From the mosque above him came the sudden melodious outcry of the muezzin calling the sunset prayer. The cry was taken up almost at once in various parts of the city and for some minutes the air throbbed with the resonance of devotion, mournful and clamorous, with something militant in it too, the battle cry below the prayer.

The street levelled out as he approached the mosque. He walked alongside the high enclosing wall for some distance, then crossed the street and took up a position in an angle of the low wall on that side. From here he would be able to see anyone waiting outside the mosque.

He had the wall now on two sides of him. It was about four feet high with tufts of snapdragon and camomile daisies growing along the top where the tiles had cracked and split. The street he was on ran parellel to the Divan Yolou, one of the main thoroughfares of Stambul, and he could see across to the tombs and patches of cemetery and dark shapes of cypresses that bordered this avenue for most of its length. The space between was open ground, beginning immediately below the wall where he was standing, extending to the first of the gravestones; a level, roughly rectangular expanse enclosed by the walls of the streets around it, like a large sunken courtyard.

In the deepening shadows against the walls and out some way towards the middle of the enclosure, people were sitting, some alone, most in small groups. Markham rested his arms along the top of the wall and stood looking down. Many of those below had already staked out their territory for the night, laying striped and patterned quilts and *kilims* on the earth floor. Alongside these were the bundles containing their possessions. Here and there, in the shelter of the walls, fires had been lit and smells of mutton fat and wood smoke came to Markham, mingling with the scent of camomile growing in the wall near his face. He felt suddenly envious of these people, even with the odour of their destitution in his nostrils: envious of the casual, promiscuous ease with which they huddled together. He stood there above them in his clean white linen suit, listening to the voices and occasional laughter. He heard a quick run of notes on what sounded like a flute. This was repeated after a minute or two, but now continued longer and was accompanied by some light finger-tapping on a drum of some kind. He leaned forward, trying to see where the music was coming from. One or two people glanced up at him, then looked away. The light was fading rapidly now, he could not distinguish a great deal. Occasionally flames from the fires rose high enough for him to make out the features of a face, a profile sombre or smiling.

They were peasants or artisans for the most part. Some of them had their womenfolk with them, thickly veiled in black – perhaps returning from visits somewhere. Others would be itinerant labourers without the price of a night's lodging. There were a few soldiers in drab green, probably going on or returning from leave. He made out here and there the white turbans of *softas* or theological students, that ragged and turbulent section of society.

The quick, tentative run of music sounded again. It was

coming from a group sitting near the middle of the enclosure, gypsies – the women were unveiled and ornaments glinted at their throats and in their hair; the men were ragged, thin, very dark. One of them had a drum gripped between his knees – Markham saw the quick movement of his fingers above it.

There would be people here, almost certainly, he thought, who would not welcome very close scrutiny or very much questioning about purposes and destination; and those not the usual outcast and homeless of the city, but opponents of the régime, now returning. Change was in the air, he had felt it himself. Some sense of final impotence in the vast unwieldy bulk of the Ottoman state, or perhaps simply the undisguisable whiff of decay, was bringing dissident elements of all kinds back into the city . . . Vultures of democracy, Markham thought – he had little faith in the liberal principles they brought with them, not, at least, applied to a medieval theocracy like Turkey. But they were coming back, so much was certain; coming with false identities after years of exile in remote corners of the Sultan's possessions; coming by train, tourist boat, tramp steamer, fishing caique; coming in a variety of disguises, the turban of the priest, the leather apron of the stevedore, the Albanian *fustanella*, or the rags of wandering dervishes. And the word 'Constitution', banned for thirty years by the palace censors, was in circulation among them, slogan and political programme in one . . .

Suddenly, totally unexpectedly, light fell on Markham from some source – his hands, the white front of his suit were lit up. Bewildered, he glanced up to discover where this unwelcome light was coming from. The low wall against which he was leaning met at right angles, only a yard or two away, a much higher one, evidently the courtyard wall of a *medresseh* or ecclesiastical building of some kind. This wall was pierced with a series of narrow apertures about six feet from the ground, and the light which had surprised him came through these – someone had lit gas lamps on the inside walls of the courtyard.

He was about to move away when he heard the low pattering drumbeat once again. Glancing down he saw that one of the gypsy women had risen to her feet, was looking up at him – he saw the tilted oval of her face. At the same time one of the fires below blazed up higher. Someone had put rags on it – the acrid smell of pitch rose to him. He realized, with a dull feeling of surprise, that he and the woman below had become visible to each other at the same time, more or less, by separate accidents. He knew also that she had risen to her feet because of him, because she had seen him there. Again he felt the impulse to move away, the impulse to concealment. But he was held against the wall, almost constrained, by the beginnings of a horror not yet understood, except that it concerned the light somehow, that sudden, almost festive illumination.

By the light of the fire he could see her quite clearly now. She was young, some years younger than himself he guessed, and her skin was as dark as an Indian's. Her hair was black, very long, worn without covering of any kind. There was the boldness of a savage in the high-cheekboned face, something too of the insolence of a despised race, in the way she spoke over her shoulder to her companions and laughed, still looking up at him. She wore a long, full-skirted dress, dull red in colour, and her feet were bare.

The patter of the finger drum continued – it was simply an earthenware jar, Markham now saw, with a stretched skin over the mouth. One of the others – a youth of about eighteen – raised the flute and drew notes from it in which Markham could discern no order or melody, only a wild and plaintive sequence of sounds. The girl raised her arms, took two quick steps forward.

Afterwards, when Markham went over the incident in his mind, it was the element of conspiracy in it that gave him most anguish, a conspiracy of circumstance, the feeling that everything had been arranged to attack him when he was alone and vulnerable: the girl's attention, claiming his own;

121

the sudden festive lighting of the lamps; the music gathering in volume and momentum; the dance itself. He stood there, looking down, gripping the top of the wall as if it were the rail of a prison dock.

In fact he had felt accused from the first movements of the girl's body, the first swirling notes of the music; that patter of the drum was like an interrogation, like soft insistent blows on the walls of his brain – though this was a beat of varied rhythm, to set the feet moving and the body swaying, whereas that other which he was remembering now, which he was being obliged to remember, the drumbeat which had been in his blood over all the intervening years, had been heavy, loud, a single, exactly spaced, reiterated stroke, the signal to commence the slaughter of the Armenians. With characteristic sobriety and discipline, the Turks had waited for it, then gone out into the streets of the city with their weighted clubs – there were shops in Galata that sold them during the fortnight of the killing. The killers called themselves *saporjis*, the wielders of clubs. That same heavy stroke, at nightfall, signalled an end to the day's killing – too late for them, for Miriam . . .

The woman danced slowly at first, setting her feet with evident circumspection. Her features were serious, almost sullen, the eyes downcast. Behind her the other older woman had set up a wavering song, which followed uncertainly the cadences of the flute. The hands of the drummer moved in and out of the firelight. The sound of voices – others had now joined in – seemed to rise and fall with the leaping of the light. The woman's head was lowered still: she was self-absorbed, watching her own movements.

If he had been in a crowd, if he had been a spectator among others, the effect on him could not have been the same. But he was alone, at the rail, in his patch of light – the one to be interrogated; and night was darkening round him, round the firelit enclosure below. Guided by the wavering ragged unison of the voices, with their uncertain yet wild complaint,

122

by the deliberate steps of the dancer, his mind singled out details of that other dance, moving with the terrible arbitrary skill of recall: the soft gas-light along the walls, the black-suited fiddler, Miriam's white dress. He had danced with her, the girl he was intending to marry, holding her lightly. She was in a long white dress, her body a scented mystery to him. White light, scent of the woman . . . A face suddenly now from the night outside, thin beard, moist blue eyes, a Circassian face, or possibly Kurdish. The only one to smile. He came in after the others. The light in that room of lovingly accumulated objects was different, it was full, soft, steady – the gas lamps in brackets along the wall. The energetic movements of the fiddler, but no sound – there was no sound from the past.

The men came in from the back of the house. Ragged men in faded headcloths, carrying their weighted sticks. They filled the room before he knew it, stopping the dance – she was dancing with her father. They had strained, staring faces, excited faces. We heard the music, one said, seeming abashed almost, in the soft light, among the furniture and objects of the room. As if that was why they had come. But they had come to kill Armenians. *I am not Armenian . . .*

Markham shook himself free from the memory of his voice uttering this simple truth. He opened his mouth and panted several times, softly, as if to ease breathing and memory together. He took his hands from the wall to look at his watch, noticing as he did so that his fingers felt cramped and stiff – he had been gripping too tightly. It was twenty past seven.

The voices of the singers grew in strength. The woman was dancing with raised head now, though she did not look at Markham, setting her bare feet more rapidly but with care still, the sway of her long, heavy skirt in subtle counterpoint to the movement of the hips, the tension of the abdomen sensed inside the loose material of the dress – the essence of the gypsy dance, this contrapuntal movement of the careful feet stepping within a short compass and always, however rapid,

123

selecting their place, and the subtle, suggestive movement of hip and abdomen, asserting their own rhythm against the formal steps. It was the dancing of rebels, Markham thought suddenly, and with relief at his own restored detachment, the body insisting on its own hungers and defiances against all requirements of pattern, code, law. A different matter altogether from the collective dances of the conformist Anatolians . . .

'So sorry to be late.' The voice was soft, rather sibilant. Markham had heard no sound of approach. He turned hastily to see a man of middle height, thin, in light-coloured clothes and a straw hat, standing beside him. 'Zimin,' the man said.

Markham caught the gleam of a gold tooth. 'My name is Markham,' he said. 'You speak English then?'

'Oh yes,' the other said, as they shook hands. 'My mother was of British descent.' He paused for a moment, then he said, with what seemed a desire to be totally exact, 'On her father's side, that is.' He looked down over the wall. 'She is dancing for you,' he said. 'It is a great compliment when these people do that.'

'They are hoping for some money.'

'No, no, it is more than that,' Zimin said. 'She is performing for you.' He was sharp-featured and clean-shaven with small bright eyes, very dark – they looked black in this light. There was a dark handkerchief in his breast pocket and he smelled of pomade. 'If it was only for money,' he said, 'she would not go on so long. They are *chinganés* – gypsies,' he added, as if that explained everything. He paused a moment, then said, 'It was not a good place to wait, here in the light.'

'The lights came on quite suddenly,' Markham said.

He sensed rather than saw the other's shrug. Then he was looking down again into the enclosure. The woman had come forward. She was dancing below him now, full in the light that came from the gas-lamps in the courtyard. He could see the straight parting in the oiled black hair, the gleam of the copper band at her throat, the darkened tips of her raised fingers – they were dyed with henna down to the first joint. It seemed to him that he could smell the heat and musk of her body. He was stirred now by the dance, the age-old snare and seduction, that setting of the feet with such dignity and scruple as if the body above was so charged, so burdensome with beauty, that utmost care had to be taken, even with the briefest settling of the weight.

Dance and music came to an end together. The woman stood still. After a moment she looked up at the two men standing above her. Her eyes rested on Markham. He could see the rise and fall of her breathing. He felt in his pocket, found a mejidieh, and threw it towards her. It fell near her feet. She did not move for perhaps another half minute, a longer pause than was needed for dignity, so that he was beginning to wonder whether he had caused offence, when she stooped, picked up the coin, looked briefly once more at him. Then with a toss of the head, half challenging, half disdainful, she turned away, slipping the coin into the neck of her dress as she did so. There was some laughter among those nearby and one or two people called out, but the woman took no notice, returning quietly to her place among the others.

Markham turned to the man beside him with sudden compunction. 'I'm sorry,' he said. 'I should not have kept you standing here, in the light. Perhaps I have exposed you—'

'It doesn't matter,' Zimin said. 'In any case the risk is not great from people of this kind.'

Markham was not sure this was true, but he said nothing. There was a curious and rather appealing blend of servility and hauteur in Zimin's manner that he was just beginning to notice; something to do with the rigid set of the thin shoulders, which at one moment inclined forward with exaggerated deference, and at the next, as if sensing the beginning of a rebuff, reared back affrighted.

'Can we have a drink somewhere?' Markham said.

'I know a place not far away,' Zimin said. 'It is Turkish, but quite safe. Actually the proprietor is a relative of mine.'

It was near the fish market, a tiny restaurant with half a dozen tables and a back room to which Zimin's relative, a bald bulky Turk who looked like an ex-wrestler, conducted them.

'The only thing to drink here is raki,' Zimin said. 'The wine I would not recommend.'

In the light of the kerosene lamp on the table beside them, Zimin's eyes were revealed as chestnut brown in colour and lustrous. He had thick, dark brown eyebrows, almost straight, their luxuriance rather improbable on that narrow face, as if part of a disguise.

The silent Turk brought them raki and when he had left the room again, Zimin leaned forward in his deferential way and said softly, 'What does Robert Markham, excuse me, *Captain* Robert Markham want with Arturo Zimin?'

'I want some information,' Markham said. He saw the other man's shoulders shrink back a little, in a sort of involuntary retraction. 'I thought you might be able to help me,' he said. Now that the moment had come, he felt reluctant to go on with the matter. What was it, after all, why should it concern him, a name seen by chance after all these years? For this he had brought the man opposite out of his burrow, for this he was about to expose himself to danger – a request to such a man carried danger with it, as he well knew. Yet he knew too and with a deeper, completely unswerving certainty that he was going to go through with it, not because Zimin was waiting for him, not because it was too late to withdraw, but simply because failure to come out with the name now was impossible, unthinkable. He had not foreseen, on that August evening, that all failures of nerve, all his life, would confirm and renew the one failure, convict him again of the same offence. Promptness with a name then, reticence with a name now, it was the same offence.

Zimin drank, set his glass down gently – all his movements were gentle, almost diffident. He did not speak during the long pause; nor did he, perhaps out of delicacy or desire not to seem importunate, look at Markham. A dazed white moth

126

clung to the hot glass of the lamp. Voices came from the café.

'Do you know anything about a man called Hartunian?' Markham asked, in low but distant tones, looking directly at the other.

'Hartunian?' Zimin looked down at his glass. 'There is more than one Hartunian,' he said. 'There is the one people know about, because he is rich, you understand. That is Hartunian the cotton merchant.'

'Where does he live?'

'Excuse me,' Zimin said, very softly. 'I think, before we discuss this any further, there are one or two other things to talk about first.'

'Captain Wetherby recommended you,' Markham said, as if in reassurance.

'I suppose so, yes. But if you will excuse me, it is more a question of who recommends you.'

'I am here on my own account,' Markham said. 'I am ready to pay for any information you can give me.'

Zimin was silent for some moments. Then he said, 'It is not a question of money, at least not primarily. I will be frank with you, Captain Markham. I will put all the cards on the table.' As if in earnest of this promise, Zimin took off his hat and laid it on the table beside him. His hair was abundant, springy-looking, high on his head.

'Nobody sent me,' Markham said. 'I am here on my own. This is an entirely personal matter.'

Zimin drank again, refilled his glass. 'Listen,' he said. 'The British have no reliable sources of information in Constantinople. You must know this yourself. No contacts, no agents, no *structure*. None at all. Nothing. You buy gossip from the palace – the same information that is given to journalists. You cannot find anyone, sir, because no one trusts the British. Excuse me. After three deaths there are no offers. One of them I knew. He worked in the Palace Secretariat. He died under interrogation. No one knows how the police had his name. Someone – one of you – gave it. This was before you came.'

127

'You needn't worry,' Markham said. 'I promise you that no one else will know of this meeting. This is between the two of us.'

He was beginning to wonder now whether Zimin would agree to act for him. After all he was offering no guarantees. But in that case why had the other man turned up this evening, why had he not simply ignored the note? There must be something he wanted.

'I believe you completely,' Zimin said, glancing into the corners of the room. He looked like a man who believed nobody. 'That is what I meant,' he said, 'about money not being the most important thing. Of course, money is necessary. But trust is the important thing, Captain Markham.' He leaned a little towards Markham in his stiff-shouldered, deferential way. 'Mutual trust,' he said.

'I quite agree,' Markham said. He drank some raki, watched the other man shrink back a little. He felt the heat from the lamp on the side of his face. The moth was still clinging there, more or less dead he supposed, by this time.

'Friendship is important to me,' Zimin said. 'One good turn deserves another.'

'Of course,' Markham said, 'if there is anything I can do for you . . .'

'I feel, you see,' Zimin said, 'a close affinity with the British. I understand instinctively their attitudes, the fair play, House of Commons, tea on the lawns, everything. England is Zimin's spiritual home.'

Markham nodded. 'I don't think I could get you British citizenship,' he said. 'There is a residence qualification, for one thing—'

Zimin raised a slim hand ornamented with a large gold and turquoise ring. 'No, no,' he said. 'Only what one friend can do for another. I am a Perote. What you would call a Levantine, yes? You know what they say of us: the languages of six nations and the soul of none. In a great city like London a knowledge of languages could be useful.'

'That is true,' Markham said. Of course it was only to be

expected, he thought, that men like Zimin, creatures as adapted to Abdul Hamid's monstrously corrupt régime as rats to a sewer, should feel threatened by whiffs of a clearer air. The same sense of change that was bringing back the idealists was sending Zimin scurrying. 'I could arrange for testimonials,' he said. 'Letters of introduction, that kind of thing.'

'That is what I had in mind,' Zimin said. 'But *good* ones, Captain Markham. Documents full of praises, with the official stamp on them. You know what impresses your fellow countrymen. My strong affinity with the English must be evident from the documents. That is logical, I think. Zimin is always logical.'

He said this with a humorous, almost jaunty intonation. The *raki* had loosened his tongue a little, increased the familiarity of his manner. All the same, looking into the fathomless shallows of those chestnut-coloured eyes, Markham could see nothing humorous there. They remained serious, intent, whatever the mouth said.

'That can be arranged,' he said slowly.

'I have your word?'

'You have, yes.'

'So,' Zimin said, 'you are interested in Hartunian, the cotton merchant.'

'If that is the right one.'

'He lives in Scutari, in the Yeni Mahalleh quarter. He has a big house, near the Armenian cemetery – his last journey will not be a long one. He lives alone there, except for servants. No women, or so they say. His wife is dead.'

'Recently?'

'I don't think so, no.'

'And his name?'

'The first name? Avedis.'

'It sounds like the one,' Markham said. He paused for a moment, then he said, 'What else do you know about him?'

'Not very much. Only what is common knowledge. He is said to be very rich, even for an Armenian. He travels a good deal. To Syria, to Samsun, on the Black Sea. He has land holdings there – unusual for an Armenian, but of course the land is cultivated by others. They grow tobacco there. Also he goes to Europe on business. He exports cotton, to France mainly, I think. Probably he will have other interests that I know nothing about.'

'Can you think of any reason,' Markham said slowly, 'why he should be on the police list, or a subject for investigation?'

Zimin smiled with what at last seemed genuine amusement. 'My dear sir,' he said, and he laid his hand on Markham's arm, very briefly. 'Anyone can be on the police list, with or without reason. The fact that he is an Armenian, to begin with. All Armenians are regarded with suspicion. Then the fact that he goes regularly to Europe. I don't need to remind you that the Young Turk movement has strong bases in Paris and Geneva. A person like that would make an excellent courier.'

'But what would an Armenian have to do with the Turkish nationalists?'

'Who knows?' Zimin said. 'Of course this is only speculation. I could find out more, if that is what you want.'

'That is exactly what I want.'

'There will be expenses,' Zimin said.

Markham took out his wallet and extracted ten one-lira bank notes. 'This should do to be going on with,' he said. He laid the notes on the table. 'I want everything you can find out,' he said. 'How soon can you get the information?'

'I can't promise anything,' Zimin said. 'About the quality of the information, I mean.' He reflected a moment, then shrugged. 'The day after tomorrow,' he said. 'No, better say Monday. We could meet here – do you remember the way?'

'Yes, I remember.' Markham got to his feet. 'There will be another ten for you,' he said. 'In any case.'

Zimin took the money from the table and put it in the side pocket of his jacket. 'And the documents?' he asked. 'My testimonials?'

'I will get them ready, but I will not hand them over unless I think the information is worth it. I will want to know exactly where his house is also.'

Zimin walked across to the door, opened it slightly and looked into the café. 'Better if you leave first,' he said. 'Can you come at three o'clock on Monday? It is quiet then. Make sure you are not followed.'

'Very well.'

'You will remember your promise?' Zimin said, and there was no mistaking his sincerity now. 'No word of this to your esteemed colleagues. It is between ourselves, yes?'

'Yes, of course,' Markham said. 'That is, unless you try to use the information against Hartunian.'

'What is he to you?'

'Nothing,' Markham said. 'Nothing at all.'

There were people at some of the tables and they stared as he went past, but only with what seemed normal curiosity. He nodded to Zimin's relative, and stepped out into the quiet street. He began to walk slowly down towards the Galata Bridge, thinking as he did so about the interview just finished. It seemed to him that he was reasonably safe, for the time being at least. Publicity of any sort was obviously as unwelcome to Zimin as it was to him, though he did not really understand the nature of the other's fear. In fact only that rather pathetic desire for testimonials signed by a British hand had got Zimin to the meeting at all. The fear had been genuine enough, certainly. It was as if the connection itself, the mere fact of contact, carried danger . . . He could be wrong, of course. Suspicion was always strong in men of Zimin's profession, like superstition among gamblers. The friend in the Secretariat who had been tortured – the accusation could have come from another source, not from the British at all. All the same, Zimin had seemed certain . . .

The streets were silent, almost deserted. In this predominantly Turkish quarter of Stambul there was little life on the streets after nightfall. Life went on behind the blank

131

walls of the houses, the high, latticed windows; the intensely domestic, jealously screened and guarded life of Moslem people. For his brothels and cabarets the Turk crossed over to the Christian districts on the other side of the Golden Horn.

Markham was again close to the water now, near the gaunt Customs building that stands at the quayside. There were lights on here and he could see the figures of men moving about in the great hangars, among heaps of impounded merchandise. Beyond this, eastward of the bridge, the water of the Bosphoros ran in to meet the Sea of Marmara – he was standing at the junction of two seas. The water rippled with conflicting currents, glinted black in the light of the lanterns along the bridge. Water was everywhere in Constantinople, the city was surrounded by it. He thought of the Black Sea opening wide from the neck of the Bosphoros to the north; of the miniature enclosure of the Marmara, then the Straits, much coveted access to the Mediterranean. It was these seas that first bore the Argonauts to Colchis, and the fleets of Darius to conquest; that carried the great navies of Genoa and Venice; the Godfreys and Bohemunds and Tancreds on their passage to Jerusalem and the Crusades; the galleys of the Crescent to overrun the land. Further conquests and fleets were inevitable, in spite of all the treaties in the world. He thought suddenly of the reports they had had from local sources about the fortifications of the Dardanelles. The fortresses that guarded the mouth of the Straits might be neglected and dilapidated; but they housed two hundred brand-new Krupp guns. And he himself had seen, passing through on his way out here, the white and green tents of the military permanently encamped up there. Impossible to travel through those narrow waters without having a sense of extensive preparation for war . . .

Depressed by the thought, Markham began making his way down towards the bridge. Almost at once, however, he heard the sound of horses' hooves on the cobbles behind him and turning saw that he was being overtaken by a fiacre. The driver had a passenger already, an elderly man in a fez. He did not object to Markham's getting in, although it was obvious that he didn't want to talk, and they sat in silence until he got out at Fondoukli.

It was not late when Markham reached home, not much after ten o'clock. There was a note from his wife saying that she had gone to bed early with a slight headache. Markham went to his study, where he mixed himself a whisky and soda. When he had drunk this he felt very tired suddenly, as if only now allowing himself to yield to the tensions and exhaustion of the day. He went directly to his own room without disturbing his wife – she would probably have taken one of her pills, he thought, feeling the usual worry and guilt at this.

Once in bed, however, sleep did not come to him. He lay with eyes open, staring upward through the darkness. Distantly from the city he could hear the howling of street dogs and the occasional whistles of the night watchmen. Stray images passed through his mind, unrelated except for the sense of uneasy wonder that hung over them: Miss Munro and her gesture of capturing the city; the flame of that sunset and the brief oily flame of the boat's wake; Zimin's abundant hair and shining eyes; Henry behind the sofa, detected, dishonoured . . . These thoughts slowly merged into the one image that could contain them, the one that somehow gave unity to them all: the Armenian features of Abdul Hamid in the photograph at the Ministry of War. Once again that terrible interest in the Sultan descended on him, that need to relate their lives together, which was like a sickness. Lying there in the dark he sought to spin threads that would adhere to them both. With the sort of disgusted fascination he might have felt for his own corrupted motives, he pictured the old man imprisoned up there in his artificial paradise of Yildiz, unable to sleep for his crimes, as he, Markham was . . . Markham closed his eyes as if the better to see him. After a considerable time, he slept.

133

# 7

Here and there in the grounds of Yildiz Palace, inside the first, the inner enclosure, there were small coffee-houses. Abdul Hamid was the only customer for these. Sometimes, during his late afternoon stroll, he would stop at one of them and order a coffee, while his Albanians waited outside. The waiters were members of his bodyguard. They took it in turns to do the coffee-house duty, dressing in white suits for the purpose and taking care to move with exaggerated slowness while in the vicinity of the Sultan. He ordered his coffee, however, as if it were a real coffee-house and they were real waiters. And they had instructions to behave towards him with the normal politeness due to a valued customer. The coffee was in small sealed packets and he chose a packet at random, afterwards watching closely while it was being prepared. Seated at one of the small tables with his back to the wall he would have for a while a certain illusion of normality. When he had finished he always paid for his coffee and left a tip.

On 3rd July he returned from one such expedition to find despatches from Salonika to the effect that a major by the name of Niazi Bey had looted four thousand mejidiehs from the battalion treasure-chest and led two hundred followers into the mountains above Lake Ochrida, where they had raised the standard of revolt. They were armed with Mauser rifles and well supplied with ammunition from the battalion arsenal.

This revolt of an insignificant infantry major was not one that Abdul Hamid took very seriously – there had always been trouble in Macedonia and he did not believe that a handful of discontented troops could achieve much. All uprisings, however, added to his fears, inclined him some degree further to that immobility of ultimate panic which he sensed approaching – a state he both dreaded and desired. Moreover, there were unusual features in this revolt: Niazi Bey had issued a manifesto, it seemed, speaking openly as a member of the Committee of Union and Progress and addressing himself to both Christians and Moslems alike as fellow countrymen with equal rights. Thus the mutiny was also an attack on the *Sheriat*, the Holy Law, which held Moslem supremacy as a cardinal tenet.

Abdul Hamid gave orders that Niazi should be outlawed and that Shemshi Pasha, Commander-in-Chief of the forces in Northern Macedonia, should take immediate steps to suppress the rebellion. Niazi Bey was to be taken alive, so that information as to other members of the Committee could be extracted from him.

Afterwards he went down to his shooting gallery, a brilliantly illuminated subterranean room below the Little Mabeyn. As usual he took Kiathané Imamy, his dwarf, with him. It was the latter's job to throw oranges up towards the ceiling so that the Sultan could shoot at them. Abdul Hamid waited until the orange was in the air, then he drew the revolver from his pocket and fired in one movement. The dwarf scampered over the floor, retrieving the drilled oranges, squealing to indicate wonder and admiration. Sometimes, in order to amuse his master, he pretended to slip and fall over.

At Markham's house in Beshiktash supper was finished though the guests were still seated at the table. Mehmet Agha had removed the remnants of the meal and now the white expanse of tablecloth showed only glasses and decanter and two vases of white roses from the garden. The evening was warm, the french windows had been thrown open and scents from the summer night came into the room.

Markham felt relaxed. He had drunk a fair amount of wine

135

with the meal and he had brandy before him now. His duties as host were for the moment in suspension. Conversation seemed to be flowing easily. He fell to studying the faces round the table. His wife first, sitting opposite him at the far end. It struck him again that Elizabeth was a beautiful woman. She looked her best this evening, slightly flushed, gently animated by the conversation – she was talking to the man on her right, Colin-Olivier from the French Embassy. There was no strain now on her face. She looks as she often used to look, he thought, with a sudden pang of something like sorrow. The wall lamps cast a soft glow over her cheeks and her fair hair, which she had dressed in rather Teutonic fashion this evening, in braids on top of her head. She was wearing a silk dress, dark red in colour, and the loose sleeves moved like mild flames when she shifted her arms. The Frenchman beside her, sallow, quick-eyed, attentive, slim in his dark clothes, was openly admiring. However, in spite of the rather caressing quality of his voice, the topic between them seemed to be an impersonal one.

'Confident tyrannies can never last long,' Markham heard him say. 'Fear is a great preserver, preservative, how do you say it? Power alone can never—'

The rest of this was lost in laughter from Madame Wallisch, the Hungarian lady who had been giving piano lessons in Constantinople for twenty years and knew more about the city than any of them. She was laughing at something Henderson, the American journalist, had said. He sat there now, on Markham's left, his scant hair dishevelled, his body bulky, powerful-looking inside the loose-fitting dinner jacket. He was smiling, holding a wineglass which was almost lost in his huge paw. Opposite him, on the other side of Elizabeth, was Blake, listening with a flushed, almost painful effort of attention to Madame Colin-Olivier, a voluble, rather beaky woman, very elegantly dressed. Worseley-Jones and Somerville were talking across the table to each other, Somerville in his peering enthusiastic fashion, Worseley-

Jones serious, a slight frown of perplexity on his goodlooking, still rather boyish face. Somerville was probably dazing him with the trade figures, he thought. His wife and Blake both came to a pause in their respective conversations at the same moment, and he saw them turn to each other with a relief so patent that it seemed like eagerness. They got on well together, those two, he thought, with a faint kindling of jealousy. He wondered suddenly where Miss Taverner would be, what she would be doing. He had seen very little of her since the day they had met at the Bazaar. She would be in her room, probably; reading or perhaps doing some needlework or writing letters. As always his mind, as if needing protection from its own desires, stopped short of imagining the full physical existence of Miss Taverner in her room, moving about, sitting, lying, dressing and undressing herself. He leaned forward, shutting out such thoughts, listening more closely to the conversation. This apparently had continued from Colin-Olivier's remarks about confident tyrannies.

'Fear,' Madame Wallisch said, speaking across the table to the Frenchman. 'Yes, why not? He has much to be afraid of.'

She had stopped laughing now and there was a pointedness in her tone and glance that caused a certain hush round the table. The Wallisches were residents of long standing, known to be tolerant of the régime, on which to a large extent they depended, he as an official interpreter and she with pupils in the richer Ottoman families.

'My wife,' Wallisch said in his gentle, hesitant manner, 'is referring to the states on Turkey's borders, I think. Is that not so, my dear?'

'Yes,' Madame Wallisch said, and her face relaxed in a sudden smile for him which was full of affection. 'And all the nations of Europe,' she said. She surveyed the faces round the table with her prominent grey eyes. Her fair thin hair escaped here and there from the bandeau that held it. 'I call them vultures,' she said.

137

'Vultures?' The Frenchman turned towards Markham with an affected bewilderment, which was also belittling.

'*Vautours*,' Markham said, aware that the translation was superfluous.

'France among the rest,' Madame Wallisch said. 'They sit in a row, waiting. None of them can move for fear of the others. *That* is the fear that preserves the Empire, not Abdul Hamid's.'

'Fear needs no object,' Markham said, 'only a pretext.' He had spoken at random, uneasy at the turn the conversation was taking. The Wallisches had a circle of German friends in the city and these days any dinner table could become a battlefield in a very short time.

No one appeared to take any notice of his remark. Blake, patriotic as ever, sprang at once to his country's defence. 'I say, you know,' he said, 'that is simply not true. Not of England anyway. It is the declared policy of His Majesty's Government to preserve the Empire.'

He stared across at Wallisch, his face flushed, his blue eyes in a rage of honesty. It was typical of Blake, Markham thought, to address himself to the man rather than the woman when it came to a contradiction – though the argument was with Madame Wallisch really. There was no guile whatever about Blake; his opinions were registered as directly as the blood rose to the surface of his skin. Markham felt a sudden deep and almost painful envy for this quality of the other man's, this strength of right instinct and right feeling, apparently unquestioned, unaccompanied by doubt of any kind.

By comparison the Hungarian, in spite of the gentleness of his manner, seemed grudging and pedantic. 'Are you claiming that for virtue?' he said now. 'You do not want changes because you are afraid for your Jewel of India.'

Before Blake could reply to this, Colin-Olivier said coldly, 'Germany of course has no territorial ambition in Asia Minor. Perhaps therefore she has no fears either. She is *sans peur* if not

138

exactly *sans reproche*. Why should she worry about territory when she can plunder the country without it?'

'Plunder?' Madame Wallisch leaned forward, her hair looking more than ever in disarray. The word, it seemed, was new to her. Her husband spoke quietly in Hungarian, explaining. She appeared to be gathering herself for some angry expostulation. At this point, and Markham silently blessed him for it, Henderson's deep drawling voice intervened.

'Well,' he said, 'I was here in 1899, as correspondent for the *New York Herald*, and that's nearly ten years ago, but they were still just as afraid of everything. I remember in the January of that year, they were holding the *Hirkai Sherif*, the Adoration of the Cloak of the Prophet, that they hold on the fifteenth day of Ramazan – it's Ramazan next month again, isn't it, the next new moon? Anyway, the *Hirkai Sherif* was one of the few occasions in the year when Abdul Hamid ventured out of his Palace and exposed himself to public view. Now, I don't know whether any of you have heard of chlorate potassium, but if you can collect enough of it you can make a bomb. It's been on the prohibited import list for years. Anyway, the druggists all kept small quantities for medicinal purposes. There were something like two hundred and fifty druggists in the city at that time. At dawn on the morning of the *Hirkai Sherif* the police raided all the shops simultaneously, all two hundred and fifty of them, and seized all the chlorate potassium . . . Nobody can say they're not thorough, these people.'

This story and the laughter accompanying it reduced the tension of the conversation. Elizabeth Markham took advantage of this to rise and take the ladies with her into the drawing room, leaving the men to their brandy and cigars, which Markham brought to the table from the sideboard where Mehmet Agha had left them.

'There was a time,' Colin-Olivier said, 'when at a supper party with ladies present such arguments would not have

139

come up. Now the women are more ferocious than the men.'

This was a piece of direct rudeness to Wallisch, who however made no reply. There was something implacable about the Frenchman that Markham was beginning to find disagreeable. 'These are political times,' he said. 'Back home they are fighting with policemen and having to be fed by force . . . That story,' he said to Henderson, 'the one about the chemical, strikes me as absolutely typical of the Hamidian régime. The absurdity of the fear itself, and then the efficiency of the operation. I would be willing to bet that the whole police operation was planned down to the last detail. High efficiency in a pointless proceeding is comical, isn't it? Not always, of course.'

He paused for a moment. He had begun calmly enough, but when he spoke again it was in a charged voice.

'Like the killings,' he said. 'The same sort of thing, really. I mean the massacres of the Armenians in the 1890s. That was a pointless proceeding, too, but the planning was impeccable. They began when the drums were beaten in the morning and stopped when they were beaten again at nightfall. You know, as if there were rules. Most of it was down in the Galata region – a very cosmopolitan district, yet not one Jew was killed, not one Greek. Only Armenians. Do you know why? They went round painting white crosses on all the Armenian houses.'

There was a short, uneasy silence. Then Wallisch said, 'Yes, that is terrible, but the Armenian societies make trouble for themselves. Look at the 1905 *attentat*. It is well known that the Henchak was behind that, and people were blown to pieces, let me remind you . . .'

'Well known?' Markham said. '*I* don't know it for one.' He had spoken too loudly. The faces at the table were turned to him and the stillness on them, as if expectant or alarmed, increased his sense that his behaviour was inappropriate. Some inner voice of warning spoke to him but he did not heed it. 'It could have been the Armenians,' he said. 'God knows they have cause enough to want Abdul Hamid dead. He has done away with well over a hundred thousand of them in the course of his illustrious reign. Some say half a million. But there's no proof. All the confessions they had were extracted under torture. That worthy public servant Rassim Pasha was in charge of the enquiry, if you remember. Very convenient that it should turn out to have been the work of a Christian minority group. Otherwise it might have seemed that the Turks themselves were dissatisfied with the régime.'

In pausing he was aware of a faint trembling somewhere within him. Wallisch looked with his usual slightly preoccupied composure across the table. 'But you were not even in the country at that time,' he said. He paused for a moment. 'You keep yourself remarkably well informed,' he said. He expelled cigar smoke in a gentle cloud and looked steadily at Markham through it.

There was no particular emphasis in his voice, nothing but mild surprise; yet now, belatedly, caution came to Markham. He said, 'One takes an interest, naturally.' He tried to relax his face, on which that stiffness of tension had descended.

Wallisch would have gone on but again the slow voice of Henderson broke in. 'I met Rassim once,' he said, 'way back in 1899. That was before he got his hands on any Armenians. Before his true talents were known. He was in the Board of Trade then. He asked me if I had any American cigars. I handed him one. "I meant boxes," he said. He wanted *baksheesh* for the interview.' He paused, smiling at Markham. 'He struck me at the time as a crook of the first order,' he said.

There was some quality in his smile which moved Markham. Sympathy, understanding, he could not determine what. He had liked Henderson from the first moment of meeting him at the Pera Club some weeks before, had detected, through all the difference in experience and outlook, a natural ally, somewhat cynical but humorously so, quite free of cant, open-minded in a way that most of the officials Markham worked with were not.

'Whoever it was,' Colin-Olivier said, 'Armenians or others,

141

certainly it would not be the Germans.' He was still pursuing the same theme, as if there had been no break, no anecdote from Henderson, no outburst from Markham. 'Germany does very well in the Near East,' he said. *Sans risquer rien.* Isn't that what they mean by their *Drang Nach Osten*?'

'It's a great pity,' Somerville said suddenly, 'that there has to be all this rivalry. It's stupid, apart from anything else. There is enough here for everybody, Turkey included. I wonder if you realize what enormous wealth there is in Asia Minor, a lot of it completely untapped. Resources absolutely essential to modern industry – minerals, fuel, lubricants, abrasives, oil.'

Somerville's eyes behind his glasses were shining. His small hands tapped the table before him in emphasis. 'And think of the potential for agriculture,' he said. 'A combined effort to control the floods of the Tigris and Euphrates and we could get the deserts of Mesopotamia to bloom again. The Empire could produce more grain than the Russians, if you add Syria and Iraq. Nowhere else in the world offers so much. Source of raw materials, market for finished products, field for investment – the possibilities are endless. And what do we do? I'll tell you, gentlemen. We spend all of our energies squabbling over pickings. We have made Turkey into an international danger-zone. The Government is debt-ridden, the whole country in decline. With a combined investment programme the economy could be transformed within five years.'

'I don't know,' Henderson said. 'I haven't got your faith in the salvaging power of capital, Mr Somerville. I reckon that if any European power were to undertake to finance Turkey, the whole place would be bankrupt in a week. You are an exponent of political economy, as I think it's called. But the Ottoman government has a different philosophy. They call it *ekisi gibi*, the same old way.'

'So long as the Christians pay their taxes and the Moslems provide the troops,' Markham said. He stood up with something of an effort. 'We'd better join the ladies, I think,' he said.

Not very much was left of the evening now. There was some talk about the replacement for the Ambassador, Sir Nicholas O'Connor, who had died the previous April. Sir Gerard Lowther was the man chosen to replace him, but no one knew when he would be taking up the appointment. There was a good deal of speculation about Lady Lowther, since it was on her that the quality of Embassy entertainment would mainly depend. Lady O'Connor had been very good in this respect, it was generally agreed. The Grand Ball to inaugurate the move to the Summer Embassy at Therapia had been postponed this year, and there was some doubt as to whether it would now take place at all. But the finals of the Therapia Lawn Tennis Club Tournament would be played out, as arranged, at the end of July. Worseley-Jones, who was still in the tournament, was certain of this.

It was approaching midnight when they left, and Elizabeth Markham went almost at once to bed. Markham himself remained below to smoke another cigar. He helped himself to some more Armagnac and stood at the open french window, looking out over the garden. Scents of the day and scents of the night mingled there, dry summer soil, sparse dew, odours spilt by the depredations of insects. As he stood there, however, scent was only one element in a complex act of recognition. Mind and senses seemed to brush lightly together. Light behind him, smell of cigar smoke, spirituous heat at the back of his throat. It was through a garden like this one, a summer garden in the darkness, that the men had come to kill her. They had walked through the garden towards the lights and the music . . . It was as if he had been there too, in the garden with them.

He turned his mind from this to the conversation earlier, at dinner, the animosities that stirred immediately below the surface, kept barely in check by the requirements of polite intercourse. These people seemed to find so little difficulty in identifying themselves with the larger group, with the nation, with the alliances that Europe had divided herself into. Tribal

143

loyalties really, for all the numbers involved. Why then was he without them? Why could he not feel representative of his kind, as did Colin-Olivier still dragging the humiliation of his fathers in the 1870 war, or Blake with his concern for British prestige and defence of government policy, or Somerville above all, who dreamed of collective action, collective responsibility, steadily increasing dividends for all concerned – it was the financiers these days who had idealism, not the artists, certainly not the politicians . . . Standing there, looking out over the garden, Markham knew himself completely alone. He had clutched at the illusion of belonging to a larger whole. Perhaps it was this that had made a career in the army seem attractive. Yes, it must have been this, to make him go against all previous inclinations, all ambitions professed before that – before the night they had come through the garden with their weighted sticks. In any case the illusion had not survived this second visit to the city. It had been a pretence, a temporary refuge at best. He belonged to nothing. He had belonged to nothing since that other evening, a summer evening like this one, when he had been in such craven haste to proclaim his identity, his separateness from every other person there in the room.

The terrace outside and part of the steps leading down to the rose garden were lit up by the lamps in the dining room. Behind him he heard the scrape of steps on the wood floor, sounds of movement at the table, faint clink of glasses – Mehmet clearing the last things away. He did not look round. After some moments he heard the door closing, then all was again silence.

Suddenly, towards the far end of the garden, in a lighter space among dark clumps of trees, he saw, or thought he saw, the flash of some pale material, the brief pale glimmer of what might have been a dress. Then nothing – only the darkly massed foliage with the lighter spaces between. There were pale expanses of flowers here and there, white roses, acacia flowers, jasmine, and he thought at first that what he had seen, that effect of movement, was some stirring of these, but

144

the night was still – there was no breath of wind. Then he saw it again, that brief, evanescent glimmer of some pale material among the trees, and again it was gone.

He hesitated for some moments, prescience coinciding with desire. He knew who it was, who it must be, out there. He moved out onto the terrace and began to make his way down the steps to the first level of the garden, moving slowly at first, keeping close to the balustrade. Once, on the lower steps where it was dark, he stumbled a little.

The sound of this stumbling footfall and the subsequent light sounds Markham made as he proceeded down the steps were heard quite clearly by his son Henry, whose bedroom window was open, though the shutter was closed. The boy had slept and dreamed and the dream had woken him but he could not now remember what it had been about, except that he had been in a room with no doors to it. He lay awake, wide-eyed, looking up at the dim ceiling, listening for more sounds, but Markham was on the grass now and the boy heard nothing else, except, after a moment, the sudden cry of some night bird.

He got up and went over to the window, opened the shutters and looked out. He was in time to see the dark form move across the open space of the lawn into the obscurity of the trees beyond.

Henry remained at the window for some minutes, prey to a painful indecision. He was frightened at the thought of going out into the night-time garden, yet he felt driven by the now familiar sense of necessity, the sense that he had to keep his eye on things, had to know what was happening, had to know everything, because only in this way could he control things, protect himself from some future decision even worse than the one that had brought him to this alien place. Two kinds of fear contended in him, there at the window, and it was fear of the night that proved weaker. With a slightly tremulous sense of resignation he began to put on his socks and shoes.

* * *

Markham made his way through the rose garden. He could see better now, see the different intensities of light, the dark mass of bushes and trees, the lighter sky above. There was no moon, but there was starlight, a very pale luminosity upon everything in the garden, which lent a faint incandescence to the white flowers, to his hand when he extended it before him.

Beyond the rose garden he came to the gravelled path that led past the summer-house to the denser rear part of the garden. He smelt the heavy odour of the flowering currant bushes that bordered the path on one side, and felt the brush of the leaves against his legs through the thin trousers. His excitement persisted, mingled now however with something else, some darker feeling. He moved steadily forward with a growing sense of impunity, as if there was nothing substantial to impede him, merely different tones and intensities of light, the mass of foliage and trunks of the trees simply a deepening of the darkness, like dark colouring in cloud or water. He had no sense of solid objects, things palpable that might resist him. He was moving towards something glimpsed only briefly but registered in that glimpse as necessary to appetite . . . Again, helplessly and involuntarily, he thought of those other men, moving through that other garden, and again he was one of them, sharing their excited purpose; for some seconds he entertained this notion without conscious repugnance – indeed his excitement and that sense of effortless progress were increased by it for those seconds only, just before he saw her.

He was at the end of the path now, looking towards the massed shapes of the orchard. Below the foliage, in the spaces between the trunks, it was lighter, and he saw the pale glimmer of the dress, lost it, moved forward a few paces, saw it again, now with a smaller faint radiance surmounting it, the shape of a face. He stood still, in no hurry now, looking at the form among the trees, in a moment of pure, triumphant perception.

The other was motionless too, looking towards him. There

146

was a pause, then he heard her say, 'Is that you . . . Captain Markham?' Her voice was steady, slightly sharp with enquiry, but not sounding nervous or afraid.

'Don't be alarmed,' Markham said at once, though he was aware that there had been no alarm in her voice. It was as if she too had known she was being stalked through the garden, and by whom. 'I thought I saw someone,' he said. 'I came down to have a look.'

'I smelt the cigar smoke,' she said. 'I thought it would be you.'

'Does the smoke bother you? I can put it out.'

'No, please don't. I like it.'

He was still where he had stopped on seeing her, some half dozen paces away. Now he began to advance towards her, quite slowly. She stood still. When he was about a yard away he stopped again. Her face was near enough now for him to reach out and touch if he had wanted to, though her features were still indistinct. He could see the shadowed eyes and the mouth, slightly parted, and the pale column of her neck above the wrap – she was wearing a white wrap over a dress of darker colour. It was this he had glimpsed, looking out from the room.

'It's beautiful out here, isn't it?' he said. 'Do you often come out like this?'

'These evenings, lately,' she said. 'It's so hot indoors.'

'My name is Robert, by the way,' he said.

'Robert,' she said tentatively, as if trying out the sound. 'I don't think—'

'Your name is Mary, isn't it?' he said.

'Yes.'

'Mary Taverner.' Saying the name gave him pleasure, and a return of that predatory triumph as if he were identifying something he had caught. And he *had* caught her, he was surer of this with every word – words too intimate and direct for the lonely place and the late hour. They had already exchanged enough speech, under these circumstances, for propriety:

147

every moment she stayed longer now was an admission of special interest, surely . . . All the same, some doubt remained. She had been brought up more freely than other women he had met, more unconventionally, he could sense it. Nothing he knew about her background could explain this feeling, though admittedly he did not know a great deal – he had been chary of asking his wife much, not wanting to show an interest that would have been uncharacteristic and therefore perhaps suspicious; and he had had little opportunity to ask the governess directly. She came from provincial middle-class people, that much he knew. Her father was a building contractor in a largish way, Elizabeth had said. Prosperous enough to give their daughter a somewhat superior education. They were acquaintances of Elizabeth's, not his. The girl must be independent-minded or she would not have come out to Constantinople like this. Still – and now confidence reasserted itself after these flickerings of doubt – certain conventions were understood by all women, and never broken except by intention . . .

He was aware as he leaned closer towards her of a kind of precariousness about their situation there, about the precise distance between them; aware of the dangers of shattering what had been established by a movement too precipitate – though whatever it was he sensed as fragile, it was not concerned with the girl's well-being, rather with maintaining between them a mood, a climate of feeling, necessary for his own purposes. Just for a moment, looking at the shadowed beauty of her face, he felt sorrow that his need could not encompass her welfare.

'I come out here myself sometimes,' he said. 'In the evening, you know. At about this time. Walk about a bit, after dinner. Smoke a cigar. I love this garden. I'm fond of the whole place actually.'

He was unable to keep the vibrancy of his nervousness out of his voice, and she must have sensed it: her own voice, when she replied, was self-consciously conversational in tone.

148

'It's walled in,' she said, 'and being behind the house, of course, gives it that feeling of seclusion.'

Markham looked at the pale shape of her face, lifted seriously towards him in this dutiful attempt to exchange views about the garden. 'It is peaceful,' he said. He was standing quite close to her now. He could see the dark gleam of her eyes, smell the warmth from her, part fragrance, part heat of the breathing body. 'Not much noise from the city here,' he said, 'except the steamers occasionally. And those eternal street dogs. Whatever is going on there we don't hear it. Like the shrieks of the damned which do not reach the ears of the righteous.'

'You always sound sad when you talk about this place,' she said. 'Constantinople, I mean. I noticed it before.'

'Do I?' he said.

'You said you had been here once before.'

'Yes.' Markham paused then said slowly, 'My fiancée was killed here. I saw her killed. It was at our engagement party. She was Armenian.'

He had often wondered what it would be like actually to pronounce these words to another human being, as opposed to constantly addressing them to himself. He felt distress at the terrible sound of the words, but stronger than this was a complex blend of self-contempt: contempt for the part he had played, the way he had saved his own life; contempt for the way he was presenting the episode now to the woman before him, so partially, so favourably to himself – he was using Miriam's violation and death to enlist pity, feed Miss Taverner's romanticism. And all the time, below the contempt, untouched by it, crouched his unwavering predatory purpose.

'Killed?' she said now. 'You mean an accident?'

'She was killed by some men,' he said. 'They raped her and then they killed her. I saw them do it. They held me – I couldn't do anything to help her.'

There was silence for some moments, then she said, 'That

149

is terrible. It's the most terrible thing I think I've ever heard. I'm so sorry.'

'You are the only person in the world that knows about this,' he said. 'You won't speak of it, will you?'

'Of course not,' she said. 'I wouldn't, not to anybody.'

He heard the fervour in her voice. 'I have never talked to my wife about it,' he said. 'I have never been able to.'

'You can talk about it to me,' she said, with the same fervour.

The mute oval of her face was directed towards him, as if soliciting further confidences. The urge to confess, to find some sort of temporary and shallow absolution in her sympathy, rose strongly in him. But her invitation, the very readiness to listen, defeated him. It was too free, too unforced. She would judge him. He had to be above her judgement, to conquer her judgement together with the rest, all the rest of her. Desire for this conquest filled his mind, excluding all else, so violent that he had to clench his teeth against it. For a little while he was silent, then, with conscious effort to render his tone normal, he said, 'I knew from the first that you were someone I could talk to.'

She did not reply or if she did he did not catch the words. He had glanced away from her as he spoke, glanced past the dark slopes of the hillside above them towards Yildiz; and at that moment the lights of the Palace began to go on by the score and hundred, until within a matter of half a minute a huge beacon of light was blazing out on the hill above them, discovering as if by an act of sudden, radiant creation the white roof-tops of the kiosk and pavilions.

'Of course,' Markham said softly, as if in self-reproof, as if in his absorption with the woman near him he had left something out of account. It was midnight, approximately – the sixth hour, according to Moslems. Time for Abdul Hamid's night light. 'Lighting up time,' he said.

She turned to look behind her in the direction of his gaze. He saw the turn of her head, heard the soft exclamation that sounded not so much surprised as wondering, almost pious. Again he was reminded of a child striving to meet the expectations of adults.

'I haven't seen that before,' she said. 'I've never been in the garden so late. It must cost a fortune in electricity.'

'He's not paying the bills,' Markham said.

A great tract of sky above the Palace was lit with a soft effulgence. Markham thought about the thousands on thousands of lamps blazing there, not only in the royal apartments but in all the alleys and walks of the vast, empty park, lamps strung in trees and bushes, lamps ringing the lake, lamps hanging along the outer walls and in the farthest limits of the grounds, wherever the crazed suspicions of the Sultan might fancy conspirators lurking. One small man at the heart of this prolonged flare of fear – it was a celebration of fear, he thought, renewed nightly.

'Abdul Hamid is frightened of the dark,' he said, and he saw her smile. He knew in that moment, quite suddenly, knew with a finality so absolute that the issue might never have been in question, that he was going to see Hartunian and warn him. Whatever Zimin came up with, he would do this. Hartunian was an enemy of the régime: that was sufficient reason. No, that was not the reason. He was an Armenian . . .

He looked down at Miss Taverner's face, looked for some moments without speaking. Perhaps uncomfortable at this silent scrutiny, sensing some intensification of purpose in it; or perhaps feeling they had spent too long alone together in the garden, Miss Taverner resettled the wrap on her shoulders and said, 'It is very late, isn't it? I must go in.'

'Don't go,' Markham said instantly. He reached out and put his hands on the sides of her arms, as if to prevent her. They stood thus for a moment, then she moved to extricate herself, but not with a very decided movement. He took a short step towards her and then she was in his arms and he kissed her on the brow and on the mouth, felt an answering warmth in her lips and a small leap, like fear, of her abdomen against him, then she had broken free, and he heard her quick breathing. 'Let me go,' she said, almost panted, and she moved quickly away from him, out of the cover of the trees, towards the house, making no attempt at concealment, as if rendered heedless by the disturbance of her feelings.

He stood, himself breathing heavily, watching her form recede till it passed out of sight. Gradually the night settled round him, his agitation subsided. He remembered that slight surge of her fear against him, the brief but unmistakable compliance of her body. He felt grateful, appeased almost, as at some need or appetite already assuaged. After a while he began to move back through the trees, towards the house.

Henry heard his father's voice coming through the darkness, a voice different somehow from the day-time one, saying, 'I come out here myself sometimes.'

These were the first words he actually registered, actually understood. Before that, working his way towards them, he heard voices only, no distinct words. And at first, even when he got near enough to hear properly, his own agitation, the fear of his own stealth, set his heart beating and his breath straining so that for a little while he could hear nothing. Gradually, however, a measure of calm returned, that immunity he always felt when in concealment, and the two voices, dark and light, which until then had been pure sound, like some intermittent music he was following to its source, now began to separate, and he heard his father tell Miss Taverner that he sometimes came out into the garden after dinner, and Miss Taverner comment on the fact that the garden was walled in, and behind the house.

He had managed, by keeping down among the bushes beyond the summer-house, to get quite near – near enough to see the dim forms and pale faces. It was strange to see his father and Miss Taverner standing so close together, so alone together, talking about things that did not seem interesting. It was this sense of strangeness that held his interest, rather than the words themselves, that and the curious strain he sensed in the voices, sensed without understanding. He thought of his mother who would be in her room, asleep probably, knowing nothing about this conversation in the dark. Perhaps his father would tell her. He tried to mimic in his mind his father's voice saying, perhaps at breakfast-time tomorrow morning, 'Oh, by the way, I met Miss Taverner in the garden last night and we had a jolly interesting conversation.' It did not seem probable somehow. Yet his father and mother did tell each other things. They had both known about his going out of the garden . . . Crouched down in the bushes, he stopped listening to the voices as he remembered his mother's face, telling him she knew, forbidding any further sorties of that kind. 'It's dangerous,' she had said, 'for a European child to be wandering about alone. This is not like England, Henry. You must promise faithfully not to do it again.' She had not mentioned the little girl. He had promised, not really understanding what was meant about the danger, concerned above all to remove the worry on his mother's face, sorry for her because she had this task of reproving him, because he knew it distressed her to do so, because he knew too that she was protecting him from his father's anger . . .

He could smell the smoke from his father's cigar. It mingled with the other scents of the night, the honeysuckle from the side of the summer-house, the sweetish smell of soil and dry leaves from the bushes around him. He heard Miss Taverner say, 'You said you had been here before,' and his father's slow reply: 'My fiancée was killed here. I saw her killed.' Something more about an engagement party, which he did not quite catch. Then again his father's voice, saying, 'She was a mean 'un,' or so he thought, though it was difficult to make much sense out of this, nor did he have much time to puzzle over it, because almost at once there was the sudden great glow of light on the hill and then his father saying 'Don't go,' in a sharper, less deliberate voice, and then the two forms became one form for a long moment and the two heads one head and then Miss Taverner was walking away towards the house – she found the path not far from where he was hiding and passed quite close to him. He did not dare to look but he heard her breathing as she passed, she was breathing in short breaths. His father remained there for some time longer, and this seemed the strangest thing of all to Henry when he thought about it afterwards, how his father remained quite alone there and quite still among the trees. Once he looked up towards the sky. Then he too began to move towards the house, more slowly than Miss Taverner. When he disappeared from sight Henry began at once to feel afraid, as if someone or something might now be watching *him*. It was only by a great effort that he was able to move out of the shelter of the bushes and start making his way back towards the house.

# 8

Two days after the news of Niazi's defection, it was learned that Enver Bey, one of the most brilliant graduates of the Military Staff College, had deserted from Resna with one hundred and fifty men and taken to the mountains above Lake Ochrida in Northern Macedonia, thus swelling the ranks of the rebels.

This intelligence was received on the Friday. After giving instructions that Enver Bey should be offered a pardon if he would return to Constantinople, Abdul Hamid began as usual to prepare for his weekly visit to the mosque. Religious law prescribed that the Sultan-Caliph should on every Friday, the Mohammedan holy day, be present in person to attend religious service. Fear of venturing into the open streets had become over the years so overwhelming that Abdul Hamid had had a new mosque, the Hamidie Mosque, built about a hundred yards from the outer wall of his Palace, thus reducing exposure to a minimum. Even this brief journey was a great ordeal, and guards packed the way, making defensive walls of bodies.

Before he set out there was the elaborate ritual of his toilet. He was attended in the Harem by a bevy of women. After the traditional milk bath, the hair of his beard and temples was darkened with a mixture compounded of coffee, gall-nuts and henna. His cheeks were carefully rouged, the women taking great care to work in the paint until it made a natural blend with the tones of his skin. His forehead and the areas of skin above the cheekbones were lightly tinted with walnut stain. Drops were applied to his eyes to make them more brilliant. His lips were salved. He was in his sixty-sixth year at this time, but when he saw himself in the mirror, after these

155

ministrations, he found it possible to believe that he had not greatly aged. There was no vanity in this. It was always his endeavour to achieve a state as near changeless as possible; all his rituals tended to that purpose, holding back time, slowing down motion, as though he could live forever in the frozen moment before the assassin struck. In the painted stillness of the face his eyes looked back at him, glistening and sad, like a trapped animal's.

The square below the mosque was lined with troops, the Zouave regiments in high white turbans and white uniforms braided elaborately with black cord, the lancers with their pennons flying, the marines carrying the banner of the Caliphate, a black flag embroidered with an inscription from the Koran in silver, Abdul Hamid's Tripolitan guards in green and red, his Imperial Guard in scarlet, marching with the goosestep as they had been trained by their German instructors to do, his innumerable aides-de-camp, the Ambassadors in their full dress uniforms watching from the Diplomatic Gallery above the square, the Imperial Princes on horseback, their faces covered with white powder and carefully rouged, the favourites of the Harem in closed carriages guarded by negro eunuchs, and behind the massed troops, packing every inch of the great open space before the mosque, a vast crowd of common people who had come to see the Sultan.

Towards noon a silence fell over the crowd. Then the voice of the muezzin was raised in superb modulations and the noon call to prayer fell on the ears of the assembled believers. God is great, he reminded them. There is no God but God.

When the last echoes died away, there were some minutes of profound silence, the tension of a ceremonial many centuries old. Then came a great fanfare of trumpets and two glittering officers with drawn swords appeared in the foreground and approached the steps of the mosque. A flashing movement like a wave ran through the ranks of the troops as they presented arms. The band struck up the lively strains of the Hamidish March. A dark green carriage came through the gilt gates of the Palace, its single occupant sitting well back; a hand in a white glove was raised continuously in a salute that was never quite completed, as though the effort was exhausting. Chamberlains and officials surrounded the carriage, striving to control their prancing Arab horses. The carriage stopped at the foot of the steps. A shrivelled man, in fez and grey military cloak, with dyed beard and huge insomniac eyes, stood for a moment of controlled fear on the steps, acknowledging the titles bestowed on him by the shouting crowd: Refuge of the World, Shadow of God, Slayer of Infidels. Then he went quickly up the steps and disappeared into the mosque.

Markham breakfasted alone as usual, and as usual took his tea to the corner of the windowseat, where he sat looking out at the distant gentle blue of the Bosphoros and the Asian shore, still indistinct in the early morning haze. It was on that side, in Scutari, that Hartunian lived – it was there that he himself intended to go, later that day, to see him. There was solemnity in this thought, something almost sacrificial, because the proceeding was so irregular. He thought again of Miss Taverner, her pale attentive face in the starlight – it was during his talk with her, in some way because of her, that he had decided to go over in person to Hartunian's house, to warn him; a decision that was mixed up with the scents of the night-time garden, the muted enthusiasms of her voice . . . Before that, of course, there was the meeting he had arranged with Worseley-Jones at the Summer Residence and in the afternoon there was Zimin. He had not so far had time to do much about Zimin's papers, apart from writing a personal testimonial himself – perhaps Worseley-Jones or someone at the Embassy could help.

When he had finished his tea he went upstairs to his wife's room. She was sitting up in bed with the morning tea on a tray beside her. She was wearing a blue silk peignoir – blue was a colour she often wore; nearly all her clothes were in the colour range from grey to blue, soft, rather indeterminate colours. He was relieved to see that she was looking rested and well this morning. Her face broke into a smile as he entered and she held out one hand to him.

Perhaps it was guilt on his part, the knowledge that he was unfaithful to her in desire and intention, or perhaps simply the kind of irritation that sometimes comes from long familiarity; but this smile of hers, even as he crossed the room towards her, aroused a sort of involuntary resentment in him. There seemed conscious goodwill in it, almost forbearance, as if she knew her own loyalty and sacrifice.

None of this showed on the calm, slightly smiling surface of his face. He bent over to kiss her and felt the softness of her cheek and neck, still relaxed from sleep, smelt the warm silk and flesh smell of her. Gently, with deliberate gentleness, he freed himself and straightened up, smiling. 'We shall have the tray over,' he said, 'if we are not careful.'

He could not detect any change in her expression, had no way of knowing whether his resistance to the embrace had hurt or offended her. He sat on the edge of the bed and after a moment they began talking about the excursion to the Sweet Waters of Europe which was due to take place in some days. There were ten people going and the Markhams had charged themselves with the arrangements. Now Elizabeth was beginning to worry a little about the practical aspects, food, drink, transportation. He set himself to reassure her, all the time with a half-incredulous sense of what he was proposing to do that day. It struck him now for the first time that he would have to go in disguise. It would be far too dangerous to go in his own person, dangerous both for himself and for Hartunian.

'You'll see,' he said. 'A dozen bottles will be quite enough.'

He knew immediately and with peculiar certainty what form his disguise was going to take. There was a disturbing ambivalence attendant on this – it was not choice so much as

158

recognition – which he did not wish for the moment to analyse.

'It will be all right,' he said. 'The weather is the only thing to worry about. You get these sudden squalls on the Bosphoros at this time of the year.'

As he stood up to go and as he looked back once more from the door, he seemed to detect the same expression of patience on his wife's face, the same smile; but he felt no resentment now. Partings bring out different emotions, and he had always felt sorrow of some kind when leaving his wife in the mornings – particularly here. It was as though, every morning, he abandoned her, left her to the silent house and empty garden, the heat, the crooning slave-songs of Nevres Badji, the hours of waiting for his return. Every day was an abandonment. And though the sense of estrangement between them had come only recently, only since his return to the city, it was as if the hurt of all those other mornings had been accumulative, deferred until now.

The Embassy launch was already waiting at the landing stage. Markham boarded and they headed out into midstream. It was a fast boat and they reached Ortakeui, from which Stambul is seen astern for the last time, in a matter of minutes. Rounding the headland, they passed into the narrower reaches of the Bosphoros, Bebek on the European side, Kandilli on the Asian. Markham sat in the stern watching the brief wake of the launch. Occasionally he glanced up towards the Asian suburbs. The slopes were sunlit and peaceful, with little clusters of houses set amidst trees. Unrecognizable. It was here, in these narrows, that he had been picked up by HMS *Imogen* twelve years before. He had sat among the Armenian refugees, watching the fires, hearing the screams and the splintering of glass as the killing went on in Kandilli. He had sat there in his bridegroom's suit, wet after the scramble for the boats, grateful for the coffee the sailors handed out. Even then, still numb from the first shock, before the grief and shame had started, while he still did not

159

understand the damage to himself, there on the boat he had started the necessary task of recasting, reinterpreting what had happened, to make it endurable. A process still continuing . . .

They passed below the towers of Rumeli Hissar, built by Mehmet the Conqueror in the last days of Byzantium. Here, at this narrowest part of the waterway, the launch came in close to the shore, avoiding the notorious currents called by the Turks *Sheitan akintisi*, 'Satan's stream'. They kept close inshore till they came into the bay of Therapia with its cafés along the waterfront and terraced gardens.

The Summer Residence was a tall white building on the quayside, a little northwards from the bay. Markham made his way directly to Worseley-Jones's office on the ground floor, a spacious, pleasant room looking out over the water. Blake was already there, having ridden across from Tacsim.

Worseley-Jones was dressed in a cream-coloured linen suit of impeccable cut. He greeted Markham with his usual slightly preoccupied amiability. 'Good of you to come,' he said. 'The chargé d'affaires wants to be in on this as well. I've given him an account of what happened at the conference. He should be along in a minute. And Tomlinson, I think.' Tomlinson was the senior clerical officer, a bachelor who had been in Constantinople several years. 'We need someone to take notes, you see,' Worseley-Jones said. 'Can't trust to memory. We were going to foregather in the chargé d'affaires' room but part of his ceiling has collapsed. He's living rather a makeshift existence up there.'

Markham nodded, finding nothing to say to this. From where he was standing he could see through a side window across the low shrubbery to the tennis courts. Two young men were just beginning a game in the nearest one. The windows in Worseley-Jones's room were open, and Markham could hear the voices of the players and the soft, plosive sound when the ball was struck.

'I've asked them to make coffee,' Worseley-Jones said.

160

'That was a business, the other day, wasn't it? The way they walked out like that.'

'I was tactless,' Markham said.

'I don't think it was that,' Blake said brusquely and again Markham was touched by his brother-officer's immediate protectiveness. It was no more, probably, than the old service habit of closing ranks. Still, he felt grateful for it.

'You mean they were set on walking out anyway?' Worseley-Jones paused. 'Well,' he said, after a moment, 'that is more or less the conclusion I came to myself. That's one of the things I'd like to discuss with you. All the same,' he added, looking at Markham, 'you did get into quite a paddy, didn't you?'

Markham felt the question in this, felt Worseley-Jones's eyes dwelling on his face. Mild eyes, but more than mildly interested. It was easy to underestimate Worseley-Jones. The casual, lounging manner concealed considerable shrewdness and grasp. But he saw things in terms that were too abstract, like all diplomats – or so at least it seemed to Markham. Worseley-Jones thought of Macedonia as a sphere of conflicting interests not as a place where children were being bayoneted. And he himself, did he really care about the sufferings of the people there? It was his own wrong, his own injury, that he saw reduplicated – all the rapes and murders of the Empire, crimes too manifold to relate, reduced by his monstrous egotism to one rape, one murder, one outrage done to Robert Markham . . .

'Yes,' he said, 'I'm afraid so.' He glanced out of the window at the tennis players who were calling to each other no longer, but playing with an air of great earnestness.

The chargé d'affaires, whose name was Lewin, now entered with Tomlinson at his heels, and after brief greetings, the men seated themselves, Lewin taking Worseley-Jones's seat behind the desk.

'Captain Blake thinks as I do, sir,' Worseley-Jones began. 'They had no intention of negotiating at all.'

161

Lewin nodded, compressing his thin lips. He was a sallow-complexioned man with gilt-rimmed spectacles and brown hair brushed straight back. He had great stores of nervous energy, revealed sometimes in gestures of irritation, normally kept in check by a habit of deliberate courtesy that seemed too old for him – he was in his early forties. Sometimes, when dealing with inferiors or when he was displeased, this courtesy became frigid or derisive. Markham had met him before and had not liked him.

'That is so, Blake, isn't it?' Worseley-Jones said.

Blake nodded. Becoming conscious that everyone in the room was waiting for him to say something, he hesitated for a moment or two, then plunged.

'I've noticed a change for some time past,' he said. 'I think Markham has too. I date it to the Reval Agreement at the beginning of June. I don't think we have appreciated what a blow that was to the Turks, England and Russia coming together like that and declaring their intention jointly to carry out the programme of reform in Macedonia. The Turks could feel free to do as they liked in Macedonia because we and the Russians distrusted each other too much to agree on anything. Reval changed all that. They know we mean business now.'

'But the Murstag Programme has been in existence for years now,' Lewin said. 'It was merely reaffirmed at Reval.'

'Enough to worry them,' Markham said. 'A picture of King Edward and the Czar arm in arm is enough to give Abdul Hamid sleepless nights. But it's the army that's the main trouble. They would never accept an international peace-keeping force in Macedonia, whatever Abdul Hamid said. I never thought they would, from the beginning.'

'That must have been a disadvantage to you,' Lewin said, 'in your role as negotiator.' He smiled as he spoke, but the criticism hung heavily in the air. Tomlinson, who was busy writing notes, smiled too, but no one else did.

'I suppose you don't believe in everything you talk about

162

here,' Blake said. 'But you don't stop talking because of that.'
He met Markham's eye and grimaced slightly and again
Markham felt grateful for his support.

'But why didn't you think so?' Worseley-Jones said.

'Because of the idea of European officers, mainly,'
Markham said. 'It's too much for their pride.'

'Oh, *pride*,' Lewin said, with an irritable, dismissive
gesture.

'You don't think that's important?' Markham paused for a
moment, wondering whether the contempt in Lewin's face
was for him or for the concept of pride. 'Anyone who has any
understanding of Turks,' he said, 'knows how important it is.
We have made mistakes in our dealings with them. If I may
say so, these mistakes derive from the attitude of the Foreign
Office, which still sees Turkey as a moribund imperial power,
completely static, incapable of change. This is not the case.
There's a powerful nationalist movement going on under our
noses and we ignore it completely.'

'Even assuming that you are right,' Worseley-Jones said,
'why should that affect the gendarmerie issue just at this
moment?'

'I don't know,' Markham said. 'Things may be happening
in Macedonia that we know nothing about.'

He saw Worseley-Jones glance quickly at Lewin. There
was a short silence, then Lewin said, 'In my opinion you are
going beyond what the evidence warrants.' He regarded
Markham narrowly. The latter's reference to Foreign Office
attitudes had clearly not been well received. 'Colonel
Nesbitt's opinion,' he said deliberately, 'is that you offended
the Turks by accusing them of atrocities, and that is the sole
reason why the conference broke down.'

'That wasn't my impression, actually, sir,' Worseley-Jones
said quickly.

'Mine either,' Blake said.

'Evidence?' Markham frowned slightly as he looked across
at the chargé d'affaires. 'Do you mean evidence of a

163

nationalist movement? But we have had evidence of a secret revolutionary society known as the Committee of Union and Progress since 1905 at least.'

'That's one of your pet concerns, isn't it?' It was almost a sneer.

'We've known officially of their existence since 1907,' Markham said. 'You will remember that they sent an open communication to all the European powers setting out their principles and aims. It was more or less ignored in England.'

'The Balkans are riddled with secret societies of one sort or another,' Lewin said. 'They always have been. Greeks, Serbs, Bulgarians – it's a way of life with them. Like brigandage. And they're always sending out manifestos. None of it amounts to anything. Movements of that kind never change anything. And in any case, as far as official knowledge is concerned, this gang you are talking about has no footing in Turkey. They are living in exile, mainly in Switzerland, I gather.'

The frigid nonchalance of these last words was designed to dismiss the whole subject, Markham knew that. Nevertheless, he persisted. 'We know about the people outside Turkey,' he said, 'because they set out to publicize their cause. They are mainly politicians and literary men, people who take naturally to making speeches and writing articles. And they are living in countries where they don't have to fear the secret police. Here, inside the country, conditions are different. Of course we have no evidence. How could evidence be obtained? But what intelligence we get indicates the existence of a secret society organized on the basis of the four-man cell, with its main strength among the officers of the Third Army Corps in Macedonia but also gaining ground in the Second Army Corps in Syria. As far as we know, the Sultan's agents have not yet succeeded in infiltrating a single one of their cells. I think these people are getting stronger. I think it is because of them that the military here are no longer willing to discuss an international peace-keeping force in Macedonia. They are afraid of losing the province.'

'What would you recommend?' Lewin said.

'I think we should try to contact them,' Markham said, ignoring the sarcasm. 'I think we should try to establish a channel of communication, perhaps through their people in London.'

'My dear chap,' Worseley-Jones said, 'we couldn't possibly do that, you know.'

Lewin took off his glasses and began to polish them with a white handkerchief. His eyes were small, deep-set. Tomlinson looked up for almost the first time. His face was quite expressionless. There was a short silence, during which Markham again heard the soft crashes of impact from the tennis courts outside. 'Your service,' one of the young men shouted.

'A terrorist organization?' Lewin said. 'You mustn't let your feelings run away with you, Captain Markham.'

'Feelings?' Markham was bewildered for a moment, then he realized suddenly that Nesbitt had not limited himself, in his report to Lewin, to the proceedings at the conference only. They had obviously discussed him at some length, his hostility to the régime and so on. 'My feelings are my own affair,' he said.

'Quite so,' Lewin said. 'That is more or less what I meant.'

Markham looked from him to Worseley-Jones and back again; men of widely differing style and physical type, members of the same caste – their attitude towards him now was identical. It was as if he had transgressed, broken some law, or rather, disputed some law long cherished. Illegal organizations have no existence. But it was more than that: they were *relieved* that no act of recognition was required. They had been trained to see political systems as constant, only territory was subject to change, contraction, expansion. Every diplomatic service in Europe was the same, playing the same game, following the same rules. Balance of greed, balance of fear. The last thing any of them wanted was the dynamism of internal change, any whiff of revolution . . .

165

Except perhaps the Germans, he thought: they were new to diplomacy as they were to the scramble for territory, possibly less hidebound, less rigidly subject to codes of practice – less scrupulous, these men before him would probably say.

'We won't detain you any longer, gentlemen,' Lewin said, rising. 'I am very glad to have had your views.' He looked only at Blake as he spoke.

Worseley-Jones accompanied them a little way along the terrace fronting the residence. 'Thanks for coming,' he said. 'There is one thing . . . Perhaps it bears out your theory to some extent.' He hesitated, kicking lightly against the low wall of the terrace. 'No harm in telling you,' he said. 'The fact is, we had a long telegraph message late last night. It seems there has been a military uprising of some kind up in Northern Macedonia. Fairly small-scale affair, but the officers involved are self-professed members of this Committee you were talking about. A major called Niazi Bey is the ringleader, apparently. The other unusual thing is that the civilian population seems to be on their side. To a man. The local authorities don't seem able to do anything about it. I thought I'd better let you know – you would have had the news anyway, before long. I don't suppose it's anything serious.'

'Thanks for letting me know,' Markham said. He smiled at Worseley-Jones with a sudden feeling of warmth. He thought more of the other man now than he had done before. There was a quality of diffidence in him, an absence of complacency which was attractive, after the cold professionalism of Lewin.

Before getting back into the launch, he spent a few minutes talking to Blake, who seemed depressed by the way the interview had gone.

'I thought Nesbitt would get in first,' he said. 'Lewin had obviously prejudged the whole business. I don't take to him much, do you?'

'Not really. Listen, Blake, you're not worrying about an adverse report, are you? I intend to send in a detailed report myself, you know.'

166

'That doesn't bother me,' Blake said. 'It's just that I dislike this kind of work – hate it, in fact. There's nothing I would like better than to get back to my regiment. They are at home now, you know, in Wiltshire. But I'm due for leave anyway, in just over two weeks.' He looked for a moment curiously at the man before him, noting the lines of strain on the face, the unnatural tension of the body. 'You look as if you need some leave yourself,' he said, with a sudden sense of concern. He had never much cared for Markham, disliking the slight foppishness, the cool, aloof manner, the sardonic speech. An uncomfortable fellow to be with – too clever and, in a certain repressed way, too emotional. Not the sort you usually found in the army. And then, of course, he had not liked the way Markham seemed to be treating his wife, whom he admired . . . But there was something about Markham which brought out an unwilling sympathy in him, even a kind of respect, though he could not easily define this to himself. The fellow was relentless, but not as the strong are relentless . . . 'You let things matter too much,' he said. 'You take everything too hard.'

'Things do matter,' Markham smiled. 'Why don't you drop round for a drink after work? If you've nothing better to do, that is.'

'Thanks, I'd like to,' Blake said, not pausing to examine the nature of the pleasure this invitation occasioned him. 'About six?'

'Fine.' Markham made a gesture of farewell and walked down the steps towards the landing stage where the boat was waiting.

He stepped aboard, acknowledging the salutes of the two boatmen, and the launch at once began to move upstream, back towards the city. Before long they were rounding the headland at Ortakeui, sighting once again the amazing skyline of Stambul. Seated in the bows, Markham watched the city draw nearer, noting the elements of this famous view, which custom never staled, only made more moving and effective: the domes and minarets of the city rising from the rippled blue of the waves as if created by, and resting on, the water; the line of the ancient walls – walls that had preserved Byzantium for Christendom through ten centuries of barbarian sieges – stretching westwards from Seraglio Point; the bulk of St Sophia hazed by the heat into a great devotional mound; the sparer, more attenuated forms of the Imperial mosques; the wooded parkland of the Old Seraglio; the lighthouses marking the entrance to the Golden Horn; the white tents of the refugee camps at Kadikeui; the cypresses and cemeteries of Scutari – it was up there, he remembered again, that Hartunian lived . . .

His deliberate noting of these various landmarks of the city was like a touching, delicate but assured, of parts of a feared, familiar body, a mistress capable of hurting him but for the moment supine, passive, completely subject to his will. For these few moments he felt the city belonged to him as exclusively as his own past, the beauty that he recognized and the memory that he dreaded both present at once and curiously similar. He had asked the man at the wheel to take him to Galata, and now they were in the thick of the traffic off the entrance to the Golden Horn, among tramp steamers and fishing caiques and cargo boats of all descriptions. All harbours bring the ends of the earth together and the mouth of the Golden Horn, beyond the bridges, is like all harbours in one – flags of every country fly there. Not only place but time is confused in this tangle of shipping: Markham's motor launch edged round vessels whose build and rig could have changed little since the days of the Argonauts, ships with prows curved like parrots' beaks and high balustraded sterns. In amongst these moved the ceaseless passenger traffic plying between the banks, conducted in trim skiffs, gay with carving and gilding, furnished with velvet cushions and striped awnings.

Markham, standing in the bows as they came alongside, felt the city close round him, welcoming him back into the fetid beauty of her embrace. Hearing the endless fervent clamour of her crowds, smelling her breath of tanneries and impure water and woodsmoke, he felt the relief of one returning after an absence, even a kind of eagerness as at something to be renewed or confirmed. With sudden elation he remembered the previous evening, their voices in the dark garden, the surge of her fear against him. It was her fear he was coming home to . . .

He made a mistake on his way up towards Galata Tower and found himself skirting the slums of the Jewish quarter, one of the poorest and most insanitary districts of the city. Sorties of ragged children rushed out at him from narrow entrances, whining and clamouring for kurus. Variously deformed beggars held out hands to him. He was glad to escape from this evil-smelling maze and to emerge on the wider thoroughfare of Voivode Street, with the German Post Office on the corner. From here it was a short step to his office.

It had been his intention to work for an hour or so before going out to lunch. For reasons that were quite obscure to him, the War Office in London had asked for an updated specification of the city walls, together with full diagrams, and a general survey of the land defences. Markham had replied to the effect that the land defences had not substantially changed since the Turks took the city in the fifteenth century. But this, it seemed, was not the point. They had nothing on the land defences of Constantinople and this omission would have to be repaired. In its second despatch the War Office also requested photographs. Bowing to the inevitable, Markham had delegated the job to Winters, who had spent two weeks scrambling among the decaying Byzantine walls in the guise of a tourist, making surreptitious measurements and taking snapshots. Now Markham had to assemble the material and cast the whole thing in the form of an official report.

He sat at his desk and made a beginning, but almost at once began to find it extremely difficult to keep his eyes open. He had not been sleeping well for some time past. The strain of going about his normal duties while all the time resisting the encroachments of the past and the lingering sense of present imprudence, was now becoming considerable. He fought against weariness for a while, then succumbed, sleeping with head back against the worn leather of the single armchair left there by his predecessor.

He slept for something like an hour. When he woke it was to a sense of panic in case he was too late for his appointment with Zimin. However, a glance at his watch reassured him: it was barely one fifteen. He went down the corridor past the door to Blake's office to the tiny malodorous room – little more than a cubicle – which served as both bathroom and lavatory, boasting a marble washstand and a hole in the floor with a surround of cracked white tiles. Two cockroaches scuttled for shelter down the hole as Markham entered. He washed his face in cold water, noticing as he did so that the towel needed changing.

He felt better now, refreshed. He went back to his office and applied lemon-scented cologne water to his temples and the sides of his neck. He combed his hair in the large square looking glass on the wall – the only addition he had made to the furnishing of the office. He studied the reflection of his face for a minute or two, the level, strongly marked brows, the curve of the mouth, the dark indifferent eyes. The face regarded him without kindness. He returned to his desk, spent a further minute or two quite unnecessarily filing his nails, using the miniature manicure set with mother-of-pearl handles that he always carried with him. Now at last he felt recovered from the dishevelment of sleep, ready to go out.

He usually lunched near his office at a bar on the Place Karakeui run by an elderly taciturn Kurd, where one could get toasted sandwiches and a variety of fresh fruit drinks. Today, however, perhaps because the normal pattern of his day was already broken, he decided to eat at a restaurant. He

170

walked up to the Grande Rue de Pera and went into the Nicoli, which he had been to once before and liked. It was fairly crowded, though most of the customers were getting towards the end of the meal by this time, and in fact a group left just as he entered, so that he got a table to himself near the window. He chose from the huge tray of hors d'oeuvres brought to him by the perspiring Swiss waiter – all the people who worked at the Nicoli were Swiss – and ordered the speciality of the day – breasts of fowl *à l'eau de rose*, and a half-bottle of Turkish white wine.

He watched the variegated crowd passing along the pavements outside. Turks were in a minority here, in this traditionally Frankish quarter, though there were a good number of Arabs and some Persians, the latter identified by their round Astrakhan hats.

A loud burst of laughter caused him to look inward, away from the window, and he saw a group of Turkish officers sitting together at a large table in the centre of the room. Among them he suddenly recognized Nejib, the major who had been one of the Turkish party at the last conference, who had been their main spokesman in fact. The man's face was sideways to him and he saw the short scar on his cheek, the thick, carefully cut moustache. He was smiling broadly. While Markham watched he held up his glass and said something to the others, a toast of some kind it seemed to be – it was too far to make out the words. Whatever it was, they all drank to it. Wine, Markham noticed. There was something in the attitudes of the men that told him they had drunk a fair amount already. A celebration then. No strict Moslem would drink wine, and certainly not in public. Markham recalled Worseley-Jones's words about Nejib. One of the new type of officers, he had said. Educated, patriotic, but without traditional pieties of class. This one was German-trained . . . Markham recalled that fastidious habit of the mouth, the cold eyes. Seconded from the Third Army Corps, Worseley-Jones had said. That was where this latest uprising

171

was, up there in Macedonia, Nejib might well belong to the same regiment as the rebels. Could it be that they were celebrating, and so openly? That would make it much more than a mere local affair . . .

His speculations were brought to an end by the arrival of his meal. When the waiter had departed, Markham looked across once more, and now met the direct gaze of Nejib, who had obviously just noticed him. He nodded. Nejib's smiling expression did not change, but after a moment he bowed from the waist in a rather formal manner. Then he raised his glass across the room to Markham, causing the officers with him to look in the same direction. Markham raised his glass in reply, and drank, and the men at the other table all drank too. Nejib leaned forward and spoke to them, presumably in explanation. Neither he nor any of the others glanced again towards Markham. They were still there, still drinking, when Markham left. He thought no more about them, his mind turning towards the impending meeting.

He found a fiacre almost at once and asked to be taken to the Place Emin Eunou, just across the Galata Bridge. He remembered that they had passed behind this square to go to the café and guessed it would be easier to retrace the way on foot rather than try to give the driver instructions. In fact it was easier than he had expected and within five minutes of descending from the fiacre, he was entering the café, which was completely empty and resonant with bluebottles. Zimin's torpid relative appeared from somewhere and motioned him wordlessly through to the inside room, where Zimin was waiting. He was identically dressed, and sitting in exactly the same place – it was oddly as though he had not moved.

'Well,' Markham said, as they shook hands, 'what have you got for me?'

It was an effort for him to control his breathing and keep all tremors out of his voice. This hot little room, the narrow-shouldered white-clad figure before him, had come already to represent his secret, parallel life, his departure from official existence.

'The papers?' Zimin said. 'Have you brought the papers?'

Markham saw the other man's shoulders straighten and rear back slightly in the gesture he remembered. 'They are not complete,' he said. 'I am still waiting for the Embassy testimonial. I have arranged for it to be done. It should be ready within a few days.' He took an envelope from the inside pocket of his jacket. 'There are two testimonials here,' he said. 'One which I have written for you personally, a personal reference, you understand, and the other a sort of certificate of competence, an official interpreter's certificate, with my signature on it and the stamp of the Military Commission. Together with the Embassy papers it should be sufficient.'

Zimin considered. 'A few days?' he said.

'Yes.'

'Very well,' Zimin said, 'I accept.' He held out a hand for the envelope.

'Just a minute.' Markham retained his hold on the envelope. 'You're going too fast,' he said. 'What have you got to tell me?'

'Perhaps you will be disappointed,' Zimin said, his eyes on the envelope. 'The investigation is not an official police matter, that is quite certain – I have very good contacts in the police. And I am more or less sure that it has not been ordered by the Palace. It is impossible to be quite certain of this, because the system of surveillance is very arbitrary – in fact there is no system. It could be a freelance agent.'

'Such as yourself?'

'Such as I was,' Zimin said, his eyes returning to the envelope in Markham's hand. 'But now I am an interpreter.'

'But in that case, if he were freelance, he would report to the Palace authorities.'

'He would not report at all without first trying to find a buyer.'

'I see. Have you any ideas about why this man Hartunian should be watched?'

'I have made some enquiries,' Zimin said. 'Excuse me, I would like now to read my testimonials.'

Markham hesitated a moment, then shrugged slightly. 'Very well,' he said. 'Here you are.' He put the envelope down on the table, saw Zimin's thin hand pick it up.

'Excuse me,' Zimin said again, this time in apology for being about to read. He opened the envelope and took out the papers. He put his hand into his breast pocket and drew out a pince-nez, which he perched on the thin bridge of his nose. 'My goodness,' he said after a moment, in admiring tones. 'What an excellent style . . . reliable, conscientious . . . a man of tried experience . . . no hesitation in recommending him . . . It is beautifully written, sir.' He removed the pince-nez and looked at Markham emotionally. His eyes were shining. It was not clear whether his admiration was for the writing or the fictitious character depicted in the testimonial. 'John Bull, eh?' he said. 'I will fit in well there.'

'Yes,' Markham said, though doubting this. It struck him as strange, evidence of the power of myth, that Zimin should continue to believe in the honesty of the English with this evidence of dishonesty before him – for he must know it was lies. Or perhaps he assumed that it was only inside England that the English behaved well. Markham watched the envelope being stowed away in Zimin's pocket, small change of deception added to the considerable amount already in circulation. Some day somebody might be harmed by believing his assertions about Zimin. Odd, he thought, this small ripple of evil, still moving outwards from Abdul Hamid's order to slaughter Armenians all those years before. And even those orders were not the beginning, not the plunge that caused the ripples . . .

'Well,' he said, 'so far you have told me nothing much. You can't tell me who ordered him to be watched. Have you any idea why?'

174

Zimin spread his hands, leaning his narrow shoulders forward apologetically. 'It is difficult,' he said. 'You must understand that here in Constantinople the system is breaking down. Everybody is watching everybody else. There are more spies than police. It is all what you call private enterprise these days.' He took off his hat and fanned his face with it. 'Shall we have some beer?' he said. He went to the door and shouted in Turkish. 'Everything is going to pot,' he said, returning to the table. 'That is why I want to leave this damned city. I like order, decorum. Zimin is a citizen of the old world, sir – rank, protocol, the little elegancies of life, these things matter to him.' He paused a moment then leaned forward and said in lower tones, '*Abdul Hamid bitte*. The days of the Sultanate are numbered.'

'Why do you say that?' Markham asked.

'I have lived here all my life,' Zimin said, as if that was sufficient answer.

The proprietor, whose name it seemed was Ahmet, came in with the beer and set bottles and glasses on the table without speaking.

'The city is not what it was,' Zimin said, when the Turk had gone. He drank some beer, afterwards wiping his lips with a pale mauve handkerchief which he took from his sleeve.

'I suppose not,' Markham said. He was beginning to suspect that Zimin had not much to add to what he had already said. The fellow had found out precious little. In fact it now seemed to Markham that there was a good deal of the charlatan in him, or perhaps showman was a better word, a performer of some kind: with that improbable abundance of hair and eyebrows, so like false hair donned for the occasion, and the precise, rather shrinking gestures, he put Markham in mind of a music hall performer, one of those frustrated virtuosos who attempt to play the violin while things collapse around them.

'As for Hartunian,' Zimin  said suddenly, 'his wife was killed during the massacres, and he himself nearly died then.

He has no reason to like Abdul Hamid. He is rich, he travels. His house is a meeting-place for Armenians. As I said to you before, there could be a hundred reasons for watching such a man. The gossip is that he has links with the Young Turks. That could bring him into conflict with some of his compatriots.'

'In what way?'

'The Armenian movement is very divided,' Zimin said. 'Armenia exists nowhere, there is no place on the map you could point to and say that is Armenia, not on this side of the Caucasus at least – I do not speak about the Russian side. Perhaps that is why there are so many different ideas of it. And family quarrels are always the worst.'

'What is Hartunian's idea of it?'

'He would call himself a liberal, I think.'

'I see,' Markham said. 'Better conditions for the Armenian communities, reform of the land laws, equal rights with Moslems, that kind of thing?'

'Yes. He has European ideas.'

'But still within the Ottoman state?'

'Oh yes,' Zimin said. 'Certainly. And that could make enemies for him, you see. Among Armenians, not Turks.'

There was a short silence between them, then Zimin said, 'That is all I can tell you . . . It is not much. I have brought the map you asked for.'

'It is something to go on. Here is the rest of the money.' Markham laid the notes on the table.

'And my other testimonial?'

'I will leave it with Skafidis.' Markham rose to his feet. 'Good-bye,' he said, not offering the other man his hand.

'I will pay for the beer, don't worry about it,' Zimin said with an air of generosity, thrusting the money and testimonials into his inside pocket.

'If you learn anything more I would be interested,' Markham said. 'Anything definite, I mean.'

He left Zimin sitting there and went back through the

unclean buzzing of the café. Once outside he made his way directly to the square where he had watched the barrel-organ man with his monkey. He walked along the side of the square until he came to the costumier's shop. Without hesitation he passed inside. The shop was empty. The masks stared down at him from the wall. After some moments the shopkeeper came out from some recess, blinking rapidly as if the light were too strong.

'Do you remember me?' Markham said.

The shopkeeper looked at him, head a little on one side, blinking and smiling. 'You were in uniform last time,' he said.

'That's right. I want to buy some theatrical make-up. And I want a costume. Well, it's hardly a costume really. I want the kind of clothes an Armenian from the country would wear. I'm going to a fancy dress party, you know, and I thought I'd go as an Armenian.'

# 9

On the evening of 6th July, Abdul Hamid spent several hours reading translations of articles from the foreign newspapers, prepared for him by the press department of the Palace Secretariat. He read all the material from the beginning of the previous month relating to European reform plans for Macedonia and particularly the attitude of the Powers towards the Reval Agreement which had been signed between Czar Alexander and Edward VII on 10th June. Ever since 1907, when Russia had joined the Entente, the Sultan had been worried by the signs of growing friendship between Russia and England. It was on their traditional rivalries and suspicions that his own policy of inertia had relied. Now it seemed that they were united in their determination to implement the Macedonian reforms. The *rapprochement*, induced by fear, disturbed the balance of fear existing until then.

In his felt skullcap and thick *hirka* the Sultan sat crouched forward at his desk in the Little Mabeyn, while outside light ebbed from the spaces of his park and gardens. He could hear the measured crunching steps of the two Albanians patrolling up and down the gravel walk below his window. This guard duty began immediately after the third *namaz* and continued with two reliefs until sunrise. In the nights of his insomnia Abdul Hamid took comfort from this unceasing measured tread – it was in order to have it clearly in his ears that he had had gravel put down along the paths.

All day fears had been congregating in him, since the news that Enver had joined the uprising: fears for his life, his Empire, his dynasty. Conditions in Macedonia were now such that the smallest pretext might bring the Russians and

178

the English in. This revolt, probably unimportant in itself, could provide the pretext needed. There had been no time yet to learn Enver's reaction to the offer of a pardon.

*The Times* expressed optimism and the usual moral platitudes which exasperated Abdul Hamid and made him dislike England more than he did the other powers. The *Novoe-Vremja*, regarded as England's bitterest foe, had now become an ardent supporter of the Anglo-Russian alliance. Indeed there was complete unanimity in the Russian press on the need for friendly relations with Britain. Of course Alexander had recently relaxed press restrictions, a great mistake – Abdul Hamid reflected with sad wonder that he was now the only autocrat left.

Germany, of course, was bitterly hostile. The reports spoke of imperialistic designs, policies of encirclement, threats of invasion. It was difficult to determine whether this was sincere. Germany must know that the Triple Entente was the direct result of the Triple Alliance of which she was the moving spirit, she must know that Russia had felt isolated and afraid . . . All the same, Abdul Hamid understood this language of insane hyperbole. It was a public paranoia which echoed his private one. He was not merely the sole autocrat now remaining, but the only ruler fully representative of the stasis of fear that had descended on Europe, an embodiment of it in fact.

He tried to re-read the details of the Reval meeting, tried to picture that sunny day on the Baltic, the English King and Queen stepping aboard the Russian Imperial yacht, embracing the Czar and members of his family. But his misery at the thought of these two powerful monarchs on friendly terms, dismembering the Balkans between them, was presently too much for him, and he rang for the aide-de-camp on duty and asked him to summon Djavad Agha, the Chief of the Black Eunuchs.

In due course this latter arrived. He salaamed repeatedly as he advanced into the room, with sweeping *temmenas*

179

amazingly low to the ground for one of his huge bulk, and addressed compliments to his master in his soft, quick, high-pitched voice, using the traditional flowery epithets of the Harem. His vast pendulous cheeks shook with the exertions of his duty and there was a faint shine of moisture on his brow. White eunuchs shrivel and become cadaverous, but black men who have been castrated usually get fat, and Djavad, with years of power and easy living, had grown truly enormous – the folds of his neck hung thicker than a man's arms over the collar of his Stambouli frock coat.

'O Begetter of Sovereigns,' he panted in his girlish voice. 'O Light of the Harem.'

Abdul Hamid informed him that he proposed to pay a visit later to the Harem and wished all to be made ready. Djavad retired as he had entered, torso dipping to the ground in loop upon loop of salaams.

The news of the Sultan's intended visit stirred three hundred females into an intense activity of preparation. His visits were not so frequent these days – fear had imposed a genital immobility on him, along with the other varieties. Still, the women reasoned, he was able to have children, and to be the mother of a prince was all the ambition open to them.

In the event it was a Circassian girl of fifteen, named Mesté Alem, who caught his attention. She was an *ikbal*, the gift of a provincial governor, and had been in the Harem since she was ten. She danced for him and before he left he gave her a handkerchief, a sign that she was *gozde*, in her lord's eye. From that moment she would hold herself in readiness for the day he called her. She would be given private quarters, and groomed and advised by the older women, one or two of whom had already initiated her into the ways of love – for in an establishment of so many ardent women and no men save eunuchs, it is natural for the women to make love among themselves.

\* \* \*

180

That afternoon, after his lessons, Henry Markham had gone down to the summer-house. Nowadays he was more or less confined to the house and garden. His mother sometimes took him on visits, and every Friday he was allowed to go to the Beshiktash market with Nevres Badji and look on while she bought vegetables and fruit, and help to carry things. Apart from this he rarely went out. It was a lonely, blank time for him. His father was always distant and preoccupied. His mother too seemed wrapped up in rather sad reflections, and had less time for him than before. Even Miss Taverner was not her usual self. She had changed since the night he had watched her with his father in the garden, she smiled less and her attention wandered during the lessons. Everyone seemed to be under a sort of spell which made them listless and absent-minded.

He climbed in through the window with the broken shutter, forcing back the screen of ivy as usual. He sat in the accustomed cool dimness of the little pavilion, smelling once again the familiar smells of blistered paint and dust and mould. These smells and this atmosphere had become intimately associated in his mind with loneliness and the strangeness of being alive. When he sat here and felt his own existence in this hushed place with vegetation all around – vegetation both inside and out, for milk-white stems of some plant groped upward inside the walls – the awareness of his own existence made ripple on ripple of wonder in his mind, ripples that spread outwards from this disturbance of his still, breathing body. Every impression of his senses, however random, added to this sense of wonder. He placed his hand inside his shirt against the hot flesh of his chest. The heat and stealth of his body filled his mind with the same brimming sense of loneliness and wonder. He remembered their two voices, his father's and Miss Taverner's, which he had followed like uncertain music; voices with that strange quality of meaning something more than the words they said. He had puzzled over it since, trying to find clues in that talk about the garden and people having to pay bills and the fiancée who was perhaps killed because she was such a mean 'un . . . There was something within or beyond all this that he could not fathom, felt in the pain of the voices, in the moment when the two forms had become one. The ripples that went on spreading from his still body reached this moment too, absorbed it into the strangeness of existence. His father and Miss Taverner had kissed each other. Since then she had changed.

He sought to recollect and order the symptoms of this change, but could not. He thought of Miss Taverner's regular white teeth when she smiled, and the movements of her pink tongue when she was trying to teach him the difference between *th* and *s* – he had a tendency to lisp. In the hot afternoons, during their lessons, she would shift in her chair and he would hear the delicate sound of Miss Taverner's legs shifting under the rustling of her skirts. She held the skirt of her dress sometimes a little away from her legs, pinching up the material between thumb and forefinger. Sometimes she would take off her cotton jacket and sit in her short-sleeved blouse.

He felt a sudden pang of resentment against his father, who was able to make Miss Taverner blush, who was able, with his harsh presence, his clipped voice, to change people. Even his father's glance changed everything, spoilt everything . . . Envy was mingled with his resentment, the hopeless wish to be like his father, to touch things and change them.

He had brought an apple with him to eat there and this now rolled off the windowseat onto the floor, dislodged by his squirming. He bent down to retrieve it and as he got up again his shoulder caught against the outer edge of the bench that ran below the window and he felt it give a little, as if there was a lid. This was a possibility he had not thought of before, because the bench was padded and covered with faded material in a pattern of tulips, hanging down almost to the floor.

Kneeling down, he lifted the material clear and folded it along the top of the bench. It was mildewed and gave off an acrid odour, as if smoke had been trapped for a long time in its folds. The outer edge of the seat projected slightly. He tried first to raise it near the end but found that it was fixed there – in fact the lid was only a yard or so long, right in the centre of the bench. He found this and raised it. The cavity was lined with wood. There was nothing in it except a bundle of old clothes, Turkish-looking clothes in faded colours, and a pair of old black shoes and a wooden box like a large cigarette box. He took this out and opened it. It was laid out like a box of paints, with short-handled brushes in a groove and a row of little pots of different colours. Henry moved a finger across the surface of one of them: it was slightly greasy, rather like shoe-polish. He looked at his finger: it was stained dark red.

At this moment, while he was still staring at his stained finger, he heard his name being called from the terrace. It was Nevres Badji. He knew this because of the strange wailing note she made out of the second syllable of his name. 'Henree – e – e,' she called. 'Henree – e – e!'

Quickly, before she decided to come down into the garden to look for him, he shut the box, put it back beside the bundle of clothes, closed the lid. Almost he forgot to replace the drape, but remembered at the last moment. He scrambled out the way he had got in and made his way quickly towards the terrace, keeping into the side of the garden until he was well clear of the summer-house. When he judged that the distance was enough he moved into the middle part of the garden, just above the fountain and pool. Now he could see Nevres looking huge on the terrace above him, her head encased in a dark blue turban and with a long blue apron going almost to her feet. Her eyes were discoloured, muddy-looking, in the black face. She gestured to him. '*Viens, petit gars*,' she said in her soft throaty voice. '*Ton père t'attend.*' She had picked up some French in her youth, in the house of the Pasha who had bought her as a slave.

He went past her into the house, passing directly from the terrace into the passage-way that ran from front to back of the house past the three large downstairs rooms. He entered the drawing room, but paused at the door, bewildered to see another man standing there with his father, not so tall but thicker-set, in a black suit and a fez. He had a roundish face with a thick dark moustache but no beard. He was smiling and Henry saw that his father too was smiling – he had an impression of some joke having just been exchanged between the two of them. Both of them assumed slightly different expressions when they saw him, and from the first moment he was somehow alerted by this, sensing that something concerning him had already been discussed and decided. His mother he saw last. She was sitting on the sofa behind which his father had once found him hiding. She too was smiling slightly.

He was unused to visitors, unsure of how to behave. He stood there at the door, silent, looking at them.

'Ah, there you are,' his father said. 'Come in. *Bu benim oglum*,' he said, turning to the other man. 'Henry, this is Mr Oksuz.'

'How do you do, sir?' the boy said.

The man said something which Henry didn't understand and inclined his head slightly. His expression, now that he was no longer smiling, was rather sombre. His eyes had dark shadows under them. He said some words in Turkish to Markham, then looked back towards the boy.

'He says,' Markham said, 'that he was very curious to see you, and is glad to find you such a fine-looking fellow.'

Not having the remotest idea what to say to this, Henry remained silent. He crossed the room to where his mother was sitting and stood as close to her as he could – almost touching. Watching this manoeuvre with mingled sympathy and irritation, Markham said, 'Mr Oksuz is a near neighbour of ours. He's the father of the little girl who it seems you have been in the habit of visiting. He asked specially to meet you.

184

Apparently the little girl has been missing your visits.' He stopped and looked at the floor, as if uncertain how to proceed. 'She says you make her laugh,' he said after a moment.

'We've explained why we stopped you going out,' his mother said. 'We couldn't have you wandering about, not knowing where you were.'

Markham compressed his lips, the only sign of his impatience at this irrelevance, this feminine desire to reassure the boy that all was for his sake, as if Henry's sense of this would justify her as a parent. 'We couldn't allow it,' he said curtly. 'But in view of what Mr Oksuz says . . .' Once more he stopped.

Henry, with a sense of supremacy older than his years, watched these hesitations of his father's and took pleasure in them. It was clear to him that the visitor had obliged his father to change his mind, though how such a thing had been achieved was still a mystery to him.

'The fact is,' Markham said, 'Mr Oksuz has asked us particularly to allow your friendship with his daughter to be resumed, and we have agreed. Mr Oksuz has asked me to tell you that you are welcome to visit whenever you like.'

Henry glanced now at his mother, who smiled encouragingly at him. He said, 'Thank you,' and with a sudden access of confidence, almost of triumph, he nodded his head and smiled at Mr Oksuz, to show that he understood.

The Turk threw up his hands in pleasure at this small demonstration. '*Tamam*,' he said. He spoke some smiling words to Mrs Markham, then to Markham himself, words of thanks Henry supposed. Then he shook hands. There was a kind of natural dignity in his manner that was impressive. He smiled and nodded to Henry as he left. '*Au revoir*,' he said, and added something in Turkish which the boy did not understand.

Both his parents accompanied the visitor out, leaving Henry alone. Through the window he saw the Turk, still escorted by his father and his mother, pass briefly across the front of the house and disappear from view behind the hedges of the path leading to the road. Henry remained where he was. After a few moments he saw his parents return, walking arm in arm. They disappeared into the house, then almost at once he heard his father's voice in the passage saying, 'Impossible to refuse, under the circumstances. It's obvious they give her anything she asks for.'

'Well, of course,' his mother said. 'Surely that's natural, Robert.'

'Spoiling the child can't be good,' Robert Markham said, as they re-entered the drawing room. 'Though I suppose in this case . . . I felt sorry for the chap, I must say.'

They both looked at Henry who had remained standing in the same position, near the window. He was aware at this moment of what shyness had prevented him from seeing before, that there had been something extremely unusual about the man's visit, that his parents were embarrassed and didn't quite know what to say to him.

'Well,' Markham said at last, 'I still think that if you'd been frank with us in the first place, we might have avoided all this, er, misunderstanding. You may go there at fixed times on certain afternoons – not every afternoon. I hope that's clear.'

'Yes, sir,' the boy said. He glanced at his mother and saw that there were tears in her eyes. At once he felt himself flush with distress at this evidence of her feeling, though he was ignorant of what caused it.

'You may leave now,' his father said, and Henry began at once to move towards the door.

'I'll go with him,' Elizabeth Markham said. 'We're going to copy some animals from his book.'

'Very well.' If Markham had seen any sign of tears he gave no indication of it. 'You know I'm going out fairly soon?' he said. 'I have one or two things to see to.'

'Yes, I remember you said so. Will you be late?'

'I'm not sure. Don't wait up for me, in any case.'

186

At once, as soon as they had left the room, his own purposes returned to him. He thought for a moment. His wife and son would be up in the nursery, which had no window overlooking the rear garden. Miss Taverner would presumably be in her own room, and that was at the front of the house. The servants might be anywhere, though Nevres would almost certainly be in the kitchen preparing the evening meal. He would have to keep an eye open for the gardener, of course. It didn't matter, in any case, if he was seen walking about the garden, so long as he wasn't seen entering or leaving the summer-house. The whole business, from start to finish, had bristled with practical difficulties that he had not at all foreseen. Finding a place to keep the costume and make-up, for one thing – he had hit upon the summer-house because there was only one key, and that was in his possession. The summer-house, too, was obviously a good place for him to get himself ready, there was an escape route through the gate in the rear wall. It was the timing of the thing that had caused most difficulty: he had to put on the make-up in daylight, as he could not risk a lamp of any sort in the summer-house; on the other hand, he wanted to get out of the garden unseen, and to make the crossing over to Scutari in poor light in order to avoid any close scrutiny. Now was the time he had decided on, the sunset hour; and as if to remind him or spur him on, the sound of the sunset call to prayer reached him from the small mosque near the waterfront below, to be echoed almost at once from the Imperial mosque at Yildiz high above him.

He went slowly out into the passage and along to the rear of the house. The garden had a slight smell of damp about it – it had rained in the afternoon, briefly but quite heavily, and there had not been time enough for the sun fully to dry things out. He saw no one – it was late in any case for Ibrahim to be working.

He used his key to enter the summer-house. The narrow lock opened quickly. The door was warped with the rain and sun of many years and did not give at once, but had to be pushed inwards quite strongly before it would part from the jamb. The costume and the wooden box were there where he had left them, in the *sanduk* formed by the windowseat. He had in his pocket a vanity-case belonging to his wife, taken for the sake of the small looking-glass inside.

He took off his jacket, trousers, shirt. There was something exciting about this disrobing, in the dim, musty interior of the summer-house; it was like undressing for love, the same kind of haste, the same kind of unfocused agitation. One by one he put on the things that he had bought at the Parsee's shop: the baggy black cotton *shalvas*; the collarless white blouse with the thick red waistband over it; over this the long, loose-fitting cotton garment, more like an overshirt than a jacket, with a round neck and no buttons – it was worn open. The shoes were somewhere between clogs and slippers, black, heavy and thick-soled, but heelless.

Now he began to apply the make-up, following the shopkeeper's instructions, using a peach-coloured grease-paint very slightly mixed with brown to give the skin a darker, thicker tone, remove that clear northern pallor which would have betrayed him. His hair was dark enough, and his eyes. He worked in a little rouge over the cheekbones and above the eyes to give an impression of blood below the skin – without it the colour was too uniform, masklike. Tentative at first, he soon grew absorbed, filled with a kind of elation at this gradual abandonment of himself.

He was clean-shaven, but not all Armenians wore beards. The black felt skullcap came low over his brows, secured by a long strip of dark red cloth wound round several times, serving as a thick headband. When he had finished he looked closely at himself, peering into the little vanity-case mirror in the failing light. The dark-toned face that looked back at him was unrecognizable, even the eyes somehow not his own, returning his gaze without acknowledgement.

He sat there for perhaps half an hour after he had finished, waiting while dusk occupied the summer-house and the spaces of the garden. Peering through the shutters he saw the first lights go on in the house. He had some minutes more of struggle, almost of revulsion, now that the time had come to leave, venture into the open. Then, moving quickly, he pulled the warped door towards him, stepped outside. He almost forgot to lock the door, so eager was he now to give himself no time for reflection. Then he was moving towards the rear of the garden, shuffling in the unaccustomed looseness of his shoes. He felt it to be unlikely now that he would be seen by anyone in the house. All the same he kept well to the side of the garden, moving along the wall until he reached the gate.

Once outside he shuffled quickly along the path, which was overgrown at its edges with nettles and low bramble threaded with convolvulus in flower – the white flowers held the light, resisted the encroachments of evening. The smell of camomile and fennel rose to his nostrils as he proceeded, and the faint reek from the stagnant water in the stream-bed, where the rains of recent days had made puddles here and there. No one emerged from any of the gateways on his own or the other side.

He no longer felt any apprehension. Indeed, as he proceeded along the path in the waning light, he began to experience a sense of freedom. He felt curiously at ease and protected by the loose-fitting clothes in which his body moved so easily. This feeling of immunity, like a kind of happiness, persisted as the path met the road and he turned down towards the shore. He was in full view now. No one he passed looked at him with special interest. He crossed the wide road that ran parallel to the shore and took the narrow way between the tomb of Barbarossa and the mosque. Ferries to the Asian side ran irregularly, the general practice being for the boatman to wait until he had enough passengers to make the trip worthwhile. However, Markham was lucky on this occasion. There was a *sandal* already waiting at the landing stage, and shortly after he had climbed aboard, a group of

189

children got into the boat, accompanied by a thin middle-aged woman, a teacher from the *Mekteb* probably. She admonished the children in Turkish, in a quick, breathless voice.

Darkness was in the air now, though the walls of the nearer houses could be seen still, and the tombstones in the mosque yard. Light from the mosque lay across the landing stage and a section of the water. It was a warm evening, quite windless. The sky was a deep soft indigo and had pale, dilated-looking stars in it. Markham sat in the stern. He glanced at his fellow passengers, but no one was showing any particular interest in him. There were some Anatolian peasant women, shapeless bulks in their heavy veils and voluminous clothing. A green-turbaned *ulema* sat gravely apart in ecclesiastical dignity. Two German officers in uniform conversed together in low tones – a great deal of the aid and advice that Germany was giving Turkey in military matters seemed increasingly to take the form of staffing their army with officers, Markham reflected. There were also two Arabs in white headcloths and the inevitable Turkish official in Civil Service uniform of frockcoat and fez. There was nothing untoward or particularly remarkable about any of these people. They were in fact a very representative crowd of passengers making this crossing at this particular time of day. The boatman too was typical of his kind, with shaven poll, full white drawers, white shirt open across his splendid chest. All this was normal, familiar. Yet Markham would never forget these witnesses of his disguise, nor the aspects of their faces seen in the random light of the two lanterns lashed to the gunwales in the bows of the skiff: the excited children and the women like bundles of cloth unexpectedly vocal, the aloof, broad-faced priest, the fair-complexioned Germans, the beaky Arabs, the impassive Turk in his buttoned-up *stambouline*.

The boatman bowed and rose with the heavy oar in what looked like a periodic ritual obeisance – keeping the prow always into the current. In the light from the lanterns

Markham saw long-necked, crested birds moving downstream, quite motionless – asleep perhaps. Night seemed to have descended finally, midway between the European and Asian shores. He could see the harbour light getting slowly closer and on the slopes above dark masses of trees and lighted windows here and there.

The harbour of Scutari is no more than a nick in the coast, its inner waters barely protected from the storms of the Bosphoros. The *sandal* nosed into the narrow entrance flanked by small boats of every description. Markham paid his five piastres and stepped off the boat, the first to do so. He paused for a few moments, looking up towards the high crest of the slope with its dark shapes of roofs and minarets and the overtopping wall of the great cemetery. Then he began to make his way upwards through the narrow crooked streets of timber houses. The streets here were in worse condition than on the European side, with great holes and ruts in them, and Markham's progress, in his loose shoes, was slow. He went on, past a large mosque on his right, climbing up towards the summit – the Yeni Mahalleh district where Hartunian lived was on the heights above the harbour. He knew that, without needing to refer to Zimin's map.

However, he took the wrong way, went up too high, emerging finally on the Haydar Pasha road. Stretching away on his right now were the vast spaces of the Moslem cemetery, which the Turks called the Great Field of the Dead – the biggest graveyard in Asia it was said. He could see little of it but the low stone wall that bordered it, the massed clumps of cypresses beyond. There were no street lamps but some way ahead of him he could see the light of a lamp of some kind which seemed to be resting on the cemetery wall. He walked towards this, on the other side of the road, looking all the while for a turning that would take him lower down, to Hartunian's suburb.

Far on the horizon he could see the pale lights of ships on the upper reaches of the Bosphoros, where it opened out on to the Black Sea. It seemed to him that there was a freshness in the air, not chilly – the night was warm – but clearer somehow than the exhalations of the city, tasting of barer spaces, a breath from the vast plateaux of Asia stretching away into the night beyond the cemetery. Unchanged over centuries, over millennia, these Eastern Highlands from which the Turkic peoples had come, the Osmanlis among them, ancestors of the Sultans . . . He thought of the windswept spaces, the recurrent vice-grip of winter, the torrid summers, a people unchanging in their way of life for thousands of years. Her people had come from there, Miriam's people, Hartunian's, from a village on the slopes of Mount Ararat. Indistinguishable from their Anatolian neighbours in dwelling, in work, in suffering – even, often, in language. Different only in the Gregorian Christianity to which, with no homeland of their own, they had clung for identity. And throughout all that time, it suddenly seemed to him, through all that tenacity of faith, equally tenacious, had been maturing the passions and the hands that would kill her. We take from history what we can discern as affecting us directly, and it was difficult for Markham not to feel that the whole experience of the Armenian people had been leading to this one scrambling dance of rape and murder, in a room, in a house, in the city lying opposite, across the water. His own dishonour, too, went back equally far . . .

He was roused from these thoughts by a combination of sounds that he recognized without needing to look, the whining plaint and rattling alms-box of the beggar. It had come from the opposite side of the road. He was almost level with the lamp now – an oil lamp resting on top of the low wall. The next moment he saw the creature who had addressed him, and his heart sickened at once, even though at first, in the first few moments, seeing the chalk-white patches on the left side of the face, he did not altogether believe that the man was diseased – he looked clownish, with the irregular patches of white, as if made up for a theatrical performance, deliberately bemonstered. But then, in the light from the lamp, Markham saw that the whole face was devastated on that side, eaten away under the bleached parts.

'*Bizim karnimiz ac*,' he heard the mouth say. 'We are hungry.'

The use of the plural confused him for a moment, then he remembered being told that there was a small colony of lepers living in the cemetery, in the wilderness of tombs and bushes that formed the interior. They took turns, presumably, to beg at the side of the road. In the first moments of surprise, Markham forgot what he was wearing, who he was supposed to be. As he crossed towards the beggar he clutched hastily for loose piastres where his trouser pocket should have been, but found only the thick cotton of the *shalvas*. The next moment he had recovered, found the purse on its string inside his shirt. Without looking at the face again he dropped several coins into the box that was held out to him. He walked on, hearing the leper's blessings, indistinguishable in tone from his plaints, continuing behind him.

Almost at once he saw a narrow lane leading off to the left, back towards the harbour. He took this and after some two or three hundred yards of fairly steep descent came to a broader intersecting street, very quiet. He had begun to walk down this, with the vague idea of finding somewhere light enough to consult his map, when he saw the street sign in Arabic and French. By approaching and peering closely at it he was able to make it out: it was Rue Citlenbik. He had stumbled on the street where Hartunian lived. Immediately after this realization and as though to confirm it, he saw a tall barred gate set between stone pillars with glimpses of gravestones beyond. This must be the Armenian cemetery that Zimin had spoken of.

There were no pavements on the street. A muffling of dust lay over the packed earth surface, so that Markham's steps were soundless as he made his way along. The houses were infrequent. He counted only five on his side – the other side

193

was mainly taken up with the cemetery. They were wooden houses of the old style, broad-fronted, shallow-roofed, set well back from the road and partially screened from view by the pines and larches planted before them.

Hartunian's house was the last one. In fact the street did not appear to continue beyond it, ending in high wooden fences. If there was no way through, Markham thought, that would account for the quietness, the almost abandoned feeling of the place.

There was a wooden gate and a short path through low, thickly spreading pine trees to the door. Markham stood for some moments, his hand on the top bar of the gate. So far, nothing was irrevocable. He could turn away, walk back down the quiet street in his alien costume, return home, resume the life of Captain Robert Markham, Third Gloucesters, seconded for special duties.

He looked up and down the street. It was absolutely deserted as far as he could see, but dark enough to conceal an army of watchers. He opened the gate, walked down the path to the door. Without hesitation he lifted the heavy ring, let it fall back on the round plate of copper. The sound it made was loud, startling. Light from inside the house came through the oval window above the door – he was looking up at this, with its pattern of thin wooden spokes, when the door opened. A servant girl in black stood there, looking silently at him.

'I want to speak to Mr Hartunian,' he said. 'It is an urgent matter.' He spoke in Turkish. What he would do if Hartunian turned out to be away from home was something he simply had not considered – as if the mere force and intensity of his purpose would somehow guarantee all such matters, all the conditions necessary for its fulfilment.

The girl hesitated. It was clear that she was tempted to ask him to wait there, outside, on the step. After a moment, however, she asked him to enter. The door opened on to a large rectangular hall and it was here that Markham was

194

asked to wait. There were gas-lamps in gilt brackets on the walls, several divans, a very large mirror in a heavy, carved wood frame, an alabaster table with a vase of red carnations on it – their scent hung in the air. There was an obvious ease and spaciousness here, but nothing elaborate or ostentatious. Several doors opened off from the hall, which seemed to be a connecting room for the whole house. One of these now opened and a thickset youngish man in a dark suit appeared on the threshold. He looked at Markham in silence for a moment, then advanced a few steps into the hall. He said a few words in what Markham recognized as Armenian. He had heard Armenian spoken in the streets but this was the first time since the days of his engagement to Miriam that anyone had spoken directly to him in this language – she had used it sometimes for endearments, expressions of love. Now, even coming from this not at all friendly-looking young man, the guttural sound of it affected him strongly, the clotting of consonants that he remembered – it had always struck him as an awkward language, forced out by feeling over impediment of sound.

'My business is with Mr Hartunian,' he said, guessing the intention of the other's words. 'Urgent personal business.' He had again spoken in Turkish, feeling sure, however, that by now his foreign accent would have been registered.

The young man regarded him a moment. He was clean-shaven with the widely spaced, thick-lashed eyes typical of his race. There was a coldness in his regard, however, which was not at all typical. '*Attendez un moment,*' he said. He went back through the door, closing it behind him. Markham waited in the silence of the hall. After a minute or two the young man again appeared. He did not come into the hall, but stood at the open door and made a brief beckoning gesture.

Markham followed him down a narrow passage. Halfway along, the man stopped and knocked at a door. There was the sound of a voice from inside. They entered and the man who had been writing at the desk got to his feet as they did so. He was tall for an Armenian, as tall as Markham himself, and white-haired, although the face was not that of an old man. Markham had calculated his age at fifty-two or fifty-three – if he was the right man, the man who had been at the engagement party. It was in an immediate, painful effort to ascertain this that Markham scanned the face before him, a high-cheekboned, handsome face with a short beard darker than the hair and deep-set, steady eyes. For the space of some seconds Markham looked with fearful intensity at Hartunian's face, but there was nothing in it that he could be sure he remembered. Twelve years had passed after all; and perhaps he had not looked at the face carefully even then, not looked at it in a way that would keep it in memory, or any of the other faces, except Miriam's . . .

In the brightly lit room, combination of study and office as it seemed, the two men surveyed each other, both still standing. Markham heard the door close softly behind him. He thought at first that the younger man had gone but heard him after a moment shift position just behind him. Hartunian's face was calm, slightly smiling. He said something in Armenian, not to Markham but to the man behind. Then he looked at Markham and gestured with one hand towards a high-backed chair that was set against the wall. Markham moved to this and sat down. Hartunian resumed his seat behind the desk. The other man came forward, moved round the desk and took up a position behind and a little to one side of Hartunian, facing Markham. Hartunian said something smilingly to him, which Markham thought might be some kind of remonstrance about his obvious distrust of the visitor, or perhaps simply about his continuing to stand while they sat. The other man shook his head, keeping his eyes steadily on Markham.

Hartunian now spoke directly to Markham, apparently asking some question.

'*Ermence bilmiyorum*,' Markham said. 'I don't speak Armenian.'

'*Affedersiniz.*' Hartunian shrugged very slightly. 'Why have you come here?' he asked.

'I was hoping to speak to you alone.' Markham glanced at the man standing behind the desk.

Hartunian said, 'He thinks it is his duty to stay. He is my confidential secretary. I have every trust in him.' He turned smiling towards the impassive man behind him. There was in the smile, in the warmth and directness of the manner, something simple, almost childlike. Markham saw no answering smile on the other man's face. He felt sure that the confidential secretary was armed, sure too that the man's vigilance was somehow directed towards both of them, both himself and Hartunian . . .

'Very well,' he said. He began to tell Hartunian what he knew. It did not amount to much, when shorn of speculation. There was the central fact of the surveillance. Really, that was all. He could not even say how he had come by the information; could not even voice the suspicion, almost a certainty with him now, that Nesbitt had ordered the surveillance quite independently, for purposes of his own. If this were the case, it could only mean that Nesbitt was hoping to get something incriminating on Hartunian, something to link him up with subversive activities, perhaps with one of the Armenian political organizations.

When he had finished there was complete silence for some moments. Then Hartunian leaned forward and said softly, 'Why have you come here?'

'*Effendim?*' Markham looked at Hartunian's face. It showed nothing but a simple curiosity.

'Why?' Hartunian said again. 'You do not say who you are. The information in itself is not worth much. You are not an Armenian, though you are dressed like one. You are not a Turk either, are you?'

Markham was silent.

'Why have you come here?' the secretary said harshly. 'Tell us why.'

'Yes, why?' Hartunian repeated, sitting forward, looking at him steadily.

'To warn you,' Markham said, but he knew as he spoke that this was not enough. He had known it, in a way, all along; but it was only now, hearing this reiterated 'why?', sitting here in this trap of his own contriving, that he realized it fully: it had not been for Hartunian's sake that he had come, but for his own, to see the eyes of the man who might have seen his shame. If a warning had been all that was necessary, a note or a phone call would have done as well. But no, he had had to come in person. That he would be running his head into a noose he had known too, without admitting it to himself. For of course he could not get out of here now without satisfying them as to his motives. And the only way he could do this was to say who he was. As he sat there in his paint and borrowed robes, in the intensifying silence of the room, it came home to him how devious were the desires of the heart. He had wanted this all along. The disguise had not been to protect Hartunian. It was not as an Armenian but as a witness that Hartunian mattered. He had wanted to protect himself from Hartunian's recognition, Hartunian's knowledge. And yet all the time he had been working towards this moment of exposure, when he would have no choice but to offer his own face to be looked at by Hartunian. The question, he now saw, was not whether he remembered Hartunian, but whether Hartunian remembered him.

'You are not an Armenian,' the secretary said. 'Why do you wear these clothes?' He had moved away from the wall slightly. His hands hung loosely by his sides, held a little outward from the body.

'No,' Markham. '*Ermeni degilim.* I am not an Armenian. I am English.' He raised a hand suddenly, pulled off the hat and headcloth, dropped them to the floor. He raised his head and looked straight at Hartunian. 'My name is Robert Markham,' he said.

For what seemed an eternity he sat still, enduring

Hartunian's eyes on his face. There was an effort of memory in the eyes, no recognition.

'Markham,' Hartunian repeated. Then he said in halting but quite passable English, 'I seem to know your name.'

'Yes,' Markham said. 'I think we met twelve years ago.' He paused again, then he said, 'I was once engaged to a girl called Miriam Krikorian. Her mother's name was the same as yours.'

For a moment or two Hartunian continued to regard him with the same slightly vague expression of one trying to remember. Then Markham saw his eyes widen and fix themselves in a stare that looked for a moment hostile. He put his hands flat on the table before him. 'My sister's girl,' he said. 'But she was killed.' He still had not fully understood. 'They killed her,' he said.

Markham sat waiting, saying nothing. He saw the corners of Hartunian's mouth turn down a little. Then the Armenian was on his feet and moving round the desk towards him. With a vague sense of expecting a blow Markham rose to his feet. The next moment he felt himself taken in the other's embrace. For a moment he was held thus, then Hartunian released him, stepped back. 'I know you now,' he said. Suddenly, sharply, he turned his face away. Markham in the first instant took this for a sign of aversion as if the knowledge Hartunian spoke of had come accompanied with contempt. Then he saw the movement in the man's throat. His own eyes prickled with tears, though whether these were of mourning or relief he could not have said, perceiving as he did in that moment that Hartunian did not know of his behaviour, of his words, that evening, was remembering only the deaths and the grief.

'You remember me then?' he said.

'Of course.' Hartunian turned to the secretary, who had not moved or spoken, and said in English, 'He was the fiancé of my niece, my sister's child. She was killed at the same time as my Naavik – both the sisters were killed. It was to celebrate

199

the engagement that we were all there, at my brother-in-law's house. You were only a child then.'

'I was fifteen,' the secretary said. 'I was in Bitlis, not Constantinople. There were massacres there too.' His English was fluent, with hardly a trace of accent.

'Tarquin was at university in England,' Hartunian said, with a pride in which there was again something childlike. 'At London University.' He had his emotion under control now, though there was a glint of tears still in his eyes. The control had been rapidly regained. Markham thought again of the way Hartunian had turned his head aside to conceal his tears. His people normally wept more frankly, more openly. The tallness and the narrow, high-cheekboned face were not typical either. Perhaps some admixture of races. The secretary was in strong physical contrast, with his stocky build, large, slightly upward-slanting eyes and full mouth – a more purely Armenian type.

'He came to warn us,' Hartunian said. He turned back to Markham and said, almost tenderly, 'You have darkened your skin. You came as one of us.'

'I thought it better,' Markham said. 'So as not to attract attention.'

'You became one of us twelve years ago,' Hartunian said, as if he had not heard this last remark. 'I was nearly killed too that night. They thought I was dead. I have the scars still.' He touched his head lightly.

'You they didn't harm,' the secretary said, looking at Markham. 'Why was that?'

'They killed no one who was not Armenian,' Hartunian said. 'They did not hurt any Jews or Greeks – people who sometimes resemble us.'

'Why have you come back here, to Constantinople?' the secretary said. His manner towards Markham had not changed.

'I was posted here. I am in the army now.'

'You could have refused.'

200

'Yes,' Markham said. 'Well, not refused exactly, that is not a word the army understands, but I could have asked for an alternative posting, I suppose. It would have meant explaining the circumstances. I didn't want to do that.'

'Why do you question him?' Hartunian said, and there was a note of displeasure now in his voice. 'Surely you can see why he came. He thought we were in danger and he came to warn us.'

The secretary regarded him without expression. 'That is what he says,' he said.

'Tarquin suspects everyone of bad motives,' Hartunian said.

'Perhaps he is right to be suspicious.' Markham looked up and met the cold lustrous gaze of the secretary. 'So you are not worried?' he asked Hartunian. 'About being watched, I mean.'

'No,' Hartunian said. 'We expect to be the object of police curiosity from time to time. Of course it would be useful to know just why the British Military Attaché suddenly takes this interest in us. If you find out anything more about this and if you want to help our cause you can tell us, not on the telephone please – a note would be better. But I am not worried, not now. Certainly not now. Would you like to know why?'

'Very much.'

The secretary said some words quickly and eagerly in Armenian. Hartunian replied sharply in the same language. 'He is always suspicious,' he said to Markham. 'Everyone is suspicious in this nightmare that Abdul Hamid has created for us. But I am not proposing to tell you anything that could be used against us. There would be no time now, in any case. You will have heard something about events in Macedonia?'

'The uprising, you mean?'

'Uprising?' Hartunian considered him a moment. He was smiling and his eyes were shining. His joy was suddenly almost palpable in the room. 'Perhaps that is English

201

understatement,' he said. 'I am talking about a revolution. All our reports confirm this, reports from army sources, you understand – not the creatures of Abdul Hamid. It is like a miracle. It started only five days ago with one officer and a couple of hundred men. Now throughout Macedonia one garrison after another is coming out in support. The civilian population too. Turks, Armenians, Jews, Bulgarians, Greeks – they are all united behind the movement, without distinction of race or creed. These distinctions will not matter in the new order that is coming.'

This sounded so improbable to Markham that he involuntarily looked for irony on Hartunian's face, but he saw none. The secretary's expression was unchanged; it was lowering and heavy, the full lips pressed together with an effect of sullenness.

'The whole Third Army Corps is in revolt,' Hartunian said, almost reverently. 'The strongest military unit in the Empire. I am telling you this because I am grateful, because you are a friend to the Armenians, and the news will make you happy. A new day is coming for us. We have worked for this for eight years now, since the Armenian Committees first joined forces with the Young Turks. Their interests and ours are identical.'

Markham glanced again at the secretary's face. Nothing of his employer's elation was reflected there. Some words of Zimin's came back into his mind. *Family quarrels are the worst.* These Young Turks that Hartunian was relying on, men like Niazi and Enver and the officers he had seen lunching at the Nicoli, what would men of this stamp have in common with Hartunian, with his belief in European principles of democracy and constitutional reform? Why should Armenia matter greatly to them once they were in power? They were Turkish nationalists at heart. And they were Moslems . . .

He got to his feet, aware of a feeling of foreboding. 'You pin your hopes on a return of the Constitution, then?' he said.

'The Constitution is there, ready to hand,' Hartunian said.

'It has been lying there for thirty years. All we have to do is pick it up again.'

'I hope things go as you want them to,' Markham said. He bent down and retrieved his headgear. 'I'd better go back as I came,' he said. 'As an Armenian.'

Hartunian held out his hand. 'Thank you again,' he said. 'Now that I know you are here in Constantinople we must meet again soon. I will get in touch with you. Better times are coming, when we shall be free to meet our friends as we like.'

Markham shook hands and turned away. He still bore, as he was escorted by the secretary back through the house, an image of Hartunian's gently smiling face, that expression of the eyes at once penetrating and naïve. He felt chastened for the moment, almost humbled. He had gone there with his intensely personal concern and found a man concerned for a whole people. All the same, it seemed odd to him that a man so travelled, so experienced in human affairs, should put such faith in the Constitution, a mere piece of paper after all.

The secretary accompanied him without speaking. He was led back to the main hall. Crossing it he had a glimpse through a half-open door of two men sitting at a table on which there were papers. They were both young, about the same age as the secretary. One of them glanced up over rimless spectacles, rose, closed the door. Again, like a premonition, Markham sensed the possibility of discord within the house.

He reached the Scutari landing stage without incident. This time he had to wait longer for a boat. It was colder now on the open water; a light wind had sprung up with the smell of more rain on it. Markham felt the chill through the light clothes he was wearing.

He was tired by the time he reached home, and footsore – the loose-fitting shoes had chafed his feet. He met no one in the garden, to his great relief. Miss Taverner had been the main danger, though since the night of the supper party she had given up her habit of nocturnal walks.

He changed hastily back into his own clothes in the dark of the summer-house, leaving the Armenian clothes in the *sanduk* as before. The house was in darkness except for one lamp in the living-room. He stood for a few moments in this room, aware of his weariness, feeling the silence of the house around him. After a while he went quietly along to the small cloakroom on the ground floor. This had a washstand with a mirror above it. Here he began removing the greasepaint, which turned out to be a more difficult and lengthier process than he had imagined. Afterwards he went upstairs. He paused for a second or two outside his wife's room, but there was no light there and no sound.

He passed further along the corridor and entered his own room. He got into his pyjamas quickly, without bothering to put on a light. He gave his teeth a cursory brush, using the remnants of water in his jug, then he got into bed. At once, in spite of his tiredness, he began to experience the strange certainty of sleeplessness that had been more and more frequent with him of late weeks, a sort of sterile and desolate clarity of mind. He thought of the great maw of Constantinople that had swallowed him and spewed out a facsimile, good for most purposes, functioning, so long as he was in exile, efficiently enough, but not now, now that he was back, otherwise he would never have set Zimin on, never have gone to Hartunian in person like that. Nesbitt, it was Nesbitt who had ordered the enquiry. Nesbitt, whom Elizabeth pitied because he didn't believe in anything . . . What do I believe in? Markham thought. Redressing the balance of the universe in my own favour. Nesbitt must have reasons. His little French mistress would be expensive and he was getting near retirement age. Hartunian was not a member of any Armenian separatist groups, or so it would appear. It must be the connection with the Committee that Nesbitt was interested in . . . He thought again of Nesbitt's words. *The Armenians are not our business.* Why had he mentioned Armenians? If he knew anything it could not be from official army sources. None of that was ever recorded anywhere, it did not feature in his *curriculum vitae* . . . Perhaps I have been recognized, he thought. Perhaps somebody knows me here in Turkey. A member of the family, one of the servants, one of the men who had held him – it could be anybody. In one mind among the million of the city there would surely be knowledge of him, the knowledge he had failed to see on Hartunian's face.

He lay on his back staring up at the dim ceiling. Slowly his perplexity turned to misery as he thought again of that face in those terrible moments after he had announced his identity. Only those moments, in all the interview, had any reality. And Hartunian had known nothing essential, nothing of his apostasy. 'You are one of us,' he had said, his eyes shining, unaware of the terrible irony of the words. 'You came to warn us . . .'

'I came to be recognized,' Markham muttered. His misery increased. He had been disappointed, he knew that now: beneath the surge of relief at Hartunian's ignorance there had been a sickness of disappointment.

It was the disappointment that persisted now, intensifying to an unhappiness so acute that he could no longer be still and endure it. He rose, groped for his dressing gown and stepped out into the darkness of the corridor. He had a vague intention of going downstairs and mixing himself a whisky and soda. However, when he got to the head of the stairs, without any check or hesitation, as if this had all along been what he intended to do, he carried on down the corridor, putting his hand on the wall to guide him in the darkness, and turned right at the end towards the front part of the house. As soon as he had turned into this second, shorter passage, he knew where he was going and what he was going to do, so that when he saw the crack of light below Miss Taverner's door, he was not particularly surprised that she should be awake so late, but took the fact rather as a kind of collaboration on her part, a sign of encouragement.

205

He was beginning to feel the constriction of excitement in his chest, but he did not hesitate when he reached her door, raising his hand at once and tapping lightly. There was a movement inside the room, but then no further sound. Markham tapped again, his ear close to the door. He was breathing deeply, as if he had been exerting himself. Then he heard her voice, very close to the panel on the other side.

'Who is it?' she said, on a rising note of slight alarm.

Markham brought his face closer to the door. 'It's me,' he said. 'Robert Markham.'

At once he felt moved, as if this announcement was a greater gift than either heart or hand. But horror lay just below this, slowly uncoiling: the girl behind the barrier of the door, his driven statement of identity. *I am an Englishman,* some whimper of a voice said inside him.

'Can I speak to you?' he said.

The door opened, not very wide. Light from within the room fell on him, confusing his sight a little. He had an impression of Miss Taverner's face, wide-eyed, looking out at him. She was wearing a white gown.

'I must speak to you,' he said. 'Let me in.'

'You can't come in now,' she said, the note of alarm persisting, though she spoke very softly. 'It's after midnight. We can talk tomorrow if you like.'

He had the impression that she was about to close the door. Immediately, without thinking, he set his weight against it, preventing it. 'Please,' he said. 'Please let me in.'

Unintentionally, driven by the pressure of his feelings, he had raised his voice – he only knew it when he saw her start of alarm. Simultaneously with the perception he realized his power. She would be afraid of noise, of a scene of any kind, of his wife's displeasure. She was an employee, after all, and in a precarious position . . . It was as if, in extremity, his hand had fastened on the handle of a weapon. Cunning woke in him. He was still leaning his weight slightly against the door. 'You must let me in,' he said, again raising his voice. He saw

206

something change in her face, some bitterness of acquiescence appeared there. Then the door had yielded, opened wide enough for him to step inside. He closed it quickly behind him, stood there with his back to it, looking at her intently. He saw that she was trembling a little.

'Please,' she said. 'What is it? You mustn't stay.'

'I need you,' he said, in a low but quiveringly distinct voice. 'You must listen to me. There is no one else to—'

'But what is it?' she said. 'You must go at once. You mustn't stay here any longer.' Her face had paled. One hand held the edges of her robe together at the neck.

'Don't be afraid,' he said. The pleading had been transferred, now that he was in the room. In her it was an admission of helplessness, which excited him further. He knew what he had come to do, what he had come stepping so quietly down the corridor to do. For some further moments he stood there, back to the door, looking at her. 'Don't be afraid,' he said again. His sexual excitement was now so great that he could not control his voice. He moved to her and took her by the shoulders. She strained away from him, head turned aside, saying nothing. He felt the soft firmness of her shoulders under the thin materials of the gown and nightdress. He moved his arms further round her, took her more closely into his embrace. She looked up at him now but with a curious heedlessness, as if she did not see him as an individual at all. Her face was flushed, constrained rather than frightened, as if she did not know what to do, how to behave. He pressed her against him, aware with a sort of irrepressible and brutal jubilation of his advantages: her fear of noise, of attracting attention, her awkwardness with him as her employer. Below these embarrassments, as he drew her towards him, he sensed the helpless response of her body.

His mouth sought hers. Her face was averted briefly, then turned to him in a blind questing movement of its own. He felt the warm answering pressure of her lips. She broke off the kiss abruptly, turned her face again from him. A short moaning sigh broke from her. Half guiding, half forcing, Markham brought their embraced bodies some clumsy steps nearer to the white-counterpaned bed. They staggered slightly, stood still. 'Please,' she said, in a voice full of entreaty, 'I don't want to.'

With savage disregard Markham again moved their bodies in a series of clumsy dance steps towards the bed. He had to use force to do this – her body, though not resisting his embrace, was heavy and inert against him. Two more lunging steps and they fell across the bed, still embraced together.

'I don't want to,' she panted again, and the utterance had all the helpless obstinacy of childhood in it, that childhood faith that words will brings things nearer or drive them away.

He was beyond the reach of such appeal now. He was blind and deaf, regardless of everything but the need to have her, subjugate her completely. The blood was beating in his temples, and his face and whole body felt congested, as if his skin was too tight for him. Still, however, in some cold recess of his being there was an instinct of caution: control was vital if he was to subjugate the creature below him; and his control was threatened now by the contact of their bodies through the thin coverings, the friction of the silk against him as he moved.

Miss Taverner began struggling again and pleading, moving her head and raising her knees as a barrier against him. At once, and forcibly, he took her by the shoulders, held her still. He waited until he felt her body relax, then knelt above her, inserting his knees between hers. He knelt there, looking down at her, breathing harshly. He heard her utter a sound between word and sigh. Her dressing gown had fallen open and in their struggles the nightdress had ridden up over the parted thighs.

Feeling his eyes on her, she turned away her head. 'Please,' she said. 'The light.' Her face was burning.

She was quite still now. The request amounted to surrender. All the same, Markham made no movement. He had regained his control, distanced the sensations that had

208

threatened just now to overwhelm him. He wanted to prolong it, this moment of pure power, kneeling above her mastered body. She was his to do what he wanted with. Since puberty she had known this time would come. It was printed on the psyche. Yes, he thought, I have convinced her that the time has come.

'I want the light on,' he said.

Slowly, deliberately, he moved his hands from her shoulders. He lifted the thin cotton of the nightdress up over the thighs, over the dark hair of the pubic mound, over the whorl of the navel. She kept her head turned away, but made no move to stop him. Her flush had faded. There was a look almost of pain on her face, or troubled pity.

Markham fumbled a moment with the cord of his pyjamas. Then, very slowly, looking steadily into her averted face, he lowered himself onto her. He entered her in one long slow movement. The thrust of power, the *coup de grâce*. She gave a sharp surprised cry. At once, as if this were a signal, he experienced orgasm. As he spasmed and groaned she cried again, accents of pain and pleasure mingled briefly, then there was only Markham's breathing, the faint sibilance of the gas-lamp on the wall above the bed.

Afterwards he put the light out, so he could tell her about Miriam. Now he could do it, could tell her, though in the dark; now that he had subjected her, made her his creature, put himself out of range of her contempt, he could tell her anything – immunity from contempt made him free.

Such at least had been his idea. And he began confidently enough, lying close beside her in the darkness. He described to her the room with the lamps along the walls, the dark clothes of the men, long dresses of the women, the energetic elbow of the fiddler. 'She was dancing with her father when the men came in,' he said. 'It was a waltz. There were some other couples dancing, but I wasn't – I was watching. She was wearing a white evening dress. She didn't really like dressing up, you know.'

209

Memory grew intent as he talked, recalling details random but exact. He saw the gloved hand on her father's shoulder; the narrow serious face, hair cut short in defiance of the fashion of those days; the pearl-drop earrings and the white satin evening bag set with brilliants. So ridiculously elegant, that bag, not meant to contain things, simply to be carried around. As what? Emblem of caste, servitude, identification of the female. The uselessness of the bag touched him now as he remembered it, in a way he did not fully understand. Her narrow feet in the white shoes. Perhaps because it was her intelligence that he remembered over the years, the sharp, intractable, almost irritable intelligence that questioned everything, her own status and position as an Armenian woman, educated in Paris and London but still a member of a persecuted race, and an unmarried woman in an age-old male-ordered society. It was this intractable spirit of hers that he had loved so much, a spirit quite at odds with her obligatory trappings that night of the engagement party – the bag, the shoes, the dress, the earrings, a panoply specially assembled for the occasion not really at all expressive of Miriam's true nature or sense of herself. She had been raped and killed in fancy dress.

'They came in through the garden,' he said. 'They were carrying these weighted sticks with long handles. It's odd, but somehow they didn't look dangerous to me at first. They looked like people who had come to the wrong party. Almost shy, you know. But I realized afterwards it was excitement.'

He paused, but Miss Taverner made no comment. She had not said anything since he began speaking. He looked up through the darkness. 'Her father was the first one they went for,' he said. 'He moved towards them a bit – I think he was going to try to talk to them.'

He had seen the blow fall on the grey head, and the old man's instant collapse – no staggering or struggling. Dead already, almost certainly, but the man who had struck the blow struck him twice more as he lay there. After that

210

everything was confused. He had seen one woman clubbed to her knees, blood covering her face, and the stick raised again. He wondered now if that had been Hartunian's wife. Two men had hold of Miriam, her white dress was between them and the three forms were moving in what looked like a staggering, wavering dance back towards the wall.

'They held me,' Markham said. 'There was one man, more intelligent than the others. I don't know if that's the right word. He saw more than the others – he saw what was going on. He was fair, with a thin beard. Blue eyes. His eyes were peculiar, moist-looking. He had a knife. I thought he was going to kill me.'

He fell silent. He had been intending to tell Miss Taverner everything that had happened that evening: how under the regard of those moist eyes he had betrayed Miriam and all her people, betrayed them in half a dozen words of strict factual accuracy. But he could not. Even in the protection of darkness, even with Miss Taverner broken to his will. What he had done to her gave him no privilege. Even with her whimpering beneath him he had still been vulnerable to her contempt. Perhaps he had incurred this already – she had not spoken yet.

'Of course,' he said, 'it was Armenians they were after.'

It was me, he thought, with a sense of unreality. It was this person lying here. My mind frantically searching for the Turkish words that would serve me. Nobody asked me my name or my nationality. I told them without being asked. *Ismin* Robert Markham. *Ingiliz. Ermeni degilim.*

'I saw what they did to her,' he said.

He had stood there and watched, not struggling – they had not needed to exert much strength to hold him. Like a dance. Miriam between the two men, and the blows and crumpling bodies. The man with the knife had looked closely at him, the moist eyes intent on his face. When, unable to prevent himself, he had looked back into those eyes, he had seen how relishing they were, how *interested* the man was in his fear. *You*

211

*are English? Your fiancée . . . An Armenian fiancée. Ermeni bir kizla evleniyorsun . . .* That was before they did it. He had seen it in the man's eyes, heard it in the soft, almost caressing sibilance of the Turkish words, sensed already the frightful intention.

He had said it again afterwards, said who he was. Afterwards, when she was dead. She had looked at him as the men closed round her, looked at him as he stood there, held, not struggling. He had seen what they did to her down against the wall, under the soft light of the gas-lamps, seen it all, but there were blanks in his memory; he saw the men closing round her in that curious effect of dance, then her body on the floor, face invisible to him, her thin legs in white stockings uncovered, exposed. The men had held him, as they continued to hold him, in his reins of horror. Twelve years ago, almost exactly. For the second time he had said it, the formula for his salvation, disclaiming the dead father and the guests, the violated and murdered girl. *I am not Armenian . . .*

'That man,' he said. 'If it had not been for him . . . Because of him everything that happened was done to *me*. I don't know if you understand what I mean?'

'Yes,' she said. 'How terrible, what a terrible thing.'

Suddenly he realized that she was weeping. 'I'm sorry,' he said. 'Don't be distressed.'

'Do you think that's why I am crying?' she said. 'Because of what was done to *her*? No, I don't want you to touch me now. I want you to go.'

'Very well.' He got out of bed, groped his way towards the door. No sound came from Miss Taverner but he sensed that the weeping had not stopped. He hesitated at the door for some moments but could think of nothing to say. As he walked back towards his own room, her words echoed in his mind, charged with tears: *How terrible. What a terrible thing.*

# 10

Abdul Hamid kept two revolvers in each of his sleeping rooms. There were revolvers hidden all over the imperial quarters, in cupboards, in writing desks, in linen chests. When the Sultan was deposed by the Young Turks in the following year, and his palace was searched, no less than seventy-eight pistols were found in different places. Wherever he was, at all times of the day and night, there was one always within reach. And at twenty yards, Abdul Hamid, despite his years and frailty, could trace out his name with bullets.

One reason for this excessive number was that the Sultan, when neurasthenia prevented him from working, or insomnia from sleeping, moved about the Palace a great deal, using the system of secret passages and concealed doors known only in its entirety to himself. Many nights he went sleepless, sometimes for forty-eight hours or more on end, and he passed the time wandering from one room to another, listening at doors, boring spyholes into the walls. He even penetrated the living quarters of kitchen maids and boot boys and servants who never set eyes on their master. Another reason was that he never decided in advance where he was going to sleep, always leaving the decision to the last moment and even then changing his mind several times. He would order a bed to be made up for him in one room, then in another, and so on. The purpose was to confuse assassins.

On the evening of 7th July 1908, the Sultan changed his sleeping plans no less than four times. The final change was carried out alone by the Sultan, who crept out of the room where he had officially installed himself for the night, in his felt hat and nightgown, carrying his blanket with him, and made his way down chilly passages to a small room on the other side of the kiosk where there was no bed, merely a couch and a lattice-work screen. We know this from Izzet because it was to this room that he was summoned, at the sixth hour of the night, to read to his master, who could not sleep.

The Sultan's favourite reading matter was always concerned with crime and blood. In his lighter moods he enjoyed the stories and novels featuring Sherlock Holmes and these were always instantly translated into Turkish for him when they appeared; in more sombre states of mind, as tonight, he liked listening to accounts of the famous massacres of history – not battles, but the sudden slaughter of large numbers of people. He was tense and anxious during the preparations for the killing but once the blood had started to flow he seemed soothed, relaxed, and soon afterwards he was usually able to sleep. Cruelty had long ago been exhausted as an impulse in him, though the fear that had caused it had steadily intensified. Now he found the accounts of these bloodlettings deeply satisfying, like the experience of art.

Tonight, separated from his master by the screen, Izzet read about the Massacre of St Bartholomew. He heard the Sultan's troubled breathing as he read how the weak Charles IX of France was led on by his mother Catherine of Medici to order the killings of the Protestants, how a gentleman of the court, making his way homeward that night, met small companies of soldiers marching quietly, their weapons shouldered, their matches glowing, how in one quarter he watched a man chalking white crosses on the doors of several houses . . . When, before it was light, the great bell of St Germain l'Auxerrois began ringing for matins – the signal for the killing to begin – almost with the first stroke there came shots of arquebus and pistol, and screams, and then, gradually swelling from a murmur, the baying of the fierce multitude, the Catholic rabble of the city, and bells ringing from every steeple and the glow of thousands of torches as the Protestants were hunted out.

When Abdul Hamid heard how the blood ran down the

214

streets into the River Seine he gave a deep sigh and his breathing settled to a steadier, more regular rhythm. Izzet continued reading for some time longer, then paused, but the Sultan's breathing did not falter.

He slept for three hours. Bad news came to him when he was at his early morning toilet, washing in the water brought to him in leaden jugs from his own special wells – wells always closely guarded, for he feared some poison that might kill him at his ablutions. The news came in the perfumed hands of a dandified aide-de-camp named Tcherkess, a telegraph message to the effect that Shemshi Pasha, Commander-in-Chief of forces in Northern Macedonia, had been shot dead in Monastir when about to set off against the rebels. The assassin, wearing the uniform of an infantry lieutenant, had walked up to the general at the railway station, as he was about to board the train, and shot him several times. No one, it seemed, had made any attempt to stop this happening or to arrest the young man afterwards.

Abdul Hamid reflected for a while. It was becoming clear to him that the local forces were not sufficient to quell the mutiny. Enver had not replied to the offer of a pardon. For the last week there had been stories of Turkish garrisons and Christian insurgents throwing in their lot with the mutineers. And now his Commander-in-Chief had been murdered in broad daylight. He would send two battalions of his Anatolians from Smyrna, his 'faithful Asiatics', as he thought of them. These were men quite uncontaminated by Western ideas or indeed by any ideas at all except loyalty to him, their Padishah and Caliph. They would put down the mutiny within a few hours of landing at Salonika, bring him the heads of the ringleaders . . .

That afternoon, Henry Markham was given permission to go and see the little girl. His mother offered to let Nevres Badji go with him. 'Then you can go to the front door, ring the bell and so on, be admitted in the normal way,' she said. But Henry said that he preferred to go by himself, as he had gone before, through the back gate and along the path. He expected his mother to overrule him, but she gave way at once, and this added to the air of strangeness that had hung over his relations with the little girl ever since the occasion of her father's visit.

He was aware of this strangeness as he made his way through the garden. It was not only his mother but his father too who seemed to have adopted a totally new attitude since the man had come to the house. Perhaps, he thought vaguely, they were very important people, or special in some way, and the man had pointed this out to his parents. There *was* something special about the little girl. She didn't go to school, for one thing. He didn't either, but he was a foreigner. And her clothes were special – such bright colours and the colours all mixed up somehow. He did not so much care about going, now that it was permitted, legitimized. But he had thought of something today that they could play with and this was another reason why he had wanted to go on his own.

He entered the summer-house in the usual way. The old clothes and the make-up box were in the same place but with them now was something he had not noticed before, a little flat case with sides made out of pinkish-coloured shell, which he vaguely remembered seeing somewhere before. There was a gilt clip which opened the case when pressed, to reveal a small oblong mirror set into one side.

This find effected a sudden change in Henry's plans. He had been intending to take the wooden box with the pots of paint in it to show her. Now it occurred to him that he could do more than that – he could really give her a surprise. The idea was so attractive that he did not stop to think further about it. Using his forefinger he daubed patches of white on his cheeks. He traced a thin black circle round each eye. With the red paint he extended the corners of his mouth upwards in a permanent smile. The face that looked at him from the mirror was grotesque, quite unrecognizable as his own. There was a kind of collarless white shirt among the clothes, and after hesitating a moment he struggled into this. He scented, while it was over his head, evidence of a previous wearer. It came down over his knees to the tops of his grey stockings. There was a round black hat there too, which he contrived to keep on his head by folding up the edge all the way round.

The hat fell off as he climbed out, and the voluminous clothes impeded his movements. It was only when he was outside the summer-house, among the bushes, that he realized how conspicuous he had made himself, what an astounding sight he would be to Ibrahim or anyone he met on the path outside. However, it was too late now, he felt, to change his plans. Keeping as screened from view as he could, he made his way down to the gate in the wall. There was no sign of the gardener. There was no one on the path either, though a long-legged, yellowish dog with raw-looking patches of bare skin ran off down the gully of the stream bed – he had been drinking at one of the puddles left by the recent rain.

When he reached her gate, he took a thick blade of grass from the bankside and setting it between his thumbs blew the earsplitting note on it that was the signal of his arrival. He did not climb up to look through the bars because he wanted his appearance to come as a complete surprise. Instead he waited quietly below the gate. After half a minute or so he repeated the signal. Because he was anticipating the effect on her of his appearance, it had not occurred to him that she would not be there, as if the anticipation guaranteed her presence – though on one or two previous occasions she had failed to appear; and once she had seemed so tired and languid, and shown so little interest in anything, that he had gone away again almost at once.

It had been his intention to wait at the side of the gate until she had climbed up and was peering through the bars, then suddenly to step forward and present himself. But things did not work out like this at all. For one thing, she did not climb up, but simply pushed open the gate – now, because his visits were official, so to speak, it had been left unlocked. He therefore had no chance to strike a pose before she saw him. All the same, it was by no means a failure. He had given her quite a shock, as he could tell from her face and the way she stepped back quickly inside the gate. Eager to follow up his success he made his hands into claws and raised them, baring his teeth at the same time.

'Allah, Allah!' she said, and she pressed a fist against her mouth, but he sensed that she was play-acting now, partly at least, that she had guessed who he was.

'Grrr,' he snarled, and he made a small spring forward. The movement disturbed the precarious balance of his hat, which slipped over his eyes and then fell off altogether. He grabbed at it, missed, and saw her face break into a beam of delight. As always, as on their first meeting, it was his mistakes, things that had not been on the programme, which amused her most.

She made a mockingly elaborate salaam to him, raising a thin ringed hand to breast and lips and forehead. Then with the same elaborateness she gestured for him to come through the gate. He retrieved his hat and followed her.

It was the first time he had been inside the garden. It did not seem much different from his own, except that he could not hear any water. He glimpsed through thick foliage parts of the white walls of a house. The girl stopped just inside the gate and they faced each other. She was dressed today in a long dress of the kind, in Henry's experience, that girls normally wore only for birthday parties. It was scarlet in colour and made of some satiny material that reflected the light. Her face and arms seemed very white by comparison. She wore her hair in two long pigtails, tied with red ribbon.

'*Gunaydin effendim*,' she said in her high birdlike voice. '*Nasilsen?*'

Guessing the import of this, he said in English, 'I'm very well, thank you.' Then he had a brainwave. Perhaps she too had a governess, or a teacher who came to the house, someone like Miss Taverner, only Turkish, who gave her French lessons. '*Toi?*' he said, experimentally. '*Bien?*'

'*Oui*,' she said at once. '*Je suis bien.*'

Not being able to think of anything more to say for the moment, he showed her the make-up box, opening the lid to reveal the pots of greasepaint. As she looked down her pigtails swung forward and he noticed her ears for the first time – previously her hair had always covered them. He saw that she was wearing tiny gold rings in her ears, the rings passing right through the lobes. This seemed to him another sign that she was special in some way. He could not remember seeing anyone else with earrings going right through like that. The headmaster's wife didn't have them, nor the matron, nor his mother, nor Miss Taverner. He thought of what he had overheard his father say, that the girl's parents gave her anything she asked for. She must have asked to have holes made in her ears. What kind of person, he thought with something like awe, would ask for that?

She was pleased with the make-up box. She touched the paints with her fingers. '*Où as-tu trouvé?*' she said.

'*Là.*' He jerked his head in the direction of his own house, again dislodging the hat. He clutched at it. 'In the summer-house,' he said in English.

She nodded quite eagerly, as if she understood this. What she liked really, he suddenly saw, was the sense of having a conversation. '*Viens*,' she said. She moved away and he followed her into an area of low bushes with broad glossy leaves growing thickly together. Between two of these she had made a low frame with bamboo canes, contriving a roof by draping a strip of carpet over the bushes. There was a piece of carpet also on the floor.

'*Bu benim ev*,' she said. '*Ma maison.*'

He bent down to look inside. There was a raised plank in one corner with a mirror and brush and comb on it. Near this, lying alongside the bamboo fence, was a rather bald-looking

219

broom. Memory is arbitrary, and Henry could not know that he would remember this interior all his life, light falling through the gaps in the canopy, the brush for the hair and the broom for the floor.

She bent down and crawled inside, still holding the make-up box. He was going to follow but she stopped him. She said some words he did not understand, then held up her hand: she wanted him to wait outside.

He stood in the sunshine, with his back to the entrance, waiting. He could not see much from here – she had chosen a very screened and private place for her house – but he knew his bearings and felt free from responsibility here, where he was a visitor, more so than in his own garden, where he was always on the watch, afraid of missing something, some clue or information vital to his well-being; where even what he saw and heard had meanings he could not grasp, as if it was in code of some kind.

'*Bac, bac*,' he heard the light imperious voice say from inside the shelter. He was crouching down preparatory to entering – this could only be done on hands and knees – when she appeared kneeling at the entrance. The face she presented to the daylight was a completely different face. She had darkened her eyelids and the skin just below the eyes. She had rubbed rouge on her cheeks. Her lips, normally so pale, were scarlet now. The face was vivid, garish, quite transformed. The bright lips smiled. The eyes, narrowed by the paint and brilliant with excitement, regarded him expectantly.

'*Guzel?*' she said.

'Very nice.' He experienced excitement, mingled with a deep uneasiness at the boldness of the make-up, the completeness of the change. She had somehow given herself an intenser being.

She retreated into the shelter and he followed her. They sat together side by side. He was beginning to feel rather too hot in the long shirt over his own shirt and shorts. But the costume went with the make-up and he didn't want to take it off. The

220

sunlight, coming through from above, made quivering spirals over them as the leaves stirred outside. Light moved on the girl's vivid face, glinted and shifted along the satiny folds of her dress. She rested back on her elbows, raising her legs and moving them restlessly so that the skirt fell away.

Henry began to feel slightly bored. All this was anticlimax, after the drama of their transformed appearances. He edged forward towards the entrance, trying to think of a reason for going outside. When he looked back towards her he saw that her legs had parted slightly revealing a narrow gap between her knees and along the inside of her thighs for a little way. He felt the beginnings of an excited curiosity. Idly, to see what she would do, he twitched at her skirt, moving it up a little higher. She did nothing. He twitched at the skirt again, more deliberately. All of her legs were exposed now, nearly to the tops of her thighs.

'*Ne yapiorsen?*' he heard her say, in her high voice. The sound seemed to come lazily, from far away. She was lying flat. Sunlight patterned her painted face and her dress and her white bare legs. She was looking upwards, away from him.

Henry was intent now. His curiosity had become urgent. He moved the skirt up to her waist, exposing the white cotton knickers. She wasn't wearing a vest. Above the knickers he saw her navel, like a strange intricate shell. He looked at it for some moments in wonder. He experienced, through his several layers of clothing, at the root of his being, a kind of simultaneous melting and swelling sensation. He would have liked to take the knickers down, but she seemed to resist this by pressing herself against the ground. He tugged the front of them down far enough to see the mounded flesh between the legs. Then she was sitting upright again, drawing the skirt down over her knees. She was smiling, without opening her mouth, a strange, self-conscious smile. She said nothing.

He wanted to show her what had happened to him. It was an accomplishment, after all, something to impress her with –

221

he had a desire to show off. But the moment had passed, he felt. It suddenly occurred to him that he still did not know her name.

'Henry,' he said, pointing at his chest. 'You?'

'*Ismin?*'

'Your name, yes. *Quel est ton nom?*'

'Ayshe,' she said.

Since he had not been able to give her the gift he wanted, ocular evidence of his condition, he decided on a fir cone that he had picked up in the garden. He fumbled under his waistcoat and shirt to get at the trouser pocket where he had put it. He handed it to her, but she did not seem very impressed. She looked at it indifferently for a moment or two then laid it beside her. She seemed listless suddenly, and her head drooped as if it had become burdensome. The painted face looked doll-like now, doll-like or puppet-like, the neck too weak for the head. It was time for him to go.

He crawled out of the shelter. As he did so he heard the voice of the muezzin from the mosque at Beshiktash, calling the afternoon prayer. This was echoed by more distant voices from various directions – there was a sort of vibration or hum in the air while the prayers lasted. It would soon be time for tea, he thought. He would have to try and get into the bathroom, wash this stuff off his face somehow.

She came with him to the gate, still silent and listless however. As he clambered over the stream bed she was still watching him. He saw the shine of the water where it had collected in a puddle just below where he was crossing. It was now that worry about being presentable for tea combined with the instinct of the entertainer to make Henry do a very foolish thing. He bent down and scooped up some of the water into his face in an attempt to wash off the greasepaint. And because she was watching him he allowed some of the water to trickle into his mouth, spitting it out again noisily and with exaggerated repugnance. In this process some little of the water found its way down his throat.

# 11

In due course Abdul Hamid sent for Mesté Alem, the slave who had pleased him with her dancing on his visit to the Harem. He did this not out of personal desire – something he did not feel these days – but because etiquette enjoined it upon him, once he had publicly noticed her.

Perfumed and prepared she came to the room where the Sultan, after several changes, had finally elected to spend the night. She had been bathed, shampooed, scented with attar, and driven the short distance to the Little Mabeyn in a closed brougham with two of the Sultan's deaf-mute footmen standing behind her. These attendants not only underwent in childhood the usual operation performed on eunuchs but also had their tongues slit and their ear-drums pierced. They were the guards and chastisers of the Harem and also the Sultan's torturers, trained in all manner of inflicting pain, experts with thumbscrew, rope, rack, able to administer death by *datura*, by sleeplessness, by eyestrain, by dripping water and by the thousand cuts. They were the Sultan's creatures, totally faithful to him. When they had delivered Mesté Alem they stationed themselves just outside the door, ready to remove her again instantly at a sign from their master.

This was the night of her apotheosis, the encounter she had been trained for. She was only fifteen but as specialized in her way as the deaf-mutes. One mistake of judgement and her chance would be gone for ever. It was common talk of the Harem that the Sultan rarely required intercourse now. If she simply lay beside her lord, gave him the comfort of her youth and warmth, she would be dismissed with presents the following morning and the fact that she had spent the night with him would entitle her to two slaves of her own and a small apartment – a chance to escape from the oppressive proximity of so many other women, the endless close surveillance of the eunuchs.

This was the safer course. But Mesté Alem, though young, was ambitious. She knew that if she could persuade her lord to bestow on her some of his royal seed, then she would have the chance of becoming the mother of a prince, with the status of *kadin*, and thus, if God so willed, of one day attaining the supreme rank of Sultana Valide, mother of a ruling Sultan.

Abdul Hamid had a night lamp always burning – he could not endure darkness. In the light from this the slave girl undressed, taking care to make each movement graceful, and very slow – she knew the dangers of hasty or precipitate action. He watched her from the bed, watched her unblinkingly, the eyes huge in the thin face. She stood naked before him, smiling, concealing her fear. In the silence, as she moved slowly to the foot of the bed, she heard the crunching steps of the Albanians on the gravel path outside the windows.

Slowly, with the abject ceremonial of the Harem, she began to kiss his feet, then his ankles and calves and knees, squirming by degrees higher and higher up in the bed, moving with the utmost delicacy and care. Her mouth worked kissing slowly along his old man's thighs, until she reached the sacred area which could generate all glory, all power. Here she remained. She had no sense of politics or history, no suspicion that the Sultanate was doomed, that the royal seed was royal no more. Her life, her hope for the future, the whole reason of her slave's being, dwelt in this small area of muscle and gristle and skin that her mouth had been permitted to find. The Sultan's person, anything he had touched, the very places where he walked, all these were hallowed in the girl's mind, removed from the objects and places of every day; and these, the most intimate parts of him, possessed this sacredness to an even intenser degree. So the girl's mouth and tongue were devotional as they lingered over these parts.

Abdul Hamid lay motionless, looking up at the moulded design of leaves that ran along below the ceiling. He felt no abatement of fear and suspicion, but this soft, sucking creature in his bed – who as a female had no soul and as a slave almost no identity – was quickening him with her warm lips and breath and saliva, and he permitted this to happen.

Now again, as with the first caresses, she risked his displeasure, abandoning mouth love while she squirmed higher up, straddling the still body, to receive him into her. Again there was no rebuff. Gently she moved above him until she heard the harsh sighs of his pleasure, felt the brief throb of the thin loins between her thighs, knew that she had inside her the seed of kings. She kept as still as she could, so as not to lose any of it.

She slept by his side for some hours. When she awoke it was beginning to get light. He was awake, lying in the same position. At once, when he felt her move, he ordered her to get dressed and leave. The deaf-mutes were waiting still outside the door – they had squatted there all through the night.

Later, during the investigation of Abdul Hamid's private papers, a note was found in his hand to the effect that intercourse had taken place with a Circassian named Mesté Alem. Exact details of the date and time were given. This was always the practice of the Ottoman rulers, as a check on paternity claims, since illegitimacy in itself was no bar to succession. There was no further record of any act of intercourse during the remaining months of Abdul Hamid's reign. It seems likely therefore that she was the last candidate for royal mother. Whether she bore a child or not is not recorded anywhere. But at the very moment when she must have been passionately hoping she had conceived, news from Macedonia came to Abdul Hamid graver than any so far and clearly prefiguring the collapse of his régime. No more than an hour after dismissing Mesté Alem he learned that on landing at Salonika his 'faithful Asiatics', on whom he had pinned such hopes, instead of firing on their comrades, had

225

thrown down their arms and joined in the cry for 'Liberty, Progress and Equality.'

Markham returned home to find his wife in the drawing room, writing letters at a low table near the window. As he crossed the room towards her he saw that she was dressed for going out, in a dark green silk dress with full sleeves.

'Had a good day?' she asked as he bent to kiss her.

'So-so,' he said. 'You? Been out somewhere?'

'Not been, going,' she said. She put down the pen she had been holding and turned a reproachful face towards him. 'You've forgotten, Robert,' she said. 'I'm taking Henry to the Robinsons. They've got people from England staying with them, and there are children, a boy and a girl, about the same age as Henry. It's all been arranged for days.'

'Oh yes, of course,' he said.

'You are so absent-minded these days,' she said.

'I do remember now. He doesn't see enough children of his own age, does he? You're taking Miss Taverner, I suppose?'

'No,' Elizabeth said. 'She was to have come, but she asked me this afternoon if she could stay at home. She's not feeling very well, apparently. Most unusual with her.'

Markham smiled. She had spoken as if it were something of an affront to her personally that the governess should step out of character in this way. She was so determined that people should conform to her notion of them – a notion formed early, never much modified. In a way it was what he suffered from himself, Elizabeth's confident adherence to what she thought she knew. Too late now, certainly in his own case, to ask for a revised judgement – the mould had set too hard. As for Miss Taverner, she was expected to be reliable and robust, and that was that. They would be alone in the house then, except for the servants. He felt the slow stirring of excitement at the thought.

'Anyway,' Elizabeth said, 'she spends enough time with the child and she's not strictly needed this evening.'

226

Even this was grudging. It was not that she was harsh by nature, he thought, quite the contrary; but she was put out, put off balance, when people departed from her conception of them. Her distress at his recent vagueness, the reproach on her face just now, stemmed from the same source. In her eyes as she looked at him, in the very poise of her head, there was mute appeal – it was as if she was asking him to simplify the world.

'It will do Henry good to have a change of scene,' he said. 'This relationship with the girl strikes me as unnatural. Of course, under the circumstances, we have no choice. The girl doesn't know herself, so there is no danger of Henry . . .'

'He had make-up on his face when he came in for tea,' she said.

'Make-up?'

'Greasepaint. He hadn't been able to get it all off. He and the little girl had been playing with make-up.'

'Good Lord,' Markham said. 'Did he say where he had got it?'

'He said he found it in the summer-house, with some old clothes.'

'But the summer-house is kept locked,' Markham said. 'How did he get in?'

'He didn't say. I didn't think of asking him.'

'Good Lord,' Markham said again. He tried to remember the sequence of his actions. He had changed hastily, in the dark Had he forgotten to lock the door? Setting out he had almost forgotten, but now he could remember trying the door afterwards. 'Probably left there by some previous tenants,' he said.

'That's hardly the point, Robert,' she said, frowning a little. Suddenly he realized that what was worrying her was the fact of Henry actually putting on the make-up, perhaps because she regarded it as a sign of effeminacy, but before he could take this up, Mehmet entered to tell the *Hanoum Effendi* that the cab she had sent him to get was now waiting at the front of the house.

227

'We'll get some supper there,' she said. 'There are various salad things for you and some veal pie. Mehmet knows all about it.'

'I'll be all right,' he said.

'Will you ask him to go and get Henry?'

But at this moment Henry entered the room, accompanied by Miss Taverner. Markham was confused by her appearance, and noticed little except that Henry looked quite spruce in a tie and grey flannel suit with short trousers. Miss Taverner did not look at him at all, but retired at once after handing Henry over.

Standing at the window Markham watched his wife and son disappear round the edge of the drive. He remained there several minutes longer, with a vague sense of making sure they had not forgotten something, would not immediately return. Then he went through to the rear part of the house and out onto the terrace. He caught sight of Ibrahim doing something in the kitchen garden – he could not see quite what, because the rose bushes intervened. The sun was low now and long shadows lay across the garden. Markham hesitated some moments, then went down the steps and made his way towards the summer-house. The door was quite definitely locked. He opened it and passed inside. He looked carefully at all the windows in turn. Those facing towards the house and garden were secure enough but the one on the inside had no glass in it and the shutters were warped out of shape, held loosely together by the heavy mat of ivy growing on the outside wall. Someone small enough could have got through here. With an effort he managed to bring the shutters together and drive home the bolt that secured them. When he looked below the windowseat he saw that the make-up box was not there though the clothes were. He would take them with him to his office tomorrow, he decided, keep them there. Holding the bundle on the side away from where Ibrahim was working, he made his way quickly back into the house. He deposited the clothes in his study, between the desk and the

228

wall. Then he went to the drinks tray set out in the dining room and poured himself a large whisky and water.

They would be back by nine, he thought. Better say half-past eight to be on the safe side. That gave him two hours at the most. He finished his drink quickly and went at once up the stairs to the first floor and along to Miss Taverner's room.

When she opened the door, he said nothing, merely looked at her in silence. After a moment or two she stood aside so that he could come in. She was wearing the brown dress he remembered from the day of the luncheon party when he had watched her mounting the steps of the terrace. It seemed incredibly distant, that day.

He moved towards her with the intention of taking her in his arms, but she stepped back, away from him. He stood still, reminding himself that there were forms to be followed, rituals still necessary – more necessary now that she had accorded to him what she would certainly accord to no man else. He must not seem to take her consent for granted, even though she had, at least as much as himself, engineered this meeting between them.

'I wanted to talk to you,' he said.

The same sense of a necessary ritual imposed a certain stateliness on Miss Taverner's manner. She motioned towards a small gilt rattan chair against the wall. Obediently he sat down. She herself sat on the edge of the bed. The evening light, filtered through drawn lace curtains, lay quietly in the room. Miss Taverner leaned forward a little, the stuff of her dress clinging to the line of her shoulders, moulding her knees. She was wearing black stockings, he noticed now, and no shoes. She was looking at him seriously, wide-eyed, the full lower lip parted a little from the upper. Suddenly he saw in her the schoolgirl she had been till not so long ago, sitting there on the edge of the bed, at an illicit hour, prepared for whispered confidences.

'I'm glad you came,' she said. 'I was hoping you would. I've

229

been thinking about what you told me – you know, about what happened to your fiancée and how you—'

'Yes,' he said rather brusquely; he did not want her to refer to the part he had played, not like this, with this distance between them, allowing her to scrutinize him, judge him. There was nothing she could say to the point anyway, he had been unable to tell her the really important things about that evening. He was wondering what would be the most natural way of getting up from his seat, crossing the few feet between them, sitting down beside her on the bed. Time was passing; he would have to make a move soon.

Her next words, however, drove all thought of strategy out of his mind. She looked across at him with the same expression, the large brown eyes fixed and intent. 'You are too hard on yourself,' she said.

'Too hard on myself? What do you mean?'

'I know how you reproach yourself,' she said. 'I can see it. But there was nothing you could have done.'

'Good heavens!' Markham said, almost violently. He got to his feet. 'You've missed the whole point.' He saw her expression change, become uncertain. The full lips drew together. 'You don't know anything about it,' he said.

She had worked it all out, he saw now. Her role and his. She was going to console him, restore his faith in himself. She would remove with a few well-chosen words the self-reproach of twelve years and all its cancerous tendrils. He had supposed that her decision not to accompany his wife had been because she wanted him again; but it had been for this 'serious' conversation, so she could tell him he had done nothing wrong really. Monstrous female presumption, he thought. He was suddenly filled with fury against her. He walked over and put his hands on her shoulders. 'You've got it completely wrong,' he said harshly. At once, with his touch, he felt her tremble, felt the same power over her. 'Completely and utterly,' he said. He kissed her on the mouth, began at the same time to press her backwards.

230

'No,' she said, 'listen . . . I've been thinking about you so much. I haven't been able to sleep, thinking about you.'

Grinding his teeth in the rage of his vengeance, Markham pressed her shoulders back down on to the bed. He would silence this voice of consolation which sought to make his apostasy trivial. Make it sing another tune rather. He kissed her repeatedly on the mouth and throat, moving his hand meanwhile up between the resistless thighs. She moaned when his hand found the place. 'Don't hurt me,' she said. 'You hurt me before.'

She cried out when he entered her, but not this time from pain. Not tenderness but a sort of cruelty made him prolong the act. The vengeful desire to subjugate her completely, play upon her body as upon a musical instrument, drawing gasps and panting breaths from her and cries of short duration like notes checked at once. Keeping himself well in hand he watched her face, saw the vague sorrow of approaching orgasm on it, heard the cry she uttered then, different from all the others. 'I love you,' she said. 'I love you.'

Afterwards, however, lying spent beside her, he knew with despair that he had achieved nothing, neither comfort nor peace. He had merely added to his lusts this need to subjugate a creature who knew something of his shame – her only fault. Worse than that – he sensed it dimly as he lay there – he had brought the experience into the same infected area. They had moved on the bed to a soundless drumbeat, signal for the killings. The black flags of the Prophet, the crosses on the door, the thudding clubs and the squeak of blood – he had brought them into this room; he had added to the trappings of death the sounds of their love-making, panting breath, rustling of bedclothes. He carried with him the contamination of violence. As he rose from the bed, dressed, moved towards the door, he was aware of leaving behind him that smell of blood and pain, those sprawled bodies.

She smiled at him as he left, and he envied her.

231

# 12

It was on the following day, early in the evening, that Henry began to feel unwell, or at least not quite himself. It was not unpleasant at first, a slightly muzzy feeling behind the eyes, a languorous heaviness of the limbs accompanied by a sort of restlessness.

He was alone in the nursery when he began to feel like this, trying to paint a picture of a farm with various animals grazing in the fields. He was painting on a big piece of cardboard with the idea of afterwards cutting it into different shapes to make a jigsaw puzzle, but he had been feeling increasingly discouraged because the horses, cows and sheep all looked alike. Now, when he began to feel so heavy and strange, he lost interest completely in the project. Very faintly, from below, he could hear the sound of a piano and a woman's voice singing. His parents were entertaining some people for supper, and one of the members of an English touring company at present in the city had been asked to come and sing for them. Her name was Miss Ada Lamb – he had heard his parents discussing her. A very accomplished contralto, his mother had said, according to the notices in the *Constantinople Gazette*. His father had said that he didn't know about the singing but he would give her full marks for chest development.

This remark of his father's had made Henry curious about the lady and the sounds coming up to him increased his curiosity. His head was beginning to feel rather hot now and the muzziness had intensified to a slight ache. He went out of the nursery and along the passage to the head of the stairs. The voice was much louder now.

The drawing room was forbidden territory on occasions

like this; but he knew from experience that on these warm summer evenings the sliding doors that divided the reception rooms were often thrown open and if this were the case, and if one of the passage doors were left ajar, it was possible from just below the second landing to see into the rooms.

Taking care to tread quietly, he went down the wide stairway. The voice and the piano accompaniment were quite distinct now, but he could not make out any words, and this puzzled him. Reaching the right strategic position he crouched down at the edge of the stair. At first he saw only the backs of some of the guests, but by craning his neck and pressing his forehead against the bannister rails he managed to see the pianist's head and then the upper part of Miss Ada Lamb herself. She was standing at the piano facing him, contorting her broad white face in a way that was strange and rather frightening. Sound streamed from her mouth, clear, strong, absolutely unhesitating, in strange contrast to the labouring face. Because the words she was singing were not English, they did not seem like words at all to Henry, just pure sound. Miss Ada Lamb's hair was dressed in elaborate curls and she wore a pale blue dress that left her neck and the tops of her shoulders bare. She had a large bosom, larger than Miss Taverner's. But it was her face and throat that impressed him most, the fearsome stretching of the mouth, the convulsion in the white column below. And then, in contrast, this clear, unfaltering continuum of sound.

The sense of pressure at his temples and behind his eyes increased. He began to experience a definite sense of discomfort in his limbs. He wanted to get up, escape back to his room, but felt somehow rooted there, with his head pressed against the rails, unable to move, watching this agony of Miss Ada Lamb's, which was both public and lonely. It seemed to Henry now that the sound was coiled inside her like a rope and she was labouring to let it stream out, afraid of being choked if she didn't give it passage.

Nevres Badji, passing from the rear of the house and

happening to glance upward, caught sight of grey woollen stockings surmounted by scraped knees and came up the stairs to scold him. She noted at once the discoloured whites of his eyes, the clamminess of his forehead. It was she who took him back upstairs, supervised his washing and undressing, put him to bed. Afterwards she made him a *tisane* of dried camomile. But he was restless and asked for his mother, and in the end Nevres was obliged to go into the room where the recital was taking place and whisper to Elizabeth Markham that her son was not feeling well and was asking for her.

Markham, standing by himself against the wall, saw the servant enter and whisper to his wife, saw their two faces briefly in colloquy together, the black one and the white, the soft, large but indeterminate features of the Abyssinian woman in marked contrast to the almost hectic delicacy of Elizabeth's face. Then his wife rose to her feet and they left the room together.

The incident caused no check in the singing, no change in the attitudes of the listeners. From his position against the wall he could see the faces of nearly all the people there. They expressed a sort of sleepy resignation for the most part. One or two looked preoccupied, though this might mean they were responding deeply to Miss Lamb's singing, rapture and absent-mindedness being similar in their manifestations. On the whole, however, he thought not. The singer belied too much, in the solidity of her flesh, the romantic fervour of the aria she had chosen. She looked too heavy to flee with Radames. Besides, Aida was a part for a soprano, surely, a voice that could rise clear above the grossness of sense. Miss Lamb's, though powerful, was too throaty and thick. He glanced away from the singer's rhetorical face to where Miss Taverner was sitting. As the evening's entertainment could be thought of as cultural Elizabeth had invited her to attend. Her face, in profile, looked smooth and tranquil. It seemed extraordinary to Markham that he had seen a similar rhetoric

234

of feeling on this face too, seen this calm surface distorted and sorrowing. Tonight, when everyone had gone, they were to meet in the garden – the house was getting too risky. He felt a sort of dark anticipation at this thought, almost like a feeling of sickness. Miss Lamb's voice continued through it in turgid assurance of pleasure to come:

> Là tra foreste vergini
> Di fiori profumati
> In estasi beate
> La terra scorderem.

He saw his wife return and go back to her chair. But it was not until considerably later, not until Aida had finally bid the earth farewell, that she had an opportunity to tell him that their son was unwell, had a slight temperature.

Soothed by his mother's voice and her hand on his brow, Henry sank into sleep almost at once. It was a shallow restless sleep into which there came occasional sounds from below, high notes from Miss Ada Lamb, brief rattles of applause. When he woke again the house was completely silent. His headache had gone but his face and body felt hot and he could not find a way of disposing his limbs comfortably. He tossed and turned, seeking a cool bit of pillow for his cheek. Suddenly, in a moment of stillness, he heard faint sounds like the rustles with the bedclothes he had been making, but coming from outside, from the passage outside his door. At once, as if he had been waiting for it, Henry got up, walked through the rosy dimness of the room to his door, listened against it. He heard the wince and creak of a floorboard beyond his door now, nearer the head of the stairs. Very, very softly he turned the knob of the door, opened it a fraction, squinted through the crack. He was in time to see a figure which he recognized at once as Miss Taverner's going down the first flight of stairs. The candle-lamp she was carrying threw the light upward into the deep-browed face. Her lashes were lowered as she looked downward at the stairs, which she was negotiating very carefully, as if anxious to make no noise. She was wearing a long pale-coloured summer coat.

Henry watched her disappear round the bannister. Then he went back into the room, found his camel-hair dressing gown on its hook behind the door, and put it on, taking care to tie the tasselled cord in a tight bow, as he had been taught by his mother, in order to avoid knotting it. This care and the waiting at the window seemed necessary preliminaries, as if he were involved in a ritual of some kind. After a short time there happened what he knew must happen – Miss Taverner emerged from the side of the house. She no longer had the lamp but in the starlit space adjoining the terrace the pale coat rendered her clearly visible. In a matter of seconds she had skirted the terrace, disappeared among the foliage of the garden.

With the same sense of necessary care, Henry put on shoes and socks. He felt dizzy and at the same time strangely light and insubstantial, as if his weight was not quite enough to keep him firmly on the ground. He knew beyond any doubt that his father would be there, in the garden somewhere, waiting for Miss Taverner. The effort of getting his shoes properly tied made him sweat a little. His mouth was dry, but he did not think of drinking. He was impatient to be outside, near his father and Miss Taverner, listening to the next instalment of their conversation.

He knew the way without needing a light. And he was not nervous in the silent house because he had a purpose. However, the feeling of lightheadedness persisted as he too, following the way Miss Taverner had gone, moved into the denser part of the garden. He was conscious of nothing but hush around him now, as if his passage stilled everything. He stopped to listen, but heard nothing. Looking up through the trees he saw the sky softly lit by the lamps of Yildiz Palace where he knew the Sultan of Turkey lived.

He was about to continue when he heard the murmur of

voices ahead of him, a little to the right. This was a different place from where they had met before; it was near the edge of the garden, not among the trees. It was strange because although he could hear their voices he could not see anything of them, and as he moved slowly towards the sound he began to be afraid that they were concealed somewhere and watching his approach. Disturbed by this fear, he stopped again. There were no more voices now but he heard sounds of light collision as if someone were bumping against a wooden fence. This was coming from the direction of the summer-house. Henry moved forward again. He could see the dark shape of the summer-house now, shaggy with its growth of ivy and honeysuckle. He moved round to the side where he was accustomed to enter. He had not been back to the summer-house since the day he had discovered the box of make-up and the funny clothes. Suddenly he shivered, though he felt burning hot inside the two layers of dressing gown and pyjamas – hotter even than when he had sat with Ayshe in her garden house with the long shirt on top of his own clothes. Again he heard a light thudding noise, and then Miss Taverner's voice not saying any words but merely uttering a brief humming sound, as if humming the last notes of a tune. This came from inside the summer-house.

Henry was now immediately below the window with the missing pane. He raised himself very cautiously with the intention of peering in through the gap in the shutters but found that the gap was not there any more; the shutter had been pulled together and fastened on the inside. He crouched down again. There were light scuffling noises inside, but no voices. He thought of working round to the other side of the summer-house in the hope of finding a window unshuttered; but that cautious rising had made him dizzy again and he lacked the resolution to do more than crouch there, listening. The scent of honeysuckle came down to him from the clusters round the window. When he looked up he could see the pale curling flowers. He heard Miss Taverner again but it did not

237

seem so much like part of a tune now, more like a sort of sleepy murmur. This was repeated and then followed by a sound that he did not like at all – a harsh open-mouthed breathing that he knew was being made by his father.

It was at this point that Henry began to feel frightened. It was not so much the nature of the sounds that frightened him as the silence inside the summer-house from which they emerged and the silence of the garden all around, and the fact that there were no words, no conversation to explain them. There now began a series of soft regular crashing sounds, and Miss Taverner exclaimed as if in surprise or pain, and his father's harsh breathing checked for a few moments, then resumed, and the soft thudding noise went on, more rapidly now, as if someone were shaking or beating something inside.

Henry felt his heart beating heavily like a drumbeat in his ears, duplicating the thudding rhythm inside the summer-house. His body was clammy with the sweat of his fever and his fear. In that moment a fusion of sense occurred which was to affect him always, the scent of flowers in the night, the pulse of fear in the listener, the urgent, inexplicable noises.

He had lost all certainty now as to who was inside the summer-house. The sounds emerging from there had nothing familiar about them at all. There were two creatures inside, muttering and panting, making one blended sound between them.

Hastily he got to his feet and began to move away, back through the garden. The sounds drew together as he did so, the quicker panting breaths merging with the other, harsher, almost grunted ones. He heard a moaning cry behind him. Stumbling in his haste and terror, he made his way back to the house, back to the feverish sanctuary of his room.

Elizabeth Markham, finding that her son still had a temperature next morning, finding also blood on the pillow from a nose-bleed during the night, sent for Doctor Kyriakos. He arrived shortly before midday and examined the boy. His usual, slyly humorous manner gave way to one more concerned as he noted the symptoms of fever.

'It may be nothing much,' he said. 'Keep him in bed. Give him food that is easily digestible. Try to keep the fever down with cold water on the face and body.'

Next day, however, the fever had risen; and it continued to go up steadily for the six days following. Henry began to experience abdominal pain, sometimes quite severe. On the eighth day Doctor Kyriakos diagnosed typhoid fever.

'But how could it have happened? How could he have caught such a thing?' Elizabeth Markham said, white-faced.

'Something he ate or drank containing the bacilli. Man is the only carrier in nature of *Salmonella typhi*, he is always the ultimate source of infection. Your son will need careful nursing. Above all you must try to keep the temperature down. Give him plenty to drink. Cold water compresses. He will not want to eat but you must try to get some gruel or milk slops into him.'

During the second week of the illness, Henry was in continuous high fever, burning in delirium, unable to eat. He was aware intermittently of those ministering to him, the cold flannels on his face and body, the drinks held to his lips. Faces and voices too he sometimes registered: his mother and father, the doctor's brown eyes and thin nose, Nevres Badji, her broad black face surmounted by a pink cap trimmed with lace. Once he opened his eyes to find Miss Taverner's face very close before him, wide-eyed and anxious, as when she had peered through the summer-house window, looking for him, on the day of the garden party.

But all these things tended to run together in the white room where he lay, to become one with the spiralling light on the ceiling, the faint movement of the white curtains, the thin tremulous shadows of the wisteria leaves outside the window. Shadows, reflections, wavering light – all these made shapes, and from the burning refuge of the bedclothes he spoke to the shapes, accused, pleaded. Sounds were intermixed with his

239

words and at the worst moments of his delirium the sounds from outside his room, and sounds he remembered, and his own words on his lips and inside his head, all grew confused, so that the distant barking of dogs from the city and the strange frightening noises from the summer-house were happening at the same time, now, inside his room, and he was pleading with Miss Ada Lamb to stop singing so that he could hear what his father was saying to Miss Taverner, so the harsh breathing could become words. But then the light in the room became too dazzling for him to hear anything, light drove the sounds away, they receded into quivering distances. The silence would throb with the flight of sounds and in the silence the shapes would gather again.

As life sank low in him the vitality of his deliriums increased. His eyes glittered and his cracked lips were convulsed sometimes with the urgency of what they had to utter. And his mother, who sat longest with him, but sometimes his father too, could not help hearing the voices and the sounds, though they gave no sign to each other of having done so.

In these middle days of July while Henry Markham lay poised between life and death, beleaguered by visions, and in this helpless state betrayed his father and Miss Taverner, events were moving to a head in Macedonia also, where the revolutionary forces were growing daily in strength. On the 14th of the month, at his headquarters at Stavrou on Lake Ochrida, Niazi had been joined by a general of division. One by one the scattered garrisons were mutinying, raiding the depots and distributing arms among the population, Christian and Moslem alike. Sevres came over on the 16th, Vodena on the 21st. Placards demanding the Constitution were everywhere displayed. Fifteen thousand Albanians assembled at Ferizovitch and proclaimed the Constitution.

Abdul Hamid, half-crazed with sleeplessness and fear, pursued vacillating and contradictory policies, at one moment offering amnesties and bonuses, at another declaring all the revolutionary officers cashiered. His emissaries, sent to restore order, were either killed or taken prisoner. Attempts to weaken the movement by means of bribes to individuals were of no avail. The disaffection spread to the Second Army Corps at Adrianople, then to the Fourth at Smyrna. Even the troops stationed in Constantinople itself could not be completely relied on.

On the 22nd, in a last attempt to allay the unrest, the reactionary Grand Vizier, Ferid, was dismissed and the more liberal Said put in his place. But by this time it was too late. The following day a formal ultimatum was presented to Abdul Hamid in the form of a telegram from the Committee of Union and Progress at Salonika. It stated that unless the Constitution – understood to mean the Constitution abrogated in 1876 – were restored within twenty-four hours, the troops of the Second and Third Army Corps would march on the capital. The Sultan had one night in which to meditate his reply.

It was on this night that Henry Markham nearly died. Weakened by the days of continuous fever, his brain too dull now for further hallucinations, sweated to bone and skin, he lay muttering and burning, no longer aware of the hands that bathed him, the cold cloths laid on his head and chest.

On this night too Robert Markham got up from his son's bedside and went to the governess's room, where he stayed for about an hour. He did not go out of desire for her, but because the thought that his son should die thus had become intolerable to him: it was intolerable that he should continue to sit there, with his wife, waiting for the moment she would look at him – it was her look, in the silence of the room, that he dreaded. Dazed with his guilt and his grief he got up and left her sitting there. Miss Taverner asked him not to stay – she was shocked that he should have come at all, being too young to understand the extremity of his need. But he insisted, and

241

at the first touch between them became violent, bruising her lips with the force of his kisses, taking her without preliminary tenderness of any kind.

Shortly after midnight, while this was happening, Henry's breathing changed, became deeper. All the ugly and discordant noises which had been plaguing him blended suddenly into a single song, a rope of song that contained all the sounds in the world. It went on, clear, unfaltering, effortless. Henry listened to it for a while, and then he slept, the first real sleep for many days.

The hundred clocks of Yildiz ticked away momentous hours while Abdul Hamid meditated on the ultimatum he had received. Izzet Pasha relates in his Memoirs how arriving for an audience with the Sultan shortly after midnight he heard the strains of Offenbach, Abdul Hamid's favourite composer, played by a hand that had lost control, coming from the piano in the Little Mabeyn. He knew his master well and recognized the piano-playing as an ominous sign that his nerves were at breaking point.

The piano-playing stopped and a few minutes later the Chief of the Black Eunuchs, Djavad Agha, stepping softly, for all his bulk, on his thick embroidered shoes, came to usher him into the royal presence. Drops of sweat hung on Djavad's pendulous cheeks, the sweat of fear. Like the others at that conference he was identified with the régime and stood or fell with it. All those present, with the possible exception of Tahsin, the First Secretary, had crimes to account for: they were men who had grown rich through extortion and peculation. In the mind of the people it was they rather than the Sultan – he after all was God's appointed – who were responsible for the corruption of the régime. They knew what to expect if they fell into the hands of the Committee. The knowledge was on all their faces.

Izzet spoke for them all when he advocated resistance. Force must be met with force, he said. His Majesty must deal with the Young Turks as his great ancestor Mahmud dealt with the rebellious Janissaries. He should show himself to his people, speak to them as his children, denounce the rebels as traitors. Within an hour they would be shouting for their Padishah louder than they were now shouting for the Constitution.

He spoke well, Arab eloquence combining with the sophistry of his Jesuit education. He was under no illusion as to what awaited him at the hands of the Young Turks and had made his plans accordingly. He had bank deposits in London, Paris and Berlin and a ship of the Khedival line had been chartered to take him and his family to safety in the event of an emergency. But he records that tonight he felt a curious reluctance to part from the master whose policies he had helped to shape for almost twenty years.

There was the usual silence of majesty after his words. Then Abdul Hamid, fingering his amber *tesbieh*, spoke in a voice full of weariness. He was an old man, he said, and his empire was disintegrating. But it would never be said that he brought civil war on his people.

Interpreting this to mean that he was afraid of losing, the others spoke in turn, pointing out to him that he was Caliph, that he commanded the loyalties of three hundred million Moslems. Moreover, there was the Palace Guard, his trusty Albanians; there was the First Army Corps in Constantinople, most of which was loyal; above all, there was the Anatolian peasantry, patient cannon-fodder through all the centuries of Ottoman rule – they would take up arms in his cause.

Abdul Hamid listened without comment, occasionally glancing down from the faces of the speakers to the map of Macedonia spread out on the table before him. In his loose white *entari*, with the fez pushed back on his high narrow forehead, he resembled a bird of some kind, hunched and disconsolate with fever.

Kutchuk Said, the new Grand Vizier, now arrived, driven at a gallop through the gates of Yildiz and ushered immediately into the presence of the Sultan. Abdul Hamid watched him straighten up after the salaams, noting the square set of the shoulders, the slightly truculent line of the mouth. Said's honesty he knew, though he gave it no approbation – it was merely an attribute, like the colour of his eyes, but an attribute necessary to remember. With his usual courtesy he asked for the Grand Vizier's advice. Without hesitation, and without a glance at any other person there – he detested the palace clique as heartily as anyone – Said gave it as his opinion that the terms of the rebels should be accepted, the Constitution should be restored.

It was because Abdul Hamid had known what Said's advice would be that he had been appointed. To that extent the Sultan's decision was already made. Nevertheless, when they had gone and he was alone again in his study, Abdul Hamid was prey to painful hesitation. He feared for his throne and his life. He did not trust the protestations of loyalty to him, as Sultan and Caliph, with which the rebels had prefaced their demands. As dawn rose behind the hills of Asia and lightened the minarets of Scutari, while the slaves still slept in the courtyards of the Palace and the beasts of the menagerie in their cages, the Sultan sat at his desk, listening for reassurance to the crunching steps of his guards outside.

Finally he had recourse to the traditional device of the Ottoman rulers in times of crisis: he appealed to the Sheikh-ul-Islam, the chief ecclesiastic of the state, ultimate authority on matters pertaining to Islamic Law. Could the Constitution be accepted without violation of the *Sheriat*, the Sacred Law? The answer came in the accustomed single word of acceptance: *Olur*, It may be done.

It was this that finally decided the Sultan – or this, at least, that he clutched at as deciding the matter for him. As protocol demanded, a full council of state was held early next morning at Yildiz, attended by those former Grand Viziers who had escaped exile or execution, ministers of state, heads of the armed forces. Following the custom of Oriental semi-

244

divinities, the Sultan was present but invisible, concealed by a curtain. When these purely formal proceedings drew to a close, he announced to the assembled dignitaries that he was wholeheartedly in favour of a Constitution, which it had always been his intention to restore as soon as his people were ready for it. He ordered that the Constitution should be proclaimed immediately, together with a full amnesty for all political prisoners.

An *iradé* to this effect was published in the morning papers of Friday 24th July.

Doctor Kyriakos, calling at the Markham house at nine o'clock that morning to see his patient, found the boy's temperature had dropped two degrees. Though very weak Henry seemed rested. He was breathing more easily. The characteristic flower-shaped lesions of the rash, which had still been visible the evening before, had disappeared.

Elizabeth Markham followed Kyriakos out of the room, accompanied him downstairs to the hall, where Markham himself was waiting. There Kyriakos told them that the crisis was over, that the boy was out of danger.

She nodded but said nothing. Markham made neither sound nor movement. Kyriakos looked curiously from one to the other. The English were an extraordinary people, he thought. Such reticence seemed unnatural, almost monstrous to him, like a sort of goitre on the personality. A Greek would have felt it incumbent upon him to make some demonstration, some effusion of feeling – like a libation. They have no piety, he thought. Of course, sitting with the boy, they might have seen the moment of change . . . There was something more here, however, than mere reticence. His dark, observant eyes noted the stiffness between them, the distance that was maintained even after his announcement – they did not so much as glance at each other.

'I would like to thank you,' Elizabeth said after a moment, 'for the care you have taken of him.'

'*Tipote*,' Kyriakos said. He smiled, betraying gleams of gold.

'I am very grateful,' she said. She looked at him for some moments directly. Always now, because of him, she would question certain reactions, certain prejudices of her own. The man before her, with his eyes that were too bold, his tie-pin with the pearl vulgarly large, his cuffs too prominent, his insinuating manners, she had been contemptuous of him, there had been no provision in her code for such a man. Seeing him touch her son with such care and concern, being obliged to trust his judgement, had modified her snobbery for ever. Moreover, she sensed his delight in Henry's recovery, and it touched her more deeply than she was able to indicate, at this time of estrangement from her husband, in the first shock of what she had learned during the night.

'I did very little for him,' Kyriakos said. 'Your nursing did the trick.' He smiled again, broadly, pleased with the appropriateness of the idiom. Then he glanced, with a return of curiosity, at Markham. The man's face was white, completely composed, stiff somehow – mask-like. 'You must take care of yourselves, too,' he said. 'You have been under a strain. The boy should be all right now. He will sleep a lot at first. He is very debilitated, not surprising after such prolonged fever. The bowels will be disordered still for a day or two, so be careful with food – boiled rice is best to begin with. I will come and see him again tomorrow.'

'Thank you,' Markham said suddenly, as if in response to this last assurance.

'*Tipote*,' Kyriakos said again, with the same smile.

He was accompanied to the door by Markham and took the opportunity of reminding him again that he should rest.

'You do not look well, my friend,' he said, regarding Markham's white, set face. 'Anyway, there is no point in your going to work today. Nobody in Constantinople will be working today, except the waiters and the pickpockets, of course.'

'Why is that?'

246

'You haven't seen the papers?' Kyriakos moved his head from side to side in a way that combined reproof for Markham's ignorance with pleasure at being about to impart information.

'I haven't been out,' Markham said.

'Abdul Hamid has granted the Constitution.' Kyriakos smiled satirically. 'This famous Constitution,' he said, 'that is going to heal all our ills. They are dancing in the streets already. You would not get a cab, even. Yes, it will be a good day for thieves.'

'Perhaps the thieves will be dancing too,' Markham said. He thought suddenly of Hartunian, remembering the tall figure with its slightly stooping posture, the shining eyes, the voice strong with belief. He had been right then – they had imposed the Constitution. This was what he had worked for all these years. He had lived in the narrow focus of a single overriding aim. To see it realized might not be an unmixed blessing . . .

'No,' Kyriakos said. 'They will carry on as usual. There must be some who are immune to these infections. Do you think the people know what they are dancing for?'

Markham looked at the doctor's heavy, humorous face. A man more different from Hartunian would be hard to find. Kyriakos had his being so far below the level of idealism that there was not even pain at its absence. And yet he had just helped to save a child's life. 'They are dancing for joy,' Markham said. 'It's enough reason, I suppose. Anyway. thank you again. *Evkaristo poli.*'

He usually employed his few words of Greek on the doctor as he knew it pleased him. Kyriakos smiled broadly. '*Parakalo, kyrie,*' he said. As he walked to the barouche waiting at the end of the drive, carrying his black leather bag, the doctor seemed suddenly a lonely figure to Markham, with neither belief nor suffering for company.

Later in the morning he went out himself, driven partly by curiosity, partly by the restless uneasiness he felt in the house

247

now, with his son out of danger and his wife silent and constrained with him – she had barely spoken to him since that night of their son's delirium when his relations with Miss Taverner had come spilling out through the boy's cracked lips, in a tumbled, urgent mimicry of sounds and words, more damning in their cumulative effect than any accusation could have been. He had not looked once at Elizabeth's face, but had sensed the bitter knowledge growing on it. How the boy could have known so much was a mystery still, but there was no one he could ask – certainly not Henry himself.

The streets above the waterfront were thronged with people with smiling, rather dazed-looking faces. They spoke to each other, sometimes called out, but not very loudly, passing on the news of the Sultan's *iradé*. Markham could hear the sibilant message passing among them. They were of all kinds and degrees, officials in frockcoats or the high-necked tunics of the Civil Service, officers in uniform, *hammals* and stevedores in their leather aprons. Markham saw shopkeepers among them and chefs, and policemen – no doubt having left their duties unattended. Some wore the red and white cockade of liberty, which they must have been keeping in readiness, perhaps for many years – it was surely too soon, he thought, for the shops to be selling them.

In these first hours of the proclamation, Markham saw no dancing nor any great demonstration of joy. In fact it was the absence of this that impressed him and then, quite suddenly, moved him in a way that was totally unexpected. The dazed, still not fully believing faces, the murmured repetition of the news, the mixture of classes and races and creeds unified by a sense of shared good fortune, something reverential almost in the way the word was spread amongst them, all this revived in Markham some long-obscured religious sense of good tidings, of a message that would transform human destinies. He did not believe, any more than Kyriakos, in the efficacy of the Constitution, at least in its power to do what the people hoped of it, to dispel overnight a miasma of corruption and

248

tyranny that had lain over the country for more than thirty years. Moreover, the changes envisaged were too great to be achieved without violence. Everything he knew of historical precedent and everything he sensed as probable told him that more would be needed than an ultimatum from the Third Army Corps to turn an Islamic theocracy of five hundred years' standing into a modern democratic state on the French or English model.

Nevertheless, as he walked back up the sloping streets towards his house he felt in this collective hope of the people something – and this whether it was illusory or not – that offered a term to his own isolation. He did not feel it, this shared emotion, but he felt a sort of nostalgia for it, as if it would free him from the burden of being himself, or perhaps lead him back to some truer self, before all accretions and disfigurements.

Once the crisis of his illness was over, Henry recovered strength quickly. Within three days his temperature was back to normal. Before this, while he was still rather ill, Miss Taverner came to see him. She sat beside his bed for a while, and he saw that her eyes were swollen. She said she had to go away. 'You won't forget me, will you?' she said and her eyes filled with tears. His own eyes lowered in embarrassment, he muttered that he wouldn't. She kissed him, then went out quickly. Afterwards he felt unhappy and wished he had kissed Miss Taverner back instead of holding his head away from her. He did not want to think that she had gone away for ever.

Thereafter he dozed and read or was read to through a succession of white identical days – read to by his mother, not once by Miss Taverner, who did not come into his room again. The question which this raised in his mind lingered on through the days of his convalescence, some scruple or intuition preventing him from asking until the time came when he was allowed to get up in the middle part of the day and sit in the sunshine on the terrace. Miss Taverner was not

249

here either, and one day when his mother was reading to him about Theseus and the Minotaur, he suddenly interrupted her to ask where Miss Taverner was, why she had gone away.

His mother put the book down in her lap, keeping a finger between the pages so as not to lose the place. 'Miss Taverner had to go away quite suddenly,' she said. 'She was called away.'

'Called away?'

'She was not able to say good-bye,' his mother explained, 'because you were still quite ill and there wasn't much time.'

Henry looked steadily and seriously at his mother sitting opposite him in the blue dress with the white collar and cuffs, which he particularly liked. Her fair hair was parted in the middle and framed her face softly. Her blue eyes regarded him with a seriousness equal to his own. There was a good deal here that Henry did not understand, but a tact beyond his years held him back from speaking. He saw that his mother believed the truth of what she was saying. She did not know that Miss Taverner had been to see him and cried and kissed him. But if she did not know this it could only be because Miss Taverner had concealed it from her, and why should she do that? His mother was keeping something back from him, too. It concerned his father, he knew, though he could not see exactly how. But that part of his life which had contained Miss Taverner belonged already to the past, to the time before his illness, as did the voices in the darkness of the garden, the inhuman sounds from the summer-house. All this lay at the other side of his fever, before that rope of song brought all the sound together. The world to which he had returned was a strangely elemental one, containing just a few salient features. Chief among these was the fact that he was going home to England soon, with his mother. As soon as he was well enough to travel they would be going home.

Also belonging to that blurred undifferentiated time before his illness was Ayshe, with her odd, vivid clothes and trailing songs, her made-up face serene in the sun-dappled interior of the hut, the doll-like effect of her drooping head. Still, he wanted to see her again before he left, and when he was well enough to get about on his own he asked permission to go and visit her, to say good-bye. His mother at first wanted Nevres Badji to accompany him. She could see that he didn't overdo things, didn't overtax his strength. But he didn't want to go knocking at the door with Nevres Badji; he wanted to go on his own, in the usual way by the path. And in the end all this was conceded, though it was still not like the previous visits, because he had to wear his brown knickerbocker suit and a high-collared shirt and a tie. Also, he was taking flowers, white roses from the garden, to give to Ayshe.

The flowers had been his own idea. They would be a present. He had kept a vivid memory of the day his father had come home from work early and interrupted his lesson with Miss Taverner. He had stood just inside the door, in his uniform, in one hand a large bunch of white carnations. Their scent had filled the room during the few minutes that his father and Miss Taverner had talked. His father had given Miss Taverner one of the flowers . . .

It had been a good year for roses. They were still abundant on the bushes below the terrace. Ibrahim cut the flowers for him and took the thorns off the stems, and Nevres Badji arranged them in a bunch and tied a broad piece of red ribbon round them. Before he set out he went to see his mother, who was reading in the drawing room. She inspected him carefully.

'Now remember that you have been ill,' she said, as if it was something he was likely to forget. It was afternoon and she was wearing a long gown with a trailing skirt and a pattern of lace at the front. Her face looked pale and sad, he thought, as it nearly always did these days, though she was smiling a little now as she looked at him.

'You look very nice,' she said. 'I'm sure the little girl will be very pleased with the flowers.'

'Her name is Ayshe,' he said. It sounded like a rebuke almost, but this was because he was nervous, now that the time had come to execute the first part of his plan. He had begun tugging at the roses and after a moment succeeded in pulling one out from the rest, loosening the ribbon in the process.

'What are you doing?' she said.

Henry held out the rose stiffly, at arm's length, avoiding his mother's eyes. 'This one is for you,' he said.

This gesture once performed, the rose once taken from him, he was in a hurry to get out of the room, so much so that he almost omitted to look at her face. When he did so, however, he saw at once that she was pleased. Her smile was different and her eyes were wider, more open. When she kissed him he was already turning away, glad to have done what he intended, to have carried it off. His gesture had been a success, nothing had gone wrong – that was the main thing. He was afraid always of things going wrong, of somehow behaving inappropriately; it was the fear of the imitator, who inevitably has to leave some things to chance – he could not have reproduced all the circumstances that had made his father's gift of the carnation to Miss Taverner so elegant and fine.

For some time, as he made his way through the garden and out on to the path behind, he congratulated himself. Then, thoughts of the impending visit began to occupy him; he began to plan phase two.

Ayshe was not at the gate. He put the flowers down on the edge of the path, plucked a blade of grass and made the screech with it that was their usual signal. He waited for a while, then blew again. Nothing happened. He tried for a third time. He stood for perhaps three or four minutes at the gate but there was no sign of Ayshe. Henry debated with himself as to what he should do. Normally he would simply have returned home, but on this occasion, dressed as he was and with the flowers, he was reluctant to do this. He had made up his mind what he was going to do and say. The expedition had started well. He was set on success. He thought of making a platform of stones so that he could look through the bars of the gate. Then he remembered that on his last visit the gate had not been locked at all, Ayshe had simply pulled it open. There was no handle on his side, but when he set his weight against the gate it began to swing inward at once and after a moment he was able to slip through. However, the process had to be repeated because he had left the roses on the path outside.

The garden was large, more open and orderly than his own, once the shrubbery near the gate had been traversed. A broad path, laid out in a pattern of black and white pebbles, went straight through the middle, and Henry followed this, past a small marble fountain and a little dark grove of mulberry trees. The long white façade of the house rose before him. There were steps up to a terrace, a green wooden door. He was at the rear part of the house.

Here, clutching the roses, he hesitated. No sound came to him from the house. Alone there, he felt his resolution falter. Suddenly he heard the lonely outcry of the muezzin from the mosque below at Beshiktash, calling the third prayer of the day. It seemed like a warning. He was on the point of retiring, of retracing his steps through the garden, when a woman in black dress and black headscarf came round the corner of the house on to the terrace. She uttered an exclamation and made the usual gesture of modesty in the first moment of seeing the male stranger, drawing the *tcharshaf* more closely about her face. But then, seeing that he was no more than a child, she walked towards him and spoke to him in words that he did not understand.

'I want to see Ayshe, please,' he said, very clearly and distinctly. 'Ayshe.'

'*Ayshe istiorsen?*' the woman said. She looked at him a moment then nodded her head slowly. It seemed to Henry that she knew who he was. She made a sign for him to wait, then disappeared again round the side of the house. After a short while, the green door was opened and the man who had visited his parents stepped out on to the terrace.

He did not smile, but shook Henry firmly by the hand, immediately afterwards leading him through the door and along a passage that opened into a large square hall. Here Henry waited again for a few minutes. Then the man reappeared, accompanied now by a stout handsome woman in a loose light-brown dress and an embroidered scarf worn loosely over her head and shoulders.

He indicated the boy and spoke again and she nodded.

'How do you do?' Henry said, and bowed a little, as he had been taught.

The woman made a slight salaam, afterwards turning to her husband and saying a few words in a low voice. Her eyes, Henry now noticed, were puffy and swollen-looking like Miss Taverner's had been. Though of course, he thought, they might always look like this.

The three of them now crossed the hall together and started up the steps of a broad straight staircase, Henry and the woman walking side by side, the man just a little behind. On the wall at the head of the stairs there was a picture of a bearded man in a turban. Henry, still carrying the roses, was escorted a few yards along a corridor then ushered into a largish, square-shaped bedroom. On the side of the room facing the door, Ayshe was sitting propped up by pillows in a bed covered by a scarlet counterpane. Her face was as white as the pillows behind her.

The parents, after saying some words presumably to announce him, left the room, closing the door softly. Henry walked some way towards the bed, then stopped. He felt awkward and at a loss, guilty too – he had given Ayshe his illness somehow, so he assumed in these first moments. To cover his embarrassment he drew the corners of his mouth down in a ludicrous grimace. Ayshe smiled. She did not move or attempt to raise her head, but her eyes were fixed steadily on him in expectation. After a moment or two of hesitation he began to advance again, making himself look dignified and solemn, holding the roses out with both hands. When he was near the bed he pretended to stumble and made his eyes go big with alarmed outrage. As usual his loss of dignity amused

254

her. The smile deepened on her face, but her head did not move from the pillow. Beside her, in a row, their heads also resting on the pillows, were a large ginger-coloured teddy bear with glassy black eyes and a stitched-on smile, a cloth sailor-boy with rosy cheeks and a girl doll with long scornful eyelashes and a blue ribbon in her hair.

With restored self-possession Henry sat on the edge of the bed and shook hands with the teddy bear. 'How do you do?' he said. 'Keeping well?'

This ploy did not succeed as well as his pretended contretemps, partly because Ayshe's attention was now on the flowers. '*Guzel*,' she said. '*Les fleurs sont belles*.' Her voice was without force.

He put the roses down on the bed between them. She picked them up and after a moment laid them on her lap. 'What's the matter?' he said. He could not understand why she was so weak and ill. His recollections of his own illness were of heat and torment. They somehow did not correspond with this whiteness and stillness. '*Comment allez-vous?*' he asked, remembering one of Monsieur Renier's phrases from his book.

'*Je suis malade*,' she said, and there was a familiarity with the condition, a fatalism in the quiet voice that he felt without understanding. Once more at a loss he leaned over and tweaked the teddy bear's left ear with his finger and thumb.

'*Yapma*,' she said. '*Laisse-le*.'

'I'm going back to England,' he said after a moment. '*Angleterre*.' He pointed to himself. '*Moi. Dans quelques jours*. I've come to say good-bye.'

She nodded slightly. The smile had gone now. The only colour in her face was in her lips. Her hands too, he noticed, were dead white against the red of the counterpane on which they rested. One hand had four different rings on it – he counted them several times over. Once again, as when he had noticed her pierced ears, he was visited by an amazed sense of her extravagance and excess. *Four rings*. He could not see

255

whether she had the earrings on because her hair was down, covering her ears.

He could not think of anything more to say to Ayshe and the constraint of the occasion was beginning to induce a sort of solemn boredom in him, such as he sometimes felt among gatherings of adults. He was glad when he heard the door open and the voice of the mother. He got up at once and turned towards her. 'I have to go now,' he said. 'It's tea-time.' The woman was not looking at him, however, but at the bed. Her cheeks were wet. While he watched he saw her mouth, which was rather small for so large a person, tighten suddenly in a kind of grimace.

In confusion he turned back towards the bed, saw in that moment what the mother had seen. The white-faced girl with her dolls, the white flowers laid across her. Some association tugged briefly at his mind then was lost again. He remembered now that people should shake hands when parting for long periods. He turned back to Ayshe and took her hand. It was cool, slightly damp-feeling. He gave it a slight shake then dropped it. He had some idea of shaking hands with the mother too, not wanting to leave out any of the formalities of his visit; but she now uttered a brief sobbing sound that made him abandon the idea at once, and he crossed the room to the door without looking again at her. She did not follow him out but the woman in black was on the landing outside and she accompanied him downstairs. As he descended he heard the same sound again, louder now and more prolonged.

The father was nowhere to be seen. Henry parted from the woman more or less at the point where he had met her, and made his way alone back to the gate and along the path to his own house. The water in the stream-bed had almost all gone now, in the succession of hot dry days that had followed the rain, though there were patches of wet here and there, and a brackish smell of moisture still mingled with the rank scent of camomile and dead elderflower. Small clouds of greenish, glinting flies rose and fell above these diminishing areas of damp as if enjoying some special essence from them.

As Henry made his way along the path, his hands free, the flowers successfully delivered, he began to feel extremely happy. Ayshe's white face and her mother's weeping quickly faded from his mind. I'm going back to England soon, he reminded himself. Very soon now.

That his wife intended to leave, that she was making her own arrangements during the period of Henry's convalescence, Markham knew, though she did not ask his help in any way – indeed conversation between them had now been reduced to the minimum consistent with politeness. Miss Taverner's abrupt departure, to which neither of them had yet made a single reference, lay always between them, becoming more oppressive as their unnatural silence on the subject lengthened.

This domestic constraint and suppression of feeling formed a contrast, ironic to Markham's mind, with public events during these days. The quietness, the half-doubting daze of joy which he had noted on the morning of the Sultan's proclamation, had not lasted long. When there was no official denial and the news came really to be believed, Constantinople gave itself up to a frenzy of rejoicing unequalled even in the brief, halcyon days of 1876 when Midhat had introduced the Constitution – that Midhat whom Abdul Hamid had first exiled and then had strangled.

As Markham travelled to and from his office, or generally about the city, he saw scenes enacted which he would not have believed possible only a short while before. He saw Greek Orthodox priests and *mollahs* clasped in fervent embrace. He saw Turk and Bulgar, Kurd and Armenian – people whom every circumstance of history and race and geographical accident had made archetypal foes – walk arm in arm in the public squares and thoroughfares. He saw the most fanatical Moslem elements in the population wearing the red and white cockade of liberty. Crowds surged

257

constantly in the square of Haghia Sophia and before the gates of the Sublime Porte, cheering for the Sultan and the Constitution in equal measure.

The exuberance of freedom so overflowed in the newspapers that a shortage of newsprint ensued and brown paper had to be resorted to for the expression of rejoicing. At street corners and on the quays where incoming vessels had to be tied up, postcards were offered for sale bearing inscriptions in many languages, together with symbolical portrayals of freedom, not always in the best of taste – Markham saw one which depicted a melancholy Abdul Hamid being kissed by a dimpled angel, symbolizing the awakening of Turkey. It was as impossible to forget the fact of rejoicing as it was to forget the faces of the Young Turk officers who were held to be the authors of it. The Heroes of the Revolution looked down from all sides, their portraits prominently displayed in shop fronts, on the walls of houses, the stalls of street-hawkers. These were the men who had 'freed Turkey from the Frankish yoke'. Chief among them were Niazi and Enver, the two who had been first to raise the standard of revolt.

Day by day Markham moved between these scenes of public euphoria and the constraint of his home. It was not until the eve of her departure that Elizabeth broke the silence between them, and when she did so it took him by surprise. Indeed, her words of reproach rose so immediately from a trivial context that it was some time before he understood what was happening. It was as if the dialogue had been going on elsewhere and only now became audible to him.

'At a time when your son was lying critically ill,' he suddenly heard her saying. 'That is what I can't understand. I shall never understand it. That you should so disregard our son.'

'I didn't disregard him,' he said, after a moment or two. 'Just the opposite, actually.'

'He could have died.' Elizabeth looked across the room at the stiff, composed face of this man to whom she had been married for eleven years. 'I feel as if I have never known you,' she said.

'And you take that for my fault, of course. It doesn't occur to you that some of the blame might be yours?'

'Blame?' she said, with sudden, bitter contempt. 'You feel misunderstood now, do you?'

'You never associate things, Elizabeth,' Markham said in quick, gloomy tones. 'You have no imagination. When you were having Henry I was drunk, if you remember. It isn't so very different. You've always looked at things only one way. At me too. I have never been the person you thought I was.'

'I thought you had a sense of honour,' she said. 'But I suppose I lacked imagination even there. At a time when Henry's life was in the balance, you left him and went to that woman's room.'

'So you got that out of her?'

'She told me the whole story. She didn't want to at first but I got it out of her.'

'I'm sure you did,' he said. 'I can imagine it. I doubt if it was the whole story though.'

There was silence between them for a few moments. They were in the front drawing-room, both standing, facing each other across the width of the bow window. He stood straight, with his hands in his trouser pockets, presenting to her the mask-like composure of his face. She had folded her arms across her breast as if to hold and support herself during these exchanges between them.

'I just don't know you any more,' she said. 'The girl, too, so young and in such a vulnerable position. She told me what happened, how you went to her room. You took advantage of her. I felt ashamed when she told me – the shame you should have felt.'

He saw the gleam of unshed tears in her eyes. 'I can't help what you know,' he said. 'You condemn what you don't understand. You always have.'

In spite of her distress she was in control of the situation: he

259

knew that. From the first moment of discovery, during the boy's delirium, when the disjointed words and sounds had fused into unambiguous meaning, she had controlled all the elements, herself included – orchestrated them almost, he thought, with a cynicism involuntary and self-wounding. She had lost little time before confronting Miss Taverner. He could, as he had said, imagine the interview. Elizabeth, armed with outrage, would have stripped away all attempts at subterfuge or evasion, learned everything, the times, the places. The girl, having been thus reduced, must have been given instructions to pack at once. She had simply disappeared, though it had taken Markham some days fully to realize this. A kind of cowardice had prevented him from enquiring immediately, and afterwards, with each day, it had become less possible to do so.

'Where is she?' he asked.

'I'm not going to tell you that, Robert,' she said. 'She is quite safe.'

He nodded. Safe from him, she meant, of course. But she was wronged, she was entitled to her own confusions of motive. He saw her hand move to her throat, finger the silver and amethyst cross she wore there. She held it for a moment enclosed in her palm, as if vowing something on it or getting strength from the touch.

'I can't talk about it any more now,' she said. 'Perhaps later, at home, when we are away from this place.'

She relinquished the cross, moved her hand uncertainly, nervously, down the front of her dress. He continued to look fixedly at it, this simple ornament, the arms of the cross broadening a little at the ends, the soft glow of the amethysts against the smooth silver. He had seen it before – Elizabeth wore often the jewellery she liked, as she did clothes. But now it seemed emblematic of everything about her, everything she used, the delicate simplicity, the pathos of one who knew almost no personal artifice, who could not easily change or adapt, only offer herself, for ever, as she was, and whose only defence when rejected or ill-used was the control she was showing now. Suddenly he was harrowed by the thought of what he had lost in her, of what he had thrown away, for ever. She was not a woman to trust again where trust had once been broken.

'I'm sorry,' he said. 'I love you.'

She made no reply to this, and the determined resolution of her manner did not abate.

'You once said you felt sorry for Colonel Nesbitt because he didn't care about anything,' Markham said. 'Do you remember? What you said would apply better to me. Nesbitt cared about things once. I never have.' He paused, then said more deliberately, looking at her face, 'Not even about the Armenians.'

She returned his look without change of expression. 'What do you mean?' she asked.

'It doesn't matter.' Miss Taverner had not spoken then. He was suddenly sure of it. Harassed as she had been she had kept his secret, token of his trust, as she would see it – the one thing she had that the wife hadn't.

Elizabeth paused some time longer as if awaiting an explanation. Then in a tone of deliberate indifference she said, 'All the arrangements have been made for the voyage. We are leaving tomorrow, as you know.'

'Yes,' he said. 'Everything is in order then?'

'Captain Blake has helped me a great deal,' she said.

'I see,' Markham said. 'Just the man for a crisis.'

She turned away at this, shortly afterwards leaving the room. For the rest of the time that Elizabeth and Henry remained in the house conversation was confined to practical matters – that one discharge of feeling had left the surface as before, or apparently so.

He saw them off, for form's sake more than anything else, at the Galata quay. Leave-taking was brief, quite unimpassioned. Neither gave any overt sign of awareness that they were parting unreconciled. Henry shook the hand his father offered him. Care to do the right thing, to behave as he thought his father expected, eclipsed all feeling on his face, which was as set and composed as Markham's own.

Once they were embarked Markham left immediately, not wanting the pain of watching the two of them slowly borne from him. This at least was the reason he was more immediately conscious of; but below the hurt of loss as he walked away lay other feelings, to which the hurt was merely an impediment: an eagerness for isolation, an unrepentant impatience to have done, to be left alone, here in this city which hadn't finished with him yet.

# Part Two

Part Two

Markham continued to live on alone in the house at Beshiktash. He could have saved money and been more comfortable in an apartment in Pera, but it did not really occur to him to move. The house was too deeply associated with the things that had happened to him since his return to Constantinople, the slow dissolving of his defence against the past, his growing sense of isolation. The very silence of the place, with most of its rooms unused now that his family had gone, kept him aware of this isolation in a way he found necessary now, as if there was some promise in it. Moreover, he was unwilling to leave the vicinity of Yildiz, where the Sultan had continued to reside: it seemed important to him that he should still be able, from the garden and from certain windows in the house, to have glimpses of the walls and roof-tops of the palace, and to see the night sky lit up by the three thousand lamps – this nightly blaze of terror continued unabated, though many of Abdul Hamid's fears had already overtaken him: he was a constitutional monarch now, his powers curtailed, his favourites dismissed, his Civil List under scrutiny.

As the weather got colder, with mist and cold winds coming off the Bosphoros, Markham reduced his living space to his bedroom and his study on the ground floor. Mehmet Agha lit a fire for him here in the afternoons so that when he returned from his office in Galata the room was warm. Mehmet continued to bring him shaving water in the mornings, see to his breakfast, make sure that copies of the *Yeni Gazeta* and the *Tanin* were there on the table – the European papers he read at the Embassy or the Press Club in Nishantash where he quite often had lunch. In the evenings Nevres Badji would cook for him if he wanted her to, though he usually preferred sandwiches, which he had brought to the study. He did not often go out, avoiding invitations whenever possible.

Quite soon his life settled into a state of suspension. He knew that he was waiting for something to happen. He had a sense of unfinished business, some responsibility or commitment that he had undertaken and that he would one day be called upon to fulfil. As if blunted by shock, he did not feel anything much stronger than regret for the harm he had done to his wife and to Miss Taverner. This too would have to be accounted for, but as part of a more general, much more complicated accounting. He was content for the moment to await this passively. He wrote home once a week and received several letters from his wife, cool, noncommittal letters, unadorned with endearments. Henry wrote once. He was going to be the Ghost of Time Past in the school production of *A Christmas Carol*. He was working hard at his lessons. He was learning to dive.

For a while, so great was the numbness of apparent indifference into which Markham fell that he ceased almost altogether to think about the activities of the Sultan, ceased to hear the call of that demon bidding him follow Abdul Hamid through all the phases of his being. The curiosity was still there, at times like a dull underlying excitement, part of his sense of unfulfilled commitment. But it was overlaid usually by this blankness of indifference that had descended on him.

To public events he was similarly indifferent, though his work kept him informed about what was going on. These were momentous times in the city, and in the Empire as a whole, where revolutionary fervour had continued in the weeks following the military coup – a bloodless coup, or almost so, after thirty years of bloody oppression, seeming in itself to verge on the miraculous, to be a cause for special celebration. In Constantinople the common people, who had not realized the extent of the movement in Macedonia and regarded the Constitution as the free gift of the Sultan,

266

assembled in vast crowds before Yildiz Kiosk to cheer him. (He encouraged them in this belief by making frequent appearances on his balcony, with the red and white cockade of liberty pinned to the plain grey military cloak he now wore.) The dismissal of the Palace favourites was demanded and granted – in fact, those of them who did not succeed in getting away were arrested and held pending investigation into their activities. The exiled Armenian patriarch Ismirlian was restored to his flock, and the famous Fuad Pasha, in exile all this time in Damascus for protecting Armenians during the 1896 massacres, was received at the quay by enthusiastic crowds of every race, Turkish women throwing off their veils and joining in the cheering with the men. This continuing sense of racial and religious harmony culminated in a solemn memorial service at the Armenian cemetery in Scutari, in which Christian priests and Mohammedan *mollahs* prayed together for the souls of the massacred, the 'martyrs of liberty'. This, in retrospect, was seen by many as the high point in that spirit of reconciliation which was so strong in the weeks following the Revolution. Thereafter there was a darkening, barely perceptible at first except as an increasing grimness of official tone in questions concerning the minority races.

Markham was kept busy, though the volume of work had no effect on the general sense of indifference that he felt during this time. Blake, as expected, had not returned, so it fell to him to draw up the final summaries of the Macedonian gendarmerie issue. This had been abandoned for the time, though there was talk of forming militia units throughout the Empire – officered by Turks, however, not Europeans.

Other facts contributed to his burdens. Nesbitt's hours of work had become extremely irregular of late. There were days when he did not put in an appearance at all, others when despite the steadiness of his manner – the steadiness of an old soldier who shows no weakness on parade – or perhaps because of something too deliberate in this very steadiness, as also in the harsh voice, the staring eyes, it was clear that he had been attacking the bottle. Inevitably, therefore, much of the work of the Military Attaché's department fell on Markham and on Armstrong, the artillery subaltern, with whom he got on quite well, a cheerful, athletic young man with a slight stammer.

It was a time of intense diplomatic activity in Turkey, with all the powers bidding for the friendship of the new régime. In this contest Britain had considerable initial advantage. The new Ambassador, Sir Gerard Lowther, had arrived at the end of July, amidst scenes of great public enthusiasm, and declared his Government's support. *The Times* had come out with a leading article encouraging the Young Turks in their aims and policies. Britain, and the British, reached great heights of popularity during these early weeks. They were associated with the movement for liberty and with liberal institutions generally, whereas the Germans were identified with the old régime. It was official policy to exploit this situation in Britain's interests, and Markham's orders were to do everything possible to promote good relations with the Turkish military authorities. It was hoped in Whitehall that the British could supplant the Germans in the crucial role of military advisers to the Turks, though Markham himself did not believe this was possible. The German influence was too strong, especially among the junior officers. Unit formation was on German lines and the Turkish troops were drilled in the goose-step. Nevertheless he discharged his duties as ordered, attending frequent briefings at the Embassy, now back in Pera for the winter, liaising with the Turkish authorities, collecting what information he could about the attitudes of the new leadership.

However, it was not any development in public events that brought Markham out of the numbness and indifference of those weeks following his wife's departure, but an insult offered to him personally during an altercation with Nesbitt at the Pera Club.

He liked the Pera Club, which combined the best features of a Viennese café and a London club. It had a bar and a restaurant, and a reading-room with leather armchairs and long brass clips used for holding the newspapers while you were reading them. The bar was spacious and the tables were solid, square-topped affairs, not the spindly contraptions elsewhere becoming fashionable. The barman's name was Alex and he came – by obscure paths – from Beirut.

It was fairly early in the evening when Markham arrived and there were not many people in the bar yet. He asked for a whisky and soda. Through the mirror behind the bar he caught sight of Worseley-Jones sitting at a table, talking to a man in the uniform of a naval officer.

'Well,' he said to the barman, 'how is life these days?'

Alex smiled and shrugged. 'The same,' he said. 'Nothing has changed.' He had dark curly hair which he oiled with some faintly sweet substance. His eyes were raisin-coloured, with an expression flat and uncurious, though quite alert.

'Nothing changes here,' Markham said, glancing round.

'Even outside,' Alex said. 'Not so many Arab noses at Yildiz now, that is the only change.'

'Come now.' Markham deliberately avoided looking again into the mirror. 'Things are better than they were,' he said.

'People say so.' Alex picked up a cloth and began a ritual circular polishing of the bar surface, already gleaming. Following the movements with his eyes, he said, 'Where is this great improvement people talk about? Everywhere it is the same *baksheesh* that makes the wheels go round.'

'You really are a pessimistic fellow,' Markham said. 'It must be something to do with your occupation.'

'I hear things,' Alex said, with dignity. 'I have an uncle in the catering trade, he has the concession for olive oil to the First Army Corps here in Constantinople.'

'Very profitable, I should think,' Markham said. 'Give me another whisky, will you?' Once again he found himself wondering about Alex's country of origin. Beirut, it seemed, had been only a staging post from somewhere else. Speculations about the barman's nationality always seemed curiously irrelevant: he was a composite figure somehow, as if all the races of the Empire had gone into his being. 'Well, what about this uncle?' Markham said.

'He tells me a lot.' Alex narrowed his eyes meaningfully. 'The troops are not happy,' he said. 'Their pay is in arrears still. They regard the officers of the Committee as atheists, without respect for the Koran and the *Sheriat*. Moreover they have now to spend such long hours on drill that they have no time for their *kaif*, their coffee and cigarettes, nor to wash their clothes. They have not even time for their prayers, they say. They are getting very unsatisfied, Captain Markham.'

'They were too idle before,' Markham said. 'You can't run a modern army and allow two hours' *kaif* every day in addition to meals and regular breaks for prayer.'

At this point two men, Levantines in Western clothes, came up to the bar and Alex moved along to serve them. Markham thought for some moments about what the barman had said. It was true of course that disillusionment had followed in the wake of the revolution, and not only among the troops. No foreigner living in Constantinople during this autumn of 1908 could be unaware of deterioration once the first phase of euphoria was over. It was a slow process and there were differences of course as to when it became apparent, each person noticing it in his own way; but almost everyone had small, disquieting experiences to relate, insolence on the part of the soldiery, intransigence of an official, some return to the brutal contempt for the *giaour*, the infidel. At the same time the tone of domestic politics had grown more bitter and vituperative. The Palace archives were currently being investigated, the millions of words of secret correspondence sifted through, reports of spies from every province of the Empire, dating back to the 1870s, which the mania of the Sultan had prevented him from destroying. Daily lists of implicated persons were published in the press. Those accused, when they could be found, were taken into custody and held while their cases were being prepared for trial. Accounts of the swindles of the Palace pashas had also now started to appear in the newspapers. Unable to accuse the Sultan directly because of the reverence in which the mass of people still held him, the Committee sought by these public exposures of corruption to discredit him along with his instruments. At the same time, on one pretext or another, they had gradually reduced his establishment: by the end of October his private theatre at Yildiz had been closed, his three hundred musicians dismissed, his two hundred and ninety aides-de-camp whittled down to a mere thirty and his famous Arab stud farm taken over by the state . . .

'That is not the only thing,' Alex said, moving back along the bar towards him. 'There was a gentleman in here last night who works at the Banque Ottomane.'

But Markham was destined not to hear anything further about this person, because Alex's attention was claimed by another customer and he was obliged to break off to serve him; and while this was happening Markham looked across the room and caught the eye and smile of Worseley-Jones, who instantly raised a hand to beckon him over. Seeing no alternative, Markham carried his drink over to their table. Worseley-Jones introduced the man with him as Lieutenant-Commander Phelps.

'Phelps has come over with Admiral Saunders,' he said, 'on the naval commission.'

Markham nodded. 'Plenty of scope for advice, I expect,' he said.

Phelps laughed. He was a thickset man of about forty-five, clean-shaven, with a florid good-humoured face. 'I should say so,' he said. 'First job has been to get the decks cleared of vegetable gardens. There were whole families living on some of the ships.'

'No chance of the army doing the same?' Worseley-Jones said. He was lounging back in his chair, in one of those

271

naturally elegant reclinations his body invariably seemed to fall into. As always he was irreproachably dressed, this evening in a dark serge suit of impeccable cut. And as always the slight frown, the underlying seriousness of the question, belied the lounging posture, the smooth face and smooth hair. Worseley-Jones never really relaxed, never ceased to be a member of the diplomatic corps.

'You mean living on the decks of the battleships?' Markham said.

'No, of course not,' Worseley-Jones said, the slightly worried look on his face remaining. 'I mean the army getting a chance to advise on Turkish military reorganization. We've got English irrigation engineers advising in Mesopotamia, English experts putting the Customs in order, an English admiral superintending the reorganization of the navy. The army is the only gap.'

There was a note almost of reproach in his voice, as if Markham were somehow responsible for this weak link in the otherwise perfect chain of English influence.

'The Germans are too strongly entrenched,' Markham said with some acerbity. 'You know that yourself. They were early in the field.'

'Yes.' Worseley-Jones pondered a moment. 'I don't think they like us that much anyway,' he said. 'The Young Turks, I mean – the people like us well enough for the moment. It's worrying.'

'Another drink?' Phelps asked. He tapped on the table for Adriano, the waiter. Markham asked for whisky and soda, Worseley-Jones for a gin and tonic, without ice. 'I don't like ice in drinks,' he said in the same thoughtful tone, as if this too had something to do with the threat to British influence.

'Are you a submarine man or a dreadnought man?' Markham asked Phelps. He was beginning to feel the effects of the whisky now.

'I'm not quite sure what you mean,' Phelps said. He was smiling, but he spoke rather stiffly.

'Or like your chief do you manage to be both?' Markham said. He caught sight of his French opposite number on the gendarmerie commission, Major Godard, standing alone at the bar, and waved to him. He saw the Frenchman start moving towards them.

'I don't know what you mean,' Phelps said.

Markham stood to introduce Godard to the others. 'We were talking about the navy,' he said.

'Which navy?' Godard asked, with a slight smile. He was a slim, tense man with pale eyes and a moustache waxed into points.

'The British navy,' Phelps said. 'The French haven't got one, as far as I know.' He smiled as he spoke, but his eyes rested steadily and without particular kindness on the Frenchman.

'*Vous vous trompez*,' Godard said with acid politeness.

'Have a seat,' Markham said. 'He says you are mistaken,' he said to Phelps who had not understood.

'*Il plaisante*,' Worseley-Jones said, also addressing Godard. 'He is joking. Here's Adriano. What about another drink?'

They all ordered drinks except Godard, who explained that he had to leave almost at once. He was going to a reception at the French Embassy.

'I suppose you were talking about Fisher just now?' Phelps said to Markham.

'Yes,' Markham said. 'Extraordinary man. Says he believes in the supremacy of the submarine and then proceeds to build iron-clad warships, which are the submarine's born victims. I suppose you'll admit there is a contradiction there?'

He had spoken in his usual clipped, sardonic manner, aware of the naval man's growing dislike, not much caring.

'We're building submarines too,' Phelps said. 'We've got over fifty already.'

'That only makes the contradiction worse, it seems to me.'

'Dreadnoughts are marvellous ships,' Worseley-Jones said, with instinctive tact. 'They're a mixed blessing, though – they encourage German emulation, for one thing. In order to keep our lead we have to go on building more and more of them. There's no end to it. And they are terribly expensive.'

'Asquith wants to keep us short so he can spend more on his precious social service schemes,' Phelps said.

Godard leaned forward, looking across at Phelps. 'France is not interested in your navy,' he said.

'Indeed?'

'*Pas du tout*. Your ships will not help us. Ships did not help us in 1870. Can you take them up the Rhine? We had to fight on land then and it is the same now. We need soldiers from our allies, not ships.'

'If you think,' Phelps said, 'that we are going to sacrifice our advantage at sea simply in order to put troops at your disposal to be shot to ribbons on the Continent, then you are mistaken.'

The good humour had vanished completely from his face. It was absurd really, Markham thought, to assume such attitudes. Phelps would obey his orders, like anybody else. He was talking now as if policy decisions rested with him alone. Markham glanced round the room. There were more people now and he saw several faces that he knew. Henderson, the American journalist, entered the bar and paused just inside the door, glancing round the tables. Godard, his drink finished, stood up and took his leave, formal and polite as ever.

'Can't say I take to that fellow,' Phelps said. 'Colleague of yours I gather?' He managed to infuse the question with disapproval.

Markham felt a sudden impatience with the insular, self-righteous tone, the appeal to their common Englishness to justify prejudice. 'Yes,' he said. 'I like him. And I think he's absolutely right. Ships aren't going to keep the Germans off Paris.' He got to his feet. 'Excuse me,' he said. 'There's someone over there I want to speak to.'

Henderson had established himself on a stool at one end of

the bar, leaning comfortably against the wall. His loose black jacket hung open to show an expanse of burgundy-red waistcoat with large gilt buttons. His glass was almost lost in his huge hand. He smiled broadly when he saw Markham.

'Have a drink,' he said. 'What'll it be?'

'Whisky and soda, please,' Markham said.

'Alex has just been telling me about a relative of his.'

'He's got relatives everywhere,' Markham said. 'This one was his uncle, I suppose, the olive-oil man.'

'Yes, how did you know?'

'He told me the same story.'

Henderson laughed. 'So much for the exclusive sources my newspaper talks so proudly about.'

'You've been away, haven't you?'

'I've been up in Salonika,' Henderson said. 'Having a look at some of the men of the hour. Very interesting, very instructive.'

'In what way?'

'Well, it's a different thing entirely from Constantinople, you know. Those people up there, they really mean business.'

'The army, you mean?'

'The army and the middle class generally. There's a very strong professional element there, basically Jewish. They are behind the new régime to a man, just about. So the Committee has got guns and money and that is a winning combination.'

'I would have thought they'd won already,' Markham said.

Henderson's expression of genial sagacity deepened. He shook his head a little. 'There are plenty of people here who would like to see the autocracy restored,' he said. 'The Sultan's secret police, the *khafie*, for example, most of whom are still in the same positions they were before. Then there's the multitude of sacked spies, fifty odd thousand of them, their bread gone. They talk to the troops whenever they can, spreading disaffection. Even the army is not altogether reliable. I gather – at least, not here. But you would know more about that.'

'No, you are right,' Markham said. 'The First Army Corps has always been the one most loyal to the Sultan. And they're distinctly fed up at the moment because some of their units are under orders for the Yemen, which is a very unpopular posting, as you can imagine, with fever and Arabs to contend with. It is really what they call the *alailis*, the ranker officers, who are the main trouble, as far as we can make out. They're an ignorant, bigoted lot. And fanatically Moslem, of course. The school-trained officers are quite different. But it's the *mollahs* who are the greatest danger I think. The Young Turk officers are not taking enough care to show respect for the Holy Law. They're being called atheists by their own men. If religious feeling gets inflamed there could be trouble.'

'It's unlikely, I think, unless something happens to bring it all together. People get disillusioned, but that's only natural – they had very exaggerated notions of what liberty would mean. There was one case, up in Salonika while I was there, a Bulgarian Moslem who was being tried for murdering a Christian. When they found him guilty and sentenced him to death he made a great scene in the courthouse. "But we have liberty now," he said. "You promised us liberty." He was furious.'

Markham laughed, as much at Henderson's expression as at the story. 'They're refusing to pay the toll on the Galata Bridge, for the same reason,' he said. At this moment he felt a heavy hand on his shoulder. He half-turned on his stool to see Nesbitt standing beside him, a Nesbitt, for the first time in Markham's experience, dressed not in uniform but in a dark, double-breasted suit, which his thick body strained tight across the chest.

'Well, well, well,' Nesbitt said. 'If it isn't young Markham.'

His voice had the usual, derisive grating quality, but when Markham glanced at his face he saw that the pale eyes under their heavy brows were glazed-looking, not properly focused.

'This is Colonel Nesbitt,' he said to Henderson. 'The Military Attaché here. Mr James Henderson, sir. Mr Henderson is a correspondent for the *New York Herald*.'

'All papers print lies,' Nesbitt said. 'Nothing but lies. What are you drinking?' Without waiting for a reply he said to Alex, 'Same again for all of us.'

Alex complied. There was no particular expression on his face but it was somehow apparent that he did not like Nesbitt very much.

'How goes it with the gendarmes?' Nesbitt said. 'Pretty much of a dead duck by now, eh?' His drink was neat brandy.

'For the moment, yes.' It was the first time Markham had spoken to Nesbitt, except for the barest official exchanges, since their disagreement at the conference. He recognized the need to be wary, but the drink he had consumed lowered his guard somewhat. 'Everything takes time in this country, as you know,' he said.

'I hope you're not going to say anything against Turkish methods of conducting business,' Nesbitt said, in what seemed to be intended as a joking tone. 'Let's go and sit at a table. These bar stools are bloody uncomfortable.'

Markham had a vague idea of rejoining Worseley-Jones and Phelps at their table, mainly as a way of diffusing Nesbitt, spreading his disagreeableness thinner; but they had gone, the table was now occupied by other people. They found a small table against the wall and sat down at that.

'American, eh?' Nesbitt said to Henderson.

'All the way from Baltimore,' Henderson said in his slow deep voice. He was relaxed, sitting back in his chair, looking across at Nesbitt.

'He said you were from New York,' Nesbitt said, with a motion of his head towards Markham. He had finished his drink already. Markham saw his tongue protrude very briefly at the corner of his mouth, as if to make sure that the mouth was still intact. He realized that Nesbitt was drunker than he had thought. Or perhaps it was this last drink that had tipped him over.

277

'It's a New York newspaper,' Henderson said. 'But they are broadminded – we've even got a feller from Alabama on the staff.'

Nesbitt's expression did not change. 'Don't listen to this chap,' he said, again indicating Markham without looking at him. 'He's got a soft spot for certain sections of the population.'

'What do you mean?' Markham asked quickly. 'What soft spot?'

Nesbitt said nothing more for the moment, merely continued to look with a sort of ponderous shrewdness at the American. Henderson drank some of his brandy and soda, afterwards keeping his large head with its close-cut grey hair lowered for a while as if in some process of degustation. Then he looked up. His eyes were deep-set, hazel-coloured – unexpectedly fine eyes in the big, rough-featured face.

'I listen to everybody,' he said mildly.

'He'll tell you everything is marvellous, now that his precious Committee of Union and Progress is in power. Christ, what a title.'

'Of course things are better.' Markham looked with steady dislike at the side of Nesbitt's face presented to him, with its blunt nose, bristling fair moustache, prominent vein at the temple. 'After thirty years of institutionalized evil how could they not be?'

'Twaddle,' Nesbitt said. 'Sentimental socialist twaddle.' He had spoken loudly and several people at nearby tables glanced round. 'I'll tell you how far things have changed,' he said – still, with peculiar offensiveness, addressing himself only to Henderson. 'Last week, outside the mosque at Beshiktash, a Moslem mob killed a Greek youth. They tore him to pieces, literally. His crime?' He paused and sat back for effect. 'He was engaged to a Turkish girl,' he said. 'The police stood by and watched. That is your racial harmony under this gang of a Committee.'

'Nothing to do with the Committee,' Markham muttered.

278

There was a recklessness in Nesbitt's speech which he did not feel the drink could altogether account for. To express such public hostility to the new régime was almost grotesquely indiscreet for a man in his position.

Henderson was looking at him with a sort of speculative interest. 'I was here back in the 90s,' he said. 'Marriages between Greeks and Turks were not uncommon then, at least not in Constantinople.'

'That's what I'm saying.' Nesbitt raised a hand and snapped his fingers in an attempt to attract Adriano's attention. 'Where *is* the bastard?'

'You're missing the point, I think,' Henderson said. 'If they are going to lynch people now, it must mean the people have been worked on in some way, their religious feelings, I mean.'

'With this war scare,' Markham said, 'it's a wonder there aren't more such incidents.'

'There will be,' Nesbitt said. 'How about another drink?' He rapped loudly on the table with the bottom of the glass.

'Not for me,' Markham said. He paused briefly, then he said, 'You seem to take a good deal of pleasure in the prospect, Colonel Nesbitt.'

Now at last Nesbitt turned his head. Markham saw the small eyes narrow suddenly. His first feeling was one of regret for having allowed himself to be provoked. Then, characteristically, the sense that he had been unwise angered him more. Rage, as always with him, took the form of a cold, rigid demeanour masking inner tumult.

'That is not your business,' Nesbitt said. He paused, as if at a loss. Markham too was silent, trying to control his agitation. Then Nesbitt said, 'Quite a firebrand, aren't you, old chap?' All his hatred of rebellion was in the words. 'At a stage or two from the scene of action, of course,' he said after a brief pause. His voice was thicker now and his whole bearing had become slacker and more careless. He seemed to have deteriorated without having drunk more – evidence of a long course of drinking beforehand.

279

Markham looked at him a moment. 'You know what I think of Abdul Hamid,' he said. 'His rule has been a record of crimes. He's a criminal – one of the great killers of history. The harm he has done to the minds and bodies of his subjects is beyond calculation. And you sit there defending him. Anyone who defends him is a criminal too, an accomplice.' Suddenly, as he uttered this last word, a tiny crystal of certainty about Nesbitt formed in his mind. He looked straight into the other man's eyes. They were grey, he now noticed, with a strange, dispassionate particularity, not blue, and they had small greenish flecks round the pupils. 'An accomplice,' he said again. 'At a stage or two from the scene of action, of course.'

'An accomplice?' Nesbitt appeared to ponder a moment. Henderson spoke in his usual unhurried drawl, but neither Nesbitt nor Markham paid any attention to the words. They were looking narrowly at each other. Then Nesbitt advanced his face a little nearer to Markham's. 'We haven't all got your weakness for Armenians,' he said.

Markham felt the blood drain from his face. He saw Nesbitt raise one arm, apparently in an attempt to attract the attention of Alex behind the bar. 'No, just a minute,' he said. 'What do you mean?'

Nesbitt turned his unfocused stare back from the bar to Markham's face. 'Cowardly lot,' he said, and his lips twisted suddenly in a contempt that resembled a sudden stab of pain. 'They let themselves be butchered like sheep,' he said. 'I was here too – he's not the only one. They didn't raise a finger. Able-bodied men, *young* men, lying down offering their throats to be cut by a few skinny Kurds. I've seen rows of them, *tidy* rows, all dead. Despicable people. If you won't fight for your life you're not fit to live.'

'Courage is a mighty various thing,' Henderson said. 'There are different brands of it. Those young men could have saved themselves by accepting Islam. All they had to do was raise a hand and say a few words. Not many did.'

'No guts,' Nesbitt said, ignoring this. He glanced at Markham then looked away with an effect of indifference. 'Perhaps that's why they appeal to you,' he said. He placed both hands flat on the table as if about to lever himself up. 'I don't know which is worse,' he said, 'the cowardice of the men or the ugliness of the women.'

Markham heard Henderson's voice again, raised in expostulation, but he did not listen to the words. His vision blurred, then cleared. There was time enough, in this split second, for him to feel the pain of the insulted, which lies in the recognition that one has been specially singled out. He saw Nesbitt's face opposite him with extraordinary distinctness: dark red, blank-eyed, the vein prominent at the left temple. With a rapid but at the same time almost casual movement, Markham flung the contents of his glass straight into Nesbitt's face.

After this gesture in which impulse and act had achieved a perfect fusion, Markham's impressions were fragmentary. He stood up after a further moment and took a pace back from the table. Henderson had been the first on his feet – he was halfway round the table now, between the two men, as if to prevent them coming to blows. Nesbitt, however, sat quite still for some moments, not attempting to mop his face. He blinked several times as though the alcohol was stinging his eyes. Then he pushed back his chair with sudden violence. Henderson was close beside him now, bending his bulk solicitously over him. Markham saw the American take out a large white handkerchief. After standing there stiffly for a moment or two longer, he turned and left the bar, walking with head up through the hush that had fallen on the place.

He walked through the streets of the city for a length of time he did not measure. It was light still, and the sky beyond Seraglio Point was suffused dark pink, aftermath of the sunset. The evening was mild. He walked quickly at first, then more slowly; through the maze of narrow streets lying behind the Grande Rue, then down from the heights of Pera to the

281

crumbling-edged shelf of a street above the Little Field of the Dead. Here he stood for a while, looking over the cypresses of the cemetery to the vista of the Golden Horn and the domes and minarets of Stambul. Above the glint and haze of the city, crows wheeled in a gusty billow against the fading glow of the sky.

Gradually the tumult of his feelings quietened. But the conviction remained that somehow he had betrayed Miriam once again, just by allowing the insult to escape from Nesbitt's lips – his response had come too late, like all his responses, all his efforts to compensate. There was no compensation.

However, in the measure of calm that now returned to him, his thoughts turned with a more particular curiosity to Nesbitt himself. The man had been drunk, but it was more than drink that had made him so reckless. Nesbitt was a veteran of many drinking bouts, he would have learned discretion in his cups as a factor in survival. No, it was some particular combination that had led him on this evening, led him on to the brutal rudeness which he had not been able to resist and in yielding to which he had exposed his own throat. For it was true certainly that he had given himself away. The imputation of cowardice, the references to Armenians, these could only have come from Nesbitt's private sources. Nowhere in existence, on any document, in any file, was there an official record, provided by Markham himself, of his connexion with the Armenians. Nesbitt must have informants among them, or at any rate contacts with people close enough to get that sort of information. It had been on his own account that Nesbitt had had Hartunian watched. But what had driven him to show his hand so grossly tonight?

Markham resumed his walking, seeking as he did so to recall something in Nesbitt's face and manner that would give him a clue. He made his way past the small theatres of Pera. In front of one of them there was a poster advising the public of the coming visit of an Italian company to perform *Aida*. He thought of Miss Ada Lamb at the piano, monumental in her pale blue dress. The powdered shoulders, strong throat – her throat too, exposed. *Là tra foreste vergini.* All that belonged to the time before his son's illness, before he had seen the hurt and incomprehension on his wife's face. He was suddenly swept with misery at the thought of the wreckage he had caused, escaped from it in renewed thoughts about Nesbitt. There were no virgin forests for Nesbitt to flee to. Retirement on half pay in Frinton or Lyme Regis, that was the best he could hope for – unless he had quite a bit of money put by, of course, which was unlikely, in view of the fact that he was keeping a woman in a separate establishment, had been for some years. A young woman, Wetherby had said. There would be a report on her, though Markham hadn't seen it. She was French, from Marseilles, that was all he knew. But young women were expensive when you got to Nesbitt's age . . .

He was in Galata, just above the noisome reaches of the shore. He walked along the quay towards the Arsenal buildings. It was dark now and the first stars were out, at once soft and brilliant as they are in the Thracian autumn. He felt tired suddenly and began to think about securing a fiacre to take him back to Beshiktash. There would be a cab-rank higher up, on the Top Hane road.

As he began to mount towards this he was visited by a totally unexpected feeling, an excitement so intense as to constrict his breathing, at the thought that Nesbitt might know the full details of his apostasy and shame, that they might be there at this moment in Nesbitt's consciousness. He felt for these few minutes as he had felt on his visit to Hartunian, the same pain, the same anticipation of relief, the same dark joy of being looked at and known. This feeling passed, leaving behind a faint nausea of self-contempt. But in its wake, and exactly as if his mind had just been dipped in some sensitizing fluid, he understood the third element in the combination which had puzzled him, the element that had driven out caution: Nesbitt had been afraid. It was fear that had conspired with drunkenness to put venom into the insult, fear that had set Nesbitt drinking in the first place, almost certainly; a fear which had coincided with the collapse of Abdul Hamid's régime and the investigation of the Palace papers . . . Setting one foot steadily before the other as he mounted the dark narrow street towards the lights of Top Hane above the headland, Markham set his thoughts in steady order too, and by the time he reached the thoroughfare he knew quite clearly what he should do.

Next morning, however, immediately on waking, he experienced doubts. It could after all be some purely private trouble that had thrown Nesbitt off balance. Catastrophic things could happen to people, quite unrelated to public events, blows that the rest of the world could have no means of suspecting. A letter, he thought, staring up at the ceiling, a stray word, perhaps even simply a glance intercepted. Any one of these things, or any of a thousand others, could do mortal hurt. In his own case a simple statement of fact, uttered for the wrong reason, to a particular man at a particular time, the shame of it made insupportable by a return to the place where it happened. Who could suspect that in this there had been cause to wrench the whole frame of his life out of shape? How could he have explained that man's knowledge of him, the mortal taint of it, his own failure over what seemed half a lifetime to forget or repudiate or absorb the offence? Who could know that the fastidiousness, the care with dress, the composure of face and manner were simply the outward signs of that failure, just as Nesbitt's drunkenness and truculence might be signs of his?

All the same, Markham decided, he would go ahead with his idea. Gambling on there being some connection – a dishonest one – between Nesbitt and the Palace, and trying to bluff a confession out of him, was the only way he could see at present of finding out what Nesbitt really knew about him and about the past. There was a fair chance of success, if he acted soon. And if he was wrong, Nesbitt would show it by the way he reacted. There was really nothing to lose . . .

However, an item in the *Tanin*, read during his breakfast, drove out all thoughts of Nesbitt for a while. The *Tanin* was the official organ of the Committee. These days, and increasingly, it was devoted to propaganda of one sort or another – rhetorical articles about the resurgence of Turkish national spirit, the rights of Ottoman subjects irrespective of race or creed, favourable statistics and prognostications about the economy, attacks on the Austrians for their seizure of Bosnia and Herzegovina in defiance of the Treaty of Berlin, denunciations of supporters of the old régime, together with detailed accounts of the peculations of Palace favourites. Interspersed with this were lists of persons arrested and charged with crimes against the state – the precise nature of the charges were not specified. On this particular morning, Markham, looking idly down the list, saw there the name of Avedis Hartunian.

For some moments he could not believe that he had read the name right – the Turkish was printed in Arabic characters and it was therefore quite easy to make mistakes, especially with proper nouns; but it was true enough, the name was there, near the bottom of the list. It was the second time that he had stared at this name in disbelief since his return to Constantinople, but his feelings now were quite different. It was instantly clear to him that a mistake had been made. Hartunian could not possibly be guilty either of collusion with the Palace or of conspiring against the new régime. He had been working for years to bring the Young Turks to power, to restore the Constitution. He had risked everything for this – his life included. Sitting there, with his glass of tea going cold before him, Markham remembered Hartunian's face on the evening of his visit, the utter conviction in it, the glow of idealism, the happiness at the fulfilment of his work. What was it he had said? 'The interests of the Committee are identical with our own interests.' He recalled the face of the

285

other man in the room, heavy, watchful, reflecting none of his employer's enthusiasm. The secretary might conceivably be hostile to the Young Turks, but not Hartunian – it simply was not possible.

He resolved at once to make representations on Hartunian's behalf but was not sure whom he should approach, or how he could help the Armenian most effectively. The new leadership was extremely sensitive to any hint of outside interference, and the British were by no means as popular now as they had been three months previously, mainly through a long course of inept diplomacy, or so it seemed to Markham.

As it happened he was able to make informal enquiries that same day, after the weekly conference at the War Ministry. These were lengthy and boring meetings at which Turkish staff officers and provincial officials discussed the local difficulties of supplying the army in various parts of the Empire. It was regarded by the British as important to have at least one officer present on these occasions, 'holding a watching brief' as they put it; and as Markham knew Turkish, this duty had devolved on him. But the role was a purely formal one. Both he and his superiors knew perfectly well that it was in private sessions with their Geman military advisers that any real decisions were made by the Turks concerning the organization and deployment of their army.

It was at the end of the meeting, on stepping out of the conference room into the corridor leading into the vast entrance hall, that Markham came face to face with Nejib, the staff officer with the duelling scar, who had been present on the occasion of his quarrel with Essad Pasha, and whom he had seen celebrating at the Nicoli, some days afterwards, in a fashion contrary to the injunctions of Mohammed. Nejib was carrying a sheaf of papers and was obviously in something of a hurry. He nodded and would have gone on down the corridor. On an impulse, Markham said in English, 'You haven't got a few minutes to spare, have you?'

It had occurred to him that Nejib might know something about Hartunian's arrest. Why he thought this he did not know exactly, except that Nejib had seemed from the first to be conversant with power somehow. His relative youth and juniority did not make it any less likely: almost all the Committee officers were of field rank or below. He saw the Turk hesitate a moment, saw and remembered the slight, apparently humorous twitch of the mouth beneath the carefully trimmed moustache. He was in battledress – the Young Turks had abandoned dress uniform, it was said – but the uniform was obviously tailored to his figure, and he was scented and barbered with care.

'If you like,' he said. 'If you will wait here a minute while I deliver these papers, we can go to my office.' His English was harsh, rather guttural, but quite fluent. He smiled, without particular warmth, and went on down the corridor, disappearing through the swing doors at the end.

He was back very shortly and led Markham a little way along the corridor in the other direction, into a small uncarpeted office mainly occupied by a heavy rectangular desk strewn with papers. Nejib sat down behind the desk and motioned Markham towards the only other chair, an old-fashioned, high-backed affair upholstered in dark green leather.

'Do you smoke?' Nejib asked, standing again to offer Markham cigarettes from a black onyx box.

'Thank you.' Markham took one of the thick, slightly flattened cigarettes, and Nejib came round the desk to light it for him. There was a grace in his movements almost feline, disturbing to the prejudices of an Englishman, but with no trace of effeminacy. He gave an impression of tension and energy held under control.

'Well,' he said, when he was again seated, 'how can I be of help to you?'

There was something in the dutiful phrasing of this that recalled to Markham the declared Young Turk policy of good

287

relations with foreigners. He said, 'There is someone I am interested in. I thought you might know something about him.'

'Who is that?'

Markham paused, experiencing the usual reluctance to commit himself. Thin blue smoke from their cigarettes hazed the air slightly. Light from a small window behind Nejib fell on his closely cut brown hair, making it seem fairer. His pale eyes regarded Markham attentively but without warmth. It was a Caucasian face – nothing of Asia in it.

'His name is Hartunian,' Markham said. 'Avedis Hartunian.' He waited a moment but Nejib seemed not to know the name. 'He is on today's list of arrested persons. That is why I am asking about him.'

'I don't quite understand,' Nejib said courteously.

'You see, I think a mistake has been made,' Markham said. He realized, belatedly, that he could not properly explain why he thought this without revealing too great a degree of personal involvement.

'He is an Armenian?' Nejib said. 'Ah, yes, just a moment. That is the banker, isn't it? Is he a friend of yours?'

It seemed to Markham that the other was regarding him now in a different way, with something more of interest or expectation. 'Not exactly a friend,' he said. 'But I know him. I am sure that he could not have been conspiring against the state – he is a great supporter of the Constitution and the new movement. I am sure that some mistake has been made.'

'It is always distressing,' Nejib said, with the same cold courteous manner, 'when one's friends are found to be implicated in such things.'

'But it's more than that,' Markham said. He paused, at a loss how to proceed. There was danger in seeming to know too much about Hartunian's activities. He felt it in the air of the office, in the quality of the attention Nejib was giving him. 'He's not exactly a friend,' he repeated.

'You saw his name and thought you would speak on his behalf?'

Markham saw the other's thin lips stir humorously – it was an ironic, oddly civilized-looking mannerism, probably quite unconscious. 'Something like that,' he said. He regretted now having raised the matter with Nejib at all: he had merely exposed himself to the other's curiosity.

'It is just a feeling then, on your part,' Nejib said, 'based on what you know of the man. You have no evidence of any kind?'

'No.'

'Just your sense of the man's character,' Nejib said. 'I see.' He glanced down at his desk then looked back steadily and somehow expectantly at Markham.

'You ask me if I have any evidence,' Markham said. 'I don't even know what he is charged with. Would it be possible for you to tell me that?'

'Not at this stage.' Nejib again stood up to offer the cigarette box to Markham, who this time refused. 'His case is being prepared, you see,' he said. 'Along with all the others.'

'Meanwhile he is in prison?'

'Oh yes, certainly. But a man of Mr Hartunian's means will find it quite comfortable in prison.' Nejib smiled suddenly, showing very white and even upper teeth. 'Old ways die hard,' he said. 'In our Turkish prisons money still buys a great deal. He will live as at home. Of course these abuses will have to be reformed, in time. But that will not be soon enough to affect your friend.' The last word was uttered with a certain emphasis.

'So he will be brought to trial soon?'

'I did not say that. There are many such cases now, and the preparation of the evidence takes time. In the interests of justice the facts must all be carefully looked at. We do not want to make mistakes.'

'Yes, I see,' Markham said. 'It could be months then.'

Nejib moved his head slightly from side to side, as if considering this, but he said nothing.

'And visits?' Markham asked. 'Is he to be allowed visits?'

'That could be arranged. Not until he is formally charged, of course.'

Markham nodded. He was beginning to understand. 'That too might take some time, I suppose,' he said.

'It might,' Nejib agreed. 'The courts are busy, you see, these days. I could arrange for you to be notified, when the time comes.'

'Thank you,' Markham said. He met the pale eyes, which still regarded him with the same cold attentiveness. Nejib had spent time in Germany, Worseley-Jones had said. That would be where he had acquired the duelling scar. The close-cut hair and the bearing too were German, though not the dancer's grace of movement – that was all his own. He had been in Macedonia with the Third Army Corps until shortly before the revolution – one of those sent in advance to Constantinople, to gauge the situation in the capital. A key man then, and certainly a member of the Committee. And it was the Committee who was conducting these prosecutions; only officers of the Committee had access to the Palace papers on which the prosecutions were based, only they would be the ultimate judges of the authenticity of any documents whatever, found or planted there . . .

Markham rose to his feet. 'There is a law in England,' he said, 'which makes it quite impossible to hold a person indefinitely without formulating charges. We regard it as one of the most fundamental of our liberties.'

'Your country is known for her democratic institutions,' Nejib said. He too had risen and the two men stood facing each other across the desk. 'We are in a different situation. We are struggling to preserve the gains of the revolution. Besides, my dear Captain Markham, your writ does not run here.'

He had spoken courteously enough, but Markham felt the

hostility in his voice, as sudden and unmistakable as the drawing of a sword.

'You will notify me then?' he said.

'Of course.'

There had been no mistake, Markham saw that very clearly now, at least not on the part of the authorities. It was Hartunian who had been mistaken. Again those words of his came into Markham's mind. *The interests of the Committee are identical with our interests.* But he could not have been thinking about men like Nejib. Perhaps it had never been true. Certainly it had not taken long – barely four months – for those interests sharply to diverge. The nature of the divergence, precisely why Hartunian had become a threat, or perhaps merely a nuisance, was something that Nejib was certainly not going to tell him . . .

The question, however, the nature of Hartunian's offence, remained in his mind throughout the rest of the day. When he got home in the evening, over his whisky and soda he looked again at the names of those arrested. He could find no common factor. There was one other Armenian on the list and two people with Italian names, Levantines probably. The rest were Turks, all obscure except one, whom he had heard of but not met, a Professor of Turkish literature known for his progressive views. All these people had offended the new régime in some way. All of them, presumably, would remain in prison while their cases were being prepared – indefinitely, in other words.

After supper, instead of settling down by his study fire, Markham spent some time walking about the cold, silent rooms of the house. There were remembered presences everywhere in it, the faces of his wife and son and the governess. Different parts of the house evoked different, characteristic attitudes of theirs, his son's vulnerable composure – so like his own – when he had been caught listening in the drawing room; his wife turning with that quivering brightness from her dressing table; Miss Taverner blushing as she rose from the interrupted lesson, her earnest desire for self-improvement, her uncontrollable cries of pleasure – they seemed almost to sound now again as he paused outside the door of her room. It was at these times, when the memories came strongly but without reassurance, that he knew himself to be completely alone.

This evening, however, as he wandered about the house, he experienced a steadily growing tension, something between excitement and foreboding, which ended by obliterating the wraiths of his solitude. He knew from this, rather than from any sense of having made a conscious decision, that he was going to see Nesbitt that evening. Still, however, he allowed himself to think that he might not go – even as he dressed to go, even as he was walking along the drive away from the house.

It was a cold night, gusty, with a smell of rain in the air. Dead leaves of acacia and *platane* drifted knee-high across the roads. Markham kept the collar of his overcoat turned up and his dark felt hat pulled down low over his eyes. The few people he passed were similarly muffled up, as far as he could make them out – the new system of street lamps installed by an Italian company at great expense had not been a success: those that functioned at all cast a mere pallid pool of light round their own base. He got a cab near the Beshiktash mosque and asked to be taken to the district of Azap Kapou, which was where Nesbitt lived. He knew the house, having been twice before, in the days following his arrival in the city, before the antipathy between the two men had become clearly manifest to both.

It was a square-built, single-storey wooden house, not very large but quite secluded, standing on its own among larch trees with a long, overgrown garden in front. The wind made leaping shadows across the front of the house as Markham approached and the thick bay tree near the wall shivered and hissed. There was no light showing at the front of the house, but almost as soon as Markham let the heavy metal knocker

292

fall, the pane above the door was lit up, and a few moments later Nesbitt appeared on the threshold, blinking down. He was wearing a dark blue dressing gown.

'Who is it?' he said. There was aggression in his voice and something else – an edge of anxiety.

Markham smelt the brandy on his breath. 'It's me, sir,' he said. 'Markham.' He raised his face so that the light from inside fell on it.

Nesbitt appeared to hesitate some time longer, as if he still had not recognized his visitor. Then he moved to one side to allow Markham to enter. 'Good God,' he said. 'I didn't expect to see you of all people. Come in.'

He led Markham into a small sitting room at the rear of the house where a wood fire was burning. 'My sanctum,' he said. 'Let me take your things.' The room was warm and had an agreeable compound odour of woodsmoke and cigar smoke and brandy.

'Thanks,' Markham said, allowing himself to be helped off with his coat. 'I hope you don't mind my breaking in on you like this.'

'Come and sit down,' Nesbitt said. 'I don't get many visitors. Mind? No, I don't mind. I don't believe it's a social call, for one thing.'

It seemed to Markham that he could still detect that edge of apprehension or anxiety in the other's voice, despite the challenging forthrightness of the words. Nesbitt's brusque hospitality had touched him, rather, without making him waver in what he intended to do.

'I haven't come to apologize, you know,' he said.

'For throwing your drink in my face? I don't think you ought to apologize. I was drunk. I said too much – more than I wanted to say. There's something about you that acts like a red rag to me. I don't like you, Markham. But I don't think you should apologize. In any case apologies don't matter a damn to me. If I felt myself slighted five minutes alone somewhere would settle it between us.'

293

'Then it is just as well you don't,' Markham said. The other must be well over fifty, probably fifty-three or four, he thought. But he was as strong as a bull still.

Nesbitt made a sound between a grunt and a laugh. 'Not many things worth fighting about,' he said. 'What will you have to drink? You like whisky, don't you?'

'Whisky and soda, please,' Markham said.

While Nesbitt was busy with the drink he made a brief survey of the room. It was scrupulously tidy, quite bare – there was very little in it to suggest the tastes, or the past, of its owner. A pair of old-fashioned duelling pistols on one wall, a stuffed kestrel in a glass case, one or two framed photographs of groups of young men in uniform. Three silver cups stood on a low cabinet to one side of the fireplace.

'What are the cups for?' he asked.

'Those? They're for boxing. I was in the Army Team. '69 and '70. Long time ago now. I joined the army at seventeen. I rose from the ranks. But you would know that, of course, wouldn't you?'

Markham was silent. The more knowledge Nesbitt attributed to him now the better.

'Forty years,' Nesbitt said. 'It's a bloody long time.'

He poured more brandy into his glass. In the silence that fell between them now Markham could hear the wind in the trees outside – it seemed to be increasing in strength.

'I'm tired of it,' Nesbitt said, and there was a slightly snarling note now in his voice, a snarl of disgust or disillusion.

'Well,' Markham said, 'our occupation here is almost gone, mine anyway.' I'm quoting someone, he thought, but he couldn't remember who. Perhaps it would not be necessary to tell any lies. Nesbitt seemed amenable this evening. It was almost as though he was making a bid for sympathy. Perhaps he would give the information that Markham wanted freely, without coercion. Certainly it was worth trying. However, he found himself, at this ultimate moment, unable to phrase a question to Nesbitt. How could he look into the man's face, and ask him, Do you know, do you really know, how I behaved that night, what I said? And if Nesbitt said, Yes, I know, how could that be endured?

'My sense of occupation,' he said slowly, 'is probably not as strong as yours, in any case.'

'How do you make that out?' Nesbitt's glass was again empty. Markham watched him refill it. The man was drinking twice as fast as he was himself. He still showed no real sign of drunkenness; but Markham remembered that sudden deterioration the previous evening at the club.

'Well,' he said, looking down into the pale depths of his whisky and soda, 'I've only got ten years' service, for one thing. Ten years is a longish time I suppose, but I still don't think of myself as a professional soldier. It's odd, but there it is. Perhaps I need to put in another ten years.'

'No, no,' Nesbitt said, and for a moment his face was empty of all derision – a square, heavy face, sensual and dogged. 'No,' he replied, 'it isn't a question of years. It's how you see yourself. You came to the army for your own reasons, Markham. You just took it up. For me it was different. There was never any alternative for me. The army was my way out.' He paused for a moment, then he repeated, 'You just took it up. Perhaps that's why I don't like you. You aren't typical, Markham. You're not what one would expect. I don't like abnormalities. Why did you do it?'

'Do what?' Markham asked. He watched Nesbitt pour more brandy into his glass.

'What happened to you?' Nesbitt said. 'You changed course. You were a student. Oriental languages, wasn't it?' He took a cigar case from his dressing-gown pocket, selected a cigar, then as an afterthought extended it to Markham.

'No, thanks,' Markham said. 'I'll have one of my cigarettes instead if you don't mind.'

'You volunteered for the International Brigade on the Greek side, in 1897,' Nesbitt said, puffing at his cigar. 'You fought in the Thracian campaign. When that was over you went back home and applied almost at once for a commission – early the next year. You never completed your studies.'

'You seem to know a lot about me,' Markham said.

'This stuff is all on record.'

'Are you saying that you have no idea at all why I changed course like that?'

Nesbitt made no reply and the two men looked at each other for some moments in silence. The pine logs settled lower on the fire and a thin greenish jet of flame licked briefly round them. Markham heard the wind again, whistling in the eaves of the house. 'Anyway,' he said, 'it's only a question of time now before I am recalled.'

'Yes,' Nesbitt said, 'your job is done now, more or less, isn't it?' His voice had a thicker, slightly sneering quality now, which Markham recognized as the first onset of drunkenness.

'What do you mean?' he said quickly. A sense of urgency was beginning to possess him now. He must make his attack soon – before the brandy blunted Nesbitt altogether. 'I don't know what you mean,' he said. 'I was talking about the gendarmerie issue.'

'That was just a front,' Nesbitt said. 'Do you think I didn't know that? Blake could have handled it on his own. If they had really wanted you to do anything about that they would have posted you to Macedonia in the first place, where the action was. No, your job was to liaise with the Committee, wasn't it? Discreetly of course. Do you think I'm a fool?'

'No, I don't think that,' Markham said. 'You're right of course.' He drew on his cigarette, looking directly into Nesbitt's eyes. Lodged behind those eyes, among the myriad elements that made up Nesbitt's consciousness were certain traces he had to isolate, elicit. And the other, by an amazing stroke of luck, was helping him – this belief in his close ties with the Committee had done half his work for him in advance.

'You helped to put this gang into power,' Nesbitt said.

'Listen,' Markham said, slowly and carefully. 'There is something I want to ask you. Some time ago, when I was in your office, I saw a name on your desk, an Armenian name, Hartunian. You had been having him watched. Will you tell me why?'

'Never heard of him,' Nesbitt said. The expression of contempt on his face seemed to deepen slightly. 'Why should I waste my time on Armenians?'

'I think it was because you suspected a connexion between him and the Constitutionalists,' Markham said steadily. 'It was them you were really interested in.'

'You can think what you like.' Nesbitt reached for the brandy. 'Is that why you came here tonight?' he said. 'To ask me questions about Armenians?'

'Not exactly,' Markham said. 'Though that is part of it. I came to warn you, actually.' He drew a breath and held it for some seconds, looking at the face of the man before him. The moment for his plunge had come. Taking care to suppress all trace of feeling from his voice, he said, 'You have been passing information to the Palace for years, Colonel. I know it. Certain members of the Committee know it. Papers have been found implicating you.'

He knew at once that he had been right. Nesbitt set his glass down carefully. All colour had drained from his face, leaving it ashen. He said nothing, but he opened his mouth suddenly and Markham saw the labouring breath he took.

'This is what you have been worrying about all along, isn't it?' Markham said. 'You should be glad of my connexion with the Committee. Having found the papers they came to notify me. Otherwise you would already be under arrest.'

Still Nesbitt did not speak. He had taken up his glass again and drained it. Despite the shock his hand was steady. The room was hazy with cigar smoke now. Through the haze Markham saw the large, blunt-featured face turned towards

297

him. Again he saw the other's mouth open for that quick gulping breath.

'That old manlac,' Nesbitt said, in a voice that was grating and slow.

'He never destroyed anything, you know that.'

'There was nothing,' Nesbitt said. 'Nothing in my own hand.'

'He kept records of everything,' Markham said. 'You know that. It was only a question of time, once they started going through the papers. Surely you must have known.'

He was surprised, even now, that Nesbitt should have accepted his lie so easily. But the corrupt had their own kind of gullibility; and besides, he must have been expecting it.

'Why didn't you get clear?' he said.

Nesbitt's mouth twisted in the semblance of a smile. 'Where to?' he said. 'I haven't saved anything, you know. I've had expenses.'

Markham thought of the French girl in the apartment in Pera. Nesbitt did not strike him as an ungenerous man.

'Besides,' Nesbitt said, 'it was never all that much money.'

'There is a way out for you,' Markham said. 'They want to keep up a semblance of good relations with the British. The country as a whole is still Anglophile, as you know. Kiamil Pasha, the Grand Vizier, is pro-British, always has been. It doesn't suit the Committee just now to go counter to this popular feeling – whatever their own private views are. They don't really want a scandal with a British officer involved. They have told me that under certain circumstances they would be prepared to cover the whole thing up.'

He paused. It was essential for his purposes that Nesbitt should believe this. What he was saying was basically plausible; and Nesbitt's position was weakened by his belief that he, Markham, had a private understanding with the Committee. It was difficult to read anything on his face, which had settled, despite the pallor, into the expression of heavy contempt that Markham knew. Then Nesbitt leaned forward a little and said 'What circumstances?' and Markham heard something in his voice, a note of compliance, almost akin to hope, and knew that his worries had been groundless: scepticism, distrust, all Nesbitt's professional armoury had been swept away in the shock of finding himself known, detected, his treacheries manifest. It was what Markham himself was aware of dreading and desiring, what had brought him there that evening.

'They will want a full account,' he said.

'I am no threat to the Committee,' Nesbitt said. 'I was planning to retire next year, Markham.'

Markham lit another cigarette. 'That has nothing to do with me,' he said. 'I want to know what you gave Abdul Hamid. I want the whole story. I won't clear you with the Committee unless I get it.'

Nesbitt hoisted himself out of his chair, put more wood on the fire, replenished his own and Markham's glass. There was an elderly heaviness now in his movements, something stricken, almost. But his face had recovered some of its colour, perhaps through the hope that had been offered him.

'Forty years,' he said, after a moment. 'They sent me to this backwater. End of the line for me. Shunted here and forgotten. My wife and I separated years ago. Mutual consent. I still support her. She's in England. Then there's a little lady here who has been good to me.'

Markham said nothing, watching the contemptuous, dogged face.

'The business goes back eight years,' Nesbitt said suddenly. 'I'd already been here five years then.'

The slow voice proceeded, grating out its treacheries, and Markham listened. It was a common enough story: the small beginning of favours and thanks, the first decisive betrayal, the growing involvement. Nesbitt had ended by trading lives. And all for money: Markham could discern no principle at work other than Nesbitt's instinctive conservatism, his bully's respect for established powers. Common enough; yet there was a mystery in it, as almost always. Something had given way in Nesbitt, some private incommunicable despair had combined with the corruption to ruin him . . .

Markham grew impatient suddenly; the catalogue was too long, the lives Nesbitt had sold too remote. 'And Hartunian?' he said. 'What about him?'

'You were right. It was because I knew he was a courier for the Committee that I was interested. I was hoping he would lead me to some of the Committee people inside Turkey itself – those were the people we wanted. I wasn't interested in the Armenian movement. That was penetrated long ago in any case. Half the people in it are spies of one sort or another.'

'How did you get the information in the first place? Who sent in the report that I saw on your desk that day?'

'Someone inside the house – another Armenian almost certainly.' The contempt was back in Nesbitt's voice and on his face. 'I told you they were all spies,' he said. 'We didn't set anyone on to Hartunian, we didn't need to.' He paused, then repeated loudly, 'They are all spies,' and Markham heard the same snarling note in which disgust and the horror of emptiness seemed combined.

'Who was it?' he said.

'We don't know. Someone close to him.'

'What would be the point of it?'

Nesbitt shrugged his heavy shoulders. 'There are divisions inside the Armenian movement,' he said. 'Not just tactical questions. I mean totally different aims. Some of these people are working for an independent Armenia, with a homeland in Eastern Turkey. Hartunian isn't one of them, as far as we know. Perhaps he was in the way. This is only guesswork, of course. I don't give a damn for their squabbles.'

Markham nodded slowly. 'I see,' he said. 'Yes, I see. Now, tell me what you meant last night when you said I had a weak spot for Armenians.'

'I was drunk. I've told you that already.'

300

'Yes, I know that.' Markham's face was mask-like in its composure. The effort of control took almost all inflection from his voice; it came out flat, monotonous, deliberate. 'I know you were drunk,' he said. 'Tell me what you meant.'

Nesbitt paused a moment longer, then he said, 'The man you set on to enquire about Hartunian came to me. Zimin, yes.' He smiled bitterly. 'He was afraid not to,' he said. 'It would have got back to me anyway. He was afraid I would put the *Khafie* on to him, as a double agent. Rats like that trust nobody. You were a fool to trust him yourself.'

Markham remembered Zimin's nervousness on the evening they had met. He had set it down at the time to a simple fear of being observed.

'You must have turned others over to the secret police,' he said. 'Otherwise he would not have been so afraid.'

Nesbitt made no reply to this. He was slumped back in his armchair, looking straight before him. 'Naturally he made further enquiries,' he said. 'He scented something – rats have keen noses. Why should you show an interest in Hartunian? He talked to people, various people. In the end he found someone who remembered.'

'Remembered me?' Markham spoke more loudly than he intended. 'Remembered what?'

Nesbitt turned his head to look at him. 'Not you, exactly,' he said. 'He was little more than a child at the time – the son of the woman who did the washing in the house. The Krikorian house, I mean. Hartunian's sister married a man named Krikorian. The Krikorians had three children, one of them a girl called Miriam. The man Zimin spoke to said he thought this girl had been a student in London, that she had become engaged to an Englishman, or even married him, he was not sure. They were killed during the massacres, the man said. The girl and most of her family.'

'And that's all?'

'Yes. Zimin came to me with what he had found. He thought it might be useful. He didn't ask me for any money.

All he wanted was a testimonial. He supposed it was for the sake of the girl that you took an interest in Hartunian.'

'You're lying,' Markham said. 'There's something more.'

'I swear that what I've told you is the truth,' Nesbitt said.

'Then why did you call me a coward?'

'I didn't mean anything. I wanted to be unpleasant.'

'You're lying,' Markham said again. 'Damn you. You must know something more.'

Again his voice had risen. He met Nesbitt's eyes, saw enquiry gathering in them, like an appetite. Even in his stricken state Nesbitt caught the smell of weakness, prepared to alight, though half-disabled. Or perhaps he was acting, perhaps he knew.

'Is there something more?' Nesbitt said softly.

'An accident then? A kind of coincidence? You despise Armenians, don't you? The whole race. You don't like me. And you were drunk. You knew of the connexion and you wanted to insult me with it. That's all, is it?'

'I swear to you that's all.'

Markham looked into the other man's eyes for some moments longer. There was no way he could be sure, he realized, with sudden, sickening conviction. What Nesbitt knew or suspected would remain undeclared within him, for ever, probably – there was no way of getting at it. Perhaps – and this was as humiliating as any knowledge of his could have been – Nesbitt had simply recognized a fellow spirit, a shared corruption . . . In any case he had been foolish to think that Nesbitt would admit to any knowledge of his shame, in these circumstances anyway: Nesbitt too believed himself to be fighting for life.

'A very unlucky coincidence for you,' Markham said slowly.

'How do you mean?'

'It led to this talk we have just had, which might not have been necessary otherwise. Now that you have told me all this, I can't overlook it – I can't go back to where we were before,

before I had this knowledge of you. You are answerable for it, Nesbitt.'

'Answerable to who?' There was arrogance in the drink-thickened voice. Nesbitt was still struggling, despite the blow he had had.

'To me,' Markham said. 'You are answerable to me.'

'I have done you no harm.'

'No harm?' Markham experienced a kind of internal burst of laughter though the stiff composure of his face remained unchanged. 'You express contempt for Armenians,' he said. 'That repeats the harm done to me.'

'I don't know what you're talking about.'

'It's more than that. Take this Hartunian for example. Persecuted under the Hamidian régime, his wife clubbed to death in front of him. Betrayed by his own people. Betrayed again by those he had helped put into power. Don't you understand? It doesn't matter who is in power for people like Hartunian. It doesn't matter what the reasons are. He's a victim, in any case.'

'He played a dangerous game,' Nesbitt said.

'Yes, I suppose so.' Markham paused for a moment, then he said, 'You are one of those that make victims.'

'And you?'

'Yes, but not like you. There was no necessity in your case. A short while ago, just a few minutes ago, you admitted that you had named certain Armenians to the Palace as being implicated in the 1905 attempt on Abdul Hamid's life. On what grounds?'

Nesbitt was silent. Markham looked for some moments at the big, blunt-featured face before him, the grizzled hair, the vein at the temple. Nesbitt looked strangely ordinary at this moment, like any Englishman of his type: dull, decent, somewhat choleric.

'You must know what happened to them,' Markham said. 'You must have known what would happen. It has been in the newspapers lately anyway, in the reports of these public trials

303

they are having now. The men who buried those Armenians have been giving evidence. They were buried secretly with the whip marks and the brands of the irons on them. The chances are they had nothing to do with the assassination attempt.'

Nesbitt said nothing still. His head was lowered on his breast and he was staring into the fire. There was silence for some moments, then Markham stirred and sighed. 'I'm not going to help you,' he said. 'Did you think I would? You are going to be a victim now at last.'

At this Nesbitt raised his head, still however not looking directly at Markham. 'You promised,' he said.

'I promised you nothing,' Markham said harshly. He stood up and crossed the room to the chair where Nesbitt had laid his coat and hat. 'I won't do anything for you,' he said. He put the coat on and stood for some moments looking down at Nesbitt, who had not risen. 'I'm afraid it's the end of things for you, Nesbitt,' he said.

'I suppose the fact that we are both English makes no difference to you,' Nesbitt said. There was no note of pleading in his voice. He spoke gruffly and almost accusingly, as if he had in his turn found something to reproach Markham with. His face, however, wore a bemused and hopeless expression.

'I'd rather you didn't think of me as English,' Markham said coldly, 'if that means kinship with you.'

Nesbitt turned his head slowly. The bemused look had deepened on his face. 'You bloody pansy,' he said.

'If I were in your shoes,' Markham said very distinctly, 'I know what I would do. Think of the disgrace, Nesbitt. Think of the political repercussions. No one will want to touch you with a barge pole. Dishonourable discharge. Loss of pension rights. Back to England, fifty-odd years old, no references. Who's going to employ you? You'll be on the scrap-heap Nesbitt.' He stepped towards the door. 'I'll let myself out,' he said.

Nesbitt was watching him but still had not risen – it was as if

304

he had been immobilized there, in his armchair, by the dying fire in the orderly, characterless room. The last that Markham saw of him was the big dogged face fixed in an expression both patient and savage, reminding him suddenly of the face of the monkey he had seen that day in the square outside the Bazaar, the same bemused docility of a baited and derided creature.

He closed the door on this, and made his way out of the house. It was very dark outside and the wind ws loud in the garden. The sound of the wind, and the enveloping darkness, seemed to cancel the house at once, even before he had turned out on to the drive. It was as if the building had only existed for the purpose of this interview with Nesbitt.


So certain was Markham that everything had now been said or acknowledged between Nesbitt and himself that he ceased altogether, and at once, to think about the other man or even feel conscious of his existence. He had lied to Nesbitt, and the lie had succeeded, though only to the extent of re-affirming his own loneliness: in Nesbitt, as in Hartunian, he had failed to find a sharer.

The following morning, therefore, he did not at first register the fact that Nesbitt was absent from the fortnightly conference at the Embassy. It was not until proceedings were under way that he noticed the empty place. Even then he did not jump to any conclusions. Nesbitt had been notably erratic of late weeks. He might simply have got drunk, he thought. All the same, throughout the meeting, he was conscious of the empty chair, a little further down from him on the opposite side of the long table.

The Ambassador was not present, though he did sometimes attend these briefing sessions, which he himself had instituted. The meeting was well attended otherwise, Markham noted, with himself and Armstrong and Nesbitt's assistant, a recently arrived subaltern named Kent, making up the military

305

contingent; three members of the Naval Commission, one of whom was Phelps – he nodded to Markham but did not speak or approach him; and various Embassy officials including Lewin and Straker, the Press Attaché, but not Worseley-Jones, who was on leave in England. Somerville and a colleague from the Ottoman Debt Commission arrived just as proceedings were beginning, both armed with papers.

The first part of the meeting was taken up with routine progress reports by the Service representatives, including Markham. Then Somerville was asked for a summary of the trade figures. These he supplied with his usual blend of enthusiasm and caution. What he said had by now become familiar hearing to the men assembled there. The Alliance Powers, particularly Germany and Italy, were continuing to make gigantic strides in the volume of their trade with the Ottoman Empire.

'Their combined share of the market is increasing by something like thirty per cent per annum,' Somerville said. He paused, looking up and down the table, his spectacles gleaming. 'That is against our six per cent,' he said. 'The German business is nearly all through the banks, not private enterprises. The Deutsche Bank and the Deutsche Orientbank mainly – they have tentacles everywhere.'

Lewin frowned, obviously disapproving of this flourish of rhetoric. 'I'd back our Merchant Banks against them,' he said. It was as if he was talking about a cricket team.'

'Hear, hear,' Phelps said.

'I'd like to ask a question if I may,' Markham said.

'Wouldn't you say so, Ramsay?' Lewin looked down the table at the Embassy Dragoman. 'People like Baring Brothers and Morgan-Grenfell?'

'Ay, well, they've been here longer of course,' Ramsay said, in the grudging Lowland Scots accent that twenty years in Turkey had done nothing to change.

'Much longer,' Lewin said, with a sort of urbane triumph. 'Considerably longer.'

306

'It's not the length of time,' Somerville said, tapping his papers. 'The German banks are organized differently. They represent very diverse manufacturing industries back home. They use their capital like a battering-ram.'

'Oh come now,' Lewin said.

Markham leaned forward. 'I'd like to raise a general point,' he said. There was a large picture of King Edward on the wall facing him. He looked up to find the mild, somewhat puffy eyes of his sovereign regarding him steadily. 'If we accept Somerville's figures,' he said, 'and there is no reason not to, it must mean that the present government of Turkey is granting Germany a totally disproportionate share of new business.'

'And they are newcomers in the field,' Armstrong said. 'Relatively, I mean.'

'That is the reason,' Clissold, the Commercial Counsellor, said, speaking for the first time. 'That's it, old boy. Newcomers always bag a disproportionate share. The charm of novelty, you know.'

'Excuse me, that can't be a sufficient reason,' Markham said. 'Let me put it another way. If the government is as pro-British as we all continue to assert, why is it that all the major trade concessions are going to Germany?'

There was a short silence, then Lewin said, 'There is absolutely no doubt that our stocks are high with the government. This new Grand Vizier of theirs, Kiamil Pasha, is a staunch admirer of the British.'

'Grand old chap,' Phelps said, looking at Markham in much the same way he had regarded Godard, the French officer, at the Pera Club.

'A Turk of the old school,' Clissold said.

'You mean he's a gentleman, don't you? And he's been around a long time – like the British banks.' Markham paused, looking down the table. Again, fleetingly, he was aware of Nesbitt's empty chair. He sensed the hostility of some of the men there, the dislike for his persistence, his clipped, sardonic style of speech. 'Not like some of these upstarts, eh?'

He looked at Lewin, who at once, and pointedly, looked away. 'Well, whether we like it or not,' he said, 'it is these upstarts who have the real power now. They are not gentlemen. And they are certainly not liberals. And the trade figures suggest that they don't like us.'

'Markham's right actually, I think, up to a point,' Straker said, with a distinct note of apology in his voice. 'I covered the elections in December, you know. Out of three hundred deputies only eight are Committee men. They could have got themselves elected in droves if they'd wanted, you know, they were so frantically popular at the time. Heroes of the revolution and so forth. But they didn't. They preferred to remain behind the scenes.'

'Their job was done,' Lewin said. 'They had seen the Constitution restored. Very properly they handed over to the accredited representatives.'

'Accredited representatives?' Markham experienced again that interior burst of laughter. There was a pompous fatuity about the phrase very typical of Lewin. 'Do you really think they handed over power?' he said. 'Having led a successful revolution, imposed a constitution on the Sultan, conducted elections? With their organization still intact? There's no indication that they did anything of the sort. In fact all indications are that there are two governments at present in this country: the public government of Kiamil Pasha and the elected deputies; and the private government of the army officers and professional men who make up the Committee. And we're backing the wrong one.'

'You're exaggerating,' Lewin said, with an air of deliberate patience, and Ramsay nodded his long head in agreement.

'Possibly,' Markham said. 'But I still think we're backing the wrong horse. This government contains reactionary Islamic elements, everyone knows that. Have you counted the green turbans in the Assembly? Kiamil Pasha would be regarded as a Conservative in any other context. We could end by being identified with a government not only reactionary but without effective power.'

'I don't know about the role of the Committee,' Straker said. 'Markham may be overstressing that. But I spend a lot of time going through the newspapers, and there's no doubt that the references to Britain in the Turkish press have changed over the last two months or so. At the same time the pro-German bias is increasing. I suppose you have noticed the tendency to spell English names as if they were German?'

Lewin nodded. 'I've noticed that,' he said. 'Frightful impertinence. Isn't there anything we can do about it?'

He looked concerned, almost for the first time. It was clear that this liberty with English names was something he took seriously – more seriously, Markham thought, than the possibility of British policy being discredited . . . He did not listen closely to Straker's reply. There was little to be done. The press was controlled by the Committee now, as were the agencies inside Turkey. The astonishing – and deeply depressing – thing about it all was that most of those present knew this already, yet were unable to acknowledge what it meant. The Embassy people certainly knew it, whatever public attitudes they might adopt. But training, and the sense of caste, had made them more deeply hostile to change than any politician, apparently unable to recognize dynamic movement at all. They were like people trying to play chess on a tilting board. The pieces were sliding about all over but they somehow kept on playing. It was as if something had gone wrong with their sensory equipment – that part of it which determines the gravity of impressions. The old dynastic order of Europe, which had made the rules of the game, was everywhere collapsing. And yet to the British official mind a revolution such as had happened here in Turkey, a great wave of popular feeling and popular will, was no more than a hiccup in the throat, leaving things much as they were, in the hands of good chaps like Kiamil Pasha, serving monarchs slightly chastened but essentially the same . . .

At the end of the meeting, when people were breaking up to go their various ways, Markham found himself standing beside Ramsay near the door. On an impulse he asked him about his niece, Miss Munro, whom he had not seen since the day she had come to lunch at his house, and argued with him as to whether Constantinople could be regarded as a romantic city. In his close-mouthed, cautious manner Ramsay told him that his niece, having been home in Aberdeen for some time, was now back again in Constantinople. She was planning a further series of articles about the impact of the revolution on the lives of ordinary people. Her first series, it seemed, had been a great success. Had Markham read them? He had one of her articles at home, which he would send over.

Markham thanked him. He had a certain curiosity to see what Miss Munro had written, though he was without great expectation as to its merit. The conversation with Ramsay had delayed him rather and most of the others had by now left the conference room. Lewin and Clissold were still standing near the table, talking together quietly. Markham saw Andrews, one of the security men, enter by the other door, at the far end of the room, hesitate a moment, then cross to the two men at the table. He spoke in low tones to Lewin, who inclined his head to listen, with the urbane condescension he always showed towards social inferiors. Then Markham saw the smile leave his face. He turned his head sharply to look directly at the man who was speaking.

Markham had no time to see more, as he and Ramsay were now moving through the double doorway together and out into the corridor. However, in the entrance hall, at the small reception desk where Andrews had his chair, he saw the young artilleryman who did duty as Nesbitt's batman. He was in battledress, and came to attention as Markham crossed the hall. His face was white.

'What's the matter?' Markham said. 'Willis, isn't it?'

'Yessir.'

'Stand easy, man,' Markham said. 'Is there something the

310

matter?' There were only the two of them at present in the hall, Ramsay having gone up to his office on the first floor.

'It's Colonel Nesbitt, sir,' the orderly said. 'He's dead, sir – he's shot himself.'

'I see,' Markham said. He thought quickly. 'You found him, did you?'

'Yessir. I went over as usual this morning. He was in the armchair in his dressing gown. I thought he was asleep—'

'Did he leave a note? Did you see a note of any kind?'

'No sir. I didn't look around much – not after I'd found him.'

Markham nodded. He saw Lewin, with Andrews just behind him, emerging into the corridor from the conference room. The orderly raised his head. 'Colonel Nesbitt shot himself through the mouth,' he said, again bracing himself in the position of attention, and it was exactly as if he was delivering an official message from one officer to another, almost as if he should have prefaced the message with Nesbitt's respects, as he had done often enough before.

Markham nodded again. Willis was hardly more than a boy. It would have been a nasty thing, that unexpected sprawl of death in the quiet room stale with tobacco smoke. Messy too, probably . . . He himself felt nothing yet but a desire to get clear before Lewin came up. This was an Embassy matter. They would have to look after the security aspects.

'Take things easy,' he said to Willis. 'You've had a shock. You may have to go back there with them, I'm afraid.' He smiled at the orderly then moved away down the corridor.

He still felt no emotion as he went through the Embassy grounds towards the street. If Nesbitt had left a note it was possible that he, Markham, had been mentioned, perhaps his visit of the evening before, and what had been discussed between them. It was possible but not, he thought, very likely. Nesbitt was not a man to go in for composition before blowing his brains out. He would have sat on there, for some time, by the dying fire, thinking, gathering himself to do it . . .

It was a misty morning with shafts of luminous sunlight in which there was no warmth. The mottled trunks of the plane trees outside the gates thinned up into the bright haze. Markham walked towards the Golden Horn, looking about him with a kind of eagerness or alacrity, in search of impressions to distract him from thoughts of Nesbitt's end.

He was helped in this, though in a way he would not have chosen, by the sight of two corpses hanging in chains at the Stambul end of Galata Bridge. They dangled there, some six feet above the pavement, shaven-headed, cheaply and nondescriptly dressed, hands tied behind them, in the meek attitude of the strangled. Most of the passers-by gave them no more than a glance – there were gibbets all over the city, now that the first death sentences of the courts set up by the Committee were being carried out. Markham had seen men in similar attitudes hoisted up on the walls of the War Ministry only two days before. They hung there, noisome object-lessons to the populace . . . He shivered suddenly. The day was cold in spite of the sunshine silvering the mist. He was glad of the heavy military overcoat he was wearing.

As he left the bridge he glanced over the side, at the scores of row boats crowded together at the edge of the water, with figures sitting silent and still in them, as if somehow immobilized by the mist. He was walking without particular purpose, reluctant to return to his office in Galata, but without any idea of an alternative. On an impulse he entered a small café near the Spice Market and asked for a cup of Turkish coffee.

Almost at once, however, he regretted this. He felt ill at ease here, dressed in uniform. The two other men in the place, who looked like porters from the market, stared at him with open curiosity. He drank a mouthful of the coffee, then got up and left, leaving a handful of kurus on the table. As he was about to cross the narrow terrace outside the café, a man who had perhaps been sitting at one of the tables there walked slowly across on a course that took him at right angles to the direction that Markham was taking. He was wearing a black overcoat with the collar turned up and a black felt hat with a rather wide brim, which partially obscured his features. However, when he was directly in Markham's path and some half dozen yards away, Markham saw his face in profile and at once recognized him for Hartunian's secretary, Tarquin. So short was the distance between them that Markham expected to be recognized in his turn, but the other man, with an indifference that Markham was to wonder about later, looked neither to right nor left, continuing in the same direction until he rounded the corner of the terrace and disappeared.

Markham hesitated briefly, then turned and followed. The other man was walking quickly. By the time Markham had reached the corner he was already some fifty yards along the street, heading towards the *han* behind the Sultane Valide Mosque. He did not stop here, however, but went on to cross the intersecting *Yolu Caddesi* and plunge once more into the streets south of this.

Keeping the distance between himself and the stocky black figure more or less constant, Markham followed, possessed by ardent curiosity as to the other man's destination and purposes. In the narrow streets beyond the *caddesi* the buildings on either side rose and disappeared into the mist. Tarquin kept his head lowered. He passed by the mosque and baths of Mahmoud Pasha, skirted the edge of the Covered Market and passed finally into the courtyard of the Nuru Osmaniyé Mosque. Markham saw him sit down on one of the wooden benches, against the wall at the far side of the courtyard. He did not himself enter the courtyard but remained outside in the *meydan*, a wide triangular-shaped area formed by the wall of the Market on one side and the small *medresseh* of Sinan Pasha on the other. From here Markham could look down over the low wall of the courtyard to where Tarquin was sitting. The line of elms near the entrance to the courtyard partially screened him from view; but in any case he was safe from detection there; the mist softened and hazed everything, and the sunshine, though it seemed bound to dispel the mist later, for the moment contributed to this indistinctness, fluffing and infusing outlines, paining the eyes with its broken gleams. Though he was no more than twenty-five yards away, and in the open, Tarquin could not have known who he was.

Almost at once Tarquin was joined by another man in an overcoat and Astrakhan hat, who must have been there already, waiting. He was slim and erect of bearing. Markham could make out little of his face except that he was clean-shaven. The two men sat talking together for seventeen minutes by Markham's watch, their heads close together. Then the man in the Astrakhan hat stood up and walked across the courtyard towards the entrance. He emerged on to the *meydan* and turned towards Markham, passing within a few feet of him. As he did so he glanced up, and for the space of a few seconds the two men looked at each other. Markham had the sensation, even in this short space, of being scrutinized. The face he saw was European-looking, pale, straight-nosed, cold and impervious in expression. Then the man had passed him and was walking with quick steps in the direction of Beyazit.

After a further moment or two Markham entered the courtyard. Tarquin did not look up until he was standing directly before him. Even then he made no immediate sign of recognition.

'Don't you remember me?' Markham said, looking steadily at the broad, rather flattened-looking face, with its thick moustache, lustrous, long-lashed eyes.

There was no change in the expression on Tarquin's face, but after a moment he nodded. 'Yes,' he said. 'I remember you. Captain Markham, isn't it? It was the uniform that deceived me.' He said this without any apparent intention of sociability but merely as one states a fact. 'You were very differently dressed the last time I saw you,' he added, in the same matter-of-fact tone.

'I was indeed,' Markham said. 'Do you mind if I sit down?'

'Not at all.' Tarquin indicated the space beside him. 'What brings you this way?'

'I was just taking a walk,' Markham said. 'Weren't you with someone else just now?'

'Someone else?'

'I thought I saw someone talking to you. Here, on the bench, just a short while ago.'

'There was someone here, yes,' Tarquin said.

Opposite them, in the centre of the courtyard, two men were crouched at the fountain, their loose trousers rolled up to the thighs, performing the ritual ablution before entering the mosque. Markham watched them wash hands, faces and feet and take some of the water into their mouths.

'The mosques are full today,' Tarquin said. He had been following the direction of Markham's gaze. 'Full of devout Moslems purifying themselves,' he said. 'Now it is the month of Ramazan. Nothing must pass the lips of the true believer between sunrise and sunset.' There was a sort of sardonic hostility in the words, which the absence of inflection in the voice seemed to make more evident.

'I didn't realize Ramazan had begun,' Markham said. 'Someone must have spotted the new moon.'

'These people need more than fasting to purge their crimes away,' Tarquin said. 'Let them eat what they want when they want, and stop killing us. That would make more sense. If not, some day we will start killing them.' The semblance of a smile touched his face. 'It will not matter then,' he said, 'whether their bellies are empty or full.'

He was speaking more openly than Markham had expected, but of course he would be assuming considerable sympathy, in view of the visit to Hartunian. He knew, too, of course, what Markham had lost. Standing there behind Hartunian he had learned of it – the engagement party,

315

Miriam's violation and death. The loss he knew about, but not the shame. He knew everything but the main thing, and so he knew nothing.

'Things will be better now,' Markham said, 'under this new government.'

Tarquin made no immediate reply. The slight smile had returned to his face. He lowered his head a little. During the brief silence that now fell between them, an old ragged woman with cataracted eyes came shuffling along beside the lower parapet wall that bounded the inner area of the courtyard. She was carrying a tin tray. Markham watched her seat herself on the parapet, produce from some part of her person several packets of grain, tip the grain out onto the tray, which was level across her knees. Within seconds the wide flagged area before her was covered with eager pigeons. They came fluttering down from all directions. The air around the old woman's head was a confusion of wings. More and more arrived until the whole space seethed with them. They must know her, Markham thought, watching the strutting creatures. It was like a celebration of greed. He saw the old woman throw a handful of grain into the mêlée.

'That is quite meaningless,' Tarquin said, raising his head. 'What you said is meaningless. For things to get better is no solution – not when they are so bad.'

'I don't see that,' Markham said.

'Bad, not so bad, a little better, bad again. We have fluctuated like that for generations, Captain Markham. The total of misery and oppression remains always constant. No one but a fool believes promises that Turks make to Armenians. We will co-operate, we will stop drawing the attention of Europe to our injustices and in return they will reduce our taxes and give us a few seats in the Assembly. What good is that?'

'I suppose that was Hartunian's mistake,' Markham said. 'According to you, anyway.'

'What do you mean?'

316

'He believed the promises, didn't he?'

Markham looked straight before him at the blind woman sitting on the wall. Beyond her the grey stone walls of the mosque rose up into the mist. This was thinning now – he could make out the leaden mass of the dome, though the upper parts of the minarets were still shrouded. The courtyard of the mosque within its surrounding wall was like a great well in which mist and sunshine mingled to form a new, incandescent element. The forms of people passing against the sun were outlines only. Markham saw someone stop beside the old woman, presumably to buy grain to give the pigeons.

'Is that why you gave information against him?' he asked. 'I know you did, so there's no point in denying it, none at all. You gave information against him, to agents of the Palace, before last July, before the revolution. On your own or with others, I don't know.'

'I wasn't going to deny it,' Tarquin said. He turned on the bench so that he was looking squarely at Markham. 'You are a fool,' he said, almost casually.

'He was your fellow-countryman,' Markham said. 'He trusted completely in your loyalty and discretion – I saw that for myself. He worked for the Armenian cause, and suffered for it.'

'Suffered?' Tarquin took his hands out of the pockets of his overcoat, looked briefly at them, then laid them loosely together in his lap. They were heavy hands, with thick short fingers – peasant's hands. The thickset squat body, too, seemed bred from generations of labouring people. It came as a shock, almost, to see the considering eyes, hear the easy English.

'The suffering of individuals is not important,' he said. 'Hartunian lost his wife in the Constantinople massacres, you lost your fiancée. You think: They did this to me, to *me*! You nurse what they did to you. You think of yourself as an outraged individual. You are alone with yourself. There are

317

two million Armenians in Turkey, Captain Markham. The very great majority of them have no leisure to cultivate their personal sense of outrage in that way.'

'That's true, I suppose,' Markham said. He took care to keep his tone casual, give no indication of the degree to which Tarquin's words had affected him, coinciding as they did with his own sense of isolation.

'We must think collectively,' Tarquin said. He was looking straight before him now at the old woman sitting on the wall with her tray of grain. A pigeon bolder than the others alighted on the edge of the tray, to be at once dislodged by a sweep of the ragged arm.

'It is the only way,' Tarquin said. 'Otherwise our strength will be dissipated. There are too many differences. Hartunian is an Armenian but he has more in common with you than with me. As an individual, that is. I knew that the moment I saw you together. You are both privileged people with the same standards, more or less. Neither of you have suffered want. You talk the same language, in other words – and it is not mine. You are both soft, in a way, too. In Hartunian's case it is dangerous.'

'Why? Because he's a moderate? Because he believes in reconciliation?'

'No. Because he still thinks of his sufferings as an individual thing. He is arrogant, as well as soft. Listen, if it is a question of numbers, my loss has been greater than either of yours. I lost both parents and a brother.'

'In Constantinople, you mean?'

'Not Constantinople, no.' Tarquin turned his head and looked at Markham. Beneath the shadow of the hat brim his eyes had a cold and steady glitter. 'You think there were no killings anywhere else?' he said. 'A quarter of a million Armenians had been slaughtered before they went to work in Constantinople. I was born in the *vilayet* of Biabekir, in the east of Turkey, which once formed part of the kingdom of Armenia but which we are obliged to share now with the

318

Kurds who prey on us. It was they who did most of the things that were done there. The Kurds and the *zaptiehs*, the local militia.'

'They were set on to it,' Markham said.

'They did not need much prompting. They have always been hostile. We were settled people, the Kurds nomadic. They raided our villages and so on. It needed Abdul Hamid with his genius for adapting means to ends, to see that the most efficient and economical way of getting rid of Armenians was to form the Kurds into an irregular cavalry and turn them loose on us. In 1894, when I was fourteen, that is what he did. It was ingenious, you see – desire for loot combined with religious fervour. They heated metal pots until they were red-hot and put them on people's heads – bishops' mitres, they were called. They branded people – men and women – with the cross. They cut throats to the accompaniment of verses from the Koran. In some places the smell of burnt human flesh hung about the mountains for days . . .' Tarquin's voice was quite dispassionate. 'I was out in the streets when it began,' he said. 'I escaped by hiding in a cellar. My parents and my younger brother were not so lucky. They took refuge in the church, together with a lot of other people. The Moslems set fire to the church and all the people inside died in the fire. I lay there in the cellar underneath the sacks of grain, listening to it all.' He nodded towards the old woman. 'Watching her reminded me of it,' he said. 'Some of the sacks were torn and the grain was spilling out. The same colour.'

The old woman was in the sunshine now. She raised her face to the faint warmth of it. Her hands were never at rest. They ruffled continuously through the grain, which was the colour of wet straw. She buried her thin hands to the wrists in it, took up handfuls, poured it back in trickles, caressed the mounds level again. Markham watched while a child, a girl of ten or eleven, handed over kurus for a packet of the grain, watched the sudden flurry of pigeons as the grain was thrown amongst them. Against the grey of the mosque and the

319

courtyard walls, the pigeons seemed vivid; the pale blue of their breasts had an effect of brilliance.

'Otherwise I wouldn't have spoken of it, probably,' Tarquin said. 'It is not much to the point now.'

'Of course it is.' Markham spoke with sudden certainty, even authority. 'An experience like that determines your life,' he said. 'To try to deny that is as bad as the self-indulgence you accuse me of.'

'You misunderstand,' Tarquin said coldly. 'I do not try to deny what happened. I try to use it. I do not spend my time trying to find a meaning in it, like you. And like Hartunian. As if it were some kind of fodder for your spiritual consumption. That is disgusting. As I was lying there I could hear the village burning, a strange sound. Like prolonged applause. I could hear the cries and screams of the people and the smashing of glass. But the thing I remember most, and the only really *important* sound, was the thing that the mob kept chanting.' Tarquin paused. Then, still looking away from Markham, across the courtyard, he recited softly, as if to himself, '*La ilaha ill-Allah, Muhammedin Rasula-llah.*'

'There is no other God but one God and Mohammed is his prophet,' Markham said.

'It doesn't sound much in English. Rather dry and legalistic. But you hear it in Arabic with those throat sounds made by a lot of voices together and it is not a human sound at all. It is the ululation of blood lust, abstract, collective – always collective. What people but Moslems could use God's name in that way?' His voice had risen. He was silent for a moment, then went on more quietly. 'I heard it again ten years later, in Severek. I was being taken to the police station with two other men for operating a printing press. We had been badly beaten by the *zaptiehs* and could hardly walk – they dragged us along. There was a crowd of women at the edge of the road shouting curses at us. Suddenly, all together, they started to screech the *zelgid*, the battlecry of the women of Islam. "Lu-lu-lu-lu." Very high and shrill. There weren't many of them, but it was the same sound, the same kind of sound.'

'I don't understand quite what you meant when you said the sound was important,' Markham said.

'That is because you cannot imagine what it is like to belong to a persecuted race. Hartunian has money, but he knows it. The sound was important because I heard the centuries in it. The hate going far back and far forward. I understood then, at fourteen – and I have never forgotten the lesson – that so long as my people remain subject to the Turk there can be no reconciliation. We can make deals, but only for our advantage. The end is always the same, a free, independent state of Armenia. Any Armenian who stops short of this is either a traitor or a fool.' Tarquin's voice deepened as he uttered these last words, but he showed no other sign of emotion. 'People like Hartunian,' he said, 'with their money and European manners and this half-baked liberalism. They speak the same language as the politicians.'

'His money is not a crime,' Markham said. This was the second or third time that the other man had referred to Hartunian's wealth, and always with the same disparagement.

Tarquin looked at him a moment with an expression difficult to read. Then he said slowly, 'To live in daily fear. To see your father humiliated, your mother insulted. To have the produce of your labour taken from you without redress of any kind. To work and work and still starve. What do they know of that? And you, you know nothing of it either. In your case it does not matter, not to us. But with Hartunian it is different. We are not the only ones who think so. Have you seen the papers? Hartunian has been arrested along with others of the Liberal Union.'

Markham nodded. So that was the connexion. 'Yes,' he said, 'I know.'

'Who do you think was behind that? Not his friends in the government. They make the same bleats as he does, decentralization, more autonomy for the subject peoples. The usual rubbish. No, it is the Committee that have locked him up, the very people he had such faith in. All this talk of equality, representative institutions and so on, it deceived people like Hartunian, it still deceives the European powers, and especially England. But not us. It never deceived us. They are nationalists, these people of the Committee. They believe in the supremacy of the Turk, in a Turkish national renaissance. They are not religious, it is true, but they cover this by their talk of Pan-Islam, which is really a race movement, not religious at all, though it appeals to the *mollahs*. Oh yes, they will make concessions to the Armenians, sufficient to satisfy Europe. We will be forgotten again, after all the work and all the blood.' He stood up abruptly. 'I must go,' he said. 'I have stayed too long already. Talking is pointless in any case, I was led into it by your reproaches concerning Hartunian. Some remnant of old-fashioned morality, I suppose.' He spoke coldly.

'You probably have more such remnants than you think,' Markham said.

'Good-bye then.' Tarquin did not offer his hand.

'Just a minute,' Markham said. 'Can you stay a bit longer?'

He had spoken on an impulse, aware only of a reluctance to let the other man go. He saw the stocky figure of Tarquin hesitate before him, the sunshine fluffing very slightly the black outline of overcoat and hat. Beyond him now it was difficult to look: the sun had invaded and infused the mist, making a dazzling haze of it, though without heat. In this cold radiance the breasts of the pigeons emitted flashes of brilliance.

'There is something I want to say to you,' Markham said.

Tarquin shrugged slightly, sat down again. All the same Markham did not begin at once. He looked for some moments curiously at the sullen profile of Tarquin's face below the brim of the hat. There was something monstrous about him, the total disregard for any claim of piety or value other than the

322

collective idea. Perhaps it was this, the fact that the man was his opposite, that for the moment brought them close, created a sort of abstract intimacy between them. All Tarquin's energy was directed towards a shared aim, whereas he, in the few words he had uttered while the men held him, had repudiated and denied all groups whatever – in those minutes, claiming to be representative, he had become for ever single, which was what Tarquin had for ever ceased to be, lying among the split sacks of grain, listening to the chanting and the slaughter . . .

'You spoke earlier,' Markham said, 'about the quantity of our losses and how yours was greater than either Hartunian's or mine, as if it was numbers that mattered. What you don't seem to see is that experiences like that affect people differently. You talk about self-indulgence, but there is a kind of indulgence in being a member of a persecuted group, in being a member of anything – you can take some collective comfort in it, or refuge, at least. There is no refuge for someone who is not a member. He can't avoid the feeling that he has been struck at just because he is who he is. Not what he is. Do you see what I mean?' He paused for a moment then went on in a more vibrant tone. 'Take my case, if I may talk about myself a little. It isn't what they did to the girl I was going to marry that connects me with the Armenians, it is what they did to *me*. That man, the one who talked to me and looked into my face . . .'

Without meaning to, driven by a sort of compulsion, he began to go further into the details of that evening, speaking to Tarquin's averted face, mentioning the terrible preliminaries, the lights, the silent fiddler, the perfume of the women, the glasses of champagne, the sheepish attitude of the strangers, then their movements, like a dance. As always it was the face of the man who had spoken to him that he ended with, that moist-eyed face with the thin beard, which had come with a kind of sly ardour so close to his own, had looked at him and *seen*. 'I could do nothing to prevent it,' he said, looking at Tarquin's profile. 'There were three of them holding me, you know. No point in saying anything either – the killing had started by then.' It was a false note: he knew it as he spoke. He saw Tarquin's head turn towards him. 'If only I could find him again,' he said quickly. 'I would know his face. If only I could find him again and kill him.'

'Just that one?' Tarquin asked.

'Yes.' He met the Armenian's eyes. They were fixed on him, bright, cold, terribly intelligent. For an appalled moment it seemed to Markham that Tarquin was looking at him as that other man had looked, with total knowledge. It was minds that had knowledge of him that he wanted to kill, he knew that now, knew it in this moment, with a sickening sense of his own perverted pride, knew that even the suspicion that there was such knowledge in Nesbitt's mind had made him want the man dead, hound him to suicide. Nothing to do with justice, certainly nothing to do with the Armenian cause . . . 'Do you understand?' he said with sudden passion. 'I don't care about the Armenians. It's for my own sake.'

'You will not find him again. He is probably dead by now,' Tarquin said, and Markham realized with a strange ambivalence of feeling that he had been mistaken, that Tarquin was not thinking of the part he had played, but only in the single-minded way characteristic of him, of what he had just declared, namely his readiness to kill.

'He does not matter,' Tarquin said. 'But there are others. I am glad we have had this talk.' He rose to his feet, and stood looking down at Markham. 'It doesn't matter either,' he said, 'whether what you do is for your own sake or for us. The only question is whether you would be ready to help us if the time came.'

Markham was aware of the squat bulk of the man before him, black and definite in the cold haze of sunshine. 'Yes,' he said, without thought, without volition. 'Yes, I would.'

Tarquin nodded once then turned and began to move away. Markham watched him pass out of the courtyard into the *meydan* beyond. He himself remained for a few minutes longer. He lit a cigarette and smoked for a while. Briefly and precariously he was at peace.

It was late in the afternoon, when he was getting ready to leave for home, that the phone call came. Armstrong was passing down the corridor at the time and he answered it, poking his head round Markham's door a few moments later to tell him the call was for him.

He went out into the corridor and took up the receiver. 'Hallo,' he said. 'Markham.'

'Captain Markham?'

'Yes. Who is that, please?'

'We talked this morning at the Nuro Osmaniyé Mosque.'

'Oh yes.' There was a metallic unmodulated quality in the voice, isolated thus on the phone, which Markham did not remember noticing earlier. It was obvious that Tarquin did not want to utter his own name. 'What is it?' he said. 'What's the matter?'

'I want to talk to you. It is something important.'

'Very well,' Markham said. 'Perhaps we could meet somewhere tomorrow. I'm just about to leave for home now.'

There was a pause at the other end of the line, then Tarquin said, 'No, it must be today.'

'Has anything happened?' Markham asked. 'Since this morning, I mean.'

'No. But there is something we would like to discuss.'

'I see.' Markham thought for a moment. He had not missed the switch to 'we'. Tarquin had conferred with others then. He ought to have expected it. Perhaps he had, in a way. He had known, sitting there on the bench in the mosque yard, in that fluffy radiance of sun and mist, known with every word, that he would have to purchase his release from whatever it was that held him in thrall to the Armenians. He would not get it free. Perhaps that too had been part of the

325

motive, part of the impulse to confess, an impulse always frustrated – by pride or shame, he did not know. Yes, he thought now, holding the receiver, of course this was only to be expected. It was the shortness of the interval that had surprised him. 'You can come here,' he said. 'I suppose you know the address?'

Again there was a brief pause at the other end. Markham had the feeling that Tarquin was conversing with someone, someone beside him there.

'There will be no one here in half an hour,' he said. 'My colleague is leaving soon. There are only the two of us on this floor, the first floor. There is a café on the ground floor, but if you go straight up the stairs you will not be noticed.'

He waited. Armstrong came out of his office into the passage. He was dressed for the street, with a trenchcoat over his uniform. Markham watched him lock his door. Tarquin's voice came over the line, almost without inflection: 'In about half-an-hour, then.'

Markham replaced the phone and turned back towards his office.

'Aren't you coming?' Armstrong said. The two men often had a drink together, these days, on the way home, usually at the bar of the Imperial near Galata Tower. A certain friendship had grown up between them despite considerable differences. On Armstrong's side this was mainly because he was still fairly lonely in the city, though he was beginning to make friends now among the foreign community. Markham for his part found that the younger man's uncritical, easy-going temperament reduced the level of his own tensions. It was with distinct regret that he told Armstrong now that he had work to finish that would keep him there some time longer.

He sat at his desk, listening to the sound of Armstrong's descending steps on the uncarpeted stairs. After this there was silence. He was aware of the life of the city around him as a vibrancy, a continuum not broken by brief, particular sounds

326

from the street outside – voices, rattle of wheels on cobbles – but somehow absorbing them into this continuous resonance, to which the life of his own body added its dues of pulse and breath.

After some minutes he got up and went to the window. The courtyard below was deserted, the stables empty. The mist had gone now and the sunshine with it. Banks of cloud had built up over the Marmara. Against the dark slate colour of the clouds, high above the city, Markham saw a pair of kites wheeling slowly. Already he could sense a faint graining of darkness in the air. Shadows were deepening in the courtyard – the cobbles looked black almost.

He looked across at the disused fountain against the far wall, its beautiful fan-shape of marble greened with ancient deposits but with the decorative carving in the side panels still discernible. There long before the wall was built, he thought. Perhaps there already in the days of Ottoman greatness, when Sinan was building the mosques and Suleyman's Janissaries were at the gates of Vienna. The consciousness of power and wealth had scattered small masterpieces throughout the city in those days; crumbling and half-ruined now, like this fountain. The whole of Constantinople was an elaborate ruin, he thought, and it was on afternoons like this, when light seemed to retreat from the city, that the signs of dereliction were most evident – sunshine always cast a veil of melancholy or nostalgia over the decay . . .

He thought suddenly of Abdul Hamid, something he did quite rarely these days. Hunched and disconsolate, a bird with its wings clipped, in his cage of Yildiz. He had been the last autocrat of his race, a dealer in death on a large scale – a quarter of a million, Tarquin had said, though the figures of course were not really known. What would he do now after such crimes? These laid their own obligation, surely, compelled some further action, even if merely one of self-definition. In a way, like Tarquin, lying among the sacks listening to the sounds of murder. Or like himself, held by the

327

intruders that night, a grip that had never really been relaxed. After thirty years in the grip of his power and his fear, it would be difficult for Abdul Hamid to acquiesce in his role as constitutional monarch. Perhaps even now he was preparing to reinstate himself. The city was tense these days, with rumours and alarms. The recent establishment of a Girls' High School at Kandilli had inflamed Moslem fanaticism. The daughters of good Moslems were being corrupted, it was said; such a thing could not have happened in the days when 'Baba Hamid' had the power. A few days previously, towards dusk, a man had run through the streets of the Grand Bazaar, shouting at intervals, 'They are coming!', exciting such panic that shops had been closed and shuttered, and children trampled underfoot in the rush to get clear. Whether the man was crazed or an agent of disorder nobody knew . . .

He heard the sound of footsteps mounting the stairs. Obeying some instinct of self-defence, he moved quickly back behind the desk and sat down. It sounded like more than one man. He waited for them to find his name on the door. There was some scraping of feet, then the knock. 'Come in,' he called.

There were two of them, Tarquin and another, a slighter man with a short beard and rimless glasses, whom he introduced as Missakian. They sat against the wall on the upright chairs which were all Markham had to offer them.

Missakian said, 'They do not give you very luxurious offices.' He spoke English with an American accent.

Markham smiled, consciously relaxing his face in order to do so. 'They think we should be glad it's not tents,' he said. 'If I were a government official it would be different.' He felt suddenly sure that he had seen Missakian before somewhere.

Missakian nodded, returning the smile. He had gentle, myopic brown eyes, magnified by the lenses of his glasses, and the general look and complexion of an indoor man. 'Yes,' he said, 'they look after their own.'

328

'Missakian has been abroad for some years,' Tarquin said in his harsh voice. 'In the United States.'

Markham said nothing to this. After a moment or two Missakian said, 'I have been editing a newspaper there, an Armenian paper, the *Gotchnag* – perhaps you have heard of it?'

'No,' Markham said. He met the other man's gaze, which was fixed on him with a sort of gentle attentiveness.

'We have a lot of support in America,' Missakian said. 'The paper was not allowed here, of course. Before the revolution, I mean. The word "Armenian" was itself on the prohibited list. Like "dynamite" and "constitution". What an absurd thing!' His face still wore the same gentle smile.

Markham stood up. 'I'm sure you'd like coffee,' he said. 'I'll get the *kahvehci* to come up.'

'It would be better not,' Missakian said. 'We do not want to draw attention to ourselves.'

'Very well,' Markham reseated himself behind the desk. 'Well, gentlemen?' he said. 'What do you want of me?'

It was Tarquin who spoke first. 'We want you to do something for us,' he said.

'I gathered that. Who is the "we"?' Suddenly he knew where he had seen Missakian before. He remembered leaving Hartunian's house, the glimpse into the small room with the table. Missakian had been one of the two men sitting there.

'Our people,' Tarquin said brusquely.

'Come now,' Markham said. 'I must know who I am dealing with.'

'We are members of the *Henchak*,' Missakian said quietly.

'Our information is that the Armenian Societies have disbanded themselves,' Markham said. 'In return for the guarantees offered by the government. Or at any rate that they are preparing to do so.'

'That is not true,' Tarquin said. 'It is those who do not belong to us who advocate this.'

'People like Hartunian?'

Neither of the Armenians answered this immediately. Then

Missakian said, 'You are concerned about Hartunian, I believe. You needn't be. He has plenty of money.'

He lifted his hand and made the gesture of rubbing forefinger and thumb together. His voice had been as quiet as ever, but Markham sensed the contempt in it, directed less at Hartunian himself than at the notion of his wealth. The same tone, though fiercer, had been used by Tarquin during their conversation in the mosque yard when he had spoken of Hartunian as the privileged outsider. There was some element in it that Markham found difficult to understand. He looked at Missakian's face, the pallor, the high forehead, the gentle eyes behind the clerkly glasses. The face had the composure of one who has answered certain questions to his own satisfaction for ever. Suddenly it seemed to Markham that this man was more formidable than Tarquin. 'It is hard for the rich man to enter the kingdom of heaven,' he said. 'We have that on good authority.'

'We are not interested in guarantees of reform,' Missakian said in the same quiet tone.

'No, I suppose not.' Markham took out his cigarette case and offered cigarettes. Both of the men accepted. 'What is it that you want of me?' he said again.

It was Missakian who answered, confirming Markham's growing sense that it was he rather than Tarquin who held the authority.

'It is something only you can do,' Missakian said. 'There is a man here, Hassan Fehmi, the editor of the *Serbesti* – do you know this paper?'

'Yes,' Markham said. The *Serbesti* was a reactionary newspaper, a self-appointed guardian of Islamic morality and custom. Of late months, with the growth of Moslem hostility to the new government, it had become increasingly scurrilous, though still taking care to pay lip-service to the democratic ideals of the Young Turks. 'Yes,' he repeated. 'I know the paper you mean, but I don't know the man.'

'He is the editor,' Tarquin said. 'A man of no principles

330

whatever.' His mouth tightened with disgust under the thick moustache. 'Very evil life,' he said.

Missakian looked briefly at him as if in warning or reproof, then continued, 'Lately, for reasons which we do not understand, the *Serbesti* has been printing a series of attacks on the Armenians. Have you seen them?'

Markham shook his head.

'They take two forms. First there are gross and abusive items about the Armenian race itself. They accuse us of perverted practices, unclean habits and so on. The idea of this is to make us seem disgusting and even sub-human to the Moslems. This may seem crude to you, Captain Markham, but they are ignorant people and they are already prejudiced against us on religious grounds. Secondly we are accused of scheming to take power. It is almost incredible, but people believe it. The *Serbesti* tells them that when we are in power we will pay off old scores. They know what that means: old floggings, old rapes, old murders. So fear of us reinforces disgust in the popular mind. You see?'

'Effective in its way,' Markham said. 'Given the ignorance and the bigotry.'

'It is during the last few weeks only that this material has been published. We want to know who is behind these articles.'

'But why should you think there is anyone behind them? Other than the staff of the paper, that is.'

'Staff?' Missakian's smile deepened. 'There is not much staff,' he said. 'There is only Hassan Fehmi, who is a known scoundrel. His only principle is to keep favour with the Palace and the reactionary elements that surround the Sultan. People pay him to put things in his paper, and people pay him to leave things out. That is how he lives.'

'And you want me to find out what is behind this anti-Armenian stuff?'

'Yes,' Missakian said simply. 'That is what we want.'

'Why ask me?'

331

'It cannot be done by one of us There are few outside the organization whom we can trust. Besides, he would be suspicious of most people, or at least on his guard. But an Englishman, that would be different. The English are highly respected, Captain Markham. Hassan Fehmi would be flattered by the acquaintance. He grew up in Egypt, if you understand what that means. Perhaps he will let something out. A few words could be enough to set us on the right path.'

'And if not?'

'Well, there will be no harm done,' Tarquin said.

Missakian leaned forward. 'We are asking you to do this for us,' he said. 'It will be distasteful, we know that.'

Markham looked from one to the other, from the heavy features and deceptively melting eyes of Tarquin to Missakian's high forehead and dilated gaze behind the glasses. They were very different in physical type. But the same ardour of expectation seemed to possess them both now, as they looked at him, though what precisely they were expecting was still not wholly clear to him. A few stray words, confidences that he might or might not succeed in eliciting from this man Fehmi, whom he did not know: the proposition was a vague one. Perhaps the more genuine for that, he thought. They had seen that he could be used and they had lost no time. Once involved he could be used again, perhaps for some larger purpose. He knew that he was going to agree – his assent had the force of a prior commitment, immediate and unquestioned. Once again the old irony touched his mind: by his one denial of them he had made himself helpless, like something wilfully disabled under the shadows of vultures' wings. He would have acceded to anything, almost, that they had asked him – perhaps he should be glad the task was not more demanding. All the same, there remained in the back of his mind some feeling of oddness about the thing they were asking him to do, not a suspicion exactly, more like a feeling of discrepancy, some failure of correspondence.

'He speaks French fluently, and English too, though

332

probably not so well,' Missakian said. 'He is from Alexandria.'

Markham nodded. 'What else can you tell me about him?'

'You agree then?' Missakian expelled a breath. It struck Markham with distinct surprise that the other had been in doubt of the issue.

'Well, I'll see what I can do,' he said.

Tarquin put a hand into his inside pocket and drew out a postcard-sized photograph. 'This is Fehmi,' he said. Markham found himself looking at the head and shoulders of an extremely corpulent man in a fez. It was a studio photograph and the subject was facing the camera with a prepared expression of blandness. It was a huge face, fleshy and heavy-boned, with something negroid in the thick, slightly everted lips, the setting of the eyes in their bony sockets.

'I'd better keep this,' Markham said.

Tarquin began speaking steadily in his harsh, barely inflected voice. 'Hassan Fehmi was born in Alexandria in 1867 or 1868,' he said. 'He is illegitimate. His father was a Turkish consular official. He was still in Egypt when the British took over – he probably learned his English during this period. Afterwards he lived in Tunis and then in Antioch, in Syria. In both those places he worked ostensibly as a journalist, but it is thought that he collected information about the Young Turk movement for Abdul Hamid – he posed as an exiled patriot, you understand. He came to Constantinople three years ago. Six months ago he took over the editorship of the *Serbesti*. He is a member of the Mohammedan League, which is an extreme reactionary society, dedicated to the preserving of Islamic law and tradition. The offices of the *Serbesti* are in Galata, in Saray Street.'

The harsh voice ceased and there was silence for a short while. Then Missakian got to his feet. 'We will leave you to manage things,' he said. He looked at Markham with the

333

same composure, at once mild and implacable. 'We will not forget this,' he said, holding out his hand. Tarquin too shook hands, though saying nothing and barely looking at Markham.

He sat at his desk, listening to their retreating steps on the stairs. There had been an element of unreality about this interview – when the sounds had died away it was difficult somehow to believe that the two men had really been there at all. As he sat there, in the silent aftermath of the visit, still holding Fehmi's picture, he heard the booming of the cannon on Seraglio Point, signalling to the faithful the end of the day's fasting, and he remembered that it was now the month of Ramazan.


The feeling of unreality persisted throughout the following days. Perhaps because of it he made no immediate move to establish contact with Fehmi. He waited, as if for some sign. Nesbitt's death was given out as accidental – he had had an accident while cleaning his service revolver. Kyriakos, who was one of the doctors on the Embassy list, certified that the injuries were consistent with this version of things. The whole affair was handled with the sort of shocked competence characteristic of British officials when avoiding a scandal. Nesbitt had left no note behind, it seemed – nothing. At least, no one showed any knowledge of the visit Markham had made on the night of Nesbitt's death. And once the official enquiry was over Markham himself soon ceased to feel much personal responsibility. The impulse of cruelty that had risen in him at the other man's despair, the words he had spoken to Nesbitt, words that had made him an accomplice in the suicide, were now equally difficult to recall, as if erased somehow by the shot that had blasted Nesbitt's brain. It was not indifference but a sort of saving numbness, similar to that which had blunted remorse over his dealings with Miss Taverner and his wife and son. It was as if he had energy only for present purposes, obscure as these still were to him. And as with the governess and his family, so with Nesbitt: all that remained were the random impressions of sense – the settling of logs on the fire, the maniacal wind in the night outside, the smell of brandy and cigar smoke, Nesbitt's dogged face turning slowly, and his voice with the snarl of death in it.

However, the very vividness with which he recalled these things constituted a sort of guilt perhaps, or at least obligation, because a week or so after the enquiry he paid a visit to the apartment off the Rue des Postes where Nesbitt's mistress was still living.

The apartment was on the second floor of a large wooden house with heavy shutters and narrow balconies of wrought iron. Markham climbed the stairs and rang the bell. He had to wait a considerable time. Then a woman came to the door. She looked about thirty or so, with pale freckles over the bridge of her nose and wide blue eyes and a loose unhappy mouth. She was wearing a white wrap over what seemed fairly scanty attire, and her fair hair was in disarray.

He explained in French who he was and she answered in the same language, but she did not ask him in. He was silent. He did not know why he had come. Perhaps it was simply curiosity, a desire to see the woman that Nesbitt had spoken of with tenderness, for whose sake, partially at least, he had needed money badly enough to betray men to their deaths. But of course there was nothing in her face that could have explained this, nothing in those small features, both ailing and sensual, that could ever help to explain why Nesbitt had done what he did. One does not do such things for other people.

She stood holding the door open, looking at him with a sort of blank enquiry. He could think of nothing to say. He looked past her into the room. It was small, cluttered-looking. Suddenly, from the room beyond, presumably a bedroom, he heard a man's voice raised. '*Qu'est-ce que tu fais? Dépêche-toi.*' It was the voice of the client, unmistakable the world over. The

335

woman moved the door forward a little, cutting off Markham's view. She showed no sign of embarrassment or anything else. '*Mon cousin*,' she said.

Markham nodded and smiled and turned away. It was fitting, he thought, as he went back down the stairs, that she should have men in the apartment that Nesbitt was paying for still, though dead. No doubt the lease still had some time to run. Nesbitt had nothing to complain of either – he had paid for his solace with blood money . . .

He had been intending to return directly to his office, and had in fact reached the lower end of Iskander Street, which led up to it, when he heard a female voice call his name and saw, on the opposite corner, Miss Munro waving and smiling. She was accompanied by a huge Albanian *kavass* in hotel livery.

He crossed over and they shook hands.

'Your uncle told me you were back in Constantinople,' he said.

'Yes,' she said, with that slight, bridling self-importance which he suddenly remembered, 'I wanted to see how things are under the new dispensation.'

He nodded, taking care to keep his expression free from any hint of scepticism. 'Good idea,' he said.

'It's lucky we should have met like this,' Miss Munro said. 'I was just on my way to call at your office.'

'Oh, were you?'

'I wanted to ask for your help.'

She glanced at the tall, magnificently moustached *kavass* standing quietly a few paces away, with his tasselled cap and broad red sash from which knives of various sorts protruded.

'I won't need him any more,' she said, 'now that I've met you. You can go,' she said to the Albanian. 'You can go back to the hotel now. This gentleman will accompany me.'

She had taken his assent for granted, in a way that only very pretty and spoilt women usually do. But with Miss Munro, he thought, her own purposes were sufficient substitute for beauty. All the same, he did not mind. 'You can go now,' he told the guide. *'Kadine bakicilik yapacagim.* I will look after the lady.'

The man bowed his head gravely and began at once to move away.

'It's a question of the language,' Miss Munro said. 'I don't really think that he could have translated properly.' She nodded after the departing Albanian. 'My uncle is away, you see,' she said.

'Abdullah's is just along the street,' Markham said. 'Perhaps we could have coffee, or a drink of some kind, while you tell me what it is about.'

She assented to this, though with what seemed slight suspicion, as at something not envisaged, and they moved off down the street together.

The café-bar would normally have been quite full at this late-morning time but now, during the period of Ramazan, it was practically deserted. They found a table near the window. Miss Munro said she wanted orange juice.

'Well,' Markham said, 'so you have come to do some more articles?'

'Yes,' she said, 'I've been commissioned to write a further series. My first series were well received. They aroused a great deal of interest.'

She spoke with that slight, probably unconscious bridling, as if to meet some anticipated derision on his part – the self-importance was defensive, he now saw. She would be remembering the disparaging nature of his remarks on the former occasion – the only other time that they had met. She would always remember all disparagement. In her dealings with the world of men she was permanently embattled. He felt a sort of nostalgia at this spikiness of hers, at the muted Edinburgh accent: they belonged to that golden age of the previous summer, when his wife and son had still been unbetrayed, Miss Taverner unsullied, Hartunian's name not glimpsed. When he still had the illusion that his life was whole.

337

In appearance she was exactly as he had remembered: the same unwavering grey eyes, the same fashionably bobbed hair, unsuitable for that long, serious face, a Victorian face somehow, he thought, for all her modern self-assertion, recalling tones of sepia, hands in the laps, patience, subjection. She was dressed very soberly, too, in navy blue, as if ready for a formal photograph.

'You won't have anything stronger?' he asked, seeing the waiter approaching. 'A sherry, or a glass of wine?'

'At this time of day?' There was reproof in her voice, and the kind of relief that comes from having been able to normalize relations, from having, after these dangerous civilities, found something to disapprove of.

Markham ordered the orange juice and a glass of sherry for himself. When the waiter had gone, he said, 'So you are going to write about the new Turkey, that kind of thing?'

'That kind of thing, yes,' she said rather tartly. 'The eyes of the whole world are on Turkey at the moment. What has happened here is one of the most extraordinary things in modern times. People don't seem to realize it. Here you have a five-hundred-year-old theocracy, centre of a vast Empire, ruled over by a man who is not only a hereditary autocrat but the Caliph of Islam with spiritual authority over three hundred million Moslems.'

Miss Munro's voice had fallen into the rhythms of the school-room. Her rather sallow cheeks had flushed.

'The most absolute autocracy in Europe,' she said. 'With a paraphernalia that hasn't changed essentially since the Middle Ages, the artifical world of the Palace with its retinue of slaves, eunuchs, court favourites, harem women. In a matter of a few days all this has been turned into a constitutional monarchy. And with hardly a single drop of blood spilt. Can you think of a parallel to it?'

Markham did not reply immediately. Miss Munro's sudden rush of enthusiasm had irritated him a little, though he could not have said exactly why. She seemed presumptuous, somehow. Perhaps it was just prejudice on his part against independent women, as his wife had said.

'The patient and long-suffering Turk has given a lesson to the whole world in bloodless and glorious revolution,' Miss Munro said, sipping her orange juice.

Last time they had talked, he suddenly remembered, she had expressed sympathy for the Sultan as a lonely and maligned potentate. 'Bloodless?' he said, smiling to cover his irritation. 'Hardly bloodless, surely. It has taken thirty years to make this revolution. That's how long it is since Abdul Hamid abrogated the Constitution. In those thirty years there has been a drop or two of blood spilt, I think you will agree.'

'We always seem to argue about words,' she said with an air of resignation.

'Anyway, you are going to write about all this.'

'Not exactly.' The look of resignation vanished abruptly. Miss Munro drank some more of her orange juice. 'No,' she said, 'what I want to do is look at ordinary lives, see how the change has affected them. You get a great shift like this, like an earthquake, and when the earth has settled again people find themselves in a different landscape.'

Markham had the impression that she was echoing the style of her articles. He said, 'I see, yes.'

'I want to try and convey what that experience has meant to people,' Miss Munro said. 'The guardsman, the concubine, the pageboy.'

'Ordinary people,' Markham said, but Miss Munro was too absorbed in her subject to notice the irony.

She waved a hand briefly, a strangely unexpected gesture in one so prim and repressed in movement. 'Oh,' she said, 'people who go to make up the motley kaleidoscope of Constantinople life. That brings me to why I was coming to see you. I have made contact with a very obliging and knowledgeable person here, and he is arranging various things for me. I have an appointment with him later today as a matter of fact. He's putting me in touch with various

339

people.' Miss Munro paused, then said in a voice of studied casualness, 'He is introducing me to a eunuch this afternoon.'

'A eunuch?' Markham felt slightly dazed for a moment. 'I see, yes,' he said.

'One of the Palace eunuchs. The Sultan has been asked to reduce their numbers, as you know. So this one has become redundant. It should be interesting to see what views a highly specialized person such as that takes about his future.'

Markham gazed at her. She had finished her orange juice now. Her hands were in her lap. Her grey eyes, small and rather close set in the long face, regarded him expectantly. There was something monstrous about her, he decided suddenly, something that went beyond hypocrisy, in the way the careful language covered a curiosity that was doubtless every bit as prurient as that of her readership.

'That is where you come in,' she said.

'I don't quite see—'

'There may be some difficulties, it is not very familiar territory for me,' she said, still in the same judicious tone.

At last he understood. She wanted him to go along with her and attend the interview. She had arranged things and then presumably got cold feet. In short, she wanted his protection.

'Well,' he said cautiously, 'I've got various things to do this afternoon, you know. We are quite busy these days, what with one thing and another.' There must be someone at the Embassy who could help her. One of her uncle's assistants, for example. They might not speak Turkish, of course. 'This person,' he said, 'the man who has arranged the interview for you, surely he knows Turkish well enough to act as interpreter?'

'Well, yes, I suppose so. Actually, yes, he does, but I wanted—'

'Someone who would be on your side?'

'Yes,' she said simply. 'Not that he isn't a marvellous man. He has been so helpful and obliging.'

'What time are you meeting him?'

340

'At five this afternoon.'

'Right,' Markham said with resignation.'I'll come with you. You've got the address, I suppose.'

'Yes, it's in Pera. A little street off the Grande Rue. On the same side as the cemetery – the one they call the Little Field of the Dead. Passage Oriental, the street is called. The room is over a café.'

'We'll find it,' Markham said. 'It's a bit of a warren on that side. Suppose we meet somewhere beforehand? Do you know the Russian Embassy? That's not too far away from it. We could meet there. Say at twenty to five?'

Miss Munro nodded briskly and at once rose to her feet. 'I'll be there,' she said.

Outside Markham hailed a fiacre for her and saw her on to it. She was returning to the hotel. After saying good-bye to her he walked up Iskander Street to his office, where he spent what remained of the morning working at his desk.

He had made what enquiries he could since the visit of Tarquin and Missakian but had not been able to add much to what they had told him about Hassan Fehmi. There was a file on the Mohammedan League with details of some of its members. Markham went through it again now. It had been founded by laymen, not by ecclesiastics, though Markham had no doubt that *mollahs* formed a considerable part of the membership. There was no doubt either that the financial backing came from the Palace. One of the royal Princes, Burhaneddin Effendi, was a founder member, as was Nadir Agha, the Second Eunuch. There was little about the aims of the League, other than general religious conservatism, and nothing at all to connect it with the *Serbesti*.

He lunched at the Pera Club and spent an hour or so afterwards looking at the English newspapers, four days old already when they arrived.

There was a review in *The Times* of Strauss's *Elektra*, which had just been performed in London for the first time to scenes of immense enthusiasm. The reviewer, while admitting the

341

brilliance of the music, spoke darkly of its 'sense of limitless power and arrogant defiance of order.' German music, like everything else German, was regarded with suspicion now, as if it were all part of that country's *weldpolitik*. The Germans themselves did nothing to lessen this suspicion: here, in the same issue, was Chancellor Von Bulow announcing publicly in the Reichstag that Germany would refuse to discuss disarmament at any future peace conference. Mere sabre-rattling really, but it served to top up the fear level in Europe, already dangerously high.

The real focus of anxiety, of course, continued to be the situation in the Balkans. Austria's annexation of Bosnia and Herzegovina had brought Russia close to a declaration of war. Here too Germany was playing a dangerous game of power, giving full support to Austria in this flagrant breach of the Treaty of Berlin. Serbia, newly emerged as a nation, like some reckless moth, was doing her best to provoke collisions. All the signs seemed to indicate that Izvolsky was preparing to back down. But it was a humiliation for Russia, suffered at Austrian hands. She had lost face with her fellow Slavs. She would not soon forget it. Nations were like individuals in that respect, Markham thought. They received such hurts and appeared to absorb them; but an internal festering went on long after the skin was smooth again, went on sometimes for generations, directing attitudes, provoking atrocities in remote areas. Sitting there in the heavy leather armchair, Markham remembered the Greek volunteers whom he had fought alongside in 1897 in that short disastrous war, with their task of the *megali* idea, the recovery of Constantinople – an injury five hundred years old, never forgotten; the loss of Alsace and Lorraine, so grievous to the French, was only yesterday on that scale of time – no wonder they still sang their songs of revenge. Now it was Russia's turn to smart. But when next Serbia asked for protection, or Austria made threats, fear might prove insufficient restraint . . .

These thoughts depressed him, but the afternoon was a

busy one and he had little time for dwelling on them. A delegation from the Balkan Committee, including two Members of Parliament, had come from London on a short visit. They were shortly to take off on a tour of the Northern Provinces and it was Markham's duty to give them all the information at his disposal about the situation in Macedonia. This had deteriorated since the July revolution. The period of racial harmony, what the Young Turks referred to as the process of Ottomanization, had not in fact made much impression up there. The bandit groups, both Christian and Moslem, had never surrendered their arms, and now, the euphoria over, they had returned to their customary rapine. It was an age-old way of life, after all, not a question of political principle – though it was precisely this that Markham found most difficult to explain to the members of the Balkan Committee, Englishmen of liberal and enlightened outlook, who could not easily understand that in certain parts of Macedonia banditry was regarded as an honourable profession, and that the incessant raiding and killing could not be stopped by legislation alone, however right-minded.

These discussions took longer than he had expected, and Miss Munro was already there when he arrived, standing alone in a felt hat and grey tweed coat at the foot of the steps leading up to the Embassy gates.

Together they walked up the Grande Rue for a little way, then turned off into the maze of twisting narrow streets between that thoroughfare and the Rue Mahmoudieh. People in doorways stared at them as they passed and children called out after them. Numbers of the yellow-brown Constantinople street dogs, made mild by long undernourishment, rooted about in casual heaps of refuse.

'These dogs,' Miss Munro said, with veiled distaste. 'They're quite a feature of the city, aren't they?'

'Their ancestors are said to have followed the tribe of Osman all the way here from the Asian Steppes,' Markham said. 'No self-respecting Moslem would harm them. In fact they give them food – never enough of course – and I've seen people putting out bundles of rags for the bitches to have their litters on.'

'Very enlightened,' Miss Munro said, compressing her lips in an involuntary expression of repugnance. She was pale, and it appeared to Markham that the squalor and bad smells in these streets were affecting her considerably. He had to ask several people before he found anyone able to direct him to the Passage Oriental, which was a very short and narrow street, little more than an alley, though it had a wider, circular area about halfway along with a small fountain and a café, and a dark workroom hung with saddles and harness.

'That's probably the café,' Markham said. 'There won't be another one in such a short street as this.'

They went up the short flight of stairs to the second floor. There was only one door and this had a small copper bell hanging on a wire. Markham rang the bell and after a few moments the door opened and a face that Markham knew, a narrow face, surmounted by a quantity of dark, springy-looking hair, peered out at them.

Zimin must have recognized Markham at once, but he made no sign of recognition. With an agility of mind no doubt bred from countless evasions he greeted Miss Munro only.

'Captain Markham,' Miss Munro said. 'Mr Zimin.'

'How do you do, sir?' Zimin said, inclining his body in the deferential manner Markham remembered. He did not look very happy, however.

With a certain feeling of unreality, Markham shook hands. 'I hope you don't mind my coming along,' he said. 'I was interested, and I thought the lady might need some help with the language, you know.'

'It was a private arrangement, actually,' Zimin said. 'But never mind, never mind, come in, you are welcome. *Hosh geldenes.*'

344

'*Hosh bolduk*,' Markham said, making the conventional response.

The room Zimin led them into was very small, and the three of them, together with the figure who rose at their entrance, seemed to fill it completely.

'This is Narsan Bey,' Zimin said. The figure advanced no further but made a practised *temenna*, then straightened and stood there waiting.

He was a plump, middle-aged negro. His fez was tipped back on the large head and the buttons of his frockcoat strained tight across the bulk of his stomach. He looked from face to face smiling broadly. His teeth were stained with betel juice.

'Please be seated,' Zimin said. 'Can I offer you coffee? Turkish coffee can be brought up from the café below, if that is acceptable.'

Both Miss Munro and Markham said they would like coffee, and Zimin went out of the room. As they sat there they could hear him shouting down from some point on the stairs to the people in the café below.

The room was very bare. Against one wall was a narrow iron bedstead with a striped quilt over it. There was a small table and two upright chairs. Like everything associated with Zimin, the room had a makeshift, improvised appearance. It seemed strangely like a stageset to Markham, as if it had been assembled for their visit only.

The negro continued to smile. Miss Munro, no doubt disliking the silence, said, 'Tell him I am very grateful to him for giving me his time like this.'

Markham translated, suppressing from his voice any hint that he found the sentiment absurd. It was clear that the man had been induced to come by an offer of money. Nevertheless, he responded politely, laying one surprisingly delicate hand over the region of his heart, and bowing his head.

Zimin returned and took up a position leaning against the wall near the door. Markham too had remained standing.

345

Miss Munro took out of her bag a notebook and a pencil, and the interview began. She asked Narsan Bey where he was from, and he said he had been told that he came from Kordofan. Others, older than himself, who had made the journey with him, had later told him this. 'That is the upper reaches of the White Nile,' Zimin said. The negro's voice was soft and slurred, as if his thick-lipped mouth was not quite properly shaped for speech.

'He came trekking from up there,' Zimin said. He said a few words quickly in Turkish, and the negro giggled a little, lowering his large, bloodshot eyes. There was a shout from below. 'Ah, the coffee,' Zimin said. 'Excuse me.' He was out of the room for a few moments then returned with the coffee in tiny blue cups on a tin tray. 'Useful,' he said, 'having the café so near.' He essayed a smile to indicate how fortunate he felt this proximity to be. Then, as if conscious that the smile had been a failure, he straightened his shoulders with the spurious dignity typical of him.

Now that he had leisure to observe him fully, it seemed to Markham that Zimin lacked the shine of former days. There was a certain sunken quality about the face which had not been there before. His cuffs and the collar of his shirt had a seedy look. His appearance seemed to have suffered some wilting process. With his thin, somehow obsessive face and that abundant hair, he was more than ever like a music-hall virtuoso – one whose piano stool would collapse at the wrong moment.

'So you were young at the time?' Miss Munro sat on the hard chair, pencil poised, knees pressed close together under her tweed skirt.

Narsan said he thought he was eight years old or perhaps nine.

'How did it happen? Can he tell us how he was caught and made to come here?'

'He was sold,' Zimin said, after some moments of conversation with the negro. 'He was sold to the slavers by the

346

chief of his village. Several boys and girls of his age were sold at the same time and also some older people.'

Miss Munro wrote busily for a while. Then she looked up and smiled sympathetically at the eunuch. 'He was sold by his own people,' she observed to Markham.

The eunuch, presumably taking Miss Munro's smile for approbation, began again to speak, his soft, slurred tones occasionally rising to that brief, high-pitched giggling note.

Zimin said, 'He went in a boat up the river. Then in a bigger boat across the sea. Many of them together. It was dark in the boat. The river he means is the Nile. He is an ignorant man and does not know the names. I, Zimin, tell you the names. He came up the Nile to Alexandria. Then to Constantinople, where he was sold in the slave market.'

'I know he is no longer employed,' Miss Munro said, 'now that the Sultan has been obliged to make economies, but can he give us some idea of what his former duties were?'

'Looking after the women,' Zimin said promptly, without referring to Narsan. 'Watching them, you know. Stop them passing messages, stop them fighting, stop them doing things with each other. Excuse me, I say this. Sex, nothing but sex in the Harem. And singing and passing messages. You know what I mean? He patrols around.'

'Yes, I see.' Miss Munro wrote hurriedly. She seemed confused. Watching her, Markham wondered how all this was going to be put for people back home in England. She looked up again, hesitated, then in a rather plunging way said, 'And where exactly . . . at what stage in the proceedings did it happen?'

Zimin, unaccustomed to such indirectness, looked blank.

'The operation,' Markham said.

'Ah, yes.' He spoke again to the negro, who listened with eyes downcast then answered briefly.

'He says he does not know,' Zimin said.

'But surely,' Miss Munro said. 'Such an important thing . . . I mean, his whole life has been affected by it.'

They all sat looking at Narsan, who after some shy reciprocating glances folded his hands on his stomach and settled his chin on his chest as if about to take a nap. He seemed to have only very limited powers of concentration.

'What it is, you see,' Zimin said, 'the operation is not performed by Turks. They regard the practice with distaste. Also, it is against their laws. But the eunuchs were needed for the harems, large numbers of them. So it was done by the slave-traders, usually Arabs – they have no law but profit. It was done on the way to the main markets for the slaves, Beirut, Jeddah, Mecca, Constantinople. So they did this to Narsan somewhere along the Nile route, Khartoum maybe, or Gondokoro. But how would he know? He was only eight. Also, he is an ignorant person.'

The negro said a few words in a mumbling undertone.

'Yes,' Zimin said. 'The other boys died. He thinks there were three other boys, the same age. They died.'

'I see, yes,' Miss Munro said, bending her head over the notebook. 'I would like to ask him how he views his present position, bearing in mind that—'

Without waiting for her to finish, the eunuch began speaking again, still with that strange giggling undercurrent in his voice. Zimin said, 'He is speaking about the operation. He is saying what was done to him. He is going into the detail of it.'

'I think we can take that as read,' Miss Munro said. 'I want to pass on to the present.'

Zimin made an attempt to break in, but the negro seemed not to notice, and the soft, eager monologue continued.

'Why don't you translate?' Markham said suddenly. His face was set and he looked angrily at Zimin.

'The lady,' Zimin said, shrugging his narrow shoulders.

'It was the lady who arranged all this.' Markham looked at Miss Munro. 'You arranged for this man to come here,' he said. 'Now you just want to listen to what is palatable in the

348

poor fellow's experience. Like picking food out of a dish. You can't select like that. I'll translate if he won't. I'll fill in a few of the gaps myself, because his account is somewhat sparse . . .' In fact he had not been able to follow completely the soft, slurred syllables of the eunuch. He had understood enough, however, to feel the outrage, to want to ram some of it into the consciousness of the woman sitting there, chaste knees together, in the sensible tweed suit.

'Mr Zimin,' she said, 'would you ask him—'

'This is what they did to him,' Markham said loudly. 'They took him off the boat where he had been lying half dead with fear, crowded with all the others in the dark. They took him to some riverside shed. They bound the lower part of his abdomen and the upper part of his thighs – that would be to prevent too much haemorrhage.'

'Captain Markham,' she said, and there was something of appeal now in her voice.

'He says he remembers the white cloths they used to bind him and the white headdresses of the men who did it – the same colour. Of course he had no idea why they were doing this to him. When they had bound him they cut off his genitals, the whole lot, testicles and penis, with one sweep of the knife. He doesn't say how they cauterized the wound or what they used as a styptic – Nile mud perhaps. Then they covered it up and left him.'

He paused for a moment. Miss Munro was silent now, vanquished, the violation of her hearing accomplished. Her eyes were fixed on the small dusty window opposite her. Her face wore the same expression as when she had noticed the street dogs.

'That is what they did to him,' Markham said. 'Some men held him while others did it.' He glanced at Narsan, who was looking sleepy again. 'He doesn't know how long they left him,' he said. 'Three or four days perhaps. Then they took the bandages off and took out whatever it was that had been

349

holding in his urine. Of course, if he hadn't been able to urinate he would have died a very agonizing death. Perhaps that's what happened to the others, the other boys.'

'The mortality rate was high,' Zimin said uneasily. 'But also prices were high. Very high prices for castrated boys.'

Miss Munro put notebook and pencil back into her handbag. 'You have ruined my interview,' she said. Her face was pale, her lips compressed. 'I relied on you for help,' she said. She got to her feet. 'I must give you what we agreed.' she said to Zimin.

Markham moved to the window and stood looking out. Behind him he heard the rustle of paper. 'Here is the testimonial I promised you,' Miss Munro said in a voice that sounded close to tears. 'And here is the money.' His anger was gone now and he felt the beginnings of regret. He turned inwards to look at Narsan again. The negro seemed to have lost interest in the proceedings, now that there were no more questions. More terrible, Markham thought, than the terror and agony of that distant occasion, the white cloths, the knife, the days of pain, were the consequences they saw now, the sense of lasting damage, the note of hysteria lying below the soft African voice. Men had held Narsan helpless and done this . . .

The transaction was finished now, Miss Munro was moving towards the door. Markham fell in behind her. He did not want Zimin to give him the slip, now that he had found him again, but the duties of escort were imperative. His role as protector, which had not restrained him from hurting Miss Munro's sensibilities, operated insistently now. He had the man's address of course; but the room promised no permanence or even continuity of occupation from one day to the next. He said good-bye to the two men, without offering to shake hands, and followed Miss Munro down the stairs. The conventions weighed more heavily on her; however much he had offended her she could not dispense with him, alone as she was in such a neighbourhood.

She did not look at him or speak until they had reached the broader thoroughfare. Then she said, 'I can get a cab from here. I will not take up any more of your time.'

The dependence of her situation and the defiant loneliness of her words touched him now with something deeper than regret. Earlier in the day, over their drink, there had been a time when they had seemed like friends. Now she would remember that he had spoilt her enterprise, humiliated her before the two others, or Zimin at least – Narsan probably did not register such things. He had wanted to punish her, for what offence he did not know.

'I'm sorry,' he said. 'My son is about the same age as Narsan was when that was done to him.' But he knew immediately that this had not been the reason for that impure rage of his; it was not Henry that he had been thinking of. 'That's not it,' he said quickly.

She raised an arm to signal a passing fiacre. This drew up at once, the driver leaning over to enquire where they wanted to go.

'I did not think it right somehow,' Markham said, 'for the thing to be dished up in bland form for your readers in Bicester or Barnsley. There was nothing personal in it, you know.' That's not it either, he thought.

'Will you get out of my way?' Miss Munro said. 'Hotel Imperial,' she said unrelentingly to the driver. She got into the cab. 'Hotel Imperial,' she said again, fierce in her desire to be rid of him. She looked rigidly before her as the vehicle moved away.

He was left standing there on the narrow pavement. After a moment or two he turned and began to make his way back towards the Passage Oriental. He walked as quickly as the uneven cobbles and the other people would allow, anxious to catch Zimin before he disappeared again.

He was relieved when, in answer to his tug at the bell, the narrow, dark-browed face appeared again at the door. Zimin was now wearing his panama hat, and Markham guessed that

351

he had been on the point of departure. There was no sign of Narsan, who had presumably taken his share of the money and gone already.

'I thought you might come back,' Zimin said with resignation. 'Shall we have more coffee?'

'No thank you. Listen, I know you went to Nesbitt, he told me. You let me down completely, but I don't want to go into all that now. Nesbitt is dead.'

'I know it,' Zimin said. 'I was afraid he would find out you had used me.'

'You made enquiries about me.' Markham took out his cigarette case, offered it to the other.

'Quite normal,' Zimin said, taking a cigarette.

'Normal in your world, maybe,' Markham said. He met the close-set, emotional eyes of the other man. 'You found things out,' he said.

'Very little. It was gossip that I took back to Nesbitt. He knew it too.'

Markham nodded. Zimin did not know, of course, the extent of Nesbitt's confidences. There was nothing to be gained by telling him.

'And now he is dead,' Zimin said. His face in the shadow of the hat brim was calm, almost unlined – he was still quite a young man, Markham realized with something of a shock.

'He's dead all right,' he said. 'For all you knew at the time, you were endangering my life. Didn't that worry you?' Perhaps it was this, he thought, more than anything else, which had brought him hastening back: the desire to scrutinize this man so different, it seemed, from himself. Zimin's whole diet was betrayal, whereas for himself one gulp had proved poisonous.

However, Zimin must have heard, or thought he heard, more than curiosity in the question, for after a moment he said quietly, 'I am armed, Captain Markham, please note.'

Markham made no reply to this and there was a short silence between them. Then Zimin said, 'There are exceptions, but most of us live unheroic lives. We fall into the stream and we try to swim. Where I fell in it is a swamp. Is that my fault? I have been avoiding to sink since I can remember.'

'Survival is a more complicated matter for some of us,' Markham said.

'You are like the Pharisee in the temple, Captain Markham. Oh yes, Zimin knows his Bible. There are not only the sins you yourself disapprove of. You did violence to the lady. You think Zimin is a crook, but he is sensitive. You did violence to her when she had no defence. Do not pretend to yourself it was for Narsan's sake. You are a man of violence.'

There was another, longer silence between them. Then Markham made a short sound, between a grunt and a sigh. 'Yes,' he said. 'I see you are a psychologist. You are still gathering testimonials too, I notice. I thought you'd have been in England now, your spiritual home, working as an interpreter.'

'That was my intention.' Zimin drew on his cigarette and trickled the smoke out through his nostrils. 'I left things too late,' he said. 'To get a visa now is difficult. Since the revolution. They ask questions, go into all the circumstances.' Zimin smiled sadly and shook his head. 'I don't like that,' he said. 'Those who have money can get a visa. Everything is possible with money. Turkey has not changed in that respect – they say the bribes are even higher now, under the Young Turks. But I have no money, Captain Markham. You see how I live.' Zimin made a gesture that comprehended the shabbiness of the room and of his person. 'That is another result of this glorious revolution,' he said. 'There is not much to do now, for people like me.'

'I don't want to appear unsympathetic,' Markham said, 'but that seems rather like a mark of progress to me.'

Zimin shrugged. 'There are a lot of people who are dissatisfied with this régime,' he said. 'These men of the Committee, they are unbelievers. A lot of people do not like that. They believe in God and the Sultan, not in parliaments.'

353

'I don't believe it matters a scrap to you whether the Committee people are unbelievers or not,' Markham said. 'What matters to you is that you can't get a visa.'

'That may be,' Zimin said with dignity. 'But the feeling against them is strong here in Constantinople, stronger than perhaps you think.'

Taking care to keep his voice casual, Markham said, 'Certainly there are elements of the press that criticize the government these days. Obliquely, of course. This paper the *Serbesti*, for example. They publish stuff that goes pretty near the line.'

Zimin nodded. 'Hassan Fehmi's paper,' he said.

'Hassan Fehmi? The name is familiar. I believe I've met him somewhere.' Markham frowned slightly as if trying to remember.

'You would not forget him,' Zimin said, but there was no suspicion in his voice. 'A very big, very fat man, without hair on his head at all.'

'That's right. I know where it was now. It was at the Press Club. Quite a character, isn't he? High up in the Mohammedan League, I believe.'

'I do not know. Did you say it was at the Press Club that you met him?'

'Yes. They'll be out in force tomorrow night, I suppose. All these pillars of the establishment. It's the twenty-seventh day of Ramazan tomorrow, isn't it?'

'Yes,' Zimin said. 'Tomorrow night is the *Leil-ul-kadr*, the Night of Power. They will go to Haghia Sophia for the prayers.' He shot a quick glance at Markham's face. 'Strange that Hassan Fehmi should be invited to the Press Club,' he said. 'His paper has no standing.'

'It was a sort of conference,' Markham said. He got up and held out his hand. 'Well, good-bye,' he said. 'I don't bear you any grudge. Perhaps we'll meet again some day – in London. When you are one of the chief interpreters.'

'I hope so, very much,' Zimin said.

354

Markham looked for a moment or two longer at the thin face below the hat-brim. 'How old are you?' he asked on an impulse.

'Thirty-three.'

'We are the same age,' Markham said. He took out his wallet and extracted five one-lira banknotes. These he laid on the table. As he went out Zimin said something, some form of thanks. He did not catch the words.

As he walked back towards the Grande Rue he heard the cannon of Seraglio Point thundering out its signal that the sun had set, the day's fasting was over.

He passed a restless night. He had not slept well since the visit to his office of the two Armenians. In the early hours of the morning he fell into a light sleep, only to be awakened by the chants and drum-beats of the 'Awakeners' taking their way through the streets of the Turkish quarters shortly before dawn to warn those who were sleeping that it was time to arise and partake of the *sahor*, the last meal before sunrise.

He was fully awake at once and lay for a while in the dark, listening. The drumbeat was repeated four times at exact intervals outside each house where Moslems were known to be, and followed by a brief chant, at once plaintive and wild. Markham experienced a sense of apprehension or foreboding, lying there, listening to the sounds getting closer as the men made their way upwards through the suburb. The notes of the drum, urgent and monotonous in the darkness, the imagined pause before selected houses, carried him straight to the edge of nightmare – always, despite all efforts of his conscious mind, such signals and selections were preludes to atrocity, the strangers in the lighted room, violation like a clumsy dance . . .

He got up and went to the window. Below him, a little further down towards the shore, he could make out the random flashes of their lantern. He heard the chant again, much nearer now – they were at the side somewhere; out of sight, but near enough for him to distinguish the words: 'Mohammed is the Guide, the Apostle of Allah.' The plaintive sweetness of the chant lingered in the air for some moments, until broken by the further tapping of the drum. Markham had the sudden irrelevant notion of someone out there trying to find his way, the tapping like a blind man's stick . . . He shivered a little in his thin pyjamas – he had allowed himself to get cold, sitting there.

He moved across the room in the darkness to where his dressing gown was hanging behind the door. When he returned to the window the chanting sounded more distant, as if farther away along the street. Perhaps they had stopped near the gate to deliver their message, at some point invisible from the window.

He remained where he was, however. He felt disinclined to return to bed. It would not be much before dawn now – half an hour, perhaps. Time for the faithful to have their meal before the day's fasting began. He could hear nothing from below, but Mehmet Agha and Nevres would be up and about, preparing to eat the *iskembe corba* and pilaff left ready the evening before.

Markham sat at the window, listening to the sounds recede. He knew, without being aware of conscious decision, that today he was going to set about doing what Tarquin and Missakian had asked of him. He was no more convinced than before that these gentlemen had been fully frank and open with him, but this did not matter: as when he had gone to warn Hartunian, it was personal necessity that drove him on, a sort of personal momentum which had to be maintained. His greatest fear now was of being obliged somehow to stop, stand still.

All the same, he reflected, the fact that today was the twenty-seventh day of Ramazan might have something to do with it. Always, since the earliest days of his interest in Arabic, he had been fascinated by this day in the Moslem year. There was nothing like it in the Christian calendar. It was the Night of Power, when the Koran had been revealed to Mohammed, the night above all others in the year when Allah was liable to intervene in human affairs, a time charged with the miraculous for Moslems, especially in the hours after sunset – many spent the night of *Leil-ul-Kadr* in prayer, believing that there was a moment between sunset and sunrise when Allah granted all requests.

Markham was not a religious man. He had no skill in translating his needs into requests, nor indeed much impulse to do so; but as he sat there at the window looking out into the darkness, he felt vaguely the possibility that so much intercession, the lips and hearts of multitudes pleading with Allah, might shape his own course somehow, give him a favourable wind. He thought of the mysterious verses from the Koran that had so intrigued him as a student: *Verily we sent it down on the night of power. And who shall make thee know what that night is! The night of power is better than a thousand months. In it descend the angels. It is peace till the rising of the dawn . . .*

Such peace seemed highly desirable to him. The meeting with Hassan Fehmi, which he was now determined on, seemed unlikely to produce it, however. He thought again about the scraps of information he had managed to obtain from Zimin before the latter's quick look of suspicion had warned him off. It was possible that the Mohammedan League was financing Fehmi, at least in part. The League had some influential people in it. A son of Abdul Hamid, Prince Burhaneddin Effendi, had lent it official support, though the Sultan himself had given it no overt sign of recognition. It was dedicated to the maintenance of Moslem supremacy and the safeguarding of the *Sheriat*, the Holy Law of Islam, from the impious innovations of the present government. Attacks on the Armenians would accord well with such policies, Markham thought. But if it was the League that was funding the paper, surely Missakian would have known it . . .

He was roused from these speculations by the booming of

357

the cannon on Seraglio Point, signalling the beginning of the fast. Dawn had occurred, apparently, though he could see not the slightest glimmer of light in the sky. Everywhere in the city the devout would be rinsing their mouths, sealing them for the long hours of abstinence. Markham moved away from the window and lit the lamp beside the bed. He would read for a while, he decided, at least until it was full daylight. He would go early to the office, get through most of the work in the morning, leaving himself free to do as he pleased later.

He adhered to this plan, though he had to retrace his steps almost from the Beshiktash landing stage in order to get a pair of binoculars – he had suddenly remembered the vast spaces of Haghia Sophia and the height above ground of the galleries. It was typical of the Mohammedan League that they should choose this former Byzantine cathedral, one of the greatest Christian monuments, as the scene of their mass prayers. Possibly of course he would not need the binoculars: Zimin might be mistaken, Fehmi might not go with the others, he might go to a smaller mosque, alone, or perhaps not go to prayer at all, though this was unlikely in view of his position.

Routine matters kept Markham occupied until mid-afternoon. At about four o'clock he left his office and made his way to the small *brasserie* on the corner of Rue Aliotti almost opposite the *Serbesti* offices. He had already, on a previous reconnaissance, singled this out as a good place to watch for Fehmi since it gave a clear view of the office front. As he had expected, the place was almost deserted. There was little business during the fast, though this was more than made up for after the sunset gun, when all such places would be thronged with people. Now, apart from himself, there were only two other customers, two grave-faced Jews speaking Spanish together.

Markham asked for tea. He had chosen a table at the side of the window so that he could keep the *Serbesti* premises in view. A certain mood of irresponsibility, almost of indifference,

358

descended on him while he waited. He was here; he had put himself in the way; now events must take their course. There would be no harm done if he did not see the man today, another day would do as well.

However, as he waited and no one at all resembling Fehmi appeared, this mood began to give way to one of impatience. He was alone in the place now, the two Jews having long since departed. It was well after five and he began to wonder whether there was anyone at the office at all that afternoon. Finally, unable to sit still any longer, he got up to go. He was already moving towards the door when he saw a big man in a pale suit and a fez standing alone on the narrow pavement outside the office. He knew at once that this was Fehmi – there was no mistaking that height and bulk, and the face was the one in the photograph, broad, thick-lipped, at once gaunt and fleshy. He had presumably stepped out on to the pavement at the moment when Markham was looking away, preparing to leave. Now he seemed to be hesitating there, or perhaps waiting for someone. Markham remained where he was for some moments, keeping to the side of the window, looking out. After a further few moments Fehmi was joined by another man, who came down the two steps from the office door – a colleague perhaps, or someone at least who worked in the same building. He looked diminutive beside Fehmi whose height was accentuated by the crimson fez, unfaded and new-looking.

The two of them began to walk down the street together in the direction of the harbour. After waiting a moment longer Markham left the shelter of the doorway and followed. They were about fifty yards in front of him, like some extraordinary knight and squire, the bulky Fehmi with his light, somehow billowing clothes and portly, rolling gait, and the other, thin, dark-suited, reaching barely to his companion's shoulder.

Markham followed, keeping the same distance between them. But at the end of Rue Aliotti they paused again and he saw Fehmi raise an arm to hail a fiacre. Markham looked rapidly up and down the street but there wasn't another cab in sight, and he had the mortification of seeing Fehmi and his companion disappearing in the general direction of Rue Arab Kapi and the shore of the Golden Horn.

He experienced a sense of disappointment at their disappearance that was quite disproportionate to the cause. After all, he had not been given a time limit by Missakian; tomorrow or the next day would do just as well for effecting his meeting with Fehmi. Moreover, he had formed no actual plan of action, either for scraping up the acquaintance or for how he would conduct himself afterwards. He was prepared to leave everything to the chances of the encounter, the main thing being that this, when it happened, must seem unpremeditated and accidental to Fehmi.

Still no second fiacre had appeared in the street. It would be too late now, in any case, to follow them. Markham hesitated some moments longer. He thought briefly of giving up the enterprise for that day at least, returning home to Beshiktash. But he was unwilling to do this. Tonight was *Leil-ul-Kadr*, night of miraculous interventions. It was not a night to skulk at home. Zimin had said that the luminaries of the Mohammedan League would congregate at Haghia Sophia for the *Teraweh* prayers, which took place two hours after sunset. If he was right, Fehmi might be among the worshippers.

Markham began to walk back the way he had come, back towards Pera. He would go to the club, he had decided. He could have a shower there and a drink or two afterwards, then something to eat. By then it should be time for the prayers.

The club was more crowded than it usually was at this early time of evening. There were a good number of Europeans having drinks before going on to an *iftar* somewhere, one of the elaborate Ramazan suppers held in the homes of well-to-do Moslems after sundown. Markham saw several faces he knew but he remained alone at the bar. He chatted for a while with Alex, who was as confidentially gloomy as ever, this time about the concessions given by Abdul Hamid to the Germans for the construction of the Baghdad Railway, details of which had only recently been published, although the concessions had been granted early in the previous summer, before the restoration of the Constitution. The present government, aghast at the ruinous liberality of the terms, was withholding assent.

'Imagine it,' Alex said, his neat dark head lowered over the bar. 'Imagine the folly of a kilometric guarantee. It is unbelievable. For every kilometre of the line they are to get a fixed sum in credits from the Ottoman Bank. What will prevent the Germans to make great loops in the line?'

'That's a shortsighted view,' Markham said. 'It's unworthy of you, Alex.'

Alex cast a glance of cosmic gloom along the bar and over the tables beyond. 'All views are shortsighted when it is a question of profit,' he said. 'They will not bother to make tunnels, they will just go round and round.'

Turning slightly aside Markham saw Kent and Armstrong, both in civilian clothes, standing together talking at the far end of the bar. It was obvious that neither of them had seen him yet. He felt a sudden disinclination for company, theirs or anyone else's. He finished his drink quickly. 'I'll be getting along,' he said to Alex. He nodded in reply to the barman's 'Good evening' and left, taking care not to look in the direction of his colleagues. He was half afraid that one or both of them, seeing him go, would follow him and corner him while he waited in the cloakroom for his coat; but this did not happen and a minute or two later he was outside, walking back towards Galata with a sense of release.

The sunset gun had sounded while he was still at the club and the streets were beginning to fill up. Restaurants too were crowded, many of the customers not having eaten since sunrise. Already, in some of the larger cafés, small groups of musicians had formed, and Markham heard as he passed the

361

broken rhythm of the music, with its insistent sounding of the minor key.

He chose a restaurant that he had never used before, a smallish place with a Turkish proprietor, above the Pont Mahmoud, overlooking the Golden Horn. Here, after *mezzaliks* of a variety that only Turks can command, and round flaps of the hot unleavened Ramazan bread, he had swordfish, cut into sections and grilled over charcoal – a dish vouched for by the *patron* with that curious gesture Turks use to denote things pleasing to the senses, like plucking at an invisible string before the face. It was indeed good, as was the Turkish wine which accompanied it. Markham, ordering his coffee, felt a glow of well-being and optimism, partly induced by the food and drink, partly by a sense of adventure, a sense of being cast on the currents of the evening, willing to be directed but still with his own purposes. That these purposes were vague to him still, that what he had been asked to do still lacked some element of plausibility, no longer mattered now: the vagueness was part of the promise of the night.

Three male dancers, a man and two boys, all heavily made up, came into the restaurant and took up positions in the cleared space in the middle. They were Turks, dressed alike in wide black trousers, dark red girdles and black fezzes. The man crouched on his haunches and began to play a wavering melody on an instrument like a primitive flute. The two boys, who were no more than twelve or thirteen years of age, danced within the narrow confines in the centre of the floor, marking out a slow rhythm by clicking the small wooden discs secured to their fingers. Their bodies were upright, their movements formal, clearly prescribed by long usage and tradition. There was, however, an extraordinary sexual suggestiveness in the movements of their hips and abdomens, a quality of provocation that worked an immediate effect – evidenced by brightened eyes and guttural exclamations – on a good many of the diners. Coins clattered onto the floor, ignored for the moment by the dancers. There were no

362

women at any of the tables, Markham now realized. There would only be certain places where the dancers came. Enthusiasm was rising among the audience; he saw one or two men spit on coins and stick them to the boys' foreheads as they slowly turned in the dance. There were loud voices of praise here and there among the tables. No consciousness of this appeared on the boys' faces, which were rendered expressionless by the thick layers of powder and rouge applied to them, giving them a staring doll-like quality, dehumanized and sad. These would be the *alimeh*, Markham thought, whom he had heard of but never seen before, a caste of dancing boys trained from infancy, invariably effeminate, perpetuating a custom which must be at least as old as the satyr dances of India or the Phrygian dance of Cybele. The music too was ancient in its infinite repetitions and wavering quarter-tones. There was a swirling savagery in it, in the midst of the melancholy; but the note to which it always returned was the monotone of a primitive life, like the day-long beat of camel bells, the mood of Asia, so rarely understood elsewhere, neither lightness nor despair.

The music ceased abruptly and the boys stood still for some moments, heads downcast. Listening to the renewed exclamations of applause, watching the flute-player gather up the coins, Markham felt regret for something broken, even though an illusion merely. He saw several men speak to the flute-player, perhaps making offers for one or other of the boys, but no deal was made, at least as far as he could see, and the three dancers went out together.

Markham himself left shortly after. It was time to cross into Stambul, make his way to Haghia Sophia for the prayers. It was quite dark now, and the streets were crowded. He saw several family parties, led by the father with a lantern, moving down towards the Galata quayside, presumably intending to go over the bridge and hear prayers at one of the Imperial mosques in the Old City.

The area adjoining the quay on the Stambul side was

363

brightly lit with rows of lanterns along the walls, and singers and acrobats were entertaining the crowds there. A little apart, but still in earshot, a *hafiz* was reciting verses from the Koran. Braziers glowed here and there and stalls had sprung up, selling sherbet and various sweet drinks. The air was pungent with charcoal smoke and roasting chestnuts.

Turning his back on this, Markham began to mount towards the royal mosques on the heights above the harbour. He looked steadily towards the dark shapes of dome and minaret looming above. There were hundreds of the moving lanterns now, the streets were lit by them. Markham could hear the insistent rhythm of drums in the distance. Suddenly, above the dimly lighted houses, above the mass of moving lanterns, a circle of light came into view, high up in the dark blue of the sky, tracing out in a slender ring of lamps the balcony of a minaret. Immediately afterwards there was another, then another. As he walked on, with his face towards the skyline, loops and bracelets and chains of light multiplied silently and with amazing speed, like luminous creatures breeding in the sky, and now he saw that the lamps not only picked out the galleries of the minarets but were slung from one minaret to another and arranged in softly effulgent shapes of boats and flowers.

As he turned down the Bab Alti Caddesi, he heard the voice of the muezzin from the little mosque of Ahmad Agha raised in sudden melodious celebration. '*Allah Akbar, Allah Akbar,*' the voice intoned, high and full-throated. The call was taken up at once from every quarter of the city. It was immense, all-pervasive, a pulsing devotional outcry raised in the night, like the collective prayer of the whole city. The lights in the sky seemed to pulse with it, now stronger, now fainter.

The prayer had ceased, fallen into a vibrant aftermath, when he crossed the *meydan* of Haghia Sophia and entered the narthex. He was admitted to the gallery by a green-turbaned *ulema*, whose gravity of manner did not conceal a certain hostility. There were some people up there already,

Europeans of both sexes, but they seemed very few to Markham, lost in that broad gallery against the legendary vastness of the interior – even here in the gallery, high above the floor of the cathedral, the spaces above were without visible limit, pillar reaching into arch, arch into vault, vault into dome, in a series that seemed endless, duplicating the infinity of God. Within a few moments Markham had ceased to be aware of his fellow-spectators, absorbed as he was in what was happening below.

The gold mosaic, the cornices of the galleries, the vast spaces of the nave, all familiar to him from previous visits, were transfigured now, illuminated by thousands of lamps, whose, clear, soft flames in glass cups of oil were reflected in the variegated marbles of the walls. Below these the congregation of worshippers stood in ranks, close packed together, waiting for the prayer to begin. They were difficult to see in detail from this height above, through the haze of light diffused by the three huge central chandeliers. These were scallop-shaped, intended to symbolize the microcosm, but resembling now enormous water-lilies floating in their medium of dusky gold. Below them in the luminous haze were ranks of worshippers, filling the nave, men all, all shoeless, standing one close to the next, hands folded and head down.

Suddenly, in this silence, came a single, exquisitely modulated voice raised in the great opening call of the prayer, '*Sal-li-a-la Mohammed!*' Immediately thousands of pairs of hands came fluttering up, pale in the light, like large moths, to rest at the sides of the worshippers' heads, touching the ears, while the first formula of the prayer was recited. 'I extol thee, O God . . .'

Markham listened to the reverent gutturals of the prayer. So many voices, murmuring, made a sound like distant thunder. Their combined exhalation, too, as they raised their heads, caused flickers in the lamps above them, so that the haze of light through which Markham was gazing down at

365

them, and in which they were immersed, seemed to pulsate to the breath of their devotions.

The *imam*, with his back to the congregation, facing towards the Holy City, led the prayers. Markham could see him only indistinctly, a figure in white, arms outstretched. To his right, on a raised platform, a choir of at least a hundred sat cross-legged, chanting responses in a minor key of almost unearthly sweetness. It was the *Fatiha*, the first chapter of the Koran: 'In the name of God, the Merciful, the Compassionate. Praise be to God, the Lord of the Worlds . . .' Like a field of tall grass swept by wind, the worshippers swayed forward, fell to their knees, prostrated themselves with foreheads to the ground, the thousands of these individual collisions making a reverberant muttering like low gunfire through the cavernous length of the nave.

Markham found himself unexpectedly moved by this spectacle of reverence and faith, the tremulous haze of light enveloping the worshippers, the faultless precision of their movements, thousands moving as one. Perhaps as a refuge from this feeling, which was after all irrelevant, he took out the small binoculars that he had been carrying all this while in the pocket of his overcoat. He trained them down through the golden light on to the heads and faces of the congregation, who were standing again, hands crossed on breasts, in readiness for the next prostration.

In thinking to pick out Hassan Fehmi with the aid of the glasses, Markham had not bargained for so many people, such serried ranks to scan, nor for such a spreading suffusion of light. However, it occurred to him now that if Fehmi was indeed among the worshippers, as a pillar of the Mohammedan League, he would have chosen a prominent position for his devotions, up towards the front, as near as possible to the *mihrab*. Accordingly he trained the binoculars there. For some moments his eyes were lost among the soft flares of the lamps, the banners of conquest draped over the high pulpit with its hooded canopy. Then he made out the small groups of *mollahs* in their white turbans and black gowns, sitting facing the congregation, swaying to the rhythm of the chants. The faces he was able to see clearly all had the transparent pallor and hectic eyes of those severely fasting. Below them were the front ranks of the congregation. Markham moved the binoculars slowly. He could see only the backs of heads, indistinct in the opalescent light. Abruptly the line appeared foreshortened as the worshippers dropped once more to their knees. Then suddenly, in the few moments that they remained thus, in that position of the *rikat* immediately before prostration, Markham picked out the bulk of Fehmi, a head taller than those on either side of him, the thick hairless nape below the fez, the fawn jacket of his suit – he was wearing the same clothes as earlier. A second later he was lost to view as the whole great mass of forms bowed down to the ground, causing again the brief sullen reverberation that reminded Markham of gunfire.

He lowered the binoculars, stowed them away again in his pocket. He had no doubt at all that the person he had seen was Fehmi – it seemed almost that the glimpse had been vouchsafed to him in the midst of the random movements he had made with the binoculars among that great crowd. He was impatient now for the prayers to be over, so that he could follow the man, effect a meeting somehow.

Perhaps because of this impatience his mood of earlier was broken; he was no longer held by the ritual obeisances, the soft pulsations of light, the high sweet chanting. Indeed these things began to strike him now as hateful in some way, especially the concerted movements, the absolute precision of rising and falling of so vast a crowd, the continual rhythmic thud and rustle. Mind was in abeyance here. Below the worshipful decorum there was something blind, frantic almost; in such uniformity of movement lay corporate mania, something he knew now that he had always detested – he was reminded of all the drills and parades of his career, all the orderly swarms he had seen. An accumulated repugnance for

367

army life, for all forms of collective movement, swept over him. This passed, to leave one clear vivid image in his mind: regimental bayonet drill, done by numbers, the men advancing dead straight in a line. One screaming shout, one stamp of the left foot, one line of light running along the blades, one thrust forward, twist and out.

He was glad when the last throbbing '*Amin, amin,*' signalled the end. The congregation remained kneeling for some time, while the *imam* descended from the high pulpit. Markham moved quickly along the gallery and down the steps into the dim vestibule. There was no one watching there now, and he was able to slip outside before the congregation had started to leave. He took up a position a little to one side of the main gates, those that looked out over the *meydan*. Fehmi was bound to pass through these gates eventually, even if he left the cathedral by a side door.

He was in darkness here, though there were lamps hanging up inside the courtyard. He stood quietly, keeping close to the outer wall, watching the people passing through the gates. They were in the light for these few moments and he had no fear of missing Fehmi, in spite of the size of the crowd. Many of the faces had an expression that he recognized from somewhere, that curious look of absent-mindedness following upon strong emotion, like a convalescence.

He saw Fehmi coming through the gates, the tall fez, the broad, thick-lipped face, the form in the bulky fawn suit. It was not possible for the moment to tell whether he was accompanied because of the press of people all around. After following him across the square for some moments, however, Markham saw that there were two men with him, one dressed in European style except for the fez, the other in the long black robe and white turban of a *mollah*. They crossed the square and stood for some time talking on the opposite corner. He saw Fehmi gesture widely. The *mollah* raised his head, smiling. Then the three of them moved along the far side of the square and turned right in the direction of Rue Mahmoud

Pasha and the Ministry of Public Instruction.

Markham followed, keeping close – there was no danger of detection with so many people about. He guessed that Fehmi and his companions would have to walk, at least for some distance, as all the cabs in the square and the adjoining streets would have been taken by those out of the mosque first. They were back on the Bab Alti Caddesi now. At the corner opposite the gateway to the Sublime Porte, the *mollah* left the other two after a brief handclasp, making his way alone round the side of the government buildings. The other two men continued down the Caddesi. They went into a café-bar near the railway station while Markham waited fifty yards further down the street. He experienced no impatience at this delay. He was fixed and intent upon his quarry now, ready to wait there half the night if necessary. In fact the two men remained in the bar for about half an hour. When they emerged the Caddesi was practically deserted. This area of the city was not much frequented after dark even on the nights of Ramazan, the inhabitants, almost entirely Moslem, preferring to cross the Golden Horn into Galata for their pleasures.

It was in this direction that Fehmi and his companion were now moving. As they descended towards the shore, the glow of lights on the other side was clearly visible – the sky was softly lit with them. Markham watched the swift traceries and showering descents of the imperial fireworks, far over towards Yildiz where the Sultan, having prayed at the Palace Mosque, would have ordered this traditional display.

He had to keep farther back in these less frequented streets; but neither Fehmi nor his companion glanced behind, and Fehmi in particular was not difficult to keep in view, with his bulk, the loose and billowing effect of his clothes, the lordly gait and set of the head. Markham had been supposing that the two men were bound somewhere together; but at the Galata side of the bridge they separated, Fehmi continuing in the direction of Galata proper, the other turning aside towards the Marmara waterfront.

Markham continued to follow. He had no plan of action, not the faintest idea of how to contrive a meeting with the man in front. His whole energy for the moment lay in not losing him.

Fehmi made his way steadily upwards in the direction of Galata Tower. There were more people again now, more cosmopolitan, more obviously pleasure-seeking than in the Turkish quarter. Markham heard the sound of tambourines from somewhere just off the street and a man's voice singing. He kept his eyes fixed on the bulky form before him, hardly glancing at passers-by, as if afraid that he might lose him if he looked away. Fehmi turned right along Rue de Galata, then almost at once left again, down a side street barely two yards across.

Markham followed, though slowing his steps rather, so as to put a little more distance between them. They were in a different world now, though still not far from the lights of the street they had just left. Here lights were infrequent, though there were occasional lamps set over doorways, illuminating a name or a number or a painted sign – Markham saw a peacock over one door, a single eye over another. There were women in some of the doorways who spoke to Markham as he passed. Fehmi pursued his lordly way without appearing to pause, as if he knew exactly where he was going; and Markham followed him deeper and deeper into the warren of streets. They were in a district that Markham knew by repute but had not visited before, that between Rue de Galata and Rue Kemmer Alit, something like a square kilometre in area, given over entirely to brothels and drinking places and cabarets, most of the establishments in fact combining all three functions. Here, it was said, all tastes were catered for, just as all races were represented.

The streets seemed to get narrower if anything, as they proceeded. The windows so nearly met overhead as to form tunnels. There were smells of impure water and charcoal smoke and jasmine. A woman spoke in Arabic to him from a

370

lighted window and glancing up quickly he saw that she had the collapsed, mumbling face of the very old, though her cheeks were thickly powdered and rouged and her eyes ringed with *kohl*. The sound of a pianola came faintly from somewhere behind her.

Markham pressed on, keeping a constant distance between himself and the man in front. He did not know what he hoped or expected, and still had no idea how a meeting could be effected without arousing Fehmi's suspicion; but the idea of losing him was as difficult to endure as ever.

It was now that accident helped Markham, an accident which, though tiny and obscure in the scale of things, seemed afterwards to him to have had some tincture of the miraculousness with which the faithful believed this night to be charged; an infinitesimal motion of God's finger, but enough.

At first, though, it seemed like a disaster. He was still about fifty yards behind Fehmi when the latter turned into a passageway with a red-shaded lamp overhead but no other sign or number. Markham was obliged to quicken his steps, so as not to risk losing the other if the passage turned out to be a short one. For this reason he was moving quite quickly as he came round the corner into the passage – too quickly to check or retreat when he saw Fehmi standing close to the wall a few yards farther on, talking to another man, little more than a youth it seemed. Beyond them the passage continued into obscurity.

Whether this was someone who had solicited Fehmi or someone he already knew, met by chance there, Markham was never to discover. For a second or two he hesitated. Fehmi had his back turned and could not have seen him yet, but the other must have done so – he had been directly below the light as he turned into the passage. To retreat now would look distinctly suspicious. At any moment Fehmi might turn and see him. There was a door, surmounted by an iron grill, in the wall near the two men, almost opposite them but not quite

– a couple of yards on Markham's side. Barely checking in his pace he went forward along the passage until he got up to the door. Fehmi still had not turned. Markham heard the mutter of his voice but distinguished no words. He saw the young man glance towards him again. He pushed against the door and it swung open. Without hesitation he passed inside and found himself at once descending a flight of red-carpeted stairs. At the foot of these was a glass-fronted cubicle, from which emerged a shortish but very powerfully built man, with the shaven head and thick moustache affected by professional wrestlers. He greeted Markham unsmilingly but without surprise and offered to take his coat.

So far he had had little time to think. He had acted instinctively, in his desire to avoid being seen by Fehmi. Now, however, as he was divested of his coat and led along a short corridor towards another, more ornate door of heavy carved wood, he felt the beginnings of dismay. He had lost Fehmi: that much seemed certain. And something in the demeanour of the person conducting him made him suspect that it might not be so easy to get out of this place as it had been to get in. This man now opened the door for him, ushered him in, closed it behind him, remaining on the outside.

A large woman came smiling towards him. Beyond her he had a hasty impression of other women sitting about the room in subdued pinkish lighting amidst glints and reflections of glass from the walls – the place seemed full of mirrors. The air was heavy, smelling of musk and sandalwood.

The woman spoke to him in Turkish, giving him the '*hosh geldenes*' of traditional welcome among Moslems. Then, seeing his foreignness, perhaps also mistaking his bewilderment for something else, with the tact of long experience she laid a puffy gemmed hand on his sleeve and said, '*N'ayez-pas peur, monsieur.*' She was very fat and the red velvet dress she was wearing left her shoulders and the upper part of her enormous bosom bare. Markham could see the grains of white powder which the heat and the transpirations of her skin had caused to coagulate in damp patches here and there. Her breath was sweetish, spirituous. The eyes were beautiful in the gross, painted face, long and narrow and gleaming, swept up slightly towards the temples.

She led him forward into the room. '*Voilà mes filles*,' she said.

Markham stood, looking at the girls. They were all fully dressed as far as he could make out, in tea-gowns and stockings, and all were sitting upright in decorous, ladylike attitudes. All of them looked smilingly towards him except one, a girl in a black dress, whose face was quite expressionless.

'*Elles sont très bien élevées*,' the woman said, looking proudly at his face. 'Very well brought up.' Somewhere comprehended in this praise was a hygienic guarantee.

He nodded, with a rather desolate sense of resignation. 'I see they are,' he said.

He had spoken in Turkish but she must have heard something in the accent, even in so brief a form of words, because she said quickly, 'English? You are English?'

'Yes,' he said. 'I am English.'

'I am Armenian,' she said. It was clear that she was delighted to have an English client – Markham had the impression that his visit was something of an apotheosis for herself and her establishment, as if the well-brought-up girls had been waiting only for this.

'My name is Madame Clara,' she said. 'They are like English girls. Very ladies.'

Markham glanced at the girls again. None of them appeared to have moved a muscle since his entrance – a docility that was beginning to oppress him somewhat. The girl in the black dress was the only one not looking towards him. He saw her move her head, glance aside. She had short hair. Her make-up too was different, there was no colour in her face at all.

'That is Mademoiselle Irma,' Madame Clara said. 'She very nice, very *good* girl. You are English, I think.'

373

'Yes,' he said.

'Irma is Lebanese.' Madame Clara put a hand on his arm to lead him forward for a nearer view. 'She *special* girl,' she said. 'The others also, but she very special girl.'

The girl looked up as they stood before her, looked full into Markham's face, but without particular boldness. Her eyes were huge in the pale oval of the face, their size exaggerated by the liberal use of *kohl* above and below them. The only colour in the face was in the painted lips. Below the skirt of the tea-gown he saw black stockings and silver sandals.

'You like her, yes?' Madame Clara said.

'Yes,' he said, with the same sense of resignation – he could not summon the resolution to go counter to Madame Clara's evident expectation. Besides, Mademoiselle Irma interested him, the indifference of the regard, something that distinguished her from the other, carefully schooled creatures in the room. Madame Clara perhaps made a sign of some sort, because the girl now rose and stood facing him.

At this moment, as Madame Clara was beginning to say something else to him, the door was opened behind them and Markham heard a man's voice. Turning, he saw the wrestler ushering in the huge, immediately recognizable form of Hassan Fehmi looming in his pale suit amidst the pink light and reflecting surfaces of the room.

It was now that Markham felt the twinge of miraculous intervention: Fehmi had obviously intended to come here all along; he had been delayed outside just long enough for Markham to get in first, establish himself as a client, thus disarming suspicion.

Fehmi advanced into the room with his lordly gait. Madame Clara left Markham's side to greet him. They conversed together for a few moments in low tones, then Madame Clara returned. Her joy in Markham's presence had lost something of its lustre. 'This *monsieur*,' she said, again laying her hand on Markham's sleeve. 'He like Irma also. Every time he ask only for her.'

Markham nodded, his sense of the miraculous continuing. Fehmi was a regular visitor here then. 'It doesn't matter,' he said.

'He does not like to wait.' Madame Clara looked at him hopefully, her beautiful eyes opening wide in appeal. She was hoping he would offer to take one of the other girls.

'It doesn't matter,' he said again. He turned and looked for the first time directly at the other man. He had to raise his own eyes slightly in order to do this, an unfamiliar experience – Fehmi topped his own six feet by two or three inches at least. With the fez surmounting this, he looked enormous, monstrous almost, among the seated women.

'No, no,' Fehmi said suddenly. 'An Englishman? You were here first.' He spoke English with a French accent. The voice was deep, with a curious thickness in it, as if the tongue was too big in his mouth. 'You were here before me,' he repeated.

'But you have prior claims, it seems,' Markham said.

'No, no, no,' Fehmi said grandiloquently – he seemed to billow there before Markham with these self-sacrificing negatives, as if enjoying his gentlemanly role. It was as if they were both playing a part, Markham thought, in this room of muted lights and glinting surfaces, like a stage duo engaged in some protracted exchange of courtesies.

'It is a question of hospitality,' Fehmi said. He glanced at Irma who was still standing in the same attitude, looking straight before her as though indifferent. Then he smiled suddenly at Markham, a sly, somehow childlike smile of primitive conspiracy, creasing the heavy cheeks, causing the small eyes to retreat into their bony sockets. 'It's a pity, my dear, that they can only accommodate one at a time,' he said.

'Bad planning,' Markham said.

He saw the smile reappear briefly, then Fehmi said, 'I will go with one of the others.'

Markham hesitated. If he let Fehmi go now, all his advantage would be lost. 'Perhaps,' he said, 'afterwards, you

375

know, we might have a drink together. To show there are no hard feelings.'

'That is a good idea,' Fehmi said. 'One gentleman to another, eh?'

He seemed delighted with the suggestion, and once again Markham felt the beneficent force working for him. 'See you later then,' he said and turned back to the girl. 'Come,' he said.

She gave him a brief, bright-eyed, somehow vacant look then led the way towards a door at the far side of the room. He followed her into a narrow corridor with doors on either side. Halfway along, she stopped, opened one of the doors and held it open for him to pass through.

The room he found himself in was small, square-shaped, mostly taken up with a double bed. It was lit by two small gas-lamps bracketed to the wall. He heard the door close behind him and turned to find the girl already undressing, unbuttoning the front of the black silk dress. In this fuller light he saw that she was very young, no more than nineteen or twenty. The soft flare of the lamps did more than reveal this, bringing a rush of familiarity, something he sought to resist but could not. He felt a compound of reluctance and desire, both deriving from an obscure pity – pity for her youth, the slightly awkward movements of her thin fingers unbuttoning the stiff, brocaded corsage of her dress, something ancient, an age-old subjection in this undressing for the transaction of love. And again, while he still had not recognized the source, while he still resisted recognition, the familiarity of this ritual came to him, a masquerade under the soft flare of gas-lamps.

'Let me help you,' he said in English, moving towards her. She had, with an inconsequence that seemed childlike, abandoned the buttons temporarily to stoop and unfasten the straps of the sandals.

With fingers that felt clumsy, too big, he unfastened the remaining buttons at the front of the dress. He felt an urge to be rid of this black material that covered her. She submitted

376

without movement, hands held loosely by her sides. Meeting her eyes once more, in their rims of black, bright but without expression, unfocused-looking, it occurred to Markham that she might possibly be drugged – hashish was in common use in Constantinople among all classes.

He was intent still on removing the girl's dress. She helped him in this, slipping the dress off her shoulders, working it down where it was tight-fitting over the hips, until she could step clear of it. She was wearing a white petticoat below it, of the camisole type, with narrow straps over the shoulders. Still without expression she raised slender arms to the catch that held this at the nape of her neck.

'No,' Markham said suddenly, again in English, 'don't take it off,' raising his hand at the same time in a restraining gesture.

It was the gesture she understood rather than the words. She stopped at once, lowering her arms once more to her sides, and stood there patiently looking at him.

Markham stared back. He had suffered a kind of violent recognition in which all sexual desire had drained away. He knew now why the black had seemed incongruous, knew why he had noticed Irma in the first place, singled her out. The small-boned Arab face, the white shoulder-straps on the pale, very slightly sallow skin, the air of rather unwilling docility, of being in travesty, somehow . . . The very differences of this girl from Miriam made the resemblance more poignant – the thick layer of powder, the lack of animation in the face, the vacant eyes, the staring rims of *kohl*. It was like Miriam brought back but not fully alive, numbed still, expressionless with shock.

He put his arms round the girl with an instinct of protection, as if the resemblance placed her too in danger. She, however, sensing the change in his mood, fearing perhaps that he would be dissatisfied with her, moved against him and after a moment he felt her hand sliding upward into his groin. This, in spite of the recognition that had shocked him, began almost at once to have its remorseless effect. He had had no woman since the departure of his wife, and pity was not proof against the repeated caresses of the small hands – both of them now busy with him. Before he knew it almost, they were on the bed. She was wearing nothing under the petticoat and spread her legs at once for him, exposing with total lack of concern her narrow loins, the pubic area shorn nude as was customary with Moslem women. He came almost at once, without violence, in long protracted throbs while she held him in the light grip of her knees until it was over. Afterwards he lay by her side for a time he did not measure, thinking of nothing.

When he got up to go she rose with him, helped him with the adjustments of his clothing. He saw that there were marks of discoloration, slight bruises, high up on her arms. He had gripped her harder than he had realized. He took out his wallet. 'I'm sorry if I hurt you,' he said. He held out the rainbow-coloured banknote.

'Madame,' she said, speaking for the first time. 'Madame Clara.'

'No,' he said. 'This is for you.' He laid the note on the bed. She did not move towards it. Her eyes regarded him steadily and quite vacantly. Once again he had the impression that she was drugged. He smiled at her to show that he was not displeased, then moved to the door. As he closed this behind him and walked away along the corridor he had the feeling that inside the room she would still be standing there, quite still, in the white petticoat, with her bruised arms, standing where he had left her.

The scene inside the *salon* was the same – as silent still, the figures seated in the same positions as far as he could tell. Madame Clara was talking to another man, another customer presumably. Fehmi was nowhere to be seen, but as Markham moved across the room Madame Clara turned towards him and indicated the door by which he had first entered. The wrestler was waiting just outside, and Markham was conducted further along the corridor to another room where he found Fehmi seated at a table with a white cloth on which were a bottle and glasses and various small dishes. He was not wearing the fez now and Markham saw that he was completely bald.

'I took the liberty of opening a bottle,' Fehmi said, raising his glass. 'I did not know how long you would be.'

'One never knows that,' Markham said, sitting down opposite.

Fehmi poured champagne for him. '*Salut!*' he said, again raising his own glass.

'Your good health.' Markham drank a little. It was good champagne but rather too warm.

He looked across at Fehmi. The other man was half reclining in his chair, so that the difference in height between them was cancelled and his face was on a level with Markham's own. It was a remarkable face in its way, broad, pitted with the traces of some former disease of the skin, a heavily sensual face, yet there was a kind of sensitivity in it too, some quality of suffering in the thick, slightly everted lips, both upper and lower lips equally full so there was almost complete symmetry in the mouth, the lips forming the shape of a pale pink, crumpled flower. Markham wondered again if there were some negro blood in the man – those lips, and then the eyes, short-lashed, black as coals in their deep, bony sockets.

'Well,' Fehmi said, 'how did you find the girl?'

'Very nice.' Markham shut out thoughts of the silent, stricken figure in the white petticoat.

'Pliable, eh? You can do what you want with her. All the girls here are the same. That is why I come here. Some of those others . . .' Fehmi made a heavy pout of contempt. 'They think they have to do something, you know what I mean?'

'I think so, yes.'

'Writhing and cavorting about,' Fehmi said. 'They should keep still and try to understand what is wanted, like good Moslem women.'

379

'Like Mademoiselle Irma.'

'Exactly. I am glad to find we share the same tastes. Are you in Constantinople for long?'

'Not very long, no. A business trip. My name is Markham, Robert Markham.'

'I am Hassan.'

'Are you on business too?'

'No, not exactly . . . The English are great for business. Not like us. Though with us it is different.'

'How do you mean?'

Fehmi refilled their glasses. 'We are in a state of moribundity,' he said. 'In a state of moribundity you do not have business. You keep still. Like these ladies here. Just living from day to day, Mr Robert, you know what I mean? The stratagems of not collapsing.'

'You have a way with words,' Markham said.

Fehmi made no reply to this. He was busy opening another bottle of champagne – he had drunk three-quarters of the first one. There was a faint shine of moisture on his brow and cheeks. The cork exploded across the room and struck the wall. He poured the foaming stuff into Markham's glass then his own. '*A la vôtre*, my dear Mr Robert,' he said.

'Your health.' Markham was beginning to realize that the luck which had brought about his meeting with Fehmi had been only of a partial kind. The other was not going to confide much to a man met in a brothel. Apart from anything else, he would not want to take the risk of his visits to whores becoming known to his fellow-members of the Mohammedan League. He was a romantic, of a kind. Some extraordinary dream of mutual courtesy had led him to pursue the acquaintance thus far, but it did not seem likely to Markham that it would extend beyond this night and this place. He dared not ask too many direct questions, for fear of arousing Fehmi's suspicion.

'Living from day to day is also the law of Allah,' Fehmi said. 'As a Moslem I am bound to pay attention to this. In the

380

present state of things the religion of Islam is perfectly suited to our needs. It is a perfect religion for us, it fills the bill entirely. Islam means resignation, my dear Mr Robert. It is a beautiful idea but also very difficult. In the present political context it means resisting change of any kind, all attempts at reform.'

He had spoken in the grandiloquent way that Markham now recognized as characteristic, with a rhetorical cadence, tucking in his chin at the end of each sentence. Now as he poured out more champagne, Markham said, 'Your English is very good. Where did you learn it?'

'I have travelled,' Fehmi said. 'I have been in countries where English is spoken.'

At this moment there was a knock on the door. *'Buyurun,'* Fehmi shouted. They saw the door open and Madame Clara appear.

'We have the *Nautch* girls,' she said. 'Do the gentlemen want to see them?'

'Well,' Fehmi said, looking at Markham, 'do you want to see the *danse du ventre?'*

'Yes, all right,' Markham said.

'They can come in here,' Fehmi said. 'There is room for them here.'

The girls must have been waiting just beyond Madame Clara in the corridor, because they entered at once. There were five of them, Turkish girls, barefoot, in short bodices, with brightly coloured scarves round their waists and loose divided skirts. Their hair was very long, falling to well below the shoulders, and unbraided. As they began to move in the slow preliminaries to the dance, the heavy gleaming tresses swung round their heads. One of the girls remained against the wall, beating on a small drum slung round her neck, and accompanying this with a kind of wild droning or humming sound, which had hardly any break or variety of pitch. Markham saw that several of Madame Clara's girls had come in and were standing together, watching, Irma among them,

381

as serious-looking as ever. He saw the shaven poll and thick moustache of the wrestler there too. Across the table from him Fehmi poured out more champagne. With one huge, swollen-looking hand he began to beat on the table, keeping time to the rhythm of the drum.

The tempo quickened and the girls moved faster now, in the strange floating movements of the dance, varying their steps to the dancer in the centre, clearly the leader, a girl somewhat taller than the others, very dark-complexioned, with flashing eyes and a mane of reddish glinting hair that swirled about her as she swayed and lunged to the increasingly urgent measure of the drum.

Suddenly, at the height of this dance, the leader stood stock-still and the whole troupe became motionless for perhaps ten seconds, though the drumbeat and the wild nasal humming continued. Then a sort of collective tremor went over them, the leader stamped her right foot, and they were dancing again, but differently now, turning and twisting on their bare toes. As they revolved, the coloured scarves wound round their waists below the short bodices gradually unfurled and fell away like streamers, revealing their nude abdomens, decorated with a few strands of bead chains from which, very low on the hips, swung the light tinsel of the divided skirts.

The girls now were gleaming with perspiration and in a state bordering on frenzy, shuddering all over their semi-nude bodies. Again, for a few seconds, they seemed to become transfixed. The drum and the voice ceased abruptly. Then, in dense silence, the extraordinary *Nautch* movements began. The girls' bodies vibrated while the exposed stomach began slowly to gyrate as though under some entirely separate control. Then the vibration ceased, the limbs became totally inert, while the muscles of the abdomen revolved, jerked, rolled, quivered in a way that seemed horrifically powerful and autonomous to Markham, as if galvanized by some voracious appetite. He was relieved when, again without any

382

apparent signal from the leader, the belly movements stopped and the girls stood still.

They stood for some time, quivering still with the exertions of the dance. Then the leader visibly relaxed, a final violent tremor passing over her limbs. She threw back the gleaming, tangled mass of her hair and looked around at the faces of those watching. The girl who had been beating the drum now rattled a tambourine in a brief peremptory fashion. Fehmi took some coins from his pocket and threw them among the dancers and Markham did the same. Madame Clara and some of the girls also threw coins on to the floor. Bending almost double the *Nautch* girls swirled and dived to pick up the money. Then in a body they swept out laughing and talking together.

'Good, eh?' Fehmi said.

'Amazing.'

'Beautiful girls.' Fehmi finished the champagne in his glass. 'They go with each other, the *Nautch* girls,' he said. 'They do not go with men.'

Markham glanced at his watch. It was four o'clock in the morning.

'Getting late,' Fehmi said. 'Are you leaving now?'

'I suppose so.' Markham felt an immediate sense of loss.

He was delighted when Fehmi said, 'I will accompany you, we can go some of the way together. I do not want to part from you yet.'

'Good idea,' Markham said. 'I must settle up first.'

'When I take to a man I take to him on a large scale,' Fehmi said. 'I knew from the first moment, when we were having our little cross-purposes about Mademoiselle Irma. Two gentlemen having a misunderstanding together. I had a sense of affinity.'

Markham rose. 'I'd better go and see Madame Clara,' he said.

Fehmi raised a hand. 'All is settled,' he said. He began to struggle to his feet.

'What do you mean?'

'I have spoken to La Belle Clara.' He fronted Markham now, smiling, monumental, the fawn jacket and trousers loose about him, the opulent crimson of the fez, which he wore straight across his brows, completing the effect. 'Everything is taken care of,' he said. 'One gentleman to another, my dear. They know me here.'

'That is really very good of you,' Markham said. He again had the impression that Fehmi was acting a part – not out of hypocrisy or self-interest, but because he was in the grip of a myth of some kind, some archetypal situation of *noblesse oblige.*

They waited in the passage while the wrestler went for Markham's coat. Madame Clara came to say good-bye. She smiled tenderly at Markham and hoped he would come again to see them. Several of her girls, she now confided, had been educated in convents. She pressed Markham's hand and breathed warmly, spirituously upon him. The wrestler, pocketing his tip, patted Markham on the back.

Then they were outside, in the cool darkness of the alleyway. The red-shaded lamp was still burning over the entrance.

'I will have to rely on you to show me the way out of here,' Markham said. 'I'd better go down to Galata Bridge, I think, and try to get an early morning ferry to Beshiktash.'

'That is the way I am going,' Fehmi said. 'I live near the *Odoun Kapou.*'

Together they began to walk back the way they had come, towards the shore of the Golden Horn. The houses were dark now, shuttered and silent for the most part, though they heard voices and laughter from some. They met no one, but Markham thought he heard the scrape of steps once or twice behind them, and once he glanced round, but saw nothing.

This was at the start of their walk. After a little while Fehmi began to hold forth in his rhetorical fashion and quite loudly, so that his voice eclipsed all other sounds. He was talking about the degeneration of the Ottoman ruling class, how the system had kept sound peasant stock from government service, so that power had fallen out of Turkish hands into those of lower racial types.

'Our Sultan was abused,' Fehmi said, 'by those around him. Power was in the hands of Greeks, Armenians, Levantines.' He was silent for some moments then he said in a voice full of relishing contempt, 'Renegades and venal people - you know what I mean? Scum.'

'But it was Abdul Hamid himself who appointed those people,' Markham said. 'He surrounded himself with such people.'

'He was abused, our Caliph was abused. What we want now is a return to the *Sheriat*, the Holy Law, government by Moslems, a strengthening of the religious courts, whose power has declined under this infidel government . . .'

The declamatory voice went on in the dimness. Markham gave the words only intermittent attention. It was obvious that Fehmi was a Moslem supremacist and political reactionary. What he seemed to be advocating was rule by the *mollahs*, which was out of the question now, surely - the army would not tolerate that, certainly not the new officer class. He could not make Fehmi out, could not bring his impressions of the man and what he had been told about him into one comprehensive frame of reference. Blackmailer, spy, Islamic polemicist, pillar of the Mohammedan League, frequenter of docile whores . . . But it was something deeper than these apparent contradictions that puzzled and intrigued him, some quality in the man he had sensed from the moment he had sat opposite him at the table, watched him pour out the champagne with that lordly air, something Markham could not yet find words for, but certainly nothing to do with the opinions Fehmi was now expressing.

'From what I can gather of the present government,' he said, 'it is secular in its outlook.' He was hoping that this might draw Fehmi out further, perhaps lead him to speak of his newspaper and the support it commanded, but something

385

happened now to interrupt the conversation. They had emerged from the Rue Kemmer Alit area and were descending towards the Galata quayside. Suddenly, from somewhere below them, nearer to the shore, they heard the plaintive chanting of the Awakeners and the exactly spaced taps of the drum.

'Time for the *sahor*,' Fehmi said. 'It will soon be dawn.'

In fact it seemed to Markham that the darkness was going already. There were no street lamps here but he could make out the pale expanse of Fehmi's face and the glimmering of his fawn suit. They were descending the steep cobbled streets leading down to the shore. Several times he saw the dark shapes of dogs lying sleeping against the walls. No sound came up to them but Markham thought he could smell the brackish harbour water now. Again, but no nearer, they heard the chanting voice: 'He profiteth who saith there is no God but God.'

They went down past the dark bulk of the Church of the Holy Virgin and came suddenly within sight of the Bosphoros, a dim unmarked expanse, with nothing but a few scattered lights on the Asian side opposite to indicate the narrowness of the straits – though the line joining the sea and land was faintly discernible to the eye that strained for it.

They stopped at the Galata side and stood with their backs against the thick girders at the beginning of the bridge. Glancing below him Markham could make out the short-masted caiques moored side by side along the wharf. While he looked a lantern was lit on one of them and he saw a dark figure moving there, against the pallid light.

'It will soon be morning now,' Markham said. 'I'll probably be able to get a boat.' At once, as if to confirm that things were starting up again, they heard the booming of the cannon on Seraglio Point, signalling the advent of light, the beginning of the day's fast.

386

'The Night of Power is over for another year,' Fehmi said. 'They say that on this night the destinies of men for the coming year are revealed to the angels.'

'It's as well they don't tell us,' Markham said. He could see Fehmi's face more clearly now. He was smiling slightly, looking towards the open sea to the south. Markham glanced in that direction. He could see the wrinkles of the currents, the dark shapes of the Asian hills scattered with pale lights.

'Maybe they try,' Fehmi said, 'but the messages are too distilled – you know what I mean? Too pure for us, we can't hear them.'

He was smiling still as he said these words, and Markham knew now what it was he had seen in the other man's face, something there that had survived the indulgence and corruption of life. He had set it down vaguely as refinement, but he saw now that it was the knowledge of pain. Knowledge, not sympathy. Whether this was the mark of a religious or a criminal temperament Markham did not know. He knew only that it was rare – he had seen it in none of the faces he had approached with his secret, Miss Taverner's, Hartunian's, Nesbitt's, Tarquin's.

He saw it now, for all the other's fantasizing grandiloquence; and with the word 'distilled' still echoing in his mind – an unexpected word, pronounced by Fehmi with a sort of rhetorical lingering on the second syllable – the intention to confess gathered within him, precisely as if deposited by some similar chemistry in the mind, drop by drop, absolutely pure.

'I didn't tell you,' he said, 'but I have been here before. I was here twelve years ago. I was engaged at that time to an Armenian girl.'

Without more preliminaries, looking straight before him, Markham began to tell Fehmi the story of the engagement party, while daylight spread slowly over the sea and the city. He told it as it came to him, as he had started to tell the others.

387

But this time he did not stop short. 'I told them my name,' he said. 'Robert Markham. I told them I was an Englishman, not an Armenian.'

His own voice, saying these things for the first time to any other human being, seemed monstrously unreal to him. Fehmi's face was serious now, attentive. Markham could see the smoke of early fires on the slopes above the interior of the Golden Horn. There were a few people now too, moving about on the moored boats below them. The far end of the bridge was still indistinct, partly concealed by the thin mist rising off the water.

'I said it several times,' he said. 'Three or four times. I said it once before they did anything to her. If that had been the only time . . . I could have imagined it was for her sake, you know, to protect her – they might have stopped, knowing a foreigner was there. That wasn't why, of course, but I could have pretended to myself, perhaps. But I said it again, while they were doing it to her, while they were killing the others. And I said it after she was dead. *Ermeni degilim. Ingilizim.* Do you understand? I said it *afterwards.*'

Fehmi nodded his large head solemnly. 'Yes,' he said, 'I understand very well. One gentleman to another. But this thing you are telling me, my dear Mr Robert—'

'He asked me if I was the bridegroom, you know.' Markham kept his voice steady with an effort. ' "So you are marrying an Armenian girl?" – I remember his exact words. *"Ermeni bir kizla evleniyorsun?"* He said it politely – a sort of polite enquiry. He spoke quite close to my face. Then he said, *"Bac, bac"* – inviting me to watch what was happening. By that time the men had got Miriam into the corner. I said it again, while he was looking at me – he kept his eyes on my face. Twelve years ago.' Markham paused, looked up at the heavy girders of the bridge. 'They might as well have killed me there and then,' he said.

'For twelve years you have been thinking about this?' Fehmi said. 'You told them your name and your nationality, you saved your skin and you have been thinking about that for twelve years?'

Markham nodded. There were a few people passing over the bridge now: dockworkers starting early, a ragged wheezing man poking in the refuse that had collected against the big iron plates at the side of the bridge, a *hammal* bowed under sacks of grain. No one paid particular attention to the two men standing under the girders in the recess at the beginning of the bridge. 'A simple statement of fact,' he said. 'Repeated several times. But it always means the same. I don't need to translate it for you, do I?'

'No,' Fehmi said. 'But twelve years ago – that was in another lifetime, my dear.' He tucked in his chin and looked solemnly at Markham. 'We must learn to turn over the page,' he said. 'We must have *resilience*. That is a quality I value very highly. I have it myself. There have been things not much to my credit, you understand. Fairly numerous.'

'That doesn't seem possible for me,' Markham said. 'I have told you, there has hardly been a day . . .'

'Naturally there must be people like that. Human types are very various. It is a misfortune.'

Beyond Fehmi, beyond the heavy shoulders and the big head surmounted by the fez, a long, gleaming track of light had appeared on the water – sunlight was visible there before the sun itself was clear of the mist.

'The luckiest are those who have resilience,' Fehmi said. There was a haggardness about his face in this clearer light; the soft skin below his eyes was creased and livid. Markham noticed for the first time that the other's forehead was discoloured with bruises. It took him a moment or two to realize that these must have been caused by the frequent prostrations of prayer.

'But if I can advise you, my dear,' Fehmi said. 'Since you are obviously lacking in that valuable property, the worst thing you can do is try to redeem things. Turpitudes are made worse in that way. No, I do not believe in that activity at all. It

389

is a Christian attitude, very destructive. Always looking to be saved. Always looking to put things right. Nothing is redeemed – it is an illusion. Man does not hold the balance. It is not only useless, but it does harm.'

'How do you mean?'

'Harm to others. One thing leading to another, you see. Let us say that you behaved shamefully. Trying to restore your credit or your sense of justice or your *amour propre* – you involve others, you set up a cycle, you do not know where it will stop. No, it is the wrong way.'

'What's the right way, then?'

Fehmi gestured towards the far end of the bridge, Stambul rising beyond it. 'Containing the troubles is the answer,' he said. 'If you have not the luck to be resilient, what else can you do? Look at the dome of the Suleimaniyé up there. It means containment. That is another of the meanings of Islam.'

'It is foreign to my way of thinking,' Markham said.

'Well, that is a pity. It is because you try to justify yourself. The harm must stop somewhere, my dear Mr Robert. It cannot be passed on forever. Think of it as a disease. Perhaps there is something, some medical term, to describe that – the opposite of a carrier? One in whose veins the infection is contained.'

'Perhaps there is,' Markham said. 'I don't know. In any case it is an accident of constitution.'

'Well, that would be my advice,' Fehmi said. 'One gentleman to another.'

Markham glanced away towards the far end of the bridge. The toll-keepers were there now; he could distinguish them by their white clothes. Beyond them among the roof-tops, he could see storks at their ramshackle nests. The early sunshine elicited gleams of brilliance from their awkwardly balancing bodies. There were voices now from the boats moored below and from somewhere farther off the quarrelling of street dogs. But these sounds, though clear enough, were separate, accidental, not affecting the deep hush that still lay over everything – the hush that Byzans and his colonizing Greeks might have felt, perhaps on a morning like this one, rounding the horn-shaped headland from the Sea of Marmara twenty-three centuries ago, sailing quietly into this marvellous harbour.

He was struck suddenly by the immense age of the place, and by his own presumption: he had thought of it only as the scene of his 'lapse', as if all its history had tended to that obscure and ugly moment. He looked at the ancient city now, in its trance of sunlight, in the spell of its violent and complicated past. His experience had been no more than a bloodstained moment in the life of the city, that life itself no more than a breath in the sum of things.

So Markham sought to dilute his own damage in the larger one. And he had so far succeeded, at least temporarily, that it was with a lightening of the spirit that he turned back to Fehmi, even a certain feeling of gratitude to the other man for having provided an occasion for confidences. These had been all on his side, however, it occurred to him now. Soon they would be parting. In all probability Fehmi would avoid further encounters. There was not much time for finesse.

'I have told you a good deal about myself,' he said. 'I'm not quite sure why. There is possibly something that you can tell me.' He paused, but Fehmi made no answer, merely tucked in his chin and waited.

'As you will understand,' Markham said, raising his eyes to the other man's, 'I have good reason to be interested in the Armenian question. What you say about containing the harm and so on hardly applies to the way the Armenians are treated, does it? After all they have suffered they should be left alone now. Yet the press continues to incite violence against them. Certain sections of the Turkish press, I mean. I am curious to know why this is so.'

There was a short silence, then Fehmi said slowly, 'You read Turkish then? An English businessman who reads Turkish?'

391

'Tell me why,' Markham said. 'One gentleman to another.'

But there was no response on Fehmi's face. The dream of reciprocal courtesy was over. The small black eyes regarded him intently. 'So,' he said. 'You know who I am?'

'Tell me only who pays for them, who pays for the articles to be published.'

'You followed me,' Fehmi said. He reached forward suddenly and gripped Markham's forearm. 'Who set you on? You are working for the Committee, aren't you?'

'No,' Markham said. Fehmi's strength was enormous. The grip, though applied without apparent exertion, was numbing his arm already. He took a step back, endeavouring to wrench the arm free. 'Let me go,' he said. He felt the thick fingers relax, but the other's hand remained there, on his arm. 'I promised to find out,' he said. 'It will not harm you to tell me. I will pay.'

'Promised? Promised who?'

'Them,' Markham said. 'Who else would I do this for?'

For a long moment Fehmi regarded him. Then he said, 'The Armenians? Are you telling me it was the Armenians? Do you think I am a fool?'

The surprise and anger in his voice gave Markham his first intimation that things were wrong, that there had been an error somewhere. 'I'm telling you the truth,' he said. 'Now give me the information I want.'

'Either you are mad or I am,' Fehmi said. 'They know who pays for the articles. They know better than anyone who pays for them.'

'What do you mean?' Markham's sense of error grew stronger. He saw that Fehmi had begun smiling now, a curiously artificial smile.

'It is a joke,' Fehmi said. He nodded his large head several times, as if to indicate that he was not deceived. The black tassel of his fez swung back and forth with the movement. 'Everyone knows the English humour,' he said. 'It is a joke, isn't it?'

392

The shots came from behind Markham, three in rapid succession, sounding very loud. He thought he heard a small coughing noise, but he was not looking at Fehmi when the shots sounded so did not register any change in the other man's face. His own immediate reaction was to glance over his shoulder, but he saw nothing out of the way – a few people entering the bridge from the jumble of buildings behind, sunlight on their faces. They all seemed to be looking in his direction, not towards where the shots had come from. Then he felt himself gripped powerfully by the front of his coat and pulled forward to face Fehmi again. He saw that there was now a short glistening ribbon of blood extending from one corner of Fehmi's mouth to the chin. He noted, with the precise observation of nightmare, that this ribbon exactly followed the fold in Fehmi's flesh. There was blood also on the lapel of his fawn jacket. To avoid being tugged forward against this mess of blood he braced himself back against the pull of the other man's hands. He heard – though whether it was then or a little earlier, before the struggle with Fehmi began, he could not afterwards be sure – the clatter of metal on the cobbles at his feet. Glancing down between their two bodies he saw the pistol, still sliding where it had been thrown, blue-black, with a glint to it like flies' wings. It stopped near Fehmi's enormous brown-and-white shoes. The shoes were motionless, about six inches apart, planted as if to withstand a gale. Markham tried to look round again but the grip on him made this difficult. He saw that people were moving towards them, two Turkish sailors in white, others behind. Fehmi's eyes stared into his with an effect of painful concentration. The life was failing in them but the grip did not relax – again Markham was obliged to strain back against the embrace. Fehmi coughed, and vomited more blood. The movement tipped his fez to an incongruously rakish angle.

In these few seconds, struggling to retain his balance in that importunate grip of the dying man, the pistol sliding to rest within kicking distance, other people moving slowly and somehow reluctantly towards him, Markham understood that this, or most of it, had been arranged for him, and with this there came a sense of extreme danger. He heard voices now, enquiring, concerned.

'Let me go,' he said. He grasped at the thick fingers but they were too tenacious, too strong. Panic rose in him. 'Damn you,' he said. 'Let me go!' He brought up his knee, driving it with all his force into the pit of Fehmi's stomach, pushing at the same time at the wet front of the other man's jacket. It seemed to him that the voices behind changed, became sharper, more menacing. He raised one arm high in the air and using his fist as a hammer struck Fehmi between the dumbly staring eyes where he had earlier noted the bruises of prayer. The blow sent the fez flying. He felt the grip on him relax, and pushed again. Fehmi, startlingly bald now, slid down against him, turned slightly and fell face forward against the base of the girders.

At once, as if the plan had been present in his mind all the time, Markham reached down and picked up the pistol. The sailors were within two yards of him now. Seeing the pistol they gave back a little, regarding him silently. He backed to the metal parapet, climbed onto it, inserted his body through the lower girders, then swung himself through the gap. His feet found a hold on the edge of a girder below. He slipped the pistol into the pocket of his overcoat. With cautious haste he began to climb down towards the water. There were shouts again now and he saw the white uniform of one of the sailors, who had climbed onto the parapet above him.

The nearest boat was several yards away – it was difficult to judge the distance accurately from above. There was no one on it as far as he could see. Bleached fishing-net lay piled in the bow and he thought that this might break his fall if he could land on it. He was too low to be seen now by anyone on the bridge itself, but people must already be running down to the landing stage to cut him off. He edged as near to the boat as he could, swung himself back and forth several times in order to gain momentum, then jumped. He landed on the net but not in the thickest part of it, and the fall jarred him and drove the breath from his body. He lay for perhaps twenty seconds. Then he struggled up, ran the length of the boat and jumped off on to the quayside.

Once here he continued running. There were shouts behind him but he was soon in the maze of streets above the docks. In his headlong rush he scattered chickens and children and old women in black who screeched expostulations after him in Greek. He sweated heavily and his breath came in laboured gasps.

Gradually the cunning of the pursued came to his aid. If he went on running he would be caught. Pausing only to transfer the pistol to his jacket pocket, he pulled off the dark overcoat which would have identified him and left it in a bundle against the wall of an alley. The suit he had on under it was much lighter in colour, pale grey. He thought it unlikely that anyone had looked much at his face. By good fortune his steps brought him out on to the thoroughfare of Arab Kapou, where there were shops and cafés and people, though not very many yet. By an effort of will, Markham forced himself to walk unhurriedly. He walked for perhaps five minutes without looking back. No one challenged him. At the end of the thoroughfare where it curves back down towards the water, there were two fiacres waiting. He got into the first one and asked the driver to take him to Beshiktash.

Almost at once, however, he began to think that it might not be wise to return home now. Those who had arranged the trap for him might well have warned the authorities in advance. He had not had time to think much until now; and even now he could not see clearly the motives of the people who had employed him in this business with Fehmi. He had been framed for the killing, that much was certain. Up to now he had completely played into the hands of the people who had done it. He might get home to find the police waiting – and once in police hands he was done for; they could prove what they liked. The wisest thing would be to make straight for the Embassy, explain the situation to somebody there, obtain official protection. But he was unwilling to do this, for a number of reasons. It was a private matter, for one thing. He could not see himself sitting down and telling someone like Lewin about it, going into all the details of his involvement, without which it would not be intelligible; asking for shelter, like a refugee. Besides, it would mean accepting restrictions on his freedom – he would have to stay on British ground. As the cab proceeded at a steady pace through Pera it seemed clear to Markham that the only way to defeat those who had sought to trap him was to remain at large. This could best be achieved if nobody knew where he was.

Where could he go, however? Various possibilities came to him, none very appealing. He could not involve any of his colleagues. Henderson might have helped him but he was again in Salonika. Other than that, who could he trust? What he needed was a sort of anonymity for a while . . . Into his mind there came the patched face of the leper who had begged from him that dark night on the Haydar Pasha road, at the edge of the great cemetery. He thought of the wilderness of tombs and tangled vegetation, the huge expanse of the cemetery, extending for miles in the darkness, beyond the wall. Space to house a colony of lepers, space enough for all the homeless of the city – of which number he was now one.

He leaned forward and spoke to the driver's back. 'I've changed my mind,' he said. 'Take me to Top Hane, to the *iskelesi*.'


The body of Hassan Fehmi was carried off the bridge into the courtyard of the Mahmoudieh Mosque. Here they bathed the blood from his face with the water from the mosque fountain but it was soon apparent to all that he was dead. Nevertheless, someone put a rolled-up jacket under his naked head, perhaps pitying the bulk of the man, lying there on the hard stone. No one thought of covering him. An attempt was made to close his eyes but they remained half open. He lay on his back near the fountain, squinting up.

The police arrived and shortly afterwards a doctor. The contents of Fehmi's pockets were examined and his identity established – one of the policemen in any case knew who he was, having seen him about the courts. The crowd was questioned. Finally the body was lifted up into a carriage and taken to the mortuary to await formal identification. Those who had heard the shots and seen the struggle on the bridge and the subsequent flight of Fehmi's companion were taken to the police station for further questioning.

The Turkish police are not noted for speed of thought but they are painstaking and thorough and the questioning of witnesses was still proceeding as Markham reached the Haydar Pasha road and approached the borders of the Great Cemetery. He was by this time exhausted. The journey across to Scutari had taken a long time, strong currents in the Bosphoros having obliged the boatman to follow a zig-zag course which had taken them at one point out past the Saray Burun towards the open sea. Then there had been the climb up from the harbour over the rough roads. The sun was well past its zenith when he saw the spaces of the cemetery opening before him, with its dark clumps of cypresses here and there, all there was to break the desolate horizontal sweep of the place.

There were no gates, as far as he could see, certainly none in that section of the road which he was now traversing. But he was desperately impatient now to be off the road, this dusty yellowish track, constraining him to one direction. It was as if the road was all that still held him to an identity, as if abandoning it was the last act in a process of abdication. He walked for some time longer, however, still looking for a gate. A dust-cloud in the distance, seeming to denote the approach of a vehicle, finally impelled him to action. The wall on his

397

right was no more than five feet high. In a few seconds Markham was over it, crouching at the foot, amidst low, irregular mounds of broken brick and masonry.

His first impulse was to remain where he was, in the protection of the wall, and rest. But after a moment or two he began to move forward. Amidst the confusion of crumbling, dilapidated gravestones and the scrub-oak and bramble and brier bushes that grew among them, narrow paths had been worn, by animals or men, and Markham took one of these, proceeding as far as possible at right angles to the road he had just left, making his way farther and farther into the interior of the cemetery.

How long he walked thus he could not have said. It was as though his own extreme weariness came to resemble a form of energy, driving him on. Though he did not know it he had passed below the Quadrangle of Lepers and penetrated the area of neglected and abandoned tombs that lie south and east of this. It was finally the sight of another human being that brought him up short: on a descending slope ahead of him, leaning against a headstone, was a thin man, bare-legged, in short ragged tunic and dark red headcloth. He was grazing a few white goats among the tombs below him, and it was clear that he had not seen or heard anyone approach.

Markham had no wish to encounter another human being just now. However, once he had stopped he felt his weariness press heavily down on him. His head was swimming and the ragged figure of the shepherd was continually passing out of focus. A few yards aside from the point on the path where he was standing there was a shallow cavity, formed partly by vegetation, partly by some slight subsidence in the ground. The tilted slab of a grave roofed this partially over. Markham made his way through the bushes towards it and entered on hands and knees. There was enough room inside for him to lie down. A faint sunlight filtered into the place and there was an acrid smell of dry earth. In less than a minute he was asleep.

He slept heavily, without stirring, through the remaining hours of the afternoon, through the short evening and the dusk, well into dark. Cold woke him finally. He lay looking up through the gap between gravestone and bushes at a scattering of pale stars. He was shivering, but his head and face felt hot. The interior of his mouth and the glands at the sides of his neck were causing him pain. He crawled out of his shelter and stood up, overcoming the dizziness and faintness which immediately attacked him. It occurred to him that he might be going to be ill. Alone, in the darkness, in this enfeebled state, he knew that he had been unwise to come here, to this wilderness, without food or adequate clothes – he had thrown away the one garment that would have been useful. It had not been the instinct of self-preservation that had brought him here, but the desire to lose himself, to join these anonymous remains everywhere about him. In this moment of sickness, the bitter paradox came back to him again. He had bought his life with Miriam's. What had seemed worth such a price had from that moment lost all value. He had been seeking ever since in various ways to submerge it, lose it, throw it away ...

As he stood there, distantly but unmistakably, he heard the sound of human voices, and what sounded like a woman's laughter. This came from somewhere before him, in the direction he had been going when he turned aside to sleep. There was very little light – the moon of Ramazan was spent now – but he could see the line of the gap in the bushes where the path ran along. He stood a few moments longer, hesitating. But whatever the risks involved in making himself known to people in such a place, he knew he could not stay where he was, with what he suspected was a degree or two of fever. To do so would be to risk serious illness. It was early April, and the night air was cold already. He had money on him and could perhaps use it to get some sort of shelter from these people. The voices came to him again, careless-sounding, as if there was nothing to fear. Treading awkwardly over the uneven ground, Markham made his way back to the path and began to move along it in the direction of the sounds. There was silence now for some minutes, except for the cautious scrape of his own footsteps. Somewhere nearby an owl hooted. Then he heard laughter again, but brief, and glimpsed the glow of a light or fire, still some couple of hundred yards off, in the midst of a dark mass of trees or masonry that rose well above the general level.

Sick and giddy, Markham made his way cautiously forward. Occasionally he stumbled and once he fell heavily sideways into thick scrub, though with no consciousness of being hurt. He could smell the smoke from their fire and could see the red glow of it ahead of him among what he now saw were trees – a grove of trees thickly planted, forming a single dark mass.

As he approached this he stumbled and almost fell again. Wavering music played on some flute-like instrument came to him, arousing a certain vague recognition in his mind. He heard a man's voice but the tone was different, sharper: they had heard him. The next moment he had blundered into the clearing among the trees. He was aware of men rising to confront him in the firelight. He knew them almost at once, with an immediacy he was afterwards to think of as strange, phenomenal almost, though he had been helped in a way by the quality of the music. He knew them even before seeing the girl, the one who had danced for him while he waited for Zimin. She and an older woman beside her had remained seated just beyond the fire, and her features were lit by it, sullen in repose, with the high sharp cheekbones and shadowed eyes. Firelight glinted on the coppper bands at her ears.

Nobody spoke for some moments, then Markham said in Turkish, 'Can I share your fire?'

He had spoken on impulse and quickly, wanting to quieten any alarm his sudden appearance might have caused. It was a request that would have met with kindness from Moslems among whom hospitality to the stranger is felt as a binding duty. But these were not Moslems, he remembered now, seeing the motionless forms before him, the dark intent faces. They were *chinganés*, an outcast people, with no laws of hospitality, no gods of their own.

'It is a cold night,' he said. There were three men and a boy of about fourteen. Neither of the women had stood up, but he heard the older one say, '*Yabanji dir*,' and this word was repeated among the men, two of whom now came forward and brought him into the circle of the firelight. He could smell their bodies and their clothes, a smell of dust and sweat and woodsmoke. The others were around him now. Quick hands ran along the front and sleeves of his jacket, fingering the material, sliding over the pockets. One arm he kept at his side, covering the pistol. With the other he tried to brush the hands away, though without great force. Then the younger woman got up and joined the group around Markham. She said something in a language that was strange to him, though there were Turkish words in it. The men fell away a little. Markham found himself looking into the dark face of the woman. It was a striking face, savage in the firelight, taut with hardship in spite of its youthfulness, with deepset eyes and a bold vivid curve of the mouth. Her long hair gleamed with oil and fell loose round her face. He could smell her too, the same feral smell as the men, but muskier, sweetened by some scent, perhaps that of the oil she had used on her hair.

She studied his face for some moments in silence. Though nothing in her own face changed, Markham felt sure she had recognized him. She turned and spoke again to the others, and again he could not catch the words but sensed that she was reproaching them or criticizing them for their treatment of him. She seemed to have some sort of authority with them –

perhaps as the dancer, he thought, the mainstay of the troupe. They listened without interrupting, though with negligent attitudes and averted faces.

In the pause that followed her words, as they turned to look at him again, he said, '*Ben hasta*. I am ill.'

The girl advanced towards him. She raised a hand and though the movement was slow he almost flinched. A moment later he felt her hand cool on his forehead. One of the men said something and the others laughed – he guessed it was something to do with the illness being in his head. The girl laughed too and spoke, looking at Markham. He smiled, not understanding. She led him, with a light touch on his arm, round to the other side of the fire. He felt faint and unsteady again now and the girl appeared to sense this, for the pressure of her hand below his elbow increased, and she led him out of the zone of the firelight towards the trees. Here, he now saw, among the scabbed trunks of the trees themselves, were more tombstones, larger than the others he had seen, leaning at various angles of dilapidation; and here and there among them were cavernous openings dimly lit from within, leading downwards below the ground. Guided by the girl he went down one of these, descending several steps cut in the earth, and found himself crouching in a small square chamber, lit by an oil-lamp, trimmed very low and set on a stone. The earth floor was covered with a striped *kilim*, and there was a folded quilt and a cushion in one corner. Various articles, ribbons, a scarf or sash, some small bottles, lay on a short plank which had been set like a trestle on stones about two feet from the ground. After a moment he realized that it was her own sleeping place that she had brought him to. She pointed to the corner where the bedding was and he nodded. Then she turned and crouching forward made her way out. She was barefoot, he noticed as she went up the steps, the soles of her feet were earth colour and there was a thin bangle that looked like gold round her left ankle. She did not look towards him again.

Fully dressed as he was, Markham lay down with his head on the cushion and pulled the quilt over him. The chamber smelt of dry earth. He could hear the voices of the gypsies talking together, the men and the women, talking in turn. He wondered vaguely if it was him they were discussing. After a short while the girl came down again, carrying a bowl which steamed lightly.

'*Tisane*,' she said, holding it out to him at full arm's length.

He took it from her and drank while she watched him. It was hot and strongly aromatic, some kind of herbal infusion. Markham could not remember enjoying any drink more since the hot chocolate of his childhood – a taste since lost. She stood watching him drink, unsmiling. He drank it to the last possible drop, like a child. When he had finished she took the bowl from him again, reaching to take it at arm's length so as not to come too near. Again, from his warm corner, he watched her slender, dusty feet mounting the steps, disappearing.

Almost at once he felt drowsy, heavily, leadenly drowsy. It occurred to him as he sank towards sleep that there might have been some narcotic in the drink she had given him. He heard the sound of the flute again. His last action was to take the pistol and the wallet containing his money from the pockets of his jacket and put them under his pillow.

He spent the next ten hours in total oblivion. He was woken by the sound of the girl's voice. He opened his eyes to see her standing there. She had brought tea and black bread and goat's milk cheese. Daylight was in the chamber now, flooding in from the opening at the top of the steps. Again the girl did not come near enough to touch him. Conventions down here were different, obviously – among the others she had touched his face, put her hand under his arm to guide him.

'*Teshekur ederim*,' he said, smiling at her.

'*Bir sey degil.*' Her smile, when it came, transformed the face, breaking the sullenness of a harsh existence, curving the mouth upward, bringing life and expression into the eyes.

Markham ate the food, though with some difficulty – he had no real appetite. She watched him without speaking.

'Why are you doing this?' he asked. She gave no answer but she smiled again – his Turkish seemed to amuse her. Surreptitiously he slipped a hand under the pillow. The wallet and pistol were still there. The lamp was not burning now; someone must have come down when he was asleep and put it out – she probably. She had slept somewhere else that night, he guessed with the other women. It was possible of course that she belonged to one of the men, but he did not think so; her behaviour, her whole bearing, would have been different. They would be related in some way, all of them, probably, members of the same clan.

She began speaking, telling him that she and the others would be away all day, would return in the evening. She spoke Turkish now, and slowly, as if to a child or a person of simple intellect; all the same he found it difficult to follow; there were a number of unfamiliar dialect forms in it and an admixture of foreign words, possibly Kurdish – he thought it probable that she came from the eastern provinces somewhere. They were going down to Scutari, she said. He could go or stay as he liked. If he was intending to go he would have to give her the bedding now so that she could take it with her. She could not leave it unguarded for fear of thieves.

Looking into the dark eyes, with their uncivilized intentness of regard, Markham knew that a considerable trust was being placed in him. 'I will stay,' he said.

Afterwards, when she had gone he went out to relieve himself, then returned and slept again. When he awoke he made no attempt to get up, but lay watching the faint flexing of light on the earth walls of his room. His fever seemed to have left him but he felt listless still, disinclined for action of any kind and even for thought. He was in some sort of

404

artificially hollowed-out cavern, presumably the vault of a tomb. Its original inhabitant would be dust now, anything of value long since plundered. The gypsies had taken the tombs over and made apartments out of them.

He lay there throughout the day, dozing intermittently, sometimes thinking in a vague circular way about his situation. The people who had killed Fehmi had intended him to be blamed for it, or at least deeply implicated, so much was certain. Otherwise why throw the pistol at his feet? Luck had favoured them: Fehmi's tenacity of grip, obliging him to use that terrible violence on a dying man; his own action in taking up the pistol and pointing it at the crowd. But the killers could not have foreseen that he would behave thus. They could not have known, he insisted to himself, looking round the rough earth walls of his chamber, at the continuous faint coiling and uncoiling of light on the walls, on the floor, caused no doubt by some stirring of the foliage outside, though he could hear nothing. They could not have known. Not without a prescience too frightening to think of. No, he had played into their hands, there was no doubt of that. And if he had waited, allowed himself to be seized by the crowd, held for questioning? The Committee controlled the courts now. They could bring him to trial, have him convicted for murder if they wished. In the shifting allegiances of the times, it was impossible to say what the authorities would find expedient. He was an army officer, part of the British military presence in the city, a perfect vehicle for discrediting British policies, if that was what they intended. But Fehmi had been hostile to the Committee. His murder would be seen as an act of sympathy for them, how could they use it to discredit the British?

Markham's mind grew tired thinking of it. There must be some other explanation. It was Fehmi's friends, the clergy, the members of the Mohammedan League, who would be best suited by the scandal of British involvement, a Christian

405

power intervening against the Pan-Islamic movement, abetted by the godless men of the Committee. Perhaps Fehmi had been shot by his friends. That would be the biggest joke of all. He had said it was a joke. He had said that twice. His big face smiling, the tassel of his fez swinging to and fro. But there had been uncertainty behind the smile – even the beginnings of alarm. Fehmi himself had not understood the situation. *They know better than anyone.* That could only mean that it was the Armenians themselves who were responsible. That was the joke then – the Armenians providing vile scurrilities about themselves, paying to have them printed in the *Serbesti*. But Missakian must have known this already, Tarquin too, when they had come to his office that day. They had sent him on a wild goose chase. Or could the articles be the work of some other group within the Armenian movement? What purpose could they serve? Perhaps Fehmi had not meant this at all – he had not been given time to say . . .

Markham retreated from these puzzles into fitful sleep, awoke to the nightmare vision of Fehmi's dying face, that curious look of concentration in the eyes, the ribbon of blood from the mouth, himself fighting to be free, that terrible hammer blow, pushing against the wet lapels . . . With sudden recollection Markham brought his hands out from below the quilt, raised them before him, palms inward. The sweat of his fever had cleaned the palms themselves but his fingers were still red with Fehmi's blood.

He got out of bed at once, went to the earthenware jug of water the girl had left for him, poured some on his hands, rubbed them clean on his handkerchief. He still felt light-headed and somehow nerveless, without tension or grip. He had no desire to leave the chamber for the world outside. After a moment or two he crawled back under the quilt and lay still there, on his back, eyes open, thinking of nothing, watching the play of light.

The gypsies returned as dusk was falling. The girl came

down at once. He saw her outline at the entrance, heard the rustle of her clothes as she came down the steps. She went to the lamp and lit it before turning towards him.

'*Merhaba*,' he said.

She looked at him closely from where she was crouching near the lamp, but made no enquiries about his health or the day he had passed. Later she brought him more of the black bread, and some dried figs. Then she rejoined the others in the enclosure among the trees, and Markham lay alone in the lamplight, and listened to the voices and smelt the smoke of the fire.

Next morning he felt much better, clear-headed and much firmer in his movements. The exhaustion had left him and when he stood up he experienced no giddiness or nausea. However, he waited until the gypsies had gone before climbing out into the open.

He was standing in a grove of cypresses, very tall and growing thickly together, so that their branches met overhead, forming a deep shade. Morning sunshine filtered thinly through this canopy, lay in broken patterns on the yellowish earth between the tree trunks, and on the gravestones scattered about the place. Here and there the earth was heaped and mounded, the mounds overgrown with vegetation. He saw the entrance holes among these mounds which he guessed led down to vaults like the one he had been using.

Advancing through the trees, he came to the clearing and saw the dead fire with the blackened stones round it where the gypsies rested their cooking pots. Some twenty yards beyond this the trees ended and the ground stretched away as far as the eye could see, a trackless wilderness of decaying tombs amidst dense scrub, with dark clumps of cypresses rising here and there and occasional low spurs of grey rock. From where he was standing he could see no break in this vista of desolation as far as the horizon. He could hear goat-bells, however, in the distance, and guessed that in the tangled hollows and gullies of the place there might be other human beings.

He went on warily, picking his way over the broken and overgrown ground. His first need was for water, a stream or pool where he could wash. There must be water not too far away – the gypsies were well supplied with it. It was impossible to pursue a straight course for very long; subsidences and upheavals had disarranged the tombs, and gravestones, with their decorations of turbans and fezzes, lay everywhere in irrevocable disorder, festooned with bryony and ivy and honeysuckle. Several times his eye caught the whisk of a lizard, escaping at his advance, and once he saw an adder move quickly over the face of a rock. For a while his course was aimless, then he noticed a seam of fresher green running through slightly lower ground to the south, narrow-leaved trees like rowans, and some poplars. He made his way towards them and found a stream, narrow but deep, with clear water running over weeds. He stripped on the bank and climbed down. The water was cold, but the feeling of it on his soiled and sweated body was marvellously healing. He stayed there a long time, scooping the water over himself with cupped hands, repeatedly over his head and back and chest. Afterwards he dried himself on his shirt and found a sheltered place in the sun, where he lay at peace, feeling the warmth return to his body, listening to the mounting chorus of the cicadas from the thickets all around.

The body of Hassan Fehmi lay the rest of that day and the night that followed before burial. He had no wife, but he had a cousin in Constantinople, and the cousin came with his family to do what was necessary. Fehmi lay with his eyes closed at last while they perfumed the room where he lay, recited over him the verses for the dead from the Koran. A local woman who specialized in this came to wash him in tepid water and scented soap. Then the *imam* rubbed powdered camphor on the eight parts which touched the ground during prayer – knees, hands, feet, nose and forehead. He was wrapped in a long shirt and seamless winding sheet and laid on the bier with his right side turned towards Mecca. Then again the verses were recited over him, led by the *imam*: *We record the deeds of men and the marks they leave behind. We note all things in a glorious book . . . The sun hastens to its resting place, its course is laid for it by the Mighty One, the All-knowing. We have ordained phases for the moon . . .*

While all this was happening and during the hours that followed, the news of Fehmi's death spread rapidly through the city. He had had a wide acquaintance among the lower orders of the clergy. He was known also to certain people at the Palace, at whose request he had sometimes printed material favourable to Abdul Hamid. But it was among people who did not know him personally that anger at his murder grew most rapidly: among the poor and fanatical elements in the population, obliged to live in close proximity to Christian communities, and among the rank and file of the troops at the Tacsim Barracks, who for months now had been in a state of smouldering resentment at the tighter discipline imposed on them since the revolution, the drills and exercises which gave them barely enough time for their prayers. This murder of a champion of Islam became a focal point for various discontents; and when it was learned that the police had made no arrest, the anger grew fiercer, it was rumoured that the authorities themselves had had a hand in Fehmi's killing.

Next morning a large crowd assembled to follow the bier to Stambul to a cemetery near the Validé Han where the burial was to take place. For reasons that only afterwards became clear, it was decided that the procession should make a detour to cross and recross the Galata Bridge. When the point at which Fehmi had been shot was reached, all further progress was halted by the press of the excited crowd. Hundreds of white turbaned *ulemas* who had been waiting on the Galata side now joined the procession. In a matter of minutes the funeral had turned into a demonstration. The bier was draped with a green shawl bearing the Arabic verse from the Koran: *One martyr is enough for Allah*. Printed leaflets were distributed among the crowd, denouncing the Young Turk régime. The choir of priests chanted in fierce nasal descant. A dervish named Vahdeti, standing in the midst of the crowd, began preaching the wholesale massacre of Unionists and a return to the Holy Law. His words were greeted with deep-throated acclamation by the crowd. Reinforcements of police were able finally to restore some order, get the procession in motion again. But they were unable to quell the shouts of the crowd, nor that fierce chanting of the *ulemas* who followed behind the bier, their tall white turbans nodding like daisies in a wind.

The authorities were alarmed. In parliament the murder was discussed with hasty recriminations. The Committee was criticized for its failure to take action. None of this, however, affected the course of events, now moving swiftly to a crisis.

At dawn on 13th April, single armed men from the Palace barracks began to move in small groups across the Golden Horn and into Stambul, where they assembled in the square of Haghia Sophia. Among them were detachments from the White Lancers of Yildiz, some of whom had just beaten two subalterns to death and stripped and insulted their bodies, because of the pictures of half-naked women, cut from *La Vie Parisienne* and *Le Sourire*, with which the young men had adorned their rooms. A few hours later a battalion of Chasseurs marched over in a body, followed throughout the morning by other units from Yildiz and several squadrons of cavalry. By noon there were thousands of soldiers in the square, with not one officer among them – something like thirty officers had now been sabred or shot to death. The troops felt their grievances keenly and though inarticulate were in dangerous mood. The *Sheikh-ul-Islam* and other high-ranking ecclesiastics went among them and endeavoured to calm them down but they continued to utter the one cry, '*Yahassin Sheriat Peicamberi!*' – 'Long live the Law of the Prophet!'

Parliament was at once disabled, as the whole of the party of Union and Progress, main target of the mutineers, had gone to ground. Only sixty deputies were left and their panicky deliberations were brought to an end when one of their members, the young Druse deputy for Lattakia, was shot dead by troops on his way to the Chamber, not fifty paces from where they were sitting. So great was their haste to quit the premises that several of them were injured jumping from windows.

The soldiers now ruled the city, no attempt being made by the Officer Commanding in Constantinople, Fuad Pasha, to suppress the mutiny. During that first night, the mutineers fired hundreds of thousands of rounds indiscriminately into the sky, causing the accidental death of seven citizens.

Markham, sitting by the fire among the others, heard the crackling of these fusillades across the Bosphoros and assumed that fighting had broken out among different factions of the troops. He had heard a garbled account from the gypsies some nights previously of a funeral demonstration and a clash with police, but had not connected this with Fehmi at all. Today the gypsies had returned early and had talked among themselves about the disorders. They appeared to believe that the mutinous troops were to march north against the Third Army Corps in Macedonia in a bid to restore the Sultan's former powers.

Markham thought this was improbable but he did in any case listen with great attention. This was his fourth day among the gypsies, and events in Constantinople seemed

411

remote to him. He was content to remain where he was. His days had fallen into a pattern, at once blank and fleeting, mindless but not disagreeable. He seldom ventured much farther than the stream which he had found on the first day of exploration, generally finding a place to sit or lie among the rocks nearby, though on two occasions he had wandered into the more frequented parts of the cemetery on the north side, a distance of some three miles from where the gypsies made their camp. Here he had seen stone-cutters chipping at slabs of marble for the graves, sitting in groups together; and in the distance some members of the leper colony going out towards the road to beg. People were still sometimes buried in this part of the cemetery and Markham once saw yellow pariah dogs scratching about among newly dug earth, perhaps hoping to get down far enough to be able to attack the body. Being eaten by dogs must sometimes befall the dead here, he thought, since Moslems were not buried in a coffin but taken out and laid in the ground with only the winding sheet to protect them. But dogs or worms, he couldn't see that it mattered much.

For the most part though, he kept nearer home. He was still allowed to use the same sleeping place. The girl, whose name he had discovered was Mara, had constituted herself his protectress, following some code or sense of relationship acknowledged by the rest of the troupe but which he himself did not quite fully understand, though he was grateful for it. There was little speech between them but sometimes, in the evening firelight, he would find her eyes resting on him, though whether this was anything more than the bold, lingering regard of her people he could not tell. The rest of the troupe left him to his own devices. The men were morose, given to sudden violent gestures in their talk among themselves and in the course of the long games of cards they played after the evening meal. They were not unfriendly to Markham, offering him *raki* when they had it, but they did

412

not speak much to him. He felt himself more at ease, now that he had no more fears of being robbed – that first day, on his return from the stream, he had hidden his wallet and the pistol under a stone not far from the camp. Partly because of Fehmi's generosity there was a fair amount of money in the wallet still, about the equivalent of ten pounds in English money. Before hiding it he had taken out one of the banknotes. He had given this, together with all the loose change in his pockets, to Mara to pay for his keep, making sure she saw that he had nothing left. Without money he could not remain long in hiding; and unless his store was kept secret he was certain to be robbed sooner or later.

On the third day, following an impulse he did not pause to examine, he had given the husband of the older woman, and leader of the troupe, his English flannel suit, in exchange for baggy black trousers, a loose white shirt without collar and a kind of felt jacket, also black, without buttons or fastenings at the front. His beard grew and the April sunshine darkened his skin. He made no plans, nor even thought much about his situation, content to live from day to day, though always with the consciousness, like an intimation of pain, that there was something to complete or fulfil, some essential business left unfinished. He heard from the gypsies of a new wave of massacres of Armenians in Adana, news of which was beginning to come through to the capital, though the scale of the killing was not known yet. Even this, though disturbing him, did not break the sense of abeyance his life had fallen into. As before, in the period following his wife and son's departure, it needed a personal shock to drive him to action.

This came four or five days after the evening of the fusillades – he was not sure which, as the days were without distinguishing features and tended to run together in his mind. He had been sitting all morning listening to the sound of the stream and watching a great band of swifts wheeling

413

high above the waste of graves. The swifts had made him think of home, cooler English skies and the birds plunging through the long dusks of summer.

He had begun to walk back towards the grove of cypresses, though without a particular intention of returning, when he heard a man's voice call, 'Captain Markham, is it you?'

The shock of this was extraordinary. Markham had to overcome an immediate impulse to drop down, out of the line of fire, a reaction perhaps from the days of his infantry training. This impulse once ·mastered, no other form of evasion occurred to him. He walked forward steadily, still seeing no one. However, as he left the path to approach the trees, two men stepped forward into his way from the shadow of tall rocks. One, standing sullenly there, he recognized as the leader of the gypsies. The other was slender, erect of bearing, dressed in a dark suit and a fez.

'Can it really be Captain Markham?' this man said now, in English. Markham saw the pale eyes, the thin, humorous-seeming mouth below the moustache.

'Nejib Bey,' he said. 'Yes, I am Robert Markham.'

'You have *gone native*,' Nejib said, dwelling on the idiom with a sort of malicious distinctness. 'Isn't that the term? Ah no, excuse me, it is only for colonies, isn't it? Turkey is not yet a colony.'

'How did you know I was here?'

'This worthy Ottoman citizen,' Nejib said, indicating the gypsy with a movement of his head, 'in the course of attempting to sell a suit of clothes, wanting to prove the suit is not stolen, speaks of a stranger, a foreigner, living in the Great Cemetery of Scutari. Among his hearers is one of our people. The suit is looked at, the label noted. The matter is brought to my attention. This fellow conducts me, for an agreed sum. It is quite simple.' He turned to the gypsy. '*Simdi git*,' he said, with sudden, brutal contempt. '*Git budan.*'

414

The man obeyed at once, moving off rapidly down the path.

'That is the top and bottom of it,' Nejib said, with a return to suavity. 'We want to ask you to return.' He paused a moment, then he said, 'My goodness, I would not have known you. You look like one of the *chingané*. You would be glad of a bath, I suppose.'

Markham heard the mockery underlying the words. He could smell Nejib's scent. 'From what I heard,' he said, 'you people don't run the show anymore. I'm surprised that you have emerged from your boltholes at all. Do you know that word – "bolt-hole"? At least you have the sense not to wear uniform.'

Nejib was smiling still but his eyes had narrowed. 'Shall we stand out of the sun?' he said. They moved into the shade of the rocks and Nejib said, 'I see that you are not so well informed about the situation. Please listen to me for a moment. It is true that the reactionary forces are in control of the city now, but their days are numbered. The regiments from Macedonia are on the way, under Shevket Pasha. They were mobilized as soon as the news of the mutiny came through. Tomorrow, or the day after, they will invest the city.' The smile took on a faintly derisive quality. 'Your military experts said it would take three weeks,' he said. 'That was the opinion expressed in your famous *Times*. Three weeks. You did not see that, I suppose? No, you do not resemble a *Times* reader at the moment. They do not know our Turkish troops. But they will, they will know them. They are now, after only six days' march, no more than twenty kilometres beyond San Stefano in the northern suburbs. By this time tomorrow they will be in position. Thirty thousand troops loyal to the Committee. How long do you think it will take them to crush this rabble? They will hang a few hundred and everything will be finished.'

'And Abdul Hamid?'

'He will be deposed. Oh yes, certainly. He has attempted to destroy the Constitution, contrary to his oath. He encouraged the leaders of the mutiny with money and promises. All this will be shown in the courts.'

'Ah yes,' Markham said. 'Those courts of yours. You intended to get rid of him from the start, I suppose. You wanted a republic. You couldn't touch him before, because of the religious feeling in the country.'

'He supported the counter-revolution,' Nejib said.

Markham looked at him for a moment or two in silence. Things were beginning to fall into place in his mind. 'Counter-revolution?' he said. 'Where are the leaders? This whole thing has been stage-managed. You wanted an excuse to get rid of the Sultan. I thought there was something odd about it at the time, when these fellows told me, troops milling about in the city out of control. The Officer Commanding was a Committee man, wasn't he? One regiment would have cleared them, if he had acted promptly. Why didn't he? He must have had orders not to.'

'We were helped by circumstances,' Nejib said.

'You certainly were. The funeral, the thing that started it off, that was Hassan Fehmi's funeral, wasn't it? They spoke about a demonstration, but I didn't connect it with him at the time . . . Did you engineer that too?'

'That was the work of the *mollahs* and Abdul Hamid's agents, nothing to do with us.'

'They did your work for you.' Markham took a deep breath. He looked away across the wilderness of graves to where, against darkening clouds, the tireless swifts still wheeled and plunged. 'But you also did your own work, didn't you? It was your people that killed Hassan Fehmi.'

In the silence that followed he continued to look away, indifferent to any denial Nejib might make. After some moments he heard the other man say, 'It is true that we wanted him dead. Not because we thought his death would

416

have such consequences. We did not think him so important as that. In fact he was not, in himself, so important.'

'But you wanted him dead.'

'Yes, that is true. His name went on the list two months ago, after he had printed lies about us. He said in the *Serbesti* that the Unionists intended to make European headgear compulsory for men. That is very wounding to Moslem sensibilities, you know. It roused bad feeling against us.'

'I know nothing about that.'

'No, why should you?'

'But why the attempt to implicate me?'

Nejib sighed. He was standing in the shadow of the rock, leaning lightly with one shoulder against the face of it. He wore the fez dead straight, low on his forehead as if it were military regulation dress. From below it his pale eyes regarded Markham steadily. 'This decision was taken by others,' he said. 'My orders are to ask you to return to your home. Your friends are distressed at your disappearance, Captain Markham. No action will be taken against you. You have my promise.'

'I see.' They would not want any loose ends, he thought. Now that all their objectives seemed in sight of being achieved, they would not want any further embarrassments. Better to have him settled at home again, resuming his duties, as though nothing had happened. Then, after a short while, a good spell of home leave . . . 'I could not think of returning,' he said, 'without having matters explained to me. For all I know I may be putting my head into a trap.'

'If there had been any harm intended to you I would hardly have come here alone.'

'All the same,' Markham said, 'I want to know.' He saw the other man's mouth tighten a little below the neat moustache. 'I must know,' he said.

After a moment or two longer Nejib said, 'It seems that you were unfortunate. Rather like a spectator that gets into the

417

crossfire. At that particular moment – and of course the situation now has changed – it seemed a good idea to both parties to bring you into it.'

'Both parties?' But he knew already what Nejib must mean, had always known it, it seemed now to him, from the very moment Missakian had leaned forward that day in his office and spoken Fehmi's name, his eyes unwavering, myopic, behind the thick glasses, his body in the shabby suit tense with the desire that Markham should not refuse. It was this anxiety that Markham chiefly remembered, Missakian's dedicated eagerness that his treachery should succeed . . .

'Both to us and to the Armenians, yes,' Nejib said. 'Or one group of them. It was without my knowledge, as I said. There are a lot of entrepreneurs these days, Captain Markham. It is difficult to keep control. It seems that the *Henchak* wanted to involve Britain, mainly for propaganda purposes. They would have claimed responsibility, published the details of your involvement.' He paused a moment. Then he said, 'Exactly what that involvement is, we have yet to discover.'

Markham looked at the other man's face, which was at once vigilant and tranquil. It was impossible to know whether he was telling the truth. 'The killer was provided by your people, I suppose,' he said. He thought suddenly of the neat, quick-stepping man he had seen talking to Tarquin in the courtyard of the Nuru Osmaniyé.

'Yes. Not many Armenians can use a pistol. My colleagues wanted to make sure the man was killed. They agreed to implicate you because they thought it might help to discredit the Liberals, who are closely identified with Britain.'

'I see,' Markham said. 'Both sides were ready to throw me away.'

'You should not be surprised at that. You think because you were sympathetic to the Armenians they should have been grateful? They chose that way of letting you be helpful. That you would be destroyed in the process was not very

418

important to them. You make the mistake of thinking in personal terms, Captain Markham. These people are interested in the collective idea. Set against the idea of an independent homeland for two and a half million Armenians, what are you? You do not exist.'

'I have as much existence as two and a half million Armenians,' Markham said. He thought of Tarquin, on that morning of mist and sunshine in the mosque yard, telling him the same thing in almost the same words. 'Or two and a half million Turks,' he said. 'You too are interested in the collective idea, as you put it.'

'Oh yes. But it does not include an independent Armenia on Turkish soil. Nor does it include any dream of union between Turkish and Russian Armenia – many of those claiming to be Armenian patriots are socialist agitators from over the Caucasus, who would sell us tomorrow. Capitalism is the enemy for them. No, our aims are practical. Turkey for the Turks, a strong army, frontiers that we can defend.'

'Everywhere you look in Europe there are these collective ideas. One day they will all come into conflict and then there will be a war, which is the biggest collective idea of all.'

'Turkey will be ready for it,' Nejib said.

'Look,' Markham said, 'I don't want to argue. There is only one thing now that puzzles me. Why have the *Henchak* not gone through with things? Presumably they have kept my name out of it, after all.'

'They have been overtaken by events, rather. The reaction has been greater than they could have anticipated. You have heard of these massacres in Adana? Ten thousand Armenians have been killed there, in the course of three days. Once more the attention of Europe is fixed on the Armenian question. It is more than they could have hoped.'

'It's insane,' Markham said.

'Sporadic massacre suits their policy best, it prevents them

419

from being forgotten. That is why they don't want us. They don't want a unified Turkey.'

'But where did the anti-Armenian feeling come from this time? What sparked it off?'

Nejib paused for an appreciable time before answering. 'I hesitate to tell you this,' he said frankly, 'because you have a personal interest in the man. I remember that you asked me about him. But it is all over now, in any case.'

'Personal interest? You must mean Hartunian. What about him?'

'He was still in custody when the mutiny took place. His sympathy with the Constitutionalists was already known. When Fehmi was killed and no arrests were made, feeling began to rise. Abdul Hamid was back in power but he had to please the mob. What you call a scapegoat had to be found. Hartunian is a prominent Armenian . . . You see? He was interrogated by the *khafie*. He confessed to having organized the murder from prison. At least, a confession was published – Hartunian was not produced. Strange there was no killing in Constantinople. But no one has thought for anything but Shevket Pasha and his Macedonian regiments. I told you they are nearly at San Stefano.'

'Hartunian had nothing to do with it,' Markham said. 'We both know that.'

'Quite so. When the city is liberated, he will be released. I can promise you that. In the meantime, my dear Captain Markham, I ask you to return home. No action will be taken against you. If you agree, all enquiries about your connection with the Armenian societies will be abandoned.'

'And the confession? Hartunian's confession?'

'It is too late to do much about that. Go home now, Captain Markham. Make your way back to your house quietly. Stay within doors as far as possible. Tomorrow morning the troops will reach the outskirts of the city. Within two days it will all be over. You can resume your normal duties. Come with me now.'

420

'No,' Markham said. 'I won't come now. I want to say good-bye to the gypsies.'

'They will not care.'

'They have been kind to me.'

'Very well. But you will come? I have your promise?'

'That I will come back to the city? Yes, you have my promise.'

Nejib regarded him a long moment in a speculative fashion which the slight movement of his lips made seem humorous, though there was nothing humorous about the pale steady eyes. 'It is too late to change any of this,' he said. He gave a curt nod and began to pick his way over the stones towards the path, moving with the dancer's grace that Markham remembered. He watched until the Turk was out of sight, then turned back towards the encampment.

He did not stop here but went on past the grove of cypresses into the broken, trackless ground beyond, picking his way through the tangled vegetation, from time to time clambering over fallen gravestones. These actions he performed with precision but without full awareness. It was as if his physical sense of things had been obscured or diffused, leaving room only for the knowledge of what he must do. He felt no outrage, nor even much surprise at wnat had happened to Hartunian: in a world where atrocities were provoked on innocent people for the sake of some remoter good, it was fitting that Hartunian should have been the innocent cause of suffering to his compatriots. This could not be changed now, he knew that. Nejib had been right. What he was going to do would change nothing, save no one, serve as no example . . .

The pistol and the wallet were there, where he had left them, under the stone. It was with the sense of resuming a former life that he took them up. He examined the pistol now for the first time. It was a Mauser automatic with a square grip. There was one cartridge left in the chamber and one remaining in the magazine. He stuck it in the waistband of his trousers, below the jacket. He had no pocket large enough for the wallet, so kept this in his hand, first extracting, however, a single banknote which he folded up small and stowed away. This done he made his way back to wait for the return of the gypsies.

It was dusk when they came. The man who had led Nejib to him was not among them – perhaps roistering somewhere on the money he had received. Markham was impatient now to be gone. He signalled the girl to follow him, led her down into the sleeping chamber. Here, without speech and hastily, he gave her the wallet, holding it out at arm's length to her. She looked inside it and he saw her eyes widen at the sight of the money. He slipped the wedding ring off his finger and unfastened his watch, which had long since stopped. These too he handed to her, still without words.

She looked down for some moments at the things in her hands. Then she raised her face and he saw her eyes flash in the lamplight. He was about to speak when she moved quickly towards him, stood still again, close now, her head lowered. It was the first time, without the others, that she had come close enough to be touched, if he had wanted, to be taken in his embrace. She had misunderstood, he realized, noting her stillness, the submissive posture of her body; misunderstood the nature of his haste, the secrecy, the urgent gifts. She thought he was offering to buy her.

'No,' he said. 'No. *Gitmek lazum*.'

Still she did not look up. Markham's throat tightened suddenly at the dumbness, the immediacy of her acceptance, at the exigencies of a life so harsh that the few things he had thrust upon her, things for which he had no further use, would seem equal in value to her person, sufficient token of love. For these moments, as she stood there at his disposal, she was like all the exploited of the world. He put his arms round her and held her close against him, smelling the sweat and musk of her body, sensing the age that would come to her as she danced in the streets and squares of the city. 'Good-bye,' he said. 'Thank you. *Selamin Aleykum*.'

He heard her give back the salaam then he put her from him and went quickly up the steps. She would wait down there, he knew, to hide the things about her somewhere, before coming up. He shook hands with the others and thanked them. Then he moved out of the circle of the firelight, found the path and began the long walk through the darkness of the cemetery back towards the road and the distant lights of the city.

Constantinople had been in the grip of fear and suspense for days now, as the Macedonian army drew nearer. The devoutness of the mutinous troops kept them from alcohol, and their behaviour on the whole was restrained; but they were without effective leadership and lived separately in their own barracks, a number of armed bands rather than an army, not communicating much with one another, so that the threat of riot was never far away. Large numbers of people, afraid of being caught in the fighting, had already quitted the city, fleeing back across the Bosphoros to the Asia from which their marauding ancestors had come. This exodus was greatest in the neighbourhood of Yildiz where people of every class, from pashas to peasants, fearing a bombardment if the palace guards resisted, were packing their belongings and taking to the road. All kinds of vehicles, from carriages to handcarts, passed constantly down to the landing stages of the Bosphoros. The quayside was choked with slaves and household possessions waiting to be ferried across.

The streets around Yildiz were deserted, except for the dogs; the houses were empty and the odour of fear hung everywhere. The legend of the Sultan's inviolability had gone now, forever. Even the lickspittle press had begun to change its tone as Shevket Pasha's troops drew nearer. It was voicing now for the first time, what would have been inconceivable before, that Abdul Hamid's days of rule were numbered.

Hour by hour the palace staff were defecting – kitchen-staff, gardeners, doormen, even some of the guard. Those who remained had nowhere to go, no life outside the palace: the women of the Harem and the eunuchs who guarded them; the deaf-mute attendants; the entertainers – dwarfs, acrobats, dancers; and Abdul Hamid himself.

He remained motionless at the centre of the maze of pavilions and kiosks that constituted his Palace and that had itself no plan or guiding principle of construction except concealment and the fear of death. It was as if the city's fear was the apotheosis of his own, as if that long-threatened immobility of panic had now finally descended on him. With thirty thousand troops in the city loyal to him, with millions of Moslems revering him as their Caliph, he remained motionless while the army from Salonika occupied the northern suburbs of the city, three or four miles away. Light was his only requirement it seemed – every night amidst the darkness and desolation of the surrounding districts, the Palace blazed with the light of its thousands of bulbs, a great flaring conflagration, lighting up the sky like a portent, plainly visible to the Macedonian sentries stationed on the heights outside the city.

Time was running out for the Sultan and his dynasty and the moribund Empire he had inherited. But even a very sick or stricken animal will still respond to instinct and perform habitual movements, and when an unkempt man in the garb of a gypsy claiming to have important information appeared at the outer guardroom at the gates of the Palace, he was searched and afterwards locked up in one of the cells. Nothing was found on him, in this initial search, except a few piastres. He spoke Turkish but not as a Turk would speak it. To all questions he made the same reply: he had important information but it was for the Sultan only. He would not give his name or any details about himself.

Neither the corporal in charge nor any of the men on guard

duty had any idea what to do with him. None of them wanted the responsibility of taking the matter further, at a time when the chain of command as well as the administrative machinery inside the Palace was breaking down. On the other hand no one wanted the responsibility of releasing him. He spent that night, which was the night of Friday 23rd April, in his cell. The soldiers gave him a glass of tea and some *gevreks* – small hoops of bread stuck with sesame seeds. Afterwards he slept, to be woken by gunfire.

In the course of that night Shevket's Macedonian regiments penetrated the city from three sides, moving quickly and almost soundlessly in their *chariks* – the soft native shoes with which both officers and men had been issued. By dawn they were in their final positions. So rapid and silent had been this advance that the attack, when it came, took the defenders completely by surprise. Many surrendered without firing a shot. Stambul and the Sublime Porte were captured inside an hour. The fighting at the Tacsim Barracks was fiercer, artillery had to be used, but within three hours the garrison had been subdued, largely owing to the superb panache of Enver Bey's leadership – he stormed the barricades at the head of his troops under heavy shellfire. By mid-morning three-quarters of the city was in the hands of the attackers.

At this point there was a lull. The firing stopped and silence fell over the city, broken only by the barking of panic-stricken street dogs. The guard at the Palace gate had been changed earlier, and now – another habitual twitch of the disabled animal – an officer arrived at the guardroom to inspect the new guard. He was told of the prisoner in the cell, questioned him and received the same answers.

The officer was an *alaili*, one who had been promoted from the ranks. He was a devout Moslem and deeply attached to the Sultan, with whose interests he identified his own. He was extremely worried by the military situation and particularly by the fact that no adequate preparation had been made to defend the Palace – there were two battalions only, and these under strength because of desertions, between the sacred person of the Sultan and the Macedonian troops lying just south of the Dolmabache Palace not half a mile away. He could not understand why this had been allowed to happen, why the Sultan had remained inactive and allowed himself to be encircled in this way. When he looked through the bars of the cell at the set-faced man and listened to the deliberate accents of his voice, claiming to have information for the Sultan, he was visited by a kind of mingled hope and superstition: perhaps here, in this unlikely form, was what the Padishah was waiting for.

It was worth a mention, at least. The officer, whose name was Kebali, made his way through the deserted, silent park, empty of gardeners and attendants now, to the gates of the second enclosure. He was known by sight to the Albanian sentries and so allowed through without question. Here were the quarters of the Imperial bodyguard and most of the Secretariat; here too was the office of Rassim Bey, the Sultan's Chief of Security. As Kebali crossed the enclosure towards this office he heard the crash of artillery to the west, in the direction of Sisli, and guessed that the Macedonian troops were attacking the heights overlooking the Palace on that side. If they succeeded they would ring Yildiz almost completely.

He was not kept waiting long. There was no real work for anyone to do now, though people kept up a pretence of it. He told Rassim about the man in the guardroom, merely stating the fact, giving no opinion – that he had thought it worth mentioning was enough. He would not have trusted the other man with his feelings anyway. He felt compunction about delivering the man in the cell to him. Rassim was head of the *khafie*, the secret police, who were a law unto themselves, though not the force they had been before the Constitution.

426

He listened impassively, fingering his full, curly beard, his eyes on Kebali's face. When the officer had finished, there was a short pause during which both men could hear the continuing sounds of gunfire. Then Rassim gave orders for the man to be escorted to his office.

The soldiers who brought the prisoner were instantly dismissed. After some preliminary questioning he was taken by two of Rassim's men to a room adjoining the office and there stripped and searched. In this process it was seen that he was uncircumcised and therefore no Moslem, and that the skin of his body was pale, not resembling the skin of a *chingané*. It was also seen that he had an automatic pistol strapped with bits of ragged linen against the inside of his left thigh. The pistol was loaded with two shots.

The discovery of this pistol changed the whole nature of the proceedings. Up to that moment it had been a routine affair, the *khafie* men had treated their prisoner with a certain rough good humour. But now they had a man in their hands who had come of his own accord, with a concealed weapon, asking to speak to the Sultan. That he could not have gained access to the Sultan without the pistol being detected made no difference. Nor did it matter that the régime was collapsing, that these men, seeing the hourly desertion, hearing the gunfire so close, knew in their hearts that Abdul Hamid was done for, and they with him. The impulse and apparatus of cruelty were still there.

Still naked the man was taken by means of a covered passageway to the Malta kiosk, whose cellars had for thirty years been used for the interrogation of prisoners. Once more he was asked his name, his race and nationality, his affiliations. When he refused to answer he was tied down and whipped on the chest and abdomen with a riding crop, as a preliminary.

With the first blood, they grew intent. They would have been disappointed if he had given way now. But he said

427

nothing. Rassim questioned him, asking always the same questions – name, race, *memleket*. The man writhed under the strokes, but he would not answer. It was decided to try him with the bastinado.

Meanwhile Abdul Hamid had himself been informed of this latest – as it was seen – attempt on his life. The *aide-de-camp* who brought him the news found him on the rooftop of the Imperial pavilion scrutinizing with the aid of his telescopes, the sea, the distant hills, the immense horizon, where after thirty years of phantoms there had at last appeared material enemies – he could quite clearly see the Macedonian infantry and guns to the west and south of him. The heights of Sisli were taken now, the firing there had stopped. His Chasseurs were still holding out at the Tash Kishla Barracks but could not do so much longer. Soon, all that would remain to him would be Yildiz itself. The animals of the menagerie were restless, he could hear them as the *aide-de-camp* spoke to him, the shrieks of the macaws, the roaring of his leopards. Though no one had dared tell him yet, the keepers had fled and the animals had received no food since the previous day.

He dismissed the *aide-de-camp* and after waiting some time made his way by routes known only to himself to the Malta kiosk. Plots against his life drew him still, even now; he desired to hear the details of the interrogation. He could hear the man's cries. Treading softly on his slippered feet he entered the room. He signed to Rassim to continue and, without glancing at the blood-streaked man on the table, went rapidly round to the other side of the heavy wooden screen with which all the rooms were provided and sat down there to listen. He did not like the sight of blood or the signs of physical suffering. On this occasion, however, after a while he got up, approached the prisoner, and looked at him.

Markham was too far gone in pain to be aware of the entrance. They had beaten the soles of his feet with thin sticks, beating lightly, allowing the feet to swell. So charged with pain were they now that the slightest strokes suffused his whole being, clouded his vision. From some ultimate lair of the mind he held out against fainting, struggled still to hear the unruffled voice beyond him somewhere and the brief questions, couched in various languages since they knew he was a foreigner of some kind. '*Onoma su?*' the voice said. '*Memleket nerede? Quel pays? Quelle race? Ismin ne?* What is your name?'

At first he made no answer, except by sounds he was unable to suppress. But afterwards words were needed, like spells, to fight off the mist, and he heard himself shouting denials that were not answers to any questions put to him now, but part of a dialogue much older. He heard that terrible courtesy again, and felt the knowing eyes on his face. '*Ermeni degilim!*' he shouted. '*Degilim, degilim!*' Pain betrayed him finally into English, but he continued to deny all races, all countries. A voice he did not know for his own screamed that he was a man, a man, *bir adam*.

It was then that Abdul Hamid approached and gazed down; and for some moments Markham saw the Sultan's bearded face above him, white, cadaverous, the eyes huge, dilated, empty, the impulse of cruelty long dead in them with all other impulse. It seemed to him that something appeared in the eyes, recognition, compassion, he could not tell. It was enough, however, to release him. A moment longer he kept the face in focus. Then it and everything was enveloped in darkness and he heard and felt nothing more.

Though he did not know it, it was the Sultan himself who told the men not to revive him for further questioning. Otherwise they would have continued until he spoke or died. He was left there on the bench, oblivious, still naked. It was a sleep of varying levels, sometimes rising to where pain and shock attended him, sometimes far down, below all sensation. Where it most resembled death it was most healing.

While he lay thus the last phase of the battle for

Constantinople was concluded. By nightfall all resistance was at an end, and the city was in the hands of Shevket Pasha's troops. Only the Palace of Yildiz and its immediate neighbourhood remained. No orders to attack this had been issued, out of policy rather than piety on Shevket's part – he feared still to offend the sensibilities of his troops by offering violence to the Sultan's person or dwelling. But there were eighteen battalions of infantry, supported by guns, encamped on the surrounding hillsides within sight and hearing of the Palace.

All through the afternoon and evening, and far into the night, while the Macedonian troops took up their positions, the steady stream of desertion from Yildiz continued. The last of the cooks and scullions fled and the kitchen fires went out, so that the pampered *kadines* were reduced to eating cold scraps of food salvaged by the eunuchs from deserted larders. The water supply failed too – the only water available was in the lake and ditches of the park. Then, soon after nightfall, the electricity was cut off. The great beacon of light which had flared out nightly for so long was extinguished in a moment and the Palace and park were plunged into darkness. Presently one of the women of the Harem began to weep aloud, from fear or bewilderment; her cries were taken up by others in a chorus that rose higher and higher, without tears now, a contagion of hysteria in which the shrieks of the women mingled with the sustained, inhuman howling of the eunuchs. Their voices were answered from the menagerie in the park, where lions roared with hunger, apes chattered, zebras brayed and parakeets screeched the *mashallahs* they had been taught.

In order to calm his people and eclipse the sounds, Abdul Hamid ordered the remnants of his orchestra to play. By candlelight the twenty or so musicians that were left struck up with some of the Sultan's favourite tunes from *Madame Argot* and *La Belle Hélène*. But when towards midnight Abdul

430

Hamid himself retired, to sit behind locked doors in the Little Mabeyn, the music ceased. The musicians packed their instruments and departed, making their way through the deserted park and the unguarded gates to seek what refuge they could find in the streets below.

Markham was conscious when the lights failed. He was looking up at the bulb in the ceiling which had shone steadily on his torture – there were no windows in the room. He continued to lie still for a long time in the darkness. His body had stiffened and his lacerated feet gave him great pain. The sweat had chilled on him and he trembled continuously. The straps were still fastened across his shoulders and thighs and his feet were held in the twisted thongs of leather which had kept them from flinching under the strokes. He heard a frenzied outcry of screams and howls as he lay there, a lamentation almost bestial; and from somewhere on the other side of him there came brute roars and yelps and the unearthly cries of birds.

Slowly he summoned the resolution he needed to set about freeing himself. He was afraid of movement, thinking that it would increase the pain beyond the limits of what was bearable, black out his senses again. For some time he experimented, shifting his body within the confines of the straps. Then he began fumbling at the upper one, seeking for the buckle that secured it. In the dark and with fingers that had lost almost all strength, it was a long process. The rough leather chafed the wounds made by the whip. But he continued to fumble at himself, pressing back to reduce tension on the strap. It was buckled against the edge of the table. By turning slightly sideways he could reach the buckle with one hand, then with both. After an age of patient endeavour he succeeded in releasing it. He rested for a while. Then, very cautiously, he sat up. The lower strap was easier to reach, but unbuckling it took even longer as his fingers had been further weakened by the effort just made.

431

Now there was only the stick and thong that held his feet. This, which he had dreaded most, proved least troublesome: by raising his legs clear of the table he released the torsion on the thongs, thus making the loops wide enough for him to draw his feet through.

He was free. It was pitch dark in the room. He could not see, and could not remember, how high the table was from the floor. This uncertainty caused him to make a bad mistake. He swung his legs over the side, lowered them. He was half standing now, and when the soles of his feet touched the stone floor they were taking some of the weight of his body. The pain of this contact was so terrible that he toppled forward in a dead faint.

He was roused, as it seemed to him, by a renewed clamour of the animals in the menagerie. He could not risk standing up again. He hoisted himself onto hands and knees and began to crawl across the floor towards where he thought the door should be. He was wrong, however – he had to crawl along two walls, halfway round the room, before he found it. But it was unlocked, and he was able to open it and get through without having to rise from his knees.

Outside in the corridor he was astonished to find a faint reluctant daylight entering through the windows. He crawled steadily through this dimness, along the uncarpeted corridor, looking for a way out. He tried two doors on his left, kneeling up to do so, but one was locked and the other opened onto a windowless room like the one he had been in – he saw in the faint light of the windows behind him a table, the shape of a screen, blank walls.

There was a third door, further down on the same side and he tried this too, though without much hope, since it seemed clear that this side formed the interior of the kiosk. The door was unlocked but he could not open it far, no more than a foot or so – there seemed to be some obstruction on the other side.

He remained kneeling there for some time, keeping quite

still, sensing the silence and abandonment of the place, which the continuing noises of the animals across the park seemed somehow to seal and make absolute. He knew beyond question that there was no living being but himself inside the kiosk. Hampered as he was, and so much weakened, he could not force the door open further. It was unlikely in any case to lead him out of the building. He had decided already to resume his creeping way down the corridor. However, at the last moment, he leaned forward, angled his arm round the door and groped to discover what the obstruction was. He found himself touching the short, matted hair of a man's head.

He sensed with the touch that the man was dead. But at once he began to work to reach him, pushing and butting against the door in his attitude of forced supplication. After some time he was able to get both arms through and with a great effort push the body over, onto its side so that the door swung clear of it. So exhausted was he that he almost fell forward across the body, which was lying turned away from him, dressed in a suit of some dark material.

The man's hair was matted with blood. Blood covered the back of his head and neck, making, in this poor light, a tone of darkness almost uniform with the cloth of the jacket. Some feeling of premonition came to Markham as he reached forward and pulled the man gently on to his back again. The face that was now revealed to him was obscured on one side, and below the mouth, with dried blood; but he knew it at once for Hartunian's. The eyes were open, strangely placid-looking, the face untroubled in spite of the masking blood.

Markham felt no surprise. With the recognition there had come a sense of inevitability. He wondered briefly how Hartunian had reached his position behind the door. He had been dead a considerable time, several hours at least, perhaps since the previous day. He was cold, and the blood which had soaked his jacket felt only slightly damp. He must have been

433

left for dead, Markham thought, perhaps in some hasty desertion of Rassim's men, beaten and left. Then he would have tried to get out, to reach the door, collapsed and died before he could do so. There seemed to have been haemorrhage from the mouth . . .

In the light from the window behind him he looked at the face a moment or two longer. Then, as though it was a plan long since decided on, he began to undress the body, manoeuvring awkwardly and clumsily on his knees in the doorway, turning the inert form this way and that, uttering short panting groans of exertion. The labour and the pain of his feet brought sweat out again all over him. Several times he had to wait for attacks of dizziness to pass.

Hartunian's body was terribly marked with bruises and contusions. It was the body of an old man, sharp-boned, with a thin pelt of grey hair on the chest. Markham sat still for some time, gathering strength, then he began to put on Hartunian's things, the jacket first, then the trousers, lying full length for this last operation, keeping his feet clear of the floor. The clothes fitted him almost exactly. With Hartunian's shirt and underclothes he made pads for his feet, tying them round and knotting them on top, so that the thickest part was underneath. When this was done he laid his hand briefly on the dead man's brow and over the eyes that had stared placidly through this last indignity. Then he got to his feet.

The first pain was excruciating but it lessened when he was actually walking. He found that a short-stepping, shuffling walk was best, both for reducing the pain and for keeping the pads in place. In this way he proceeded down the corridor, found the door at the end of it, passed through into the daylight and the deserted enclosure.

There was no sound anywhere. Even the beasts in their cages had at last fallen silent it seemed, and there was no human voice anywhere. The gates of the enclosure lay open and unguarded, and no one challenged Markham as he shuffled through them. He was in any case less concerned about being detected than about keeping himself upright and moving forward. Remembering the extent of the ground through which he had been led by the soldiers – only the day before, but it seemed like a great space of time now to his grimly concentrating mind – he knew that he could never make it back that way. But he remembered the rifle fire from the north that he had heard then. It had been close – within range, he thought, of where he was now. The Macedonians could not be far from the outer gates.

With the same mincing steps, setting his feet as briefly as possible, he began to make his way round the outside of the enclosure, using the wall as a support. This journey was without duration in his mind, time was consumed in the effort to keep going. Rounding the wall on the far side of the enclosure he saw before him the tall gilded bars of the gates, deserted, separated from him by a hundred yards or so of gravelled drive. He set out towards them, his movements a parody of haste, the frantic intention of the feet frustrated by the obstinate slowness of the body.

From the gates the approach road sloped upward, passing through trees on either side. Here on this steeper ground his progress was slowed further. He stumbled and, in the effort to save his feet, fell heavily, lying for several minutes where he had fallen before he could force himself up again. As he struggled to his feet he glanced up through the trees and saw in the dimness there, on the crest of a low hill, the unmistakable shape of a canvas bivouac. The wrappings on his feet had loosened, the ends flapped about his ankles as he moved, but he did not attempt to retie them. He left the road and began to clamber up the slope, on hands and knees again now. As he did so he called out. He saw the shape of a man appear suddenly above him, not more than fifty yards away. He shouted that he was a friend, that he was English. Finding himself once more on a level, he got up, balancing awkwardly on his encumbered feet. He raised his arms and waved. The effort to keep his balance caused him to take a series of short, shuffling steps like a clumsy dance. Despite the pain he felt a great relief and happiness. '*Arkadash*,' he shouted again. '*Ingiliz, Ingiliz!*' He saw the figure move, change shape suddenly in a way he did not at once understand. Then he realized that the man had raised a rifle. 'No, no,' he shouted in English, again attempting to move forward. 'I am a friend.' He was light-headed now, but his feeling of happiness persisted. Moisture had formed over his eyes, blurring his vision, but he thought he saw the man's shape change again. He fell to his knees.

The sentry was nineteen years old, a peasant lad from the bleak uplands of Eastern Thrace. He could not read or write. Before joining the army, three months previously, he had never been away from the village where he had been born. His training had been rudimentary. They had not needed to teach him to shoot – he had known how to do that since he was ten, even the women of his village knew how to handle a rifle. But they had told him that the Constitution was a good thing and that the Palace of Yildiz was a source of evil and corruption, an abode of demons. Through the night he had had evidence of this. He had seen the lights of the Palace put out as if by the palm of Allah. And he had sat sleepless, listening to the sounds that came up from the haunted darkness below, terrible sounds, voices human and animal mingling, blending, strains of infidel music from the orchestra. In the first light a hush had come over things and he had fallen into an uneasy sleep. He had been roused from this by the voice below and scrambled up to see, in the dimness among the trees, what he at once took for a *djinn* from the evil Palace, creeping up towards him. He knew the marks of a *djinn*, and felt sure this was one and not a member of the human race – though it attempted to deceive him with words – because it did not move as humans do and because its

436

transformation was not complete, the feet being grotesquely misshapen. As he took aim with the rifle, the *djinn* performed a menacing dance. The sentry felt great fear. He did not really believe that ordinary bullets would be effective against a *djinn*. The uncertainty made him hesitate some moments longer and in these moments he saw that the *djinn* had stopped moving. Also, straining his eyes, he saw that it was smiling, a thing *djinns* cannot do, only men.

He was afraid still, but he lowered the rifle. There was no doubt that the face was smiling.

# Epilogue

On the morning of 27 April 1909, Abdul Hamid was informed by a deputation consisting entirely of non-Turks that the Turkish nation had deposed him; and at nine in the evening of that same day the officers arrived who were to escort him to his place of exile – a villa in Salonika, the property of a Jewish banker. On hearing where he was to be taken – that breeding ground of atheists and revolutionaries whence all his trouble had come – the Sultan fainted into the arms of the faithful Tahsin, his First Secretary. He was revived and informed that he would be allowed three wives, four concubines, four eunuchs and fourteen servants. Two of his sons were also to accompany him. Towards midnight, amid the groans of the women and eunuchs left behind, the party set off.

Most of his close associates were distinctly less fortunate, being hanged at the Stambul end of Galata Bridge within days of his departure. There was a grotesqueness about some of these executions which seemed appropriate, a fitting close to such a reign. Rassim Pasha, Chief of the Secret Police, veteran of a thousand interrogations, maintained his air of brutal contempt to the end. When he saw that his executioners were gypsies, he refused with a gesture of disdain the olive and glass of water which are proffered as a sign of peace to those about to die. He gave his cigarette case to a spectator, listened for the voice of God with fingers to his ears for some moments, then signalled he was ready. However, when they pulled the stool away, he struggled and fought and would not give up his breath – it was as if all the cruelties had fed his vitality. Two of the gypsies had to swing on his legs for several minutes before the large head with its luxuriant chestnut beard lay meek and harmless in the noose. As for Djavad, the Chief of the Black Eunuchs, he was the victim of a blunder that was perhaps malicious: because of his numerous chins he was roped round the lower jaw instead of under it, with the result that the Guardian of the Gates of Felicity died neither by strangulation nor by dislocation of the vertebrae but by an elongation of the neck due to his enormous weight. He hung there in his ropes for all to see, head distanced from body by this yard-long thread of a throat.

These deaths and the many others that followed were part of the campaign conducted by the Young Turks to divert attention from the fact that the fruits of democracy, so long promised, were still very slow to arrive. Things did not go well with the new regime. There were dissensions among the leaders. The departure of European officers from Macedonia resulted in further rioting and bloodshed. The Treasury was empty, and loans not easy to raise. In 1911 Italy seized the occasion to lay claim to Tripoli and in the war that followed Turkey lost not only her last remaining African possessions but also the Aegean islands of the Dodecanese.

Abdul Hamid lived on, with his newspapers, his beloved Angora cats, his devoted attendants; saw Turkey enter into military alliance with Germany, saw that fateful day in the autumn of 1914 when the German battleships *Goeben* and *Breslau*, escorted by a squadron of Turkish destroyers, steamed out of the Bosphoros to attack Russian shipping in the Black Sea; saw the disasters of the war, the loss of the Mesopotamian oil-fields to the West, the return of the Caliphate to Arabia. Perhaps his personal fears were at last forgotten, merged in greater ones, now that the guns sounded across the straits of Gallipoli and British submarines were penetrating the Marmara. Possibly it was this release from personal fear that kept him alive so long – against all expectation.

One thing he saw which must have given him satisfaction,

of a kind, or at least appealed to his sense of symmetry: the new régime continued his policy of butchering Armenians. At the beginning of 1915, on the plea that the Armenians had supplied information and given assistance to the Russians, Enver Bey, in agreement with Talaat, set out to eliminate the Armenian problem by eliminating the whole Armenian population. Between April 1915, when the orders went out from Constantinople, and the end of that year, three-quarters of a million Armenians perished. The procedure usually followed was to summon into a town or village, where the local *zaptiehs* had been strengthened for the occasion, all the Armenian males who had not been drafted into labour battalions, boys as well as old men. They were roped together and marched away in batches, ostensibly to some distant destination but in fact merely to the first lonely place, where bands of Kurds were waiting to hack them to death. Then some days later the women and children were gathered together, broken into convoys of a few hundred, provided with guards for 'protection' and set off on forced marches to Aleppo in Syria. Those who survived the violations and brutalities of the journey were put into concentration camps in the Syrian desert where sickness and starvation completed the work. Of a total Armenian population of two million it was calculated that less than one quarter were left in Turkey, and these almost entirely in the cities of Smyrna and Constantinople.

These appalling figures were provided by Lord Bryce and based upon the large amount of material collected and sifted by him. They were laid before the British Parliament in October 1916 by Lord Grey, then Secretary for Foreign Affairs. Grey pointed out to a shocked House that the whole business had been carried out in complete co-operation between the Turkish military and civil authorities. It was not a question of religious fanaticism, he said, but a deliberate and calculated policy of genocide, devised in Constantinople, conducted in accordance with a fixed programme throughout the eastern provinces; and neither the German Emperor, nor the German government, nor the German Embassy in Constantinople, nor any German officer in Turkey had uttered the smallest protest at this behaviour of their allies . . .

These details, as phrased in *The Times*, reached the breakfast table of a former infantry captain named Robert Markham the following morning. They confirmed him in the view, held for some years now, and the main theme of the massive book he was writing, that certain races take on an excitatory role in history, just as certain individuals within a species stimulate processes of secretion among the rest. Or colours or scents, he thought, looking out at the misty morning. Human societies were more complicated of course, the range of responses was so wide. Emulation, compassion, dread – there was no end to it. It would all have to be dealt with in the book. In this case it was the atrocity glands that were gingered up. The Armenians stimulated the atrocity glands, that was their collective historical role. He would have to file the clipping . .

His wife Elizabeth was away at the time – she was often away these days – and he was alone as he sat there at the table looking through the window, down the long vista of the orchard, the grass already coloured by the first falls of leaves, down to the white of his beehives through the faint mist that hung between the trunks. He had taken up bee-keeping at the same time as authorship, and the two things were intimately associated in his mind, more or less fused, in fact. Indeed it was through close observation of his bees that the whole cyclic idea of stimulation, secretion and historical role-playing had come, changing what had begun as a conventional book on Balkan history into a much more labyrinthine, and even mystical affair.

He was not in the fighting, having resigned from the army

six years previously, soon after his return from Asia Minor. The war seemed remote to him, even though his son Henry was now at the front. All his energy went into the book, over seven hundred pages long now and nowhere near finished. As a relief from the abstruseness of his historical themes he was also writing a monograph on bees. Those who saw much of him at this time – and they were generally friends of his wife – sensed behind the grave courtesy of the manner an indifference which they found chilling.

Elizabeth, everybody agreed, was quite different. She did a lot of charitable work connected with the war and sat on various committees, activities that intensified after Henry had gone with his regiment to France – he had joined his father's old regiment, the Gloucesters. Mrs Markham's work took her to London sometimes and when this happened she had lunch usually with Blake, a lieutenant-colonel now, still unmarried, with a desk job at the War Office. Henry Markham, sitting in the trenches, reading mail from home in that disastrous third autumn of the war, could see that his mother was happy in spite of her anxiety for him. Whether his father was happy could not have been discerned from his rare letters. It seemed to Henry, when he thought about it at all, that something had been extracted from his father, an operation of some kind had been undergone, which had soothed the inflammation of his spirit, leaving him vaguer, gentler, *lesser* somehow – as if he had needed whatever the poison was for full existence. But they had never talked much – Henry was closer to his mother. Only when he had been away from home for some time did he realize that not once, in the years since his father had returned from the army, had he heard a single expression of personal feeling between his parents, either rancorous or affectionate.

Such reflections came to him rarely; and in any case he did not want to think about what his parents really felt, or whether their relations were less than perfect. They belonged to home, which was perfect by definition, as was all England –

the sense of that perfectness was behind all the faces that he saw around him. It was the territory one hoped to recover again, oneself miraculously perfect still, unwounded, unmutilated, whole.

## Available in Norton Paperback Fiction

| | |
|---|---|
| Aharon Appelfeld | *Katerina* |
| Rick Bass | *The Watch* |
| Richard Bausch | *The Fireman's Wife and Other Stories* |
| Stephen Beachy | *The Whistling Song* |
| Simone de Beauvoir | *The Mandarins* |
| | *She Came to Stay* |
| Anthony Burgess | *A Clockwork Orange* |
| | *Nothing Like the Sun* |
| | *The Wanting Seed* |
| Mary Caponegro | *The Star Café* |
| Fiona Cheong | *The Scent of the Gods* |
| Stephen Dobyns | *The Wrestler's Cruel Study* |
| Leslie Epstein | *King of the Jews* |
| Montserrat Fontes | *First Confession* |
| | *Dreams of the Centaur* |
| Jonathan Franzen | *Strong Motion* |
| Carol De Chellis Hill | *Eleven Million Mile High Dancer* |
| | *Henry James' Midnight Song* |
| | *Let's Fall in Love* |
| Siri Hustvedt | *The Blindfold* |
| Ivan Klima | *My First Loves* |
| Lynn Lauber | *21 Sugar Street* |
| Thomas Mallon | *Aurora 7* |
| Alyce Miller | *The Nature of Longing* |
| Bradford Morrow | *The Almanac Branch* |
| John Nichols | *A Ghost in the Music* |
| | *The Sterile Cuckoo* |
| | *The Wizard of Loneliness* |
| Manuel Puig | *Tropical Night Falling* |
| Agnes Rossi | *The Quick* |
| Joanna Scott | *Arrogance* |
| Josef Skvorecky | *Dvorak in Love* |
| Rebecca Stowe | *Not the End of the World* |
| Kathleen Tyau | *A Little Too Much Is Enough* |
| Barry Unsworth | *The Hide* |
| | *Mooncranker's Gift* |
| | *Morality Play* |
| | *Sacred Hunger* |
| | *Stone Virgin* |